Acclaim for Karen Fox's previous Magical Love romances . . .

Buttercup Baby

"Fortunately fairies have their own sensuous ways, which Fox describes in exquisite detail . . . Fox's good-natured fantasy romance isn't all sweetness and light; it's spiked with suspense once a stalker discovers that Ariel weeps opals."
—*Booklist*

"A lively, enchanting love story filled with strong emotion and humor. An absolute gem as only Karen Fox can write."
—*Rendezvous*

"If you like stories about fairies, you'll enjoy this book. It has an interesting twist concerning the relationship between the world of the Fae and the world of mortals."
—*Old Book Barn Gazette*

"This cute fantasy romance brings a fairy from Titania's court to the mortal world . . . Fox has more than enough fun with the difficulties of a Shakespearean fairy learning to cope with the modern world."
—*Locus*

"Gifted author Karen Fox follows up her wonderful *Prince of Charming* with the delightful *Buttercup Baby*. Join the magic and the emotion of this special charmer."
—*Romantic Times*

continued . . .

Prince of Charming

"Finally, a heroine who's a real woman. Finally, a hero who knows what a rare find she is. Finally, a book for us all to adore. Thank you, Karen Fox, for creating the most lovable hero romance has seen in a long, long time."

—Maggie Shayne, author of *Eternity*

"Highly engaging characters . . . A realistic, plausible fantasy . . . *Prince of Charming* has proved well worth the wait."

—*Romance Reviews Today*

"A fantastical journey into the faerytale realm of myth, magic, and happily-ever-after . . . Karen Fox's fantasy romance is sweet and charming, with plenty of Fae magic to burn up the pages."

—*The Romance Journal*

"What a fun read! I zipped through *Prince of Charming*, turning pages as fast as I could . . . I urge readers of paranormal romance to pick up this book as quickly as they can."

—*Scribesworld.com*

"I breezed through this most enjoyable book and am eagerly waiting for more of the same from Karen Fox."

—*Romance and Friends*

"Fun and lively."

—*Old Book Barn Gazette*

"*Prince of Charming* is an amusing fantasy romance that will enchant subgenre fans . . . Enjoyable . . . humorous . . . Karen Fox writes a novel that is fun to read."

—*Bookbrowser.com*

"Highly enjoyable and well written. I could almost believe the magic existed . . . Here is an author that aims to please!"

—*Huntressreviews.com*

"Enchanting . . . Karen Fox has penned a warm, funny and quite delightful tale that is very special."

—*Romantic Times*

Cupid's Melody

KARKEN FOX

JOVE BOOKS, NEW YORK

CUPID'S MELODY

A Jove Book / published by arrangement with
the author

PRINTING HISTORY
Jove edition / January 2003

Cover design by George Long
Cover art by Leslie Peck

For information address: The Berkley Publishing Group,
a division of Penguin Putnam Inc.,
375 Hudson Street, New York, New York 10014.

Visit our website at
www.penguinputnam.com

ISBN: 0-515-13491-0

A JOVE BOOK®
Jove Books are published by The Berkley Publishing Group,
a division of Penguin Putnam Inc.,
375 Hudson Street, New York, New York 10014.
JOVE and the "J" design
are trademarks belonging to Penguin Putnam Inc.

PRINTED IN THE UNITED STATES OF AMERICA

10 9 8 7 6 5 4 3 2 1

To the Wyrd Sisters,
Whether near or far, you'll always be special friends,
and especially to Paula Gill and Pam McCutcheon
for critique above and beyond the call of duty

and to Eileen Winter
for providing a much-needed sanity check.
Thanks!

One

This is it. Nic Stone stood outside the tall brick walls surrounding a vast estate in the mountain town of Telluride, only able to see thick groves of pines and a pointed roof through the night darkness. Moisture filmed his palms, and he grimaced. He hadn't been this nervous since . . . since he'd first met Anna.

She'd been working in a greenhouse and had come to assist him, her hands and face smudged with soil. He'd fallen in love on sight, but he'd needed several weeks to convince Anna of his sincerity. And after that, they'd lived happily ever after.

Until he'd foolishly decided he couldn't exist without her.

Nic blotted his palms against his jeans and stared at the distant house. An upper window beckoned him. She was there. He knew it. He felt it.

He needed only a magical thought to transport himself. The smells confirmed that this room belonged to a female: floral yet definitely woman. Curled up in the middle of a queen-sized bed was the woman. He recognized the scent. Not Anna's, yet close to it.

His heart filled his throat as he sank to the edge of the bed. In the dark of the deep night he couldn't discern much, but he didn't need to see. His other senses would guide him.

With extreme gentleness, he brushed his fingers over the woman's cheek. Soft, smooth, warm. Memories washed over him with such force he had to smother a groan. By the Blessed Stones, to hold Anna again, to touch her, kiss her, love her.

He found her lips and traced their contour, finding them full and slightly parted as she slept. A slight sigh escaped her, and Nic smiled.

His Anna. His long-lost Anna.

Placing one arm over her, he bent to taste her mouth—a mere brushing of lips that instantly ignited flames within him. He couldn't hold back his groan. Desire, longing, love returned with an explosive power.

He kissed her again, releasing his passion, tasting the sweetness of her mouth, relishing the softness of her lips. He had missed this, missed her desperately. When she slowly responded, he drew her closer, raising one hand to cradle her head.

The moment he touched her hair, he froze and drew back. The hair beneath his palm wasn't long and straight. It was short and tight with curls. This wasn't Anna.

Who was she?

Before he could even guess, her fist found his jaw, startling him more than hurting him. He slid to the floor but rose quickly, only to be greeted by a foot sharp in his midsection.

He doubled over. The woman had awakened . . . with a vengeance. *Stones.*

"Who the hell are you?" she demanded. As he dared to straighten, she kicked him again, and he staggered backward. "And what are you doing in my room?"

Obviously, he'd made a mistake.

"I'm calling security," she snapped.

Nic allowed himself a deprecating smile as he put a safe distance between them. "My apologies," he murmured.

He doubted she'd even heard him, for she was busy lifting the lamp from beside the bed. He was no fool. As she rocketed it toward him with the force of a Pro Bowl quarterback, he transported himself safely outside the estate.

He must have been misdirected. That fiery woman had definitely not been who he'd expected to find. He had to investigate some more.

And discover another way to meet his reincarnated Anna.

Had he been a dream?

Stacy Fielding examined her room in the morning daylight. She remembered hitting someone. The shattered remains of her lamp attested that something had happened. But what?

She'd called the estate security personnel last night, but they'd reported no visitors, no breaks in the perimeter system. And no one could have disappeared as that man had done. She had to have been dreaming. With all the stress of Dianna's summer tour, Stacy shouldn't be too surprised.

But what a dream.

She went through her morning routine in a daze. She hadn't lived twenty-five years without experiencing a kiss or two, but the one in her dream put them all to shame. Talk about sensuous. Every hormone in her body had snapped awake to beg for more.

If a man existed who could kiss like that, she was ready to sign up. At least for lessons. The last thing she needed in her life—or wanted—was a man. None of them had proven to be worth the time and energy.

Except maybe Kevin. But he fell into a different category.

With a shake of her head, Stacy descended the wide staircase, absorbing the quiet of the empty house. Time to get to work. She enjoyed the silence while she could. All too soon the phone would ring, the fax would spit out papers, and her computer would notify her of incoming mail.

And once her sister Dianna returned home, it would be insane.

With only a few weeks left before Dianna started her summer concert tour across the United States, Stacy never lacked for things to do.

She padded into the kitchen to pour a super-size mug of coffee, then took it into her office. Staring at her desk littered with papers, the schedule tacked to the bulletin board, the overflowing in box, she closed her eyes.

She hadn't intended it to be like this. She'd had dreams of her own once, before Dianna had sung that first fateful song and climbed the beginning steps to stardom.

Stacy sighed. With luck, Kevin would be her ticket out of this chaos.

The phone's shrill ring shattered the morning stillness, and Stacy winced. It had begun.

The German-made grandfather clock in the hallway struck two before she managed to break away long enough to make a sandwich. But she'd barely spread peanut butter on the bread before the front gate's buzzer sounded.

Should she ignore it?

She couldn't. She expected a delivery of costume sketches any day now.

She pushed the intercom button. "Who is it?"

"I'm here to see Stacy Fielding. My name is Nic Stone."

Why did that name sound so familiar? Stacy straightened. Of course. "Did Brad send you?"

"Ah . . . yes."

"Come on up to the house." She released the gate, then headed for the front door, unable to deny the thrill of anticipation. She'd been waiting far too long for this.

In a surprisingly short time, the doorbell played the beginning notes of Dianna's first hit, and Stacy opened the door to examine the man before her.

He was good-looking. Far too good-looking. Blessed with Hollywood appeal, he had dark brown hair, the color of melted chocolate and equally chocolate eyes—eyes that stared at her so intently she feared he could see into her soul.

"Stacy Fielding?" His voice held a hint of accent. Irish? English?

"Yes." She hesitated to say more. Something about this man unnerved her. Was she making a mistake in seeing him? "You said Brad sent you?" she asked again. She trusted her accountant. He'd screened employees for her before.

"Yes, Brad sent me." The man's guileless gaze met hers.

"You're the new gardener?"

His smile equaled the power of a full orchestra. "Nature is my specialty."

"Good. Good." Stacy nodded, reassuring herself, then held the door open. "Come on in. You said your name was Nic? Nic Stone?"

"That's right." He stepped inside, examining the interior, yet his expression displayed only curiosity, not the mercenary furtiveness she'd learned to recognize.

"The gardens are in the back." She led him through the house to the back porch and waved her arm to encompass the gardens. "The grounds are extensive, and you'll be caring for everything: the trees, the shrubbery, but especially the flowers. Have you had much experience with alpine gardens?"

He nodded. "I have experience with all areas of gardening."

She adored her gardens. When everything else became too much, she could always escape here for a few moments of solitude and strength. Motioning Nic to follow her along the inlaid stone path, she took him to where her flowerbeds lined the walkway. Brave daffodils trumpeted their bold faces into the capricious mountain springtime, and tulips peeked out from the soil with more timidity.

The grass had finally greened up again, and the trees were lined with buds of new leaves. Winter tended to linger in the mountains, so Stacy appreciated these first signs of spring all the more.

Evidence of a not-too-distant winter lingered on the peaks looming over Telluride, the pines flocked with snow, the colors ranging from majestic purple to the hints of rocky gray of cliffs. In another month or so, green would reign there, too, but for now, she found comfort here.

"It's beautiful."

As Nic spoke, she turned back to face him, surprised to see his expression held the same love for nature that she felt. Perhaps he would be a decent gardener. Well, Brad would only send the best.

"The position includes a cottage on the grounds." A gardener for this place had a more than full-time job. "I expect a lot. These gardens are important to me."

"I promise you they will have the best of care." Nic's smile held a hint of mystery, as if he harbored a secret he wouldn't share.

Stacy frowned. "And I'm warning you right now. If you think you're going to see much of my sister, you're sadly mistaken."

"Your sister?" His sudden stillness held tension. "Dianna?"

"That's right. When she's home, she's usually busy with her music. She rarely spends time in the gardens."

"She's not home now?" Though Nic asked the question casually, something in his tone made her hesitate.

"She'll be back in a couple of days." Though Nic had a good three inches on her, Stacy faced him, toe to toe. "I'm sure Brad had you sign the confidentiality agreement. If you attempt to extort from us or use your position here in any way to exploit my sister, I'll have you prosecuted in a heartbeat. Do I make myself clear?"

He nodded. "Perfectly."

"Good." Her pulse had increased, and Stacy stepped back, needing some distance between them. Men who looked like Nic Stone usually weren't gardeners. They belonged on movie screens. "I'll show you where the cottage is."

The building nestled against the brick wall on the back edge of the estate. Though small, it provided enough space for one man.

Or did it?

Once Nic followed her inside, the main room felt smaller, the air thicker. "This is it." She turned away from him to point out each of the rooms. "The kitchen is there, and there's a bedroom and bath. Utilities are covered as well."

"It is more than I expected," Nic said, his voice tugging at her like a long-forgotten memory.

"I'll let you get your bags and settle in. You have an intercom here, which will contact the house. You can reach the front lawns by going around the side. You don't need to go inside." Jeez, she was rambling.

"I understand."

Stacy turned toward the door only to encounter his potent smile again. Smiles like that should be illegal. "I expect you to start work tomorrow."

"I'd like to walk around the grounds and get a feel for the place now, if you don't mind."

"That would be great." Stacy beamed at him. "I had to fire our last gardener for selling Dianna's underwear on the I-net, and I haven't had time to tend to things myself."

"It'll be very well cared for." Again, the hint of secrets lingered in his eyes.

"Thank you."

"Thank *you.*"

That smile. Again.

Stacy left, her emotions torn. This new gardener appeared to have an honest appreciation for the gardens, yet she couldn't shake the feeling that something was wrong. Or was it his thanks and the way he'd acted—as if she'd handed him the world on a plate and tossed in the moon, too?

She'd have to keep an eye on him for the next few days—not an altogether unpleasant chore. Grinning, she hurried back toward the house.

Nic watched Stacy return to the house, unable to believe his good luck. A gardener? He could have been anything she expected him to be, but a gardener was perfect. For once, luck was on his side. What better job could there be for a member of the Fae?

Now he would be here daily, able to see his Anna . . . Dianna. In a short time, she would be his again.

He toured the small cottage in moments, using magic to give the appearance of settling in: toiletries in the bathroom, a book—on gardening, of course—on the table in the main room, and a few clothes in the dresser and closet. There, he was unpacked.

With a grin, Nic sprinted into the vast gardens, inhaling the crisp spring air, unable to keep the joy from his step.

After all this time, he'd finally found Anna. And all he was required to do in the meantime was care for the trees, bushes, and flowers.

He paused to survey the expansive grounds. Magic would take care of most of it, but he could use some pillywiggins' help on the flowers. Scanning the blossoms, he watched and waited.

Soon, his patience was rewarded with a flicker of color and light, barely noticeable to the human eye. But then, he wasn't human.

"Columbine," he called. "Come here."

The dancing flicker paused, then rose to hover before his face. The tiny flower faery was clearly visible now, her long hair encircled in tiny columbines, her short gown glowing with translucent color.

"Nic?" She flew closer. "What are you doing here? I thought you were in our world painting Titania's portrait."

"I finished that. I'm living here now." He couldn't stop his broad smile. "I found Anna."

"Anna? Your wife?" A sudden breeze caught Columbine, and she drifted away only to circle back and perch on a nearby tree limb. "But I thought . . . I thought . . ." Her voice lowered. "I thought she died."

"She did." Nic's smile fell. Anna had died because of his stupidity. "But she's been reborn as an immortal, so now we can be together forever."

Columbine flew to his forehead and placed her tiny palm against it. "Have you been eating hollyhocks?"

"No." He shook his head and the pillywiggin zipped back to the safety of the tree. "I loved Anna so much, I couldn't bear the thought of losing her, so I asked Titania to make her immortal."

Columbine's bright blue eyes widened. "And she agreed?" She abruptly tumbled from her perch, and Nic caught her, even before she had a chance to stop her fall.

Replacing Columbine on her seat, Nic grimaced. "Provided I paint her portrait." Titania never did anything without a price. "She claimed none of the mortal artists could get it right, so that left me."

Columbine glanced up from straightening her gown. "You *are* an acclaimed artist, Nic."

"That was decades ago. I've been gone from the mortal realm for years. That life is over now. It ended when Anna . . . left me." His words emerged with a shudder, the pain still too near the surface. "I should have known it was too easy. When Titania agreed to perform the spell, she neglected to tell me everything."

He paused, waiting for the constriction in his throat to ease. "I didn't know Anna would have to die until I was holding her body in my arms. Titania never told me Anna would have to be reborn."

"But you said she's alive, that you'd found her."

"I have." Knowing that helped push away the threatening grief. "It took me twenty-five years to paint Titania's portrait to her satisfaction, but I've been searching for Anna since I returned to this world. I knew she was here in the mortal world, somewhere between twenty and twenty-five years old, and I finally found her."

"How?" Columbine's gaze grew dreamy. "I bet you knew her on first sight."

"Absolutely." Nic would never forget seeing Anna—now known as Dianna Fielding—on the television screen. He'd searched everywhere, only to have her appear before him when he least expected it. She looked the same: her straight white-blonde hair long, her blue eyes vibrant, her skin tanned and smooth, her lips wide and full. He had no doubt she was his Anna. "She's a singer now. A pop star. And she lives here." He waved his hand toward the main house. "I should have expected it. Other than her gardens, Anna always loved to sing."

"How wonderful." The faery clapped her hands. "Oh,

Nic, all you have to do is introduce yourself, and she'll be yours again."

Nic sighed. "It's not that easy. Titania said she won't remember our life together."

"But you can win her." Columbine performed a dizzying twirl in the air. "You're Fae. No mortal woman can resist you if you so decide."

That was true. But with luck, some part of Anna would remember him, something deep in her soul would recall the love they shared. He hadn't used magic to win her love the first time, and he didn't intend to use it now. Magic was for more concrete things . . . like tending a garden.

"And you can help, Columbine."

"Certainly." She hovered before him.

"I need you and some of the pillywiggins to make this the best garden on earth, so it appears I'm doing my job as a gardener."

"You're the gardener?" Her soft giggle drifted on the air. "We'll be glad to do it. What fun." She soared away as she called to the others. "Pansy, Tulip, I need to talk to you. Nic is here, and we can help him."

Nic grinned. With their help, he'd have lots of time to woo Dianna. Provided the sister didn't get in the way.

The feeling of being watched made Nic turn, and he spied Stacy in a large window of the house, her gaze aimed in his direction. Probably wondering who he was talking to all by himself in the midst of the flowers. No doubt she'd suspect him of being loony.

Off to a good start I am.

With a cocky grin, he raised his hand in greeting, and she immediately disappeared from sight.

Odd one, that sister. She presented a cool, organized exterior, yet she had to have been the one he'd kissed last night. And he'd found definite, hot passion . . . and a foot in the gut. Which, come to think of it, was a lot like Anna.

Yet Stacy Fielding looked nothing like Anna except perhaps for the nose: long, slender, turned up slightly at the end. Stacy's hair was more a honey blonde, darker than Anna's, and short, in tight curls all over her head. And her eyes were more gray than blue, almost frosty, in fact, when she'd warned him away from her sister. But her mouth was generous. She could be attractive if she smiled. Though he didn't think she did that often.

A study of contrasts was Stacy Fielding. She could make it difficult for him to get near Dianna, but not impossible. Not for him. Nic smiled again and sauntered deeper onto the estate grounds.

With magic, nothing was impossible.

Two

"What else can go wrong?" Stacy hung up the phone, then shook her head. "I didn't say that." With her luck, something worse would happen.

With Dianna due home at the end of the week, Stacy needed to have everything ready to start rehearsals for the summer tour. She could make do with two costumes not being ready in time, but having a labor dispute threaten the completion of the scenery was too much. She'd insisted on having the sets delivered as is. With luck, she could find some painters in this area to finish them.

She stood and stretched the kinks from her back, pushing her arms toward the ceiling. What a horrible day. Thank goodness it was almost over.

A gentle breeze wafted in through the partially open window, carrying the scent of spring, drawing her gaze outside. Yes, the gardens. She always felt revived after spending some time there.

And she could check up on the new gardener. She'd barely seen him in the past two days and still wasn't sure if that was a good thing or a bad thing. Just thinking about him triggered an extra beat in her pulse.

Stop it, Stacy.

The last thing she needed—or wanted—was a man in her life. Besides, Nic Stone would undoubtedly be like every other man she'd ever met—with eyes only for Dianna, not her. She grimaced as unwanted memories surfaced. After this many years, she should be used to it, yet remembering Anthony's betrayal still hurt. And made her feel stupid.

Well, she was older and wiser now.

She emerged into the back gardens, reveling in the new blossoms on the apple trees, the jonquils lining the path, and the overall fresh scent of nature returning to life after a cold, hard winter. No other season held such magic as spring.

Already her headache was fading, her weariness dissipating. Now she felt only an eagerness to work in the soil. But where? The new gardener was obviously doing an excellent job. She couldn't find anywhere that needed tending. In fact, the entire area looked revitalized, alive with energy, better than she'd ever seen it.

She paused finally beside a bed of daffodils and knelt down to run her fingers through the soil. Not a sign of a weed or a fading blossom. Amazing.

A gentle breeze tousled the branches of a nearby lilac bush, the emerging buds capturing Stacy's attention. Soon the bush would burst open with color and scent that she could bring inside to help her through her long days.

But for now, the perfect daffodil blossoms would do. Stacy snapped several flowers, then froze, sensing a presence behind her. She glanced up over her shoulder to find Nic watching her, his expression unreadable.

A short shiver of guilt ran through her, as if she shouldn't be taking the flowers. But Stacy dismissed it. This was her garden. These were her flowers. She stood and faced him, lifting her chin. "I wanted some flowers to brighten my office."

He nodded but said nothing.

"They make the day more bearable," she added, explaining even as she told herself she shouldn't have to. "If I can't be out here, at least I can have some of it inside the house with me."

"Do you draw energy from nature?" His intense gaze made her feel her answer was important. With the towering mountains behind him, he appeared almost one with them, stalwart, imposing, a part of nature himself.

"I guess I do." Now that she thought about it, she did feel better when surrounded by plants and flowers. "I've always loved growing things." She smiled slightly. "If I hadn't gone to work for Dianna, I probably would have gone into botany or something similar."

Nic gave her a slow smile that caused her pulse to skip a beat. Damn, why did he have to look so devastating? "I understand. The daffodils will bring the sunshine inside for you."

"Exactly." He did understand. "They keep me going through the chaos."

He arched one eyebrow. "Chaos?"

"Arranging Dianna's schedule, her tour, her music."

"You do all of that?"

"I try." Most often she succeeded, though lately the pressure weighed heavy on her. If she could just get this tour off smoothly, then Kevin could take over, and she'd have her first break in years.

She glanced at Nic to find him studying her, as if he could read her thoughts. Searching to change the subject, she motioned toward the budding lilac bush. "How much longer before the lilacs bloom? They're my favorite."

As she'd hoped, Nic glanced toward the bush. "Two, three days, perhaps. Lilacs?" he asked. "Not roses?"

"No." Roses were more Dianna's type. "I prefer lilacs, even if they are short-lived. They give all they have in one burst—a fantastic scent and glorious color. Roses take so long to bloom, to reach perfection, then fade away after barely allowing a glimpse of that beauty."

That brought Nic's attention back to her, a quick tingle of excitement racing through her blood. His gaze locked on hers, warm and thoughtful. He raised his hand as if he intended to touch her, then dropped it again.

"You're a most unusual woman, Stacy Fielding." He sounded amused.

Stacy blinked in surprise. She'd never been told that before. Heck, she'd hardly been noticed before except as a means of getting to Dianna. "You only say that because you haven't met Dianna."

"I imagine she has her own unique qualities, too."

His sincerity reached deep inside her, stirring a new awareness. For a brief moment, tears pricked Stacy's eyes, but she blinked them quickly away. He acted as if he honestly appreciated her, as if he saw her for her, not as Dianna's sister.

She turned away, afraid of this longing he awakened. "I need to get these in water." She took only a couple of steps, then paused, words emerging before she thought them through. "Want to join me for dinner?"

Oh, jeez. Why had she said that? Already she knew it was dangerous to spend much time around this gardener. She rushed on with an explanation. "I'm ordering Chinese, and they won't deliver if I only order enough for myself."

She waited for his answer, her chest tight. Maybe he'd refuse.

Maybe he wouldn't.

"Are you sure I wouldn't be imposing?"

"No." She didn't want to be alone in that house, not tonight. Even if she was being foolish. "I'd enjoy the company." *Perhaps too much so.*

"Then I accept. Thank you." Nic smiled again, and Stacy couldn't help but return it, inordinately pleased at his acceptance. "Let me clean up, and I'll join you at the house," he added.

He didn't look all that dirty to her, but Stacy nodded. "See you soon then." She rushed away, unwilling to listen to the voice of warning in her mind.

What was she doing, inviting him to join her for dinner? She'd never done anything like this before. Not with a gardener. Not with any man.

Especially with someone who was a stranger.

Yet something about Nic Stone intrigued her, attracted her, made her curious to know more.

She put the flowers in water and placed them on the desk in her office, then grabbed the menu for a local Chinese place, perusing it as she headed for the back door. Cashew chicken for herself, of course, with fried rice, and—"Oh!"

Opening the door, she found Nic there, his hand poised to knock, and he stumbled forward, wrapping his arm around her waist to stop himself.

Which brought his lean, muscular form tight against her body.

Stacy stared at him, her eyes wide, unable to speak. She'd never been so aware of a man's presence in her entire life.

For a moment, time seemed to freeze as Nic returned her stare, heat flickering in his own eyes. Abruptly, he released her and stepped back. "I'm sorry. Clumsy of me."

"That . . . that's all right." Stacy stepped back, the air around her cool in comparison to the previous heat. "I . . . the kitchen is this way. I need to set the table." She hurried inside, not daring to look at him, her cheeks burning.

How could something so wrong feel so right?

The phrase from a song she'd written for Dianna flickered through Stacy's mind. How appropriate. She'd vowed never to get involved with another man, and that applied even to one as sexy as Nic. *Especially* to one as sexy as Nic.

"What should I order for you?" she asked, not daring to look back at him.

"I like it all." His voice was quiet, the hint of an accent teasing her senses. "Something spicy, perhaps?"

Yes, that fit him. Definitely spicy. "General Tso's chicken?"

"That's fine."

Stacy set the menu on the counter next to the phone, and Nic came to stand beside her, not touching her, yet very much a presence, long, lanky, and very, very male. "And hot and sour soup," he added.

"Okay." She placed their order and received a confirmation. Hanging up the phone, she looked at Nic. "Thirty-five minutes."

He still stood close, far too close for her rapid pulse, but good humor danced in his eyes. "Great. I'm starved. How much do I owe?"

"Nothing. I invited you."

"I insist. I wouldn't feel right otherwise."

Interesting. Most men were glad to let her pay. After all, her sister was wealthy, so therefore Stacy must have tons of money as well. "If you insist. Half is eight dollars."

Nodding, he touched his back pocket, hesitated a moment, then produced a slim wallet. Removing some bills, he handed them to her. "Here."

His fingers brushed hers as Stacy took the money, and she barely kept herself from jerking away. Something about this man, about his touch, affected her like a perfectly played sonata. Goose bumps ran up her arms, and she looked away, taking her time to put the money together with hers to pay the delivery person.

"I like this room."

At Nic's announcement, she turned back to him. He

stood in the middle of the kitchen, surveying the light wood cabinets and countertops, the island in the center, the pans hanging on hooks, and the philodendrons spreading their leaves along the macramé plant hangers. "So do I."

She enjoyed the soft warmth of this room. It felt like home and reminded her of the happy times spent with her parents in their smaller but equally loving kitchen.

"Whose house is this?"

His question startled her. Why should that matter?

Her unease must have shown, for he gave her a broad smile. "It makes me think of you, at least this room does. Did you decorate it?"

"Most of it." Stacy paused, then plunged ahead. What did it matter if he knew what everyone in town could tell him? "The house is in my name, as Dianna wasn't of legal age when we bought it, but it belongs to both of us. Once she became famous, we needed a place like this with more protection, with the space to have a studio on site."

"Is that the large building behind the house?"

"Yes, Dianna practices for her tours there and sometimes records some songs."

"Yet she's recording elsewhere now?"

Something in Nic's voice, a carefully concealed eagerness, made Stacy look at him sharply. "She's finishing up a new album. Her record label tells her where they want it produced."

"I see." He motioned toward the doorway. "Would you mind showing me around? I bet I can tell you which rooms you decorated."

"Can you?" Stacy joined him and led him into the formal dining area, where dark red curtains draped the tall windows, and a heavy wooden table filled the room. The decorations were sparse here: a burgundy table runner providing the only color to contrast with the white walls. She gave Nic a sideways glance. "Well?"

"It wasn't you." He ran his hand over the back of a mission-style chair. "The little touches are missing."

Stacy smiled. "Right." She and Dianna had divided up the decorating of the house. This room had been Dianna's, who believed the less fuss the better, unless it came to herself.

"What about this room?" Stacy continued into the music room, where a Steinway grand piano sat before wide windows trimmed with sheer white gauze and dusty blue curtains and valance. Messier than the previous room, sheet music, staff paper, pens, and pencils littered the light oak table nearby and songbooks filled the tall bookshelf on the opposite side. Two easy chairs and a love seat perched on the edge of a cream, blue, and mauve Persian carpet, creating audience seating for the piano.

Nic paced to the middle of the room, then turned slowly. Returning to face Stacy, he let a slow, seductive smile slide over his too-sexy lips. "It's warm here, homey, lived in. Your room again."

Yes, her room. Stacy ran her fingers over the Steinway, lingering, absorbing the mystical warmth it provided. If she couldn't be in the garden, she preferred to be here. "Correct again. I write Dianna's songs here."

"You write her songs?" Nic's surprise gave way to genuine interest. "Would you play something for me?"

"Sure." She relished any chance to make music. Sitting before the piano, Stacy ran her fingers over the keys. *What to play? One of my new songs? A song Dianna would never sing?*

No, like everyone else, he'd expect the lively tune of a Dianna Fielding pop song.

She launched into one of Dianna's recent hits but refused to sing it. That was her sister's forte.

She sensed more than saw Nic drawing closer. By the time she finished, he stood just behind her. He remained silent, and she twisted to look at him, startled by his pensive, slightly confused expression.

"That bad, eh?" She kept her tone light, but—dammit—his opinion mattered.

"You wrote that?" His gaze held hers, as if he were once again reading her thoughts.

"Yes. It's gone platinum for Dianna." Defensiveness leaked into her voice. This might not be her first choice of music, but she was good at it.

"It's well done, catchy, yet . . ."

"Yes?"

"It doesn't sound like you."

She jerked back, a reflex action. How could he know that? Even Dianna refused to see that the songs Stacy had written as a teen weren't what she wanted to write now. "You think you know me so well?" she asked.

"I guess not." He sounded disappointed but produced a smile as he waved his hand toward the open arch. "What's through there?"

"The living room." Stacy closed up the piano and followed him slowly, her stomach in knots. How could he know her so well? They'd just met.

Why did he think he knew her? Nic shook his head. How could he? Yet her song had startled him. It was lively, appealing, but he'd expected something entirely different—a slow love song, perhaps.

More likely he was imagining what his Anna would have played. She'd always enjoyed the romantic ballads. For a brief moment he had closed his eyes and pictured his wife at the piano, her fingers creating the music, but the sharpness of the tune had jerked him rudely from that fantasy.

Definitely not Anna's song.

He strode into the expansive main room, barely noticing the heavy wood furniture, his gaze going immediately to a large portrait hanging over the fireplace. Anna's portrait.

His breath caught in his throat, his chest tightened. What was it doing here? Did its presence confirm that his reincarnated Anna lived in this place?

He'd left it in his house when he'd gone to the magical realm to paint Titania's portrait, and when he returned, he'd found everything gone. He'd been disappointed, but what could he have expected after a twenty-five-year absence? Besides, finding Anna, alive and loving, had been more important than relocating her portrait.

And now it was here.

"Wonderful, isn't it?"

Stacy's voice reminded him of her presence, and he nodded. "Beautiful." Anna had always been beautiful, even first thing in the morning, but in this painting, seated on a bench among her blooming flowers, she'd been radiant.

"We love Nic Stone's work." Stacy started toward the portrait, then whirled to face him. "That's why your name was so familiar. Is he a relative of yours?"

A relative? Nic grimaced. What would she say if she knew he had painted that portrait? Instead, he nodded again.

"That'll thrill Dianna. She's been collecting his art ever since she found this portrait. The resemblance to her is remarkable, isn't it?"

"Is it?" He'd thought so when he'd seen Dianna Fielding performing on the television, but staring at Anna reminded him of her vivacity, her enthusiasm for life. She'd been so much more than her beauty.

"Very much so. Dianna saw this and had to have it. She occasionally tries to say it's her, but if you look close, you can see the differences."

"Differences?" All Nic could see were the similarities.

"Just small things, and I'm probably the only one who

notices simply because I know Di so well." Stacy came to stand beside Nic as they gazed at the painting. "This woman has a dimple in her right cheek. Dianna doesn't. Her fingers are more slender than Di's. Like I said, little things."

Little things were to be expected. Nic had long ago accepted that. His Anna couldn't be exactly the same as he remembered.

"She's supposed to be the artist's wife."

Nic started, not expecting to hear that, and Stacy smiled, adding, "The woman in the portrait, I mean."

"She was." The words emerged with a huskiness that surprised him.

She raised an eyebrow. "You say that like you know."

"I do." He knew only too well.

"Well, I guess you would, being a relative of his." She turned her attention back to the painting. "It's obvious he loved her very much, isn't it?" Stacy's voice trembled as well. "Every brushstroke reflects it. It's as if this is a testament—a declaration of their love."

Nic had never seen that in the painting. More evident to him was Anna's love for him, so clearly displayed in the teasing smile on her lips, the warmth in her eyes, the come-hither crook of her eyebrows.

For a brief moment, he heard her laughter again, her gentle admonishments to let her change position, her standard response to his passionate declaration of love. "I love you more." She'd always told him that just before she melted into his embrace.

And she *had* loved him more. He'd loved her only enough to destroy her.

"I wonder what's it like to be loved that much."

Stacy's soft voice shattered his dream, and he caught the quick flash of wistfulness that crossed her face.

"I imagine you'll find out someday," he said. The

woman he'd kissed that night had too much to offer to remain single all her life.

"I don't think so." She refused to look at him and leapt forward with eagerness when a bell chimed. "That will be our food at the gate."

She rushed from the room, obviously regretting her words, but Nic remained, unwilling to leave his last vivid reminder of Anna.

Soon. He had to keep telling himself that. Soon Dianna Fielding would return home, and he'd have his Anna alive again. Soon he'd be able to hold her, kiss her, make up for all the years they'd been apart.

But what about Stacy Fielding? For some odd reason, she appealed to him. Her appreciation of nature, perhaps. In any case, he owed her something. He planned to take away her sister, change Stacy's life completely from what it was now.

Her inadvertent wish for love tugged at him. Why would she think it was out of her reach? She was attractive, personable. He nodded. That's what he could do. He'd find the right man for her. That way she could be as deliriously happy as he and Dianna.

The only problem now was who?

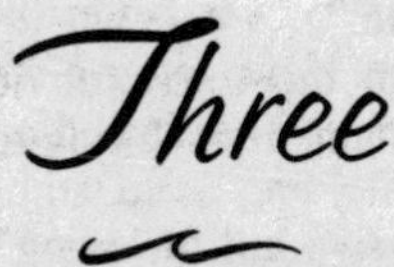

“There must be some mistake.” Stacy turned from the scenery backdrops to the delivery truck driver. “These aren’t what I ordered.”

The driver shrugged and held out his clipboard. “This is what I was given, and this is where I was told to bring it. You need to sign here.”

“Why?” Stacy struggled to keep from raising her voice. “Saying that I accept it? I don’t. I don’t accept this.”

“Either you accept it as is, or I take it all back.” The man met her icy stare, his expression devoid of emotion.

She wanted to stomp her foot like a child but refrained. This was ridiculous. Dianna’s show went on the road in a few weeks. She needed scenery for what they had planned, but this unfinished attempt was much worse than she’d been led to expect.

“What were those people doing for the past two months when they were supposed to be working on this?” she demanded.

Again the driver lifted his massive shoulders. “Don’t know. Don’t care.” He offered the clipboard once more. “You gonna sign or not?”

Stacy sighed. "If I sign this, it doesn't mean I'm satisfied with this stuff, just that it was delivered, right?"

"Suits me." Apparently, he only cared about her precious signature. Jeez.

Keeping the scenery was better than starting over, but not by much. "Fine. Here you go." She scrawled her signature on the paper, then snatched out her copy.

"Thanks, Ms. Fielding." He ambled away while she glared at the offensive bill of lading.

Studio Art and Design was definitely going to hear from her. She'd commissioned a specific set of backdrops for Dianna's tour and had nothing but some half-sketched scenery to show for it. How was she going to get this done in time? Where was she going to find artists at this late date?

Stacy stood before the backdrops, scowling. The splatters of green and brown hinted at the forest setting she'd commissioned but none of the magic nor the faery tale sense of wonder that she'd imagined.

"Damn. Damn, damn, damn." She spun around and stormed through the garden toward the house. She'd start by checking the Yellow Pages. Or perhaps Brad could help. He'd done an excellent job in finding a gardener.

In fact, she'd never seen her gardens look so beautiful. Everything was thriving wonderfully, even some flowers she hadn't expected to survive at this high altitude. Nic obviously had a magical touch with growing things.

Rounding a curve in the path, she spotted Nic, bent low, speaking to a patch of blooming crocuses. Stacy paused. Speaking? Yes, he was talking—to the flower or himself. Worse, he appeared to be listening as well.

She frowned. She'd heard of talking to plants to encourage them, but she'd never met anyone who actually listened for a response before. Of course, Nic Stone was different from anyone she'd ever met. Did that mean he was a few notes shy of a song?

"Nic?"

He straightened abruptly. "Stacy." He sounded startled.

She caught a quick flash of color out of the corner of her eye, but when she turned for a better look, nothing was there. A bird perhaps?

She looked back at Nic to find him watching her closely. What was it about this man that made her feel as if he saw into her soul?

"Do you usually talk to flowers?"

He released his devastating grin. "All the time. Works wonders."

"And do they answer?"

"Of course. The usual things: more water, get these bugs away from me."

Stacy blinked in surprise, and he laughed, a deep sound that held the warmth and richness of hot cocoa.

"I'm kidding," he added. "I listen for the sound of insects, of growth." Spreading his hands, he smiled again. "It's hard to explain."

She'd never heard of that before, but maybe that was what made Nic such an exceptional gardener. "That's all right. It obviously works." Stacy gave him a brief smile. If only her problems were that easy to solve. Her smile faded as she recalled her current scenery disaster. Finding someone to complete the backdrops wasn't going to be easy this far from a big city. "Have to go. I need to get back to work."

"What's wrong?" Nic touched her arm, stopping her.

Startled, she glanced at him. How could he know? "What do you mean?"

After a brief moment of hesitation, he spoke, "You seem upset. Can I help?"

Stacy blew out an exasperated breath. "Only if you're as good a painter as your ancestor."

Again, she felt his gaze probing, as if searching for her motives. She shook her head and pulled from his gentle hold. “Forget it. That’s just my frustration talking.”

“What’s wrong?” He sounded like he actually cared, and she responded without thinking.

“The backdrops for Dianna’s tour arrived, and they’re far from finished. I need them in place by next week, the week after at the latest.” She sighed. “I’m beginning to think this tour is jinxed. One stupid thing after another keeps going wrong.”

“Why do you need these backdrops?”

“They provide the atmosphere for Di’s road show. They were conceived to capture a mood, to package her songs.” She gave him a dry grin. “A lot more goes into these things than you’d think.”

“I’m beginning to realize that.” Nic caressed her hair, capturing a curl around his finger, and Stacy’s breath caught in her throat as she stared at him.

Why did he affect her so strongly?

“And you’re stuck managing it all,” he added, his tone soft.

Stacy tried for a casual shrug, her pulse racing. “That’s my job.” Stepping back, she forced him to drop his hand, enabling her to draw in a shaky breath. “I need to go.”

Nic fell into step beside her as she continued along the garden walk. “I can help.”

“Can you?” she asked dryly. Having an extraordinary gardener be a talented artist as well was out of the realm of possibility.

“I do paint. Quite well, I’m told. I can finish those backdrops for you.”

Stacy paused and stared at him. Though she wanted to believe him, she knew better. He probably sketched cute bunny rabbit drawings and thought that qualified him for the job. “Do you have any samples of your work?”

He hesitated, then nodded. “In my cottage.”

“Bring them to my office when you have a chance, and we’ll see.” She rested her hand on his arm. “Even if it doesn't work out, thanks for offering to help."

"It'll work out." His confidence sure didn't need any help. "I'll go get my paintings now." His muscles flexed beneath her palm as he drew away.

"Fine." Stacy watched him walk away, curling her hand into a fist. She liked touching him, the warmth and hardness of him. *Bad girl.*

Rushing toward the house, she tried to focus on the task ahead, but she kept seeing his chocolate brown eyes, his sincerity. What was it about Nic Stone? Every time she was near him, she lost a little more self-control.

She'd wanted to keep touching him, to weave her fingers into his hair, to feel his body against hers.

Heat warmed Stacy's cheeks, and she shook her head to chase away her errant thoughts. *Bad, bad girl.*

Get a grip.

She had work to do, and it wasn't going to get done if she mooned over a man. Reaching her office, she slid into her chair and stared unseeingly at the papers littering her desktop. But maybe . . . maybe after Dianna left on her tour, Stacy could spend more time with him, maybe he'd feel something for her, too, maybe . . .

Get real. She had more important things to worry about than attracting a gardener.

The scent of lilacs filled the room, and she spied a vase of fresh blossoms on her desk. Were they in bloom already? How did they get there? It had to be Nic.

She smiled, recalling their conversation in the garden. He'd remembered. Perhaps he—

Stop it. Giving herself a mental slap, she snagged the phone book and turned to the Yellow Pages. Several artists and galleries were listed, and she ran her finger down the page until she found one that mentioned commercial art. Might as well start there.

She'd just dialed when Nic appeared in her office doorway. "Stacy?"

She held up one finger to silence him as someone answered. "Hi. This is Stacy Fielding. I was wondering . . ."

Her words failed as Nic held up a small oil painting of faeries dancing among a bed of daffodils. It was magnificent. Even better, it was perfect.

She hung up the phone abruptly and rose to her feet, unable to believe her eyes. Nic couldn't have painted this. It was extraordinary. It vibrated with color, with life, with magic.

Taking the canvas from him, she stared at it, caught by the minute detail, the shimmery presence of the darting faeries. The painting transported her. Looking at it, she could almost believe in the fantasy world he'd captured.

She looked up at him. "You did this?"

Pride, amusement, and something more—something banked with heat—filled his eyes, and he nodded.

"Do you have any more?"

In response, he held up a stack of three more canvases. Her throat tight, Stacy laid them out on her desk. This was wonderful, fantastic . . . impossible.

Each painting reflected faeries in the garden—sprinkling magic on the flowers, swinging from the trees, nestled on a leaf. The color and imagery surpassed anything she'd ever seen except for the original Nic Stone portrait.

"You *do* have your relative's talent," she whispered.

"Do you like them?" Nic asked.

"I love them."

Watching her stare at his paintings made Nic smile. Pride warmed him. Pride and something more—a warmth he hadn't experienced since he'd lost Anna. She'd looked at his work like that, her face filled with awe and appreciation. He never used magic in his art, and Anna had always made him feel as if he didn't need magic for anything at all.

He stepped closer to Stacy, wanting to touch her, remembering the softness of her hair earlier. She intrigued him, drew him, touched something inside him he'd believed lost. And awakened a protective instinct he hadn't felt in ages.

If he could help her, he would. Simple.

But this need to hold her wasn't as simple. She wasn't the reason he was here. He'd come for Dianna . . . Anna. Yet being near Stacy made him forget that.

"These are perfect, Nic." Stacy turned to face him, her face glowing, and he clenched his fists to restrain the urge to pull her into his arms. "How did you know?"

"Know?"

"That I'd planned a faery theme for Dianna's tour. The backdrops are supposed to be scenes just like this. Of faeries in the forest and flowers. I want them to highlight the excitement and passion of Dianna's voice, to reflect the magic she brings when she sings."

He hadn't known. He'd merely captured moments in the garden, painting to pass the time. But the theme for Dianna's music didn't surprise him. Had enough memory of their previous life remained for her to be drawn to the Fae? "Just lucky, I guess."

Passion burned in Stacy's eyes, a passion that reminded him of the woman he'd kissed in the night. "I want you," she exclaimed.

Her cheeks grew warm as she apparently realized how her words could be interpreted, and Nic grinned, even while shifting uneasily to cover the sudden surge of desire her words had released. How was it she could so easily trigger his passion?

"To paint the backdrops," she added, obviously flustered. "I'll pay you extra for your time."

"That would be fine." Money meant nothing. He'd paint for free, but she'd never believe that.

"Don't you want to know how much?"

"I'm sure you'll be fair." He couldn't look away from the heightened color in her cheeks, the fullness of her lips.

Against all logic, he wanted a different kind of payment. He took another step closer, pausing just a hand's breadth from her, forcing her to tilt her head to meet his gaze.

He sensed her quickening heartbeat, felt the heat of her body, and caught the scent of her desire. She wanted him, too.

"Can you . . . ?" She paused to moisten her lips, and his gut knotted. "Can you get it done in time?"

"That won't be a problem." Painting wasn't a problem. Resisting her was.

He wrapped one arm around her waist and drew her against him, her soft curves meshing perfectly. Stacy's eyes widened, and he sensed her trepidation, her uncertainty, and her anticipation, so much like his own.

Raising his hand, he ran his fingers through her springy curls, then cupped the curve of her cheek. Her lips trembled, and he bent toward them. All he wanted was a brief taste. Just a taste. Surely that would be enough to ease this longing.

But the moment he claimed her mouth, he knew he'd lied. He wanted much more than that. Need jolted through him, a live fire that demanded quenching.

Stacy moaned, a quiet sound that only added fuel to his desire. She wrapped her arms around his neck, her fingers weaving through his hair, her breasts swelling against his chest, the peaks forming hard nubs.

He seduced her lips, teasing, gently nipping, swallowing her soft moans as if he could swallow all of her. He wanted more, more of the passion she gave so freely. He wanted to bury himself inside her, to experience the shattering bliss he'd nearly forgotten.

The shrill ring of the phone jerked him back to reality. He lifted his head to stare at Stacy's kiss-swollen lips, her bright eyes. By the Stones, what was he doing? This wasn't Dianna.

As the phone rang again, he pushed away from her.

This was insane. She wasn't his Anna. He ran his hand over his face even as he shook his head, trying to deny his actions, deny the feelings she stirred in him.

Stacy stared at him, disappointment then bitterness crossing her features.

At another ring, he forced a slight smile. "You'd better answer that."

Whirling around, she seized the receiver. "Hello?"

Stacy answered the phone, her voice remarkably controlled, and he studied her. She had her back to him, but the stiff line of her body told him more than he wanted to know. She was angry or hurt or both.

And he couldn't blame her.

"Yes." Stacy listened a long time. "You did the right thing. Good." Her voice softened, and Nic found himself frowning. "You said it." She even smiled. "Great. Till then."

She hung up the receiver, then turned to face Nic, meeting his gaze with eyes so cool he felt icicles form. "Dianna will be home tomorrow."

Dianna? Here? Tomorrow? Excitement pricked over his skin. Soon he'd have his Anna and escape this unreasonable attraction to Stacy. He struggled to keep his tone even. "That's good."

"That means I have even more to get done quickly." Stacy motioned toward the door. "If you'll show yourself out."

Nic nodded. To say anything now, to try to explain what he couldn't explain would only make matters worse. He made it halfway out the door when Stacy stopped him.

"You will do the backdrops?"

He didn't turn back but nodded. "I'll do them." It was the least he could do for the woman whose sister he planned to woo away.

Taking a few steps outside the door, he paused again and listened. He sensed rather than heard Stacy wrapping her arms around herself, and he frowned. He'd hurt her with his impulsive behavior.

He wouldn't let it happen again.

She was here.

Nic heard a vehicle arrive just after noon, and for a moment his heart stopped. Dianna was home. Finally.

Would she recognize him at once? Or would it be as Titania had said, that she wouldn't know him, wouldn't remember the love they'd shared?

Part of him wanted to race inside to see her. Another part feared the meeting. He wanted her to know him, to feel the same, to rush into his arms and cover him with kisses.

And if that didn't happen?

Nic swallowed to ease the lump in his throat.

Then he'd deal with it. And win her once again.

His feet took him to the house without any thought on his part. He heard voices inside and entered without knocking, moving toward them.

She stood just inside the entryway to the house, as petite and beautiful as he remembered, her long blonde hair shimmering in the light, her features perfect and animated as she spoke.

". . . excellent. Wait until you hear it, Stace." Dianna waved her hands in an expansive gesture. "I nailed every song, just the way I wanted."

"Even the ballad?" Stacy stood by the staircase, a slight smile on her face. Nic could see her affection for her sister.

"Well, no." Dianna made a flippant brush of her fingers. "It didn't really fit with the rest of the songs. You knew that. It was more you than me."

"I see." The smile left Stacy's face, but her tone revealed nothing. "What did you use in its place then?"

"That song Kev wrote for me."

"That has more depth to it than most of your songs."

"I know, but it's the direction we want to go. At least, that's what Kev said." Dianna tossed her hair over her shoulder, a gesture so familiar Nic clenched his fists to keep still, then she released a shout of glee. "And guess what, SBJ Productions asked me to write the song for their new movie. Kev told them yes, of course. What a coup."

"Oh? And is Kev going to write it?" Stacy sounded tired rather than excited, and Nic frowned, noticing the dark circles beneath her eyes.

"Of course not." Dianna went to give Stacy a hug. "You're the best, and that's what I want."

Stacy returned Dianna's hug, though she didn't appear as enthusiastic. "And where is Kevin?"

"He'll be here tomorrow. He stayed behind a day to tie up some loose ends." Dianna turned away to survey the stack of expensive leather luggage and bags in the entry. "I bought a gift for you."

Now Stacy smiled again. "You didn't need to do that."

"I know." Dianna beamed, warming Nic to his core. She was his Anna for sure. "But I wanted to." She dug into one of the large bags tossed among the pile of luggage and pulled out a wide-brimmed, floppy hat. "When I saw this, I just knew I had to have it. For you, I mean."

Dianna placed the hat on Stacy's head, and Nic smothered a laugh. The bright pink cap perched precariously on Stacy's curls. Surveying her sister, Dianna tilted her head, then sighed. "I don't understand. It looked great when I tried it on."

"Then why don't you keep it?" Stacy pulled off the hat. "I'm not much of one for hats, anyhow."

"But I wanted to get you something."

Stacy put the hat on Dianna, then gave her a quick hug. "You're home safe, and the new album is done. What more do I need?"

The hat was perfect for Dianna—as outgoing and vibrant as she was. "I did get something else. Something you're going to love."

"We'll see." Stacy stepped back, then whipped around toward where Nic stood in the shadows. She couldn't see him, not if he didn't want to be seen, yet he couldn't shake the uneasy feeling she knew he was there. Her next words confirmed it. "We have a new gardener. Brad found him."

"That's good. Now your gardens will be perfect, and you'll be happy."

"He does a wonderful job. Wait until you see how glorious the flowers are. And he's going to paint the backdrops, too."

Dianna laughed. "Sounds too good to be true."

Nic couldn't wait any longer. This was his long-lost Anna. He knew it. With merely a thought, he moved himself outside the open door to the house and peeked in. "Hello?"

A brief frown crossed Stacy's forehead when she spotted him, but she motioned him inside. "And here he is. Dianna, this is Nic Stone. Nic, my sister, Dianna Fielding."

"I'm pleased to meet you." He extended his hand and wrapped it firmly around hers as he met her brilliant blue eyes, willing her to recognize him.

But the polite smile she gave him held no awareness, no emotion. Didn't she know him at all? Surely with the love they'd shared, she'd at least feel something.

"Thank you," she murmured. She drew her hand back, then eyed him, the look of a woman seeing something she liked. "Nic Stone? One of my favorite artists. Any relation?"

"Yes." He left it at that.

A slow grin creased her rosy lips as she tilted her head

to one side. "Hmmm. Nice. I didn't know they made gardeners like you."

Nic gave her a slow, seductive smile. He was willing to start there. "I'm one of a kind."

"That's true." Stacy stepped between him and Dianna, draping her arm around her sister's shoulders. "The gardens have never looked so good."

"I can understand why." Dianna lowered her lashes, then peered at him from beneath them. A definite sign of interest. "Are you staying in the cottage?"

"Yes."

"Hmmm." A world of meaning hung in that simple sound. Did she plan to come to him? Did she remember what they'd shared after all?

"Enough, Di." Stacy glared at Nic. "Nic needs to get back to work, and you need to get unpacked."

"Oh, wait. Not yet." Dianna gave Nic a beguiling smile, one that had him ready to give her his heart on a platter. "Can you help me bring in my special present, Nic? It's too heavy for me."

"I'd be happy to." He would do anything she asked.

"Come. It's in the car." She led him to a limousine and motioned toward a tall, flat, paper-wrapped object nestled against one of the seats. "Will you carry that into the living room? Please?"

"Your wish is my command," he responded, holding her gaze for a moment. Still no recognition there, but definite interest.

Lifting the package, he followed her inside, past Stacy, to the main room where he placed the load against the wall as Dianna indicated, opposite where Anna's portrait hung.

"What is it?" Stacy asked, joining them. "Another painting?"

"Better than that. Another Nic Stone painting. I found it quite by accident and couldn't believe my good fortune." Dianna worked at the string holding the wrapping around the frame.

Nic blinked. One of his paintings? He'd done many during his last Nic Stone lifetime yet few full-length portraits, which this had to be. In fact, other than Anna, the only other portrait he'd done in the last fifty years had been . . .

"You'll never guess who this is." Dianna pulled the paper free and stood back, her face lit with excitement.

Nic's throat closed. His pulse rumbled in his ears. It couldn't be. Impossible.

"I have no idea." Stacy stepped closer to survey the portrait. "She's beautiful." She hesitated. "And somehow familiar."

"It's Titania." Dianna bounced on the balls of her feet. "Do you believe it? The queen of the Fae. No one even knew Nic Stone had painted this, but I had it authenticated. Isn't it fantastic?"

"Extraordinary." Stacy stood by her sister as they stared at the portrait.

Nic stepped back. Impossible. This couldn't be here. He'd painted Titania's portrait as payment for giving Anna immortality and left it in the faery realm. It couldn't have entered the mortal realm unless Titania wanted it here.

Which meant only one thing.

Trouble.

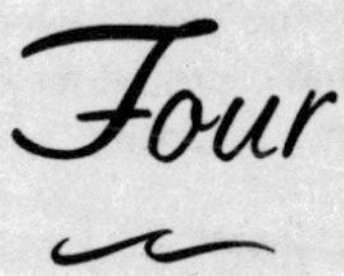

Four

Who was Nic Stone? Though Stacy was supposed to be watching the dancers practicing their backup routines for Dianna's program, her gaze kept drifting over to where Nic worked on the scenery.

The man was gorgeous, no doubt about that, yet secretive about his past. He was a fantastic groundskeeper and an incredible artist.

And the best kisser in the world.

Why *had* he kissed her?

She hadn't expected it. She'd told herself not to respond, then ended up wanting it to never end. She'd melted in his arms like a lovesick teenager only to have him thrust her away with an expression of horror, as if he'd kissed a swamp monster or something. Nothing like a little revulsion to cool one's ardor.

So, why did he do it?

For one brief moment she'd allowed herself to fantasize that he might be attracted to her, but after seeing him around Dianna, she'd quickly lost that notion. His gaze followed his sister constantly. No surprise there. The men always preferred Dianna.

Yet Stacy had hoped Nic would be different.

She dragged her gaze back to the dancers. Jermaine Silva acted as Dianna's choreographer, and he stood in front of the stage shouting directions to the four men as they practiced. Jermaine had created an excellent routine for this road show that captured the mystical feeling Stacy liked to portray. Now, if Dianna would attend practice as well, they'd be set.

Stacy had let her sister sleep in since it was her first day home, but it was almost noon. If Di didn't show up soon, Stacy was going to drag her out of bed.

"I'm here." Dianna breezed in, and instantly everyone's gaze went to her.

She was lovely. Even clad in form-fitting jeans and a T-shirt, her long blonde hair loose around her shoulders, her sister radiated beauty and sex appeal. That had helped her rise to fame, no doubt. But fortunately, Dianna had talent, too.

"Sorry to be late." Dianna beamed a smile that had Jermaine forgiving her, even as he motioned her onto the stage. "I overslept."

Stacy shook her head with a dry smile. Dianna wrapped all the men around her little finger without even trying. And if she tried—heaven help that fellow.

At Jermaine's nod, Stacy restarted the recording of her piano accompaniment to a new song, then sat back to watch. Dianna's appearance energized the group. The men's movements became sharper, more focused, as they danced behind her.

Dianna's dance talent was limited, her steps less complicated than the men's, but when she opened her mouth to belt out the tune, Stacy smiled. So much voice for such a petite woman. Dianna deserved her star status, bringing emotion to her singing that tugged at the audience.

Stacy might write the songs with an equal amount of emotion, but she could never present them with the same gusto that Dianna did. Just as well. Stacy had no desire to be up on the stage. She much preferred her place at the piano.

It was her place in the office she hoped to lose.

After an hour of practice, Stacy went to congratulate her sister. "It looks great. You're catching on to those new moves quickly."

Dianna wiped her face with a towel. "Kevin made me work on them while we were gone. The man's a task-master."

Despite her words, Dianna's tone held no anger, and Stacy laughed. "Which is just what you need," she said. "And you know it."

Lowering the towel, Dianna grinned. "Sometimes."

Nic lowered his paintbrush, unable to look away from the two sisters in conversation. Each of them tugged at him, intrigued him. Dianna's appeal he understood. She was his reincarnated Anna. But why Stacy? In appearance she was so opposite from Anna, yet her love of the gardens, her hidden passion, her ability to make music all touched a chord within him.

And her kiss . . . her kiss provided enough electricity for an entire city. He needed to kiss Dianna soon to wipe away the teasing memory of Stacy's lips beneath his. If he were wise, he'd avoid Stacy altogether.

Of course, no one had ever accused him of being wise. He was Fae, after all.

The sisters finished talking, and he met Dianna's gaze as she looked toward him. Her warm smile triggered a rush of fire through his veins, and he wiped his hands, turning to greet her as she approached.

"Your singing is incredible," he said. Her voice worked a definite magic. Perhaps it was because she'd been given immortality. Though his reincarnated Anna wouldn't have Fae magic, eternal life had to hold some special power of its own.

"Thanks." She acknowledged his compliment with a bob of her head, then surveyed the backdrop. "You're doing a great job yourself. Stacy told me how you're helping us out. I really appreciate it."

"I'm glad I could help." He'd do anything for his Anna.

Dianna started to touch the painting, then drew her hand back. "Your flowers and faeries are so lifelike. I can almost see them moving. Stace is going to rave over this."

"Not you?" Though irrational, he wanted her approval of his work, too.

"Oh, it's awesome." She gave him a smile that soothed his doubts. "But Stacy is the one who loves this faery theme. She created it for me when I first started performing."

"But?" he asked, hearing it in her voice.

"But I'm twenty-two now. I think it's time to change my image, to grow up a little more." Dianna placed her hands at the small of her back and arched, a stretch that drew Nic's gaze to her pert breasts and slim hips. "Oh well, next tour."

He couldn't stop himself from touching her shoulder. "No matter what the atmosphere, I'm sure everyone sees you for the woman you are."

He sure did. He remembered well how Anna's breast filled his palm, her soft murmurs of pleasure as he buried himself inside her.

He reached up to cup Dianna's chin. Why didn't she remember him? When would she realize they belonged together?

"Kevin!"

They both turned at Stacy's exclamation. A good-looking young man walked toward Stacy, evidently not much older than she was, yet he held himself with confidence. The smile that he gave Stacy held warmth: a more-than-casual warmth that made Nic frown.

When the man wrapped Stacy in a tight hug and placed

a light kiss on her lips, Nic dropped his hand from Dianna, irritated. Who was this guy? What gave him the right to touch Stacy like that?

Before he could even examine the depth of his feelings, Dianna let out a squeal of delight and bolted toward the man. "Kev."

The man laughed as she bounded into his arms, and he swung her off her feet. Nic frowned even more, especially when the man kissed her, a kiss of definite passion that lasted far longer than it needed to.

Who *was* this guy?

Nic started toward them, unable to stop himself, already resenting this intrusion, this violation of his Anna. When the man and Dianna finally parted, Nic met the man's gaze in definite challenge.

To his surprise, the man laughed again and came over to meet him, hand extended, the other arm wrapped firmly around Dianna's shoulders. "Hi. I'm Kevin Montgomery. You must be Nic. Stacy told me about you. Our man of many talents."

Nic accepted the firm handshake despite his reluctance. "She's told me nothing about you."

Kevin cast Stacy a teasing look. "Nothing? I'm hurt." He faced Nic again. "I'm taking over Stacy's position as Dianna's manager."

Manager? That was a pretty intense kiss for a manager.

Stacy came to join them, placing a hand on Kevin's arm. "He's also Dianna's fiancé. They're getting married after this tour."

"If we survive it," Kevin added, exchanging a warm glance with Dianna.

Dianna snuggled closer to him. "Oh, you'll survive." Mischief danced in her eyes. "And if not, it's a great way to go."

Squeezing her shoulders, Kevin grinned. "Absolutely."

Fiancé? Dianna was engaged? Nic couldn't speak. His

chest tightened. How could she even consider another man? *He* was her rightful mate.

And he would convince her of that.

Soon.

Stacy rocked back in her chair later that evening while Kevin examined the sales information thus far for Dianna's tour. The recurring fresh batch of lilacs in her office scented the air, and she drew in a deep breath. Kevin was back, and she had lilacs in her office. Things were looking up already.

"Sold out in three-quarters of the cities already," Kevin said, tapping the paper. "That's great." He twisted to sit on the edge of her desk. "I've confirmed hotels in all the cities. Dianna will have the best suites available with guaranteed privacy and security."

"Of course she will." Stacy shook her head with a wry smile. Dianna had quickly become accustomed to the best money could buy. Well, she'd earned that money. She might as well enjoy it. "What about the new album? Will it be released in time to coincide with her opening concert?"

"They say it will." A twinkle danced in Kevin's eyes. "And I made them put it in writing with a monetary penalty if it doesn't."

Stacy laughed. "You're going to be great in this business."

"Does that mean you're really going to give it up?"

"Yep." In fact, she couldn't wait. "You go with Dianna on the tour. Once you get back, it's all yours: the arrangements, the music, the whole entire headache."

"Are you sure?" Kevin leaned forward. "Really sure? I don't want you to have any doubts, Stace, as I'm not sure I'll be willing to give it back."

"Very sure. You've earned it, Kev. I wouldn't do this if I didn't trust you."

"But you made Dianna everything that she is. You raised her after your parents died, wrote her songs, created her image. I can't believe you're willing to walk away from her."

"I'm not walking away from her. She'll always be my sister. I love her." Stacy met Kevin's brilliant blue gaze. "But I need to find my own life."

"Which is?"

"To be honest, I'm not sure, but it's out there. Somewhere." She hadn't thought much past the time when she'd no longer have to arrange every facet of Dianna's career.

Kevin tugged a piece of her hair. "You'll be great—no matter what it is."

"Thanks for the confidence." Stacy smiled at him, aware—not for the first time—of how lucky her sister was. Did Dianna realize what a catch she had in Kevin Montgomery? Knowing Dianna, probably not. After all, she'd always had men throwing themselves at her.

A handsome man of twenty-seven with curly blond hair and an athletic build, Kevin not only looked the charmer but had the intelligence and heart to match. There had been a short period of time when Stacy had hoped . . . but no, as usual, all the men belonged to Dianna. Still, Stacy liked Kevin and more importantly, trusted him. Few of the male species could fill that requirement. Especially after Anthony.

The sound of a throat clearing made her look around to find Nic in the doorway, a scowl on his face. "Yes, Nic?"

"I have one of the backdrops done. I'd like you to approve it before I start the others."

"Done?" He'd only started that morning. "Don't kill yourself with this."

"I'm not." He waited, eyeing her and Kevin with a look

she couldn't quite place. Jealousy? Not likely. "Are you free right now?"

"Sure." Stacy punched Kevin's leg, and he dropped his foot from her chair so she could stand. "Want to take a look, Kev?" Next year this would be his headache.

He shook his head. "It's been a killer couple weeks. I hear a Jacuzzi calling my name."

And from the glimmer in his eyes, he wouldn't be alone.

Stacy grinned. "Just clean up after yourselves." Last time he and Dianna had shared a Jacuzzi, they'd completely flooded the room.

"Not a problem."

Stacy joined Nic, startled by the darkness in his gaze. "Let's go take a look." She touched his arm, and he turned away, stalking from the house, not even waiting to make sure she was following.

"What's wrong with you?" she asked when he finally paused on the path to the studio.

"I don't trust him."

"Kevin?" She had to laugh. "You don't trust Kevin? That's fine. You don't have to. I do."

"What do you know about him?"

"Quite a bit, actually." She paused to face him. "A lot more than I know about you."

Nic scowled. "I just think—"

She shook her head. "Stop right now, Nic. If it comes down to a choice between Kevin, whom I've worked with for two years now, or you, who has been here not even a week yet, you'll lose. Remember that."

A light blazed in his eyes, startling her with its fierceness, and she stepped back. "You're letting him take over Dianna's career?" he asked.

"He's earned that right. I hired him as my assistant a couple years ago, and he's been a hard worker with a quick mind and the instincts necessary to survive in this business. In the long run, I expect he'll do a better job with her career than I have."

"And because of that, you're giving him Dianna, too?"

"Giving him Dianna?" Stacy studied Nic closely. Was that what this was all about? Dianna? She grimaced. For a brief moment she'd actually hoped Nic had been worried for her. She should know better by now. "Nobody *gives* Dianna. She fell in love with Kevin after he came to work here, after we made our deal for him to take my place. They're perfect for each other."

"You sound certain about that."

Stacy turned away and resumed walking toward the studio. "I am." Reaching the entrance, she hesitated. "Is the backdrop really done, or was that some excuse so you could grill me on Kevin?"

"It's really done." Nic brushed past her, his tone cool, and switched on the lights. "There."

"Oh . . . my . . . God." Stacy's breath caught in her throat. She'd shown Nic the sketches of what she'd wanted, but this . . . this surpassed her wildest dreams. Unable to tear her gaze away, she walked steadily toward the scenery, not stopping until she stood an arm's length from it. "This is incredible."

The painting appeared eerily alive, the trees so real she could almost see them moving in the breeze, almost smell the fragrant flowers. Even better were the tiny fairies hovering over the blossoms and darting among the bushes. Stacy reached out to touch one, half expecting to feel the beating wings against her palm.

But it was just canvas.

She took a step back and released her breath, still unable to look away. With scenery like this, Dianna's show would take on an entire new element.

"I think you're wasting your time as a gardener," she murmured.

Nic came to her side. "I like working in the gardens." Some of the stiffness had left his voice.

"You're good at it, but this . . ." She waved her hand at the backdrop. "This is outstanding. You could make a fortune with this kind of talent."

"I paint because I enjoy it. Not for the money."

Stacy turned to stare at him, startled by his sincerity. "You're serious?"

"I don't do anything for money."

She'd heard other men say something similar, especially when confronted with their intentions toward Dianna, but none had spoken with such conviction. "Then why are you pursuing my sister?" She had to know. Wanted him to deny it. "You don't know her other than from her music."

"I know her." He spoke so softly she wasn't sure she heard him.

"So that's why you kissed me?" She had to say it, to get it out in the open and dispel her foolish daydreams. "To get to Dianna?"

"No." The word emerged with vehemence. "I didn't intend to do that. I didn't expect . . . I didn't know . . ." Nic trailed off, his gaze locked with hers, his presence exuding masculinity as Stacy realized they were all alone in the large building. "I'm sorry."

"I just happened to be available, is that it?" She didn't hide her bitterness. "Someone to make do with until Dianna came home?"

"No. I wouldn't do that." His voice took on a huskiness that twisted Stacy's stomach. "There's something about you, Stacy. I don't know what. Your passion for nature, for the gardens . . ."

She gave a harsh laugh. "Oh, this just gets better and better. You kissed me because I like flowers."

"That's not it at all." Nic paced away from her, then turned to face her from several feet away. His expression held pain. That and something more. "I like you, Stacy."

His simple declaration sent warmth spiraling through her, shattering her defenses. She couldn't trust him, but she wanted to. Oh, how she wanted to. "I thought I liked you." More than that, he'd awakened something in her too long dormant: a need she'd long ago discarded.

"Stacy, I . . ."

Awareness thickened the air as his gaze fell to her mouth. Stacy swallowed, remembering all too clearly the heady sensation of his lips on hers, the drunken stupor his touch could induce. If he tried to kiss her again, would she let him?

She should refuse. She could refuse.

But would she?

Unable to stop herself, she took a step toward him, the sudden gleam in his eyes all the encouragement she needed.

Nic stood immobile, his fists clenched at his side as if fighting himself. His indecision was obvious, but the heat won out, the fire in his gaze becoming even more intense. The rigidness left his body as he stepped closer. She could feel the internal heat radiating from him.

You're a fool, Stacy girl. Yet she didn't pause. Something about this man drew her, intrigued her, made her want what she shouldn't want.

He extended his hand to touch her cheek, then froze, his entire demeanor changing, almost as if he heard something she missed. He drew away from her. "I have to go."

"What—?"

He didn't give her time to even question him but rushed from the building. Stacy closed her eyes to hold back the sudden tears. He had no right to make her feel, to touch her emotions, then pull away like this.

Damn him.

• • •

Nic materialized in the living room, unable to deny the voice calling his name. A voice he'd never wanted to hear again.

Crossing his arms over his chest, he faced Titania's portrait, now hanging on the wall opposite Anna's. "What do you want?" he demanded. He'd known the appearance of her portrait meant no good.

A shimmer around the frame hinted at its ability to be a portal, and the appearance of Titania before him in the room verified it. Though beautiful by any standards, Fae or mortal, Titania, queen of the Fae, had no heart and no qualms about manipulating others to achieve her own purpose.

"That is no way to address your queen." At the iciness in her voice, Nic dropped to one knee and bowed his head, fighting the urge to shake her instead. She extended her hand and waited for him to place a brief kiss on it. "Much better." Her nearly translucent gown revealed as much of her voluptuous curves as it covered, but even naked she wouldn't appeal to him. "You may rise."

He stood, unable to deny the dread rising within him. Her appearance here, now, could only mean one thing. "I've found Anna, haven't I?"

"Perhaps." Titania faced him, her expression revealing nothing. "Are you sure that you have?"

"I'm positive." Dianna was his Anna. He knew it. "Otherwise, you wouldn't be here."

Her smile held no warmth. "You're right, of course. How could I miss witnessing this wonderful reunion?" Malice sparkled in her eyes. "Though you're not having much luck thus far, are you?"

"Dianna will be mine." He made the words a vow. "Even if she doesn't remember me."

"I have no doubt you can bewitch any woman you wish, my handsome Nic, but be careful." Titania approached him and drew a long fingernail down his chest. "There is a condition you must meet."

"Condition?" He frowned. "You never said anything about a condition when we made this agreement."

"Didn't I?" She gave a careless shrug of her shoulder. "It may have slipped my mind."

"Then there is no condition." Anything she thought of would not be good, he knew that.

"I'm afraid not." She ran her fingers over his face and he resisted the urge to pull away. "It just means you're lucky I thought to tell you now."

Trust her to play dirty. She hadn't told him Anna would have to die to achieve immortality, and now this. He wasn't surprised. "So what is it?"

"Only this, Nic. When you declare your love to your Anna, be very sure she is your Anna. If you tell the wrong woman you love her, then . . ."

A hard lump formed in his gut. "Then what?"

"Then you belong to me." Her smile broadened. "Forever."

"No." He never wanted to return to the magical world, especially if it meant becoming her plaything.

"No more playing in the mortal realm. No more pretending to be human." She tightened her fingers on his chin. "You'll be mine, under my command."

"I won't." Titania was the main reason he'd spent centuries in the mortal world. Under her ever-tightening reign, the magical realm was becoming more and more a prison and less the paradise it had once been.

"You don't have a choice, my artist." She squeezed his chin, then released it. "Besides, if you're so certain you've found your Anna, it won't be a problem, will it?"

"I *have* found my Anna." She was here. His inner instinct told him that.

"Very well." Titania swept toward her portrait. "Then you won't mind if I watch, will you?" With a broad swish of her arm, she disappeared, the shimmer around the frame glowing, then fading.

Nic stared at the painting, a chill permeating his veins. He should have known not to trust her. The last thing Titania wanted was for him to find happiness with Anna.

Well, he'd prove her wrong. He'd convince Dianna to love him and find some way to shake his irrational attraction to Stacy.

He had no choice.

Would she never learn? Stacy wandered the dark garden paths, wishing she could banish her disillusionment into the night, dispel her foolishness at wanting to believe so badly that someone could prefer her to Dianna.

As if.

Well, she wouldn't be so stupid again. She couldn't fire Nic, not with his talent as an artist and gardener, but she could avoid him. And she would.

Stacy plopped down on a bench tucked into the shrubbery and buried her face in her hands. Was it seeing Dianna and Kevin so happy that made her feel so needy? Ever since Nic's arrival, she'd been restless, wanting something just beyond her reach, not altogether sure what it was.

A new life? She *was* making a drastic career change. Once she passed over control to Kevin, she'd have a freedom she hadn't known since she was seventeen.

But what would she do then?

Write songs.

The songs that called to her—far removed from the pop tunes she'd been composing for Dianna. She might never sell any of them, but they'd be her music. The songs of her heart.

And would they reflect this new restlessness, this sense of loss and yearning she couldn't comprehend? She closed her eyes, listening to a new tune sing its way to life in her mind, the notes almost visual.

Oh, yes, the yearning was there, adding to the ache already inside her. She wanted . . . she needed . . . what?

A man?

But not just any man. Only the right man. The one man destined only for her.

Who couldn't possibly exist.

She released a heavy sigh, then started as a hand touched . . . caressed her hair. Jerking her head up, she stared at Nic standing before her. She hadn't even heard him approach.

Her first instinct was to order him away, but the look on his face stopped her. "What happened?" she asked. "You look like you saw a ghost."

"Worse than that," he muttered, his accent stronger than usual.

"What?" *Worse?* "Are you all right?"

His slow smile added an extra grace note to her pulse. "How like you—to worry about me when I'd more expect you to be angry."

Recalling his earlier desertion, she scowled. "I am." But the warmth of his gaze went far in alleviating that anger.

"And I deserve it. I'm sorry, Stacy." He ran his hand over her hair, then jerked it back and moved away. "You're making this much more difficult than I expected."

"Making what more difficult?" she asked. He spoke in riddles. "Am I making you do too much? Let me help."

"Not that." Though he stood, his intense gaze burned as it met hers. "The work is easy enough. It's the understanding and knowing what to do that's the problem."

"What to do about what?" Stacy stood to face him. "You're not making any sense."

"Probably not. Nothing's going as I expected." He reached for her, then stopped and turned away. "I need to go."

"Go? Why?" Was he deserting her yet again? "You can't bear to be around me?"

"Stones, no." He looked back, the fire in his eyes brilliant. "If I stay, I might not leave at all."

Her stomach lurched as anticipation tingled along her nerves. "And that's bad?"

"It could be." He closed his eyes, his inner struggle obvious. "You don't understand. I barely understand myself." Opening his eyes again, he approached her slowly, each step closer adding to Stacy's inner tumult. "There's something about you. I want to . . . but you're not the right one."

She'd lost all hope of making sense of his words, but his final statement hit home. "Yeah, tell me about it. I've never been the right one."

And Anthony had made sure she'd known she never would be. Though she'd tried to erase the memory of their last meeting, it lingered still—the way he'd gotten Di alone and tried to attack her, his anger when Stacy had stopped him, his bitter, horrible words that Stacy would always be second fiddle.

"I didn't mean that. . . ." Nic seized her shoulders, his eyes blazing. "By the Stones." He ground out the words between clenched teeth. "I can't resist, Stacy."

"Wha—?"

She couldn't finish, as his lips found hers with a ferocity that wiped all coherent thought from her mind. Now, this was what the songs were about, and even then the music could only begin to capture this sensation. Lyrics were inadequate.

Held close, Stacy could only respond, a wild rush of

desire exploding in every cell. She gave with a lack of inhibition that surprised her, demanding more, meeting the ravage of his mouth with equal force. More. She wanted more. Yet even that wouldn't be enough.

Nothing in her past had come close to this, and she suspected nothing ever would again. And the feelings his kiss generated defied explanation: desire, wanting, but more—a melding, a oneness, a sensation of coming home, and fireworks. All of it together.

She clenched Nic's shoulders tighter as he lifted his head, her breathing ragged. He gave her an apologetic smile. "I shouldn't have done that, but I won't apologize for it, either. It needed doing."

His tone suggested there was more. "But?"

Releasing her, he stepped way. "But I can't let it happen again. You're special, Stacy, but you're not her."

"Her?" Was it the continuing dizziness of his kiss that made it difficult for her to follow his train of thought?

"You're not Anna." His sad smile added to the knot in her stomach.

"Anna?"

"My wife." Nic nodded once, then hurried away, disappearing into the garden as quietly and quickly as he arrived.

Wife? He has a wife?

Stacy sank back down to the bench. And he'd kissed her like that? She brought her hand to her forehead, trying to contain her chaotic thoughts. He'd never given any indication of being married. Quite the opposite, in fact.

He'd smiled at her as if she were the only woman alive. He'd held her. Damn him, he'd kissed her with enough passion to make oceans boil.

Stacy shook her head and stood, anger mixing with her surprise. She should fire him.

But her garden . . .

The flowers, trees, and shrubbery had never looked so

vibrant, so alive this early in the season. And what about the scenery? It had to be completed soon. She'd be crazy not to let Nic finish his inspiring painting.

But she had enough sense to stay away from him.

As long as Nic did his job, he could stay. But if he stepped out of line again, then . . . then she'd have to get rid of him. Consequences be damned.

The next morning, Nic painted halfheartedly, still trying to justify a kiss that had shaken him to the core, a kiss he'd known better than to take, a kiss he hadn't been able to resist. He should have never kissed Stacy. If only she hadn't looked so lost, so hurt when he tried to explain, perhaps then he could have walked away.

No, he knew himself better than that. Anna . . . Dianna was his future, his soul mate, but he was male enough to be tempted by Stacy. Despite spending hundreds of years with the mortals, he was still Fae, still swayed by the power of desire. By getting that kiss out of the way, he could rid himself of that desire and move ahead with a clear goal.

Except that he couldn't forget the way Stacy felt in his arms, the softness of her body, her lips, the passion of her response, the stirring within that had nothing to do with the physical.

Nic scowled. He had to forget. If knowing that Dianna was Anna wasn't enough, the threat of falling under Titania's control by choosing incorrectly was more than adequate to keep him away from Stacy.

Pausing, he turned to watch Dianna practice her dance movements under Jermaine's coaching. Since the first moment he'd seen Anna, he'd been attracted to her beauty, and now was no exception. Dianna was beautiful: petite, lithe, and sexy, her clothing accentuating her slim curves.

His gut clenched, recalling the warmth that always filled him upon seeing Anna, of knowing she was his.

That warmth was missing, but not for long.

He would make Dianna his.

Jermaine called a brief break, and Nic magically produced a tall glass of fresh lemonade that he took over to Dianna. Her brilliant smile as she accepted the drink made his chest swell.

Oh, yes, soon she would be his.

"Just what I needed." She took a large swallow. "How did you know lemonade is my favorite?"

"I know." Dianna might be somewhat different from Anna, but some preferences had to carry over. "Just as I know you love spicy Mexican and hate seafood, that you prefer walks in the garden to shopping at the mall."

Dianna laughed. "Half right. I'll take shopping over walks anytime."

"That's only because you've never been on a walk with me." He spoke with confidence. With his magic, he could create a paradise for her.

Tilting her head to study him, she let mischief dance in her eyes. "Is that an invitation?"

"Yes." He wasn't about to take it slow. Too much was at stake. "Interested?"

Her slow smile tugged at him, increased his longing to draw her into his embrace and hold her tight. "I might be. We'll see."

Jermaine called for a return to practice, so Dianna drained the glass and handed it to Nic. "Thanks."

She sashayed back into position on the stage, the sway of her hips reminding Nic of other pleasurable activities. Activities he'd been without for far too long.

He hardened, recalling the many hours he and Anna had spent making love. She'd always been an equal partner, giving with as much passion as she took. Closing his eyes, he remembered the way her small breasts filled his hand, the taste of her skin, the softness of her mouth, how she welcomed him in and responded to his thrusts with fervor.

By the Stones, he needed her.

Her image appeared in his mind, so like Dianna yet uniquely Anna. He kissed her, savoring her sweetness, then drew back to stare at her. Nic frowned. Something was wrong. Her eyes were no longer bright blue but a changing hazel like—

Nic jerked himself out of his daydream to find Stacy staring at him from her position by the doorway. As soon as their gazes met, she turned away and went to speak to Jermaine. Releasing his breath in a whoosh, Nic moved toward the scenery and picked up his brush.

What was happening to him?

For a moment Anna had changed, had become . . . Stacy.

No.

He returned to his painting, unleashing the wildness inside him. He knew better. Dianna was Anna. Stacy was . . .

Trouble.

And when trouble was around, it usually meant one thing: Titania.

Of course. That would explain everything.

She was meddling as usual. Nic had no doubt she was responsible for his attraction to Stacy. After all, if he fell for the wrong woman, Titania would have control over him for eternity. How like her to manipulate things toward her favor.

Well, it wasn't going to work. He was going to win Dianna and forget Stacy, no matter what it took.

Glancing again at Stacy, he found her laughing with Kevin, who had joined her. Though his throat tightened at the sight, he couldn't deny the perfect solution to Titania's interference.

He would match Stacy up with Kevin. They were much

better suited for each other than Dianna and Kevin. Which in turn would give him free rein with Dianna and remove Stacy from his thoughts.

Perfect.

Yet as Kevin bent close to Stacy to whisper something in her ear, Nic couldn't deny the rush of irrational fury that raced through his blood. With an exclamation of disgust, he forced himself back to the work at hand.

He would escape whatever spell Titania was using to influence him. He had to.

Because involvement with Stacy would destroy him.

For eternity.

Avoiding Nic was harder than she'd expected.

Stacy left the studio and meandered to the house, needing to escape his overwhelming presence yet unwilling to return to her office and the constantly ringing telephone.

She'd spent the better part of a glorious spring day inside the studio, presumably watching Dianna put the songs and dance routines together, but unable to stop her gaze from drifting over to where Nic worked. He appeared removed from the chaos around him, concentrating solely on his painting.

Yet Stacy had noticed him casting more than one oblique glance toward Dianna. What was Nic's game? Was he simply another jerk trying to get at her sister by using her?

Stacy didn't want to believe that. She had better fantasies to think about, such as musing that Nic preferred her, that his magical kisses meant he wanted her. Had anyone ever wanted just her? Not that she could recall.

When she'd met Nic's intense gaze for just a brief moment, her heart had leapt into her throat, her pulse had accelerated. For another kiss, she'd be willing to forget he mentioned a wife.

Stupid Stacy.

She kicked a rock on the path, hating herself for her weakness. Nic Stone was an employee, nothing more. A *married* employee. He might be an excellent gardener and fantastic artist, but that was it.

So why didn't her heart believe that?

Stacy paused in the gardens to breathe in the sweet scent of blooming lilacs as she watched the sun dip behind the jagged, snowcapped peaks in the distance. The sights and scents comforted her as always. The trill of hummingbirds mingled with the echoing call of eagles. Only here could she feel at peace. And those moments had become fewer as Dianna's success had blossomed.

As it was, she couldn't afford to linger. Stacks of paperwork waited on her desk with only one redeeming feature. She could share the work with Kevin.

With a grin, Stacy resumed her stroll. Next year all this hassle would be Kevin's alone. She'd be able to linger in the gardens as long as she wanted, whenever she wanted.

Now, that was a pleasant thought.

She'd barely entered the house when she heard the front gate buzzer. With a sigh, she pressed the speaker button.

"Can I help you?"

"Um, yeah." The voice sounded young, early twenties, late teens perhaps. "This the Fielding place?"

"Why do you need to know?" Stacy grimaced. Surely the musical notes built into the large front gates gave that away. Plus everyone in town knew who lived here.

"Brad Tarrington sent me. Said you needed a gardener."

"What?" A gardener? But she already had a gardener that Brad had sent. "What kind of game is this?"

"Beats me. I got a letter from Tarrington, if you want to see it."

"I'll be right there." She wasn't going to invite him on the grounds, not until she knew more. Snaring her cell phone, she started for the gates at the end of the long, wooded driveway.

She dialed Brad's private number. She'd intended to do this long ago, to thank him for finding Nic, but she'd been too busy to do so.

"Tarrington." He answered with his typical brusqueness. An excellent accountant and good judge of people, Brad didn't say any more than he had to.

"Brad, it's Stacy. I'm calling about the gardener."

"Yeah, sorry. Took a while to find one." She heard paper rustling. "Steve Gable. Sent him your way yesterday."

"Yesterday?"

"Didn't he get there?"

"He's here now." *I think.* "What about Nic Stone?"

"Who?"

Stacy's chest tightened, her heart leaden. "Never mind. Thanks, Brad."

"Any time." He hung up without another word, but it didn't matter. Stacy wouldn't have heard it because her mind whirled with accusations.

Nic was an imposter. Brad hadn't sent him.

Yet he was undoubtedly a gardener. The best she'd ever seen.

How was this possible? And why was Nic here?

The answer arrived immediately. Dianna, of course. Why else?

Damn him. He was fired for sure now.

Jaw clenched, Stacy paused by the gate. A young man stood on the other side, his hair down to his shoulders, wearing blue jeans and a jean jacket over a faded T-shirt. Though neat, he was more of what she'd first expected when envisioning a gardener.

Nic had been too good-looking to be true. And, of course, he was. She should have known.

"May I see the letter?" she asked.

The man passed it through the gate, and Stacy skimmed Brad's familiar handwriting in a short, to-the-point letter that introduced Steve Gable and gave his credentials. She recognized Brad's style at once. This was the gardener she'd been expecting.

"You're Steve Gable?"

He nodded. "I was told you needed a groundskeeper."

"Yeah." Stacy punched in the code to open the gate. A Volkswagen Beetle that had seen better days sat on the road behind Steve. "I'll meet you at the house."

"Wanna lift?" he asked.

"I prefer to walk."

She had to do something to ease her rising anger. To hell with Nic's talent as a gardener, as an artist. He was out of here. He'd be lucky if she didn't call the police.

Though she strode at a fast pace, Steve managed to beat her by moments and waited by his car at the front door to the house. He stared at the surrounding grounds, his jaw half open, indicating his shock.

Stacy glanced again at the letter. He had experience with large estates, but apparently not one as large as this. She motioned for him to accompany her. "We'll go around back to the gardens. The cottage is there."

"Yeah, Tarrington said accommodations were included. That's great." Steve shouldered a backpack and fell into step with her. "This is a big place," he added after several moments of silence.

"Yes, it is."

"And you expect only one person to handle it?" Some of his unease carried through in his tone.

"When it's your full-time job, yes, I do." Nic was doing it. Wonderfully. Damn him.

"Ah, okay." Steve's head swiveled back and forth as they passed through the blooming flowers and neatly trimmed bushes lining the flagstone walk. "Looks pretty good. Can't tell you don't have a gardener."

"That's because I do."

"What?" Steve rounded on her, his confusion clear, as they paused by the cottage.

"And there he is." Stacy scowled as Nic walked out of the cottage. As he spotted them, his steps slowed, his gaze darting between her and Steve.

"Stacy."

"Nic." She stepped forward to confront him, frowning at the sudden jump in her pulse. "I'd like you to meet Steve Gable."

Nic extended his hand. "Hi."

"He's the gardener Brad sent me."

"Oh." The smile left Nic's face. "Oh." Realization dawned. His gaze met hers, secrets she should have seen before lingering in their depths. "I can explain."

"Can you?" Stacy crossed her arms. "I'd like to hear it."

Nic hesitated, then focused on Steve. "You single?"

"Yeah." Steve watched him, wariness mingled with his confusion.

"Girlfriend?"

"No."

"Close to your family?"

"Not particularly. Why?"

"Ever wanted to live in the Bahamas with your pockets filled with money?"

Steve laughed. "Well, yeah. Who wouldn't, man?"

Nic grinned as he lifted a hand into the air. Electricity crackled through the evening, tiny lightning bolts darting from his palm. "Enjoy yourself."

He murmured a few words as Steve spoke. "Hey, man, this—"

Before Steve could finish speaking, he'd disappeared as if he'd never stood there, never even existed.

Gone.

Completely.

Stacy stared at the spot where Steve had stood, unable to believe her eyes. A man couldn't just disappear. She turned around in a circle, searching the gardens. Maybe he'd fallen in the bushes, dashed behind a tree. "Wha—? How—? Where—?"

Glancing at Nic, she watched him lower his hand, electricity still crackling around it. What the hell was going on? Who . . . *what* was Nic Stone? He reached for her, and she jerked back. Did he intend to eliminate her next?

"Stay away from me." She cast a quick look over her shoulder. No one around. If she screamed, would anyone hear her? The house was quite a distance from the cottage. She kept moving backward, her gaze locked on Nic. What did he intend to do now?

"He's not hurt, Stacy. He's living in the Bahamas with a never-ending supply of cash."

"Tha—that's ridiculous, impossible." Her mind refused to grasp this, her thoughts whirled in endless circles. He had to be insane, dangerous. She had to get away, escape.

She turned to run, but Nic caught her arm in a firm hold. She screamed, striking out at him. "Let me go." Someone had to hear her.

"Stacy, let me explain. I—"

"Let me go." She screamed louder, increasing her struggles. Life had suddenly changed. Reality had become unreal. This man she'd kissed was something else, something frightening.

"I—" He sighed, his grip tightening.

Static shocks pricked Stacy, but before she could move, she found herself standing at the top of a mountain, looking down into the ski areas and the distant flickering lights of Mountain Village and Telluride, now resembling tiny snow-globe communities.

She gasped. Her ability to fight left. Hell, she could barely remain standing. Only Nic's hold on her arm kept her upright. She grabbed his shirt, afraid of tumbling into the rocks and trees below. "My God, what is this?"

They stood in snow several inches deep, yet she couldn't feel the dampness or the cold from the wind that howled around them. Maybe she was dreaming or had lost her mind. Overwork could do that.

Yet her imagination wasn't this vivid or wild, and she'd never felt things in a dream before. A soft glow surrounded her and Nic. Was that responsible for the warmth?

"Listen to me," Nic said. "Please, Stacy."

She stared up at him, not left with much choice, willing to believe anything at this point. "Are you an alien?"

He produced his devastating smile, but for once she was immune, her heart already pumping twice as fast as normal. "No, I'm Fae."

She frowned. *Fae? As in tiny winged creatures like Tinkerbell?* "Fae?" Surely she'd heard wrong.

"I'm a faery, Stacy. Magical."

She felt the blood drain from her head, adding to her dizziness. He'd really said *faery.* She'd dreamed of faeries, been intrigued by them all her life, but to discover they actually existed . . .

"And I mean you no harm. I promise."

His sincerity, as always, reached her heart. But how could she believe this?

"It can't be true." Yet how could she continue to deny it? Look at where she was. Snow blew around them, the wind howling.

"It is true." He spoke quietly, his gaze holding hers as if he willed her to accept his statement.

Despite all rational thought, she believed him. Hell, she had no rational thoughts left. Everything she used to think was true had just been shattered. "You—"

He eased her hold on his shirt and produced a glass of amber-colored liquid, which he pressed into her hand. "Here, drink this. You've gone completely white."

"What a surprise," she muttered, but she drank, gasping as the whiskey burned a path down her throat. But, to her surprise, some clarity returned. At least her head stopped whirling. She motioned toward the valley below. "Are we really where I think we are? Is this the top of Palmyra Peak?"

"I had to stop you from running away." Nic gave her a half smile. "I figured this would work."

"Are we safe?" She felt as if one wrong step would send her plummeting down the mountainside. Though she couldn't feel the fierce wind or the snow it pummeled against them, she still expected to tumble over the edge.

"Completely." Nic took the glass and made it disappear, much as Steve had vanished only moments earlier. Though startled, Stacy didn't feel as stunned as before. The whiskey must be working better than she thought.

"What's going on?" She tried to keep her voice from trembling but didn't succeed. "What did you do with Steve?"

"He's safe, Stacy. I promise you. Once I knew no one would miss him, I transported him to the Bahamas with his pockets full of cash. If he chooses to come home, he'll have money to do so, but I suspect he'll decide to stay there a while."

"But that's impossible. You can't—"

He lifted his eyebrows. "I can. With magic, nothing is impossible."

"Magic?" Now she knew how Alice had felt in Wonderland. "Then why are you working as a gardener? Why are you here?"

Nic briefly touched her face, brushing his fingertips over her cheek. "It's a long story, Stacy. One that you're going to find hard to believe."

She managed a dry laugh. "Harder to believe than finding myself on a mountaintop, than a man disappearing?"

"Perhaps."

What could he possibly say that was even more difficult to believe than what she'd experienced thus far? "So?"

"I'm Fae and have lived since the dawn of time."

"Uh . . . huh." He didn't look a day over thirty.

"In my last lifetime among the mortals, I used the name Nic Stone."

"Last lifetime?"

"I make a life for myself, appear to age and die, then move on to another life somewhere else as someone different." He shrugged. "I painted the portrait of Anna hanging in your living room."

That portrait was at least twenty-five years old. That Nic Stone had been famous, an acclaimed artist. "But that was painted over twenty-five years ago."

"Yes, it was." He hesitated. "By me."

"But you barely look thirty. How . . . ?"

"I'm *immortal,* Stacy. I can look as young or as old as I want."

Her mind still refused to grasp this concept. "But that portrait—the artist did it of his wife." She knew that much of its history and the love the artist had held for his wife was clearly evident.

"She was my wife. Anna." His gaze grew distant. "I painted that while we lived in Dallas, shortly after we were married."

His wife? Stacy stared at him, her chest tight. Was this the wife he'd mentioned before? The woman in the portrait? Where was she now? "What happened to her?"

Pain glazed his eyes as a muscle twitched in his cheek. For a moment she thought he wouldn't reply.

"I killed her."

Stacy's throat closed and she stepped back only to find herself slipping in the snow, toward the black chasm below. Before she could gasp, Nic snared her hand and pulled her back, close to his warmth. She could only stare at him, afraid to move.

He'd killed his wife? Yet the woman in the portrait had been loved. Stacy would swear to that. "But the man who painted that portrait loved her," she whispered.

"I did. I loved her desperately." Nic released Stacy's hand, but the despair in his voice made her want to reassure him that everything would be all right. Crazy. He should be reassuring her. "So desperately that I couldn't bear the thought of her growing old and dying, of leaving me."

"So you killed her?" He wouldn't do that. This man could never have harmed the woman he loved that much.

"I went to Titania, the queen of the Fae, and asked her to give Anna immortality. I didn't expect her to agree. Titania hates mortals."

He gave Stacy a sad smile. "But she did—as long as I agreed to paint her portrait. I was ecstatic. So much for so little?"

Closing his eyes for a moment, Nic jammed his fingers through his hair. "I sealed the bargain at once and rushed home to tell Anna that we'd be together forever."

He stopped, his gaze looking past Stacy, obviously lost in memories. If anything, he grew more somber. "I arrived home to find her dying." Moisture glimmered in his eyes. "Titania forgot to tell me that in order for Anna to receive immortality, she had to die and be reborn, this time with eternal life."

"Reborn?" So his wife was alive? Now? Was that why he was here? Did he somehow expect to find her on her estate? The only women here were herself and Dianna.

Nic continued, "Only she won't remember me in her new life. She won't recall our love, our years together. I had to let her grow up and then find her."

"Oh . . . my . . . God." The pieces of the puzzle slid together. The portrait of his wife looked identical to . . . "You think Dianna is your reborn wife."

He returned his gaze to her, nodding. "She doesn't remember anything, so I have to win her all over again."

How could this be possible? Dianna was her sister. She'd known her all her life. Dianna was . . . Dianna. "How can you be sure?"

"I'm positive. The resemblance alone is amazing, and Anna always loved music."

His confidence made her hesitate. Could it be possible? Could her sister be his reincarnated wife? Nothing in Dianna's life had hinted at this. Di loved performing, music, and—oh dear God—Kevin. What would this do to the love her sister and assistant shared?

"What about Kevin?" Stacy struggled to reconcile this new discovery with her feelings. She'd always thought Dianna and Kevin were perfect for each other.

"Don't I have a prior claim?" The sudden coldness in Nic's voice chilled her. "She is *my* soul mate, *my* wife."

Stacy's stomach knotted as a wave of despair washed over her. "Yet you kissed *me,*" she whispered. For a brief moment he'd made her believe she was special. She should have known better.

Nic hesitated. "You have very kissable lips," he said finally with a warm smile.

She didn't return the smile. Having kissable lips didn't make the hurt go away. "I think I'd like to go home now."

With a grimace, Nic nodded. A second later, they stood in the main room of his cottage on the estate. "Don't leave yet. There's more," he added.

Wrapping her arms around herself, Stacy paced to the opposite side of the room. The sudden desolation inside her rocked her foundations. This was too much to comprehend, to feel. "What?"

"I intend to convince Dianna to love me, take her with me when I leave here."

Stacy jerked her head up. "What makes you so certain she'll want to go?"

"I have my ways."

His conviction added to the sick clenching of her stomach. Did he plan to put a spell on her sister? "You cannot use magic." The words emerged before she thought, followed by a rush of fear when he frowned. What did he do to people who stood up to him?

Despite the horror of her life falling to pieces around her, Stacy wasn't about to budge on this. She hastened to explain. "If you need to resort to that to make Dianna love you, then it's not really love."

His gaze met hers, hard, blazing, then he blinked and nodded. "Of course. But I'll need your help."

"My help?" He wanted to pound the stake in her heart further. Why would she help him? Wasn't losing her sister enough? Hadn't he tortured her enough with kisses that evidently meant nothing?

"I need time with Dianna. Without Kevin around."

Stacy closed her eyes, shaking her head. This was too much. "I need to go." She stumbled toward the door, her insides roiling.

"Stacy." He caught her shoulders, forced her to look at him. Concern appeared in his eyes as he ran one hand over her hair. "I'm sorry. I didn't want to tell you this way."

"It's too late for that." She pulled free and rushed outside. She half expected him to pull her back with his magic, but he let her go. Thank goodness.

Once inside her bedroom, she dropped to her knees beside her bed and buried her face in the comforter. Faeries . . . magic . . . Dianna but not Dianna. It was too unbelievable, too fantastic.

Yet she had to believe. Unless he'd somehow hypnotized her, he'd made a man disappear, whisked them both to the top of a mountain peak. What other explanation could there be?

She should have known better. Nic had been too good to be true: a superb gardener, an incredible artist, a handsome man with sex appeal to spare and kisses that reminded her what it was to be alive, to be a woman. He'd fooled her completely. She'd actually allowed herself to believe he might care about her. As always, she was wrong. It was Dianna.

Always Dianna.

She'd been afraid he was after Dianna, but not as a reincarnated wife. This was far worse than stealing Di's lingerie or weaseling an intimate story for the gossip magazines. Worse even than coveting Dianna's fortune. He intended to claim Di's heart, to take her away forever.

But what if Dianna really was his wife, his Anna? What if they were really soul mates? What if Di was immortal?

It didn't matter. Even if they did belong together, nothing would ease this ache in her chest.

"Damn it."

Nic still saw the look on Stacy's face, long after she'd fled to the main house. Restless, he wandered the garden paths, unhesitant in the smothering darkness of night. He'd shocked her, terrified her, hurt her—all things he hadn't wanted to do.

But when had things ever gone according to plan? If

he'd thought at all, he should've expected the real gardener to show up someday.

To reveal his magic, himself, his mission so quickly, so forcefully was not the way he'd intended. He'd known he would have to tell Stacy eventually, but he'd always assumed he and Dianna would do so together after he'd convinced Dianna of his love, of hers for him, of their life together.

Now what?

Stacy had considerable influence over her sister, could convince Dianna to be wary of Nic if she so desired. He frowned, torn with indecision. He could send Stacy away, trap her in the magical realm until he'd won Dianna.

But he wouldn't.

Perhaps he was selfish, but he didn't want to lose her company. Already he'd come to like her, to respect her. She was so much more than he'd originally thought: intelligent, dedicated, loyal, and so desirable she made his gut clench.

He never should have kissed her that first night—a mistake made in the dark. That was the problem. If he hadn't held her, tasted her, desired her then, he wouldn't be tormented with such conflicting emotions now.

Dianna was the one for him. Everything pointed to it, especially Titania's arrival, her meddling. His fascination with Stacy was nothing more than a spell to confuse him, to trick him into losing his freedom. By the Stones, couldn't Titania leave him alone?

Needing to take some kind of action, he transported himself into the living room to face Titania's portrait. The house was dark, everyone long asleep. He created a simple globe of light to illuminate the room and glared at the painting of the Fae queen.

"Leave me alone, Titania."

He half expected her to answer, but only silence greeted him. Turning his back on her, he faced Anna's portrait instead. His chest ached as memories assaulted him: dancing with her, laughing with her, loving her.

"I love you so much, Anna," he whispered. He touched the painting, longing for the soft warmth of her skin, but he found only cool strokes of old oil paint. Anna wasn't there. She lived in his mind, his heart . . . and in Dianna Fielding. "We'll be together again. I swear it."

Bowing his head, he recalled Anna's smile, dancing eyes, her words: *"I love you more."*

"And I didn't love you enough," he murmured. "But I'll make it up to you. I promise."

Whirling back to Titania's portrait, he didn't hide his tears. "And you need to stay out of this. You ruin things. You caused this. This confusion, this chaos." He stalked over and slammed his fist against the frame. "Hear me, Titania. Anna and I loved each other too much not to be together again."

The portrait remained dark, silent. At this point, he wouldn't be surprised to have lightning strike, yet he lifted his head in defiance, slashing away the dampness from his cheeks. "I'm not losing her again. No matter what you do. No matter what."

"Why are you talking to that painting?"

He jumped. He'd been so intent on Titania he hadn't heard Stacy's soft footsteps behind him. As she entered the glowing circle cast by the globe, he noticed tear tracks on her face, tears he'd undoubtedly caused.

His first instinct was to go to her, hold her, kiss her. He even took one step forward before he caught himself. No. That was Titania controlling his mind, making him want the wrong sister. Holding himself rigid, he answered her question.

"Because she's in there, watching, listening."

"She? Titania?" Stacy came to stand beside him, to stare at the portrait.

Fighting the urge to touch her, Nic glanced up as well. "She's the one who made me go through this. Now she intends to interfere, to keep me from being with Anna."

"Why would she do that?"

"Because she loves to control everyone's life." He allowed his bitterness to fill his words. "And if I fail, I not only lose Anna, I lose my freedom."

Stacy placed her hand on his arm, a gentle touch that had the impact of a burning iron. "What do you mean?"

He took her hand, intending to remove it, then found himself holding it as he looked at her, immersed in the heat coursing through him, the surge of anticipation, the awakening Stacy's presence always caused. "If I fail, if I tell the wrong woman I love her, I have to return to the magical realm forever, to be Titania's slave."

In this light, Stacy's eyes were dark, luminous. For an instant he could imagine himself staring into Anna's warm gaze. He tightened his hold on Stacy's hand.

"You honestly loved your wife, didn't you?" She spoke so quietly he had to lean forward to hear her.

"With all that I was." He glanced at Anna's portrait, experiencing a rush of emotion that made his chest tighten. "I still love her."

"I'll help you."

"What?" He turned back to Stacy, uncertain he'd heard correctly.

Her eyes shimmered with moisture. Her gaze met his briefly, then dropped to the carpet. "I'll help you," she repeated, her voice barely more than whisper. "Dianna deserves someone who loves her this much—forever." She pulled her hand free and backed away, then lifted her gaze again. "*You* deserve it."

She hurried into the darkness as Nic fought against going after her. She was going to help him win Dianna. He should be excited, overjoyed.

After all, winning Dianna was everything.

Then why did he feel so disheartened?

Though Nic hadn't been certain she would, Stacy kept her promise to help by taking Kevin with her at the lunch break, claiming she had some papers he needed to look over. That left Nic free to approach Dianna.

She stood at the edge of the stage, a towel around her neck and a bottle of water in her hand, as she listened to Jermaine's final instructions. They evidently reached some sort of agreement, for she was just turning away as Nic reached her.

"Care for a picnic?" he asked, lifting the basket he'd materialized. Anna had always loved his spontaneity. Surely Dianna would respond to it as well.

She did, a smile framing her lips. "A picnic, eh? Where did you have in mind?"

"Here, in the gardens." He gathered all the charm he possessed. "At the gazebo."

"We have a gazebo?"

How could she not know there was a gazebo? Surely she spent significant time in the gardens, knew what this vast estate offered. Anna had loved her garden, the blooming flowers, the beauty of nature. "It's a short walk from here," he said finally.

Di tilted her head, as if considering his proposition, then beamed at him. "I'd love it." She linked her arm through his. "Let's go."

Nic's heart hammered as he led her along the paths to where the gazebo reigned amidst a circle of wildly blooming flowers—petunias, pansies, lilacs—each producing its own unique fragrance. The gazebo was small, barely two meters in diameter, and circular, with a railing around the edge. Bright flowers had been painted on the main posts, while real ivy climbed the latticework around the base. The building managed to convey a sense of seclusion, of being shut away from the rest of the world.

A place of nature, of seduction, yet close enough to the house so Dianna would feel safe.

She wore a simple leotard and stretch pants, her feet clad in dance slippers, her blonde hair pulled up in a ponytail. Her resemblance to the Anna he'd first met was incredible. How could he doubt this woman was his wife reborn?

Yet something was missing.

He pushed away that thought and concentrated on winning her heart, teasing her, making her laugh, as he laid out his magically prepared meal. Fried chicken, one of Anna's favorites, accompanied by German potato salad and rich chocolate torte.

Dianna's eyes grew wide. "Good Lord, there must a million calories in that."

"What?"

"I rarely eat this kind of stuff." She ran her hand over her hip. "I have to maintain my figure, you know."

"I thought you'd enjoy it." He hadn't expected this reaction. Anna had always enjoyed her food, and it hadn't affected her figure.

"Oh, I would, but it would go directly to my hips."

He eyed her, lingering on the slim curves. "Trust me. It won't hurt you."

Dianna laughed. "Easy for you to say. I'm the one up on the stage, facing millions of judging eyes." But she sat beside him on the gazebo floor and lifted a wing. "Oh, well. I'll just have a little and work extra hard this afternoon."

As she nibbled at her food, Nic studied her. The mole on the curve of her slender neck was new, enticing. And she lacked Anna's dimples, something he hadn't realized until this moment.

"You're staring at me," Dianna said. She met his gaze with a flirtatious lift of her brows.

"You remind me of someone I once knew." Eventually he would tell her the whole story.

After she'd fallen in love with him again.

"Oh?" Dianna licked the chicken grease off her fingers, one at a time, slowly, seductively. "A former lover?"

Nic swallowed the sudden lump in his throat. "You could say that."

"What happened? Why did you leave her?"

"She died."

Genuine sorrow glimmered in her eyes. "I'm sorry."

He shook his head, not wanting to remember that now. "It was a long time ago. Besides, you're here, looking exactly like her."

Dianna stuck her finger into the chocolate torte icing then slowly slid the finger into her mouth, moaning in pleasure. Nic's loins tightened. Perhaps she did recall something of their life together, teasing him this way. Her eyes held a mischievous gleam. "I'm not sure if I should be flattered or not."

"I consider it a very high compliment." Nic shifted to ease the fit of his slacks.

"But a woman wants to be considered unique, not merely a copy of someone else." Dianna rose to her feet before Nic realized she was serious.

He leaped up to catch her arm. "But you are unique.

You're much more than how you look." Even as he spoke, something in the words rang deep inside him. He was missing something . . . something just out of reach. Something important.

"Am I?" Mischief danced in her eyes.

"You're talented, intelligent, sexy." He had to clear his throat when his voice became husky.

"Oh?" She kept staring at him, her gaze hot enough to melt chocolate.

Enough banter. He wanted to touch her. Had to touch her. He created music, a slow waltz, that filtered from among the trees and pulled Dianna into his arms. "Dance with me."

Surprise flitted across her face, then gave way to delight. "You're a surprising man, Nic."

He grinned now. "You have no idea."

She fit against him perfectly, as he'd known she would, her head nestling below his chin, her body soft along his. And her scent was so similar to Anna's. If he closed his eyes, he could imagine—

But Dianna stumbled in following his lead, breaking the spell before it had hardly begun. "I'm not used to this kind of dancing," she murmured.

"Just follow me." He would lead her . . . now and always.

She relaxed, and he moved her around the gazebo, making the meal disappear before they could step in it. She never noticed. Her heart pounded in her chest. He could hear it, feel it.

She would be his.

Running his hand over her hair, he waited for the usual desire to surface, that overwhelming need to claim this woman. But it failed to rise. He frowned and pulled her tighter. By now, the passion should burn so hot they'd be pulling clothing off each other. Perhaps they needed more time together. Perhaps he needed to adjust to this new Anna.

She paused and eased back. "Let me breathe." Her tone

was teasing, but hesitancy lingered in her eyes.

"Dianna." He ran his hand along the curve of her face, lingering at her chin, lifting her mouth up—those gorgeous, full lips.

The hesitancy vanished to be replaced by another emotion. Triumph? Satisfaction? No matter. She gave him a smile designed to capture a man, and it worked.

"Kiss me, Nic," she whispered.

He didn't need a second invitation. He bent to capture her lips, to taste the sweetness he'd too long been denied, to burn in her fiery response.

Only to find disappointment instead.

Oh, she responded, and the kiss held warmth, but none of the wild fire he remembered. What was wrong? It wasn't supposed to be this way. He drew back, puzzled. Was Titania blocking his emotions, too?

Dianna eased out of his hold. "Well, that was nice." Though she presented an air of casualness, he sensed her underlying unease. "I think I need to get back now. Jermaine will want to start again." Not giving Nic a chance to protest, she hurried away.

He stared after her, then ran his fingers through his hair. That hadn't gone well at all. From the first moment he'd kissed Anna, he'd known he would never want anyone else. Within days they'd made love for the first time, within a week, he'd asked her to marry him.

Yet kissing Dianna felt like kissing a close friend. Nothing more.

Stones. He glared in the direction of the house. It had to be Titania's work. She had no intention of letting him find his Anna again.

By the Stones, he wouldn't let her destroy his life again.

Stacy laughed as Kevin related his dealings with one of Dianna's groupies he'd encountered outside her recording studio. They'd long ago finished up discussing the few questions she'd managed to think up about the upcoming tour but had continued talking.

She liked being around Kevin. Over the past couple years he'd become a good friend.

Her stomach knotted. If only he wouldn't be so hurt when Nic won Dianna.

"You okay?" he asked.

"Hmm? Yeah." She produced a reassuring smile.

"For a moment there, you looked like something hurt."

"Probably an ulcer." She sat on the edge of the desk and gestured toward the stacks of paperwork. "Believe me, I won't miss all this fuss and bother at all."

A twinkle appeared in Kevin's eyes. "Yes, you will, but I imagine you'll learn to live without it."

"I'm sure I will." Though she kept her tone light, Kevin's expression turned serious, and he placed his hand on her shoulder.

"Tell the truth, Stacy. Is giving this up what you really want?"

She nodded without hesitation. Placing Dianna's career in someone else's hands was difficult, but she needed to do it. "It's time I find out who I am. I want to be someone other than Dianna Fielding's sister."

"I always thought it was the other way around—that Dianna was your sister."

"Oh, yeah? I think you're the only one who believes that."

Kevin grinned, then pulled Stacy into a hug. "I understand."

Stacy knew he did understand. At one time, Stacy had truly envied Dianna, had even mused about a relationship with Kevin herself, but that had long passed. Now he was a best friend and the brother she'd never had.

Who would undoubtedly leave, once Nic claimed Dianna's affections.

And then what?

"Well, excuse me."

At Dianna's sarcastic tone, Kevin released Stacy and turned to give his fiancée a smile. "Just reassuring Stacy she'll survive without you."

"But will I survive without her?"

Despite Dianna's flippancy, Stacy heard more. A tension, a wariness that came from more than jealousy. Something had happened. Something with Nic.

Was this it? Was this when Dianna decided she no longer wanted Kevin? Dianna's next words fed that theory.

"I need to talk to you, Kev." Dianna aimed a glance at Stacy. "Alone."

"Sure." Kevin crossed to her and wrapped his arm around her shoulders. "Let's go."

As they left, Stacy's gut protested, while the image of Nic and Dianna together appeared in her mind. They made an attractive couple, but did they belong together? Really?

She sank into her office chair. She couldn't deny the fervency of Nic's emotion as he'd talked to Anna's portrait. He truly loved her. If Dianna was his reborn wife, Stacy had to help him.

But she didn't have to be happy about it.

She rested her elbow on the desk, cradling her forehead against her palm. Part of her wanted to run away from all of this: the tour, the music, the deception.

Instead, the phone ringing shattered the quiet. Against that small inner voice that told her to ignore it, Stacy answered the phone. It could be important.

"Hello, Miss Stacy Fielding?"

She didn't recognize the deep voice. "That's me."

"Bob Edwards here from the Pepsi Center in Denver."

"Yes?" The Pepsi Center was where Dianna intended to kick off her cross-country tour. The arrangements had been finalized months ago. What now?

"Bad news, I'm afraid."

If anything, Stacy's stomach tensed even more, her throat closing. "What?"

"We had a fire in the Center last night. There's not much structurally wrong, but the smoke damage is incredible. There's no way we'll be able to get it ready in time to host Dianna's concert. I'm sorry."

"Sorry?" Stacy tightened her grip on the receiver, her knuckles turning white. "And where am I going to find another arena at this late date? Dianna's supposed to be there in three weeks."

"I know, and I feel terrible, but it can't be helped. It's not like we planned this."

"No, of course not." Stacy didn't want to hear any more. "Good-bye, Mr. Edwards." She hung up on his apologies. Apologies weren't going to fix this problem. How could she possibly find a place for Dianna's concert in Denver now? Every place was already booked, had been booked for months.

She crossed her arms on her desk and dropped her head onto them. "Damn. Damn. Damn." What was she going to do? She needed a miracle.

Dianna burst into the office and flung herself in the side chair. "I hate Kevin."

Stacy lifted her head just enough to peek at her sister. "What?" Had Nic managed to win Dianna so completely in just one afternoon?

"He says I'm being unreasonable because I want us to go away somewhere for the weekend." Dianna crossed her arms, her lovely face set in a scowl.

"Go away?" Stacy sat upright. This was a surprise. "Why do you want to do that? You'll have months together on tour."

"That'll be work. I want something private for just the two of us. A chance to be alone." Dianna stared at the opposite wall, not meeting Stacy's gaze.

Stacy eyed Dianna, noting the obvious signs of guilt. "Has something happened?"

What had Nic done to make Di feel guilty?

"No." Her sister's denial came quickly—too quickly. "I just want a break. Is that asking too much? Instead, he says I should be more professional. That I have work to do."

"Well, he's right." Dianna still didn't have all the dance steps down, and since she'd insisted on including a new song in the performance, she needed to memorize the words and choreography for it as well.

"Figures you'd stand up for him." Dianna stood. "Well, he's not the only fish in the sea, you know."

Stacy's immediate impulse was to explain how Kevin was only looking out for her sister's best interests, but she bit back the words. "You're probably right," she said instead. Wasn't this what Nic wanted? "There are plenty of other fish."

Dianna scowled. "Stay away from Kevin." Venom dripped from her words.

"What?" Stacy stared at Dianna.

"I see what you're doing. You just want Kevin for yourself. Well, you can't have him. He's mine." Dianna glared at Stacy, then stalked from the office, her back stiff.

That did it. Tears pricked at Stacy's eyes, and she pushed away from the desk. She had to get out of here, get fresh air, jump off a cliff. Anything.

I can't do this anymore.

The fun was gone. The excitement had fled. Even the thought of writing her own songs had disappeared. To hell with Dianna, with Kevin, with the concert, with Nic. She was so tired that all she wanted was to escape, to get so far away from here that no one could ever find her.

Instead, she stormed onto the garden path only to slam into Nic's chest. He caught her arms to steady her, but she jerked free. "Let me go." She intended to push by him, but he held on.

"What's wrong?"

"Nothing."

"That's a lie." He captured her chin and lifted her gaze to his. "You're crying."

"It's none of your business." She didn't want to talk to him, to see him. Or anyone for that matter. She wanted to be alone. Stacy struggled to pull free. "Let me go."

He only tightened his grip. "What is the problem?"

She glared at him. "You. You're the problem."

That news stunned him enough to loosen his hold, and Stacy ripped free. If she could make it to the gazebo, she could relax.

She only managed a few steps before Nic captured her arm again, swinging her to face him.

"By the Stones, Stacy. What does that mean?"

"Anything you want it to mean," she snapped. She shouldn't have said anything.

"I want to know what it means to you." He held both her arms now, forcing her to stay. "Tell me."

"Go to hell."

He scowled. "Tell me, Stacy."

"Or what? You'll turn me into a toad or something? Go ahead. It's got to be better than the life I'm living now."

Instead of the anger she'd expected, concern filled his gaze. "What happened?" His voice was gentle now.

To her horror, fresh tears spurted free. She could deal with anger, but his gentleness destroyed her defenses. "Everything. I'm trying to help you, and I'm going to end up hurting Kevin, a man I like and respect. But my sister thinks I'm trying to steal Kevin away from her, so she hates me. The concert is falling apart. I can't sleep at night." *From remembering your kisses.* "And my stomach hurts."

"Stacy." He pulled her into a hug, and she let the tears of frustration flow, soaking his shirt, as she trembled, knees weak, head pounding.

"Now will you let me go?" The words sounded as weary as she felt, and she made no move to leave his embrace.

"When did you eat last?"

That was a change of subject that had nothing to do with anything. She looked up at him. "What?"

"When did you eat last? Did you have lunch?"

"No, I was keeping Kevin busy so you could seduce Dianna. What happened? She came in upset."

He frowned. "That's not important. We're talking about you. How about breakfast?"

"I had some juice."

"Dinner last night?"

She struggled to remember. She'd been ironing out the final details on the stadium for Dianna's last performance while struggling to reconcile the amazing story Nic had told her. "I think I had a sandwich."

"I see." A look of determination crossed his face, increasing her wariness. "Foolish Stacy, I'm taking you to dinner."

"I don't want dinner. I just want to be alone to have some quiet time." Though she couldn't deny the sudden leap in her pulse at the thought of dinner with him. "Besides, dinner is hours away."

"Not in Paris."

She'd barely opened her mouth to question him when she experienced an abrupt tingling, and the scenery changed around them. Though still held in Nic's arms, she found herself standing behind a large tree near the end of a large, rectangular pool. Night had fallen, but it remained warm.

Though the tree shielded most of the view, she twisted her head to see more. Twinkling lights in the distance caught her attention.

She blinked. Was that the Eiffel Tower? It couldn't be. Could it?

She glanced at Nic, who gave her a lazy smile. "*Bienvenue à Paris,* Stacy. Welcome to Paris."

Eight

Nic grinned at Stacy's amazement. She needed this. She'd been working nonstop. No wonder she was near exhaustion.

"We're really in Paris?" She stepped away from him to the side of the pool, then rotated in a slow circle. "I don't believe it." Pausing, she tilted her head toward a nearby conversation taking place in rapid French. She looked back at Nic with a smile that bumped up the temperature a few degrees. "I've always wanted to visit Paris."

"Good." He extended his hand. "Let me take you to dinner and a tour."

"I—" She reached out to place her hand in his, then stopped and stared down at her clothing. Apparently she'd finally noticed the change of apparel he'd made for her.

He'd always known she was taller and curvier than Dianna, but he hadn't expected those curves to be quite so intriguing. He'd created a sleek gown of a rich jade that accented the subtle red highlights in her honey-blonde hair and made her eyes even more vibrant. The gown was backless and dipped low in front, creating a vee between her generous breasts. The skirt was full, dropping to several inches above the knee to reveal a very attractive pair of legs.

Nic's throat went dry while the lower part of him went completely stiff. Perhaps he should have thought more before creating this dress. He'd wanted Stacy to feel pretty. He hadn't expected her to be so beautiful.

"Do you like it?" he asked, his voice raspier than he'd intended.

She looked at it in awe, then ran her hands over the sides, creating a path he ached to follow, before she met his gaze. "Do you?"

"Oh yeah." He liked it a lot. Probably far more than he should.

He noted the pink tinting her cheeks even in the dim lighting and grinned. "Shall we go to dinner?"

This time she did place her hand in his. "I'd love to."

With a brief flash of magic, he transported them to Maison d'Amour, an elegant but small restaurant tucked in a narrow alley that had existed in Paris for centuries. The food here was always excellent and the atmosphere relaxing.

And seductive, he decided, as he faced Stacy over the single lit candle at their table tucked into an alcove. She glowed in the soft light from the flame and the magic only Paris could produce, laughing as she struggled to translate the menu. By the Stones, he wanted to kiss her.

No. He had to remember, this was Stacy, not Dianna. He was helping her relax, nothing more.

After they'd placed their order, she beamed at him. "Thank you, Nic. This is unbelievable. How did you know I'd always wanted to come to Paris?"

"Lucky guess." He hadn't known, but Anna had always loved Paris. He would bring them here often for a meal or a weekend. In fact, Maison d'Amour had always been a favorite of hers. His spirits sank.

"What's wrong?" Stacy reached across the small table to touch his hand.

"I just remembered. I proposed to Anna here." And she'd accepted, making him the happiest Fae in existence.

"I'm sorry. Would you like to go somewhere else?"

"No." For some odd reason, he didn't mind seeing Stacy across from him in Anna's place. "No. The food here is excellent."

"You're sure?"

Her concern made him smile. "I'm certain."

And the food was excellent. He waited for her to finish before he mentioned her earlier outburst. "Do you want to talk now?"

Finishing the last bite of her chocolate mousse, Stacy sighed, then nodded. "I'm sorry. I shouldn't have taken my frustration out on you."

He shrugged. At least he could do something to ease the tension for her. "I'm willing to listen."

She twisted her lips, making a moue, triggering a sudden urge in him to taste those lips. Nic pulled in a deep breath. He was going to listen. Nothing more.

"Looking back, some of it seems silly. If I got upset every time Di was angry with me, I'd never have any peace."

"But?"

Her frustration reappeared, lingering in the depths of her eyes. "I received a call from the manager at the Pepsi Center in Denver, where Di's kicking off her tour. They've had a fire and won't be able to host her concert."

"And this is bad?" He had no clue what was involved in putting together a concert. Only that it kept Stacy busy.

"Very bad. At this late stage, all the other arenas that could hold a concert are booked. We'll have to cancel this appearance." Stacy extended her hands in a gesture of helplessness. "And it's not just refunding all the money for the tickets, but all the people we'll be letting down, who count on Dianna opening her tour there. She's always had a special relationship with Denver."

"Is the Pepsi Center badly damaged?"

"Some structural, he said. Mostly smoke damage."

Nic hesitated. As a rule, he refrained from the blatant use of his magic. Of course, if no one saw him . . . A slow grin took shape. "What if the Center wasn't damaged any longer?"

Stacy produced a dry smile. "As if. It would take a mir . . ." She trailed off, her eyes growing big. "Oh. You can do miracles, can't you?"

"I wouldn't call it a miracle, but I may be able to help." Nic pushed back his chair. "I'll be back in a few minutes." He headed for the rest room, waiting until he entered to transport himself to Denver.

Stacy watched the doorway through which he'd walked, still surrounded by a total sense of unreality, not completely sure she wasn't dreaming. She'd actually forgotten who he was—what he was—for a while. How could she, when she was sitting in Paris? She sipped from her glass of Merlot, letting it flow over her tongue, the fullness of it verifying she was actually here.

Sharing dinner with Nic was wonderful. He made her laugh, made her think. She felt as if she'd been transported to another world, another time when all that existed was her and Nic.

She grimaced. Now that *was* a dream.

Nic was being a friend, nothing more. If all went as he planned, she'd be his sister-in-law. That thought didn't help raise her spirits. She liked him. She liked him a lot. Too much, in fact.

Dammit.

"Ready to go?"

She jerked back as Nic appeared beside the table and tossed some bills onto the tablecloth. "I . . . yes."

He pulled back her chair as she stood, then offered his

arm to lead her into the warm Parisian night. He didn't say a word, but she sensed his inner excitement.

As soon as they emerged outside, she turned to him, unable to control her enthusiasm. Had he really done it? "What did you do?"

Amusement filled his eyes. "Do?"

She grinned. "Yes. Do." Catching his shoulders, she made him face her. "Time to confess."

His slow smile made her heart lose a couple of beats as an equally slow heat oozed through her like warm caramel. "Your manager is going to be very surprised when he visits the Pepsi Center again."

"You fixed it?" Her voice squeaked. She couldn't help it. This was too unreal, too wonderful.

"Good as new. Better. I cleaned up the trash, too."

They wouldn't have to cancel the tour kickoff. Stacy threw her arms around his neck in an enthusiastic hug. "You're fantastic. Thank you. Thank you. Thank you."

He wrapped his arms around her to return the hug. "You're more than welcome." He sounded husky, a sound that added to the clenching in her stomach.

Or maybe it was the escargots he'd made her try. Yes, that's all it was. Stacy eased away, despite her reluctance to do so. It felt so right to be in Nic's embrace. Too right for a man who was destined for her sister.

"What's next?" She struggled to keep her tone light.

"Whatever you want to see. Paris rarely sleeps."

"Everything." She threw out her arms. "I want to see everything."

"And you shall."

Notre-Dame. Sacre Coeur. Montmartre. Moulin Rouge. Arc de Triomphe. Place de la Concorde. They saw it all, transporting from one spot to another, appearing in dark doorways or behind signs and bridges to remain initially unnoticed, then Nic would provide firsthand knowledge of that spot's history. They strolled along the Seine, the moonlight slicing through the shadows over the water.

Incredible. All too incredible for words. And despite the lateness of the hour, the city was still alive with people and lights and music. Even the street vendors continued to hawk their wares, and Stacy made Nic stop to listen to a young man playing a guitar, his words, though unintelligible to her, were romantic and sad all at the same time, echoing the feeling she tried to capture in her music.

When they reached the outside of the Louvre, Stacy could only sigh. The former palace was as beautiful at night as during the day. "Too bad it's closed." She'd always wanted to see the statue of *Venus de Milo* and the *Mona Lisa.*

"It doesn't have to be." Mischief danced in Nic's eyes.

"What does that mean?" She eyed him warily. "They're not about to open up for us."

"I was thinking of a private tour." Nic took her hand in his, his clasp warm, building on the trickle of excitement running rampant inside her.

"But the security—"

She didn't get to finish as the outside gradually became the inside, dimly lit and very empty.

"Stay close." Nic tightened his hand around hers. "I'm shielding us from the security systems."

Stacy didn't respond at once. She was too busy trying to see everything. The building itself was majestic, a work of art, and the statuary, paintings, and displays down the distant hallway promised even more.

With Nic by her side, Stacy wandered up one hallway and down the next, exclaiming with delight when she found art by recognized artists. "I can't believe I'm here." She smiled up at Nic. This was a dream come true.

"You're here, but you'll never see everything unless you stay all night."

She grimaced. He was right, but she hated to miss any

of the historic treasures. "I have to see the *Mona Lisa*," she said.

"This way." He led her to a small room and motioned toward a painting on the wall, a roped-off area in front of it. "That's it."

"That's it?" The portrait was much smaller than she'd imagined, but the familiar face of the lovely woman with the enigmatic smile was all she expected it to be. "It's incredible. Can I go closer?"

"Just don't touch anything." Nic held up the rope so she could pass through. "I could get us out of here before any security showed up, but why ruin their night?"

Stacy stood for several minutes, studying the painting, the colors, the brushstrokes. "It almost feels alive," she whispered.

"Leonardo did good work." Nic wrapped his arm around her shoulders. "He always tried to paint the soul rather than the body."

"You knew him?" How could she forget that Nic was tremendously old? Probably because he looked so young, so damned handsome.

"Only by reputation. I never got to meet him, but I spent a lot of time studying his work."

"But you're as good as he is." She'd seen his amazing portraits of Anna and Titania. They were comparable to this one.

Nic laughed and squeezed her shoulders. "Thank you. I'm not sure others would agree, but thank you."

"Were you ever famous? Other than as Nic Stone? Do you have paintings here?" She could easily imagine one of his lifelike portraits adorning these walls.

"None here, I'm afraid." He lifted the rope again so they could leave. "Besides my few years of notoriety as Nic Stone, the last time I was well-known was when I had the name Nicholas Hilliard several centuries ago."

She'd heard of the name but knew nothing more.

"Where are those paintings?" To see his old work, to know the man beside her had crafted it hundreds of years ago, boggled her mind.

"They're mostly in England." Nic gave her a warm smile. "I'll take you there someday."

"I'd like that. I've never been there, either." And she longed to see London and Stonehenge, along with so many other places. She'd spent so much time caring for Dianna and working that traveling for pleasure had never been a priority.

"Then it's a date."

A date? Her heart jumped into her throat. He couldn't have meant that the way it sounded. Stacy glanced at Nic, only to have him pull her close, her body smashed against his. "Wha—?"

"Ssh. Don't move."

She heard the footsteps, then. A security guard? Yes, and he was heading straight for them. She buried her face against Nic's shoulder. Why didn't he transport them away? If they were caught in here . . .

Afraid to move, she could only listen as the steps grew closer. Nearly upon them. Her breath caught. Surely they could be seen where they stood in the hallway.

The footsteps paused just behind her. When someone—a man—coughed, Stacy jumped, and Nic tightened his hold. Then, slowly, far too slowly for her peace of mind, the steps retreated, faded, and were gone.

Releasing her breath, Stacy glanced up at Nic. "Why didn't he see us?"

"I cast a bit of glamour to make us appear invisible." Though he smiled, the intensity of his gaze held her captive. With fear gone, she felt the male awakening of his body, which acted as a wake-up call to hers.

She didn't move away, couldn't move away. All her senses sprang to life, eager to respond.

His gaze dropped to her mouth as he ran one hand over

her bare back, leaving a burning trail beneath his touch. She moistened her suddenly dry lips, anticipation making her sway forward.

Nic groaned, then shut his eyes and eased her away. Though he continued to hold her shoulders, he didn't look at her for several long moments—moments in which she fought herself to keep from grabbing him, from demanding the kiss she craved. Finally, he opened his eyes again and gave her a rueful smile. "The statue of Apollo is over this way. It's Hellenistic, first century B.C."

Despite the trembling of her limbs, she followed him to where the statue stood, proud and muscular, but after what she'd just experienced, it lacked the same thrill as being near Nic's muscular form. "It's nice," she murmured.

Nic only raised one eyebrow, then led her to the *Venus de Milo*. "What about this?"

"She's beautiful." The meticulous sculpting somehow managed to add life to stone. Stacy glanced around the room at all the other displays they wouldn't have time to see. "Can we come back someday?"

"Of course. We could even try it during the day next time."

Stacy had to smile. "That would be great."

"Anything else you want to see here?"

"Too much, but we should be heading home. Dianna will be worried about me."

"Okay, one more place then."

Before Stacy could blink, Nic transported them to an empty doorway facing a wide avenue lined with shops and bustling with traffic and pedestrians. Stacy struggled to take it all in, the sights, the sounds, and the scents. Though overwhelmed, she felt certain she'd never forget this evening.

They walked arm in arm along the Champs-Elysées, as busy at midnight as it would have been at noon. The scents of perfume and wine permeated the air, and the French conversations around them were mingled with those from tourists, creating a unique melody of its own.

"Thank you for this, Nic." She squeezed his arm. "It's been more than I could ever have wished for."

"It's not over yet." He led her to a brightly lit doorway with music throbbing inside. "Do you like to dance?"

Not giving her a chance to answer, he pulled her inside. Stacy gulped. Dance? She hadn't danced in . . . forever. Yet the dimly lit interior, the couples swaying on the tiny dance floor, the seductive charm of the music persuaded her to stay.

And Nic taking her in his arms erased any doubts. He held her formally at first and steered her among the other couples. Stacy found him easy to follow—a sign of his skill, not hers. That was certain.

As the music changed, grew richer, deeper, aching with lost love and passion, Nic drew her closer until their bodies melded together as one. Stacy drew in a deep breath, his touch reigniting senses that had barely cooled. She rested her head on his shoulder, moving without even being aware of it. All she could do was feel, every sense tingling with anticipation, with want.

His body was solid against hers, growing even firmer as they danced. His hands skimmed over her bare back, enticing, burning, stoking the fire centered deep in her gut. Her breasts swelled, her nipples tightening until the slight pressure of movement from Nic's chest made her tremble.

She tried to draw back. This was dangerous. Too dangerous.

But Nic refused to release her, his grip remaining firm. She tilted back her head to meet his gaze and found fire dancing in the depths of his eyes. "The music . . ." Her closed throat made it difficult to choke out even those words.

"It's more than the music," he murmured. He bent toward her, and she knew he intended to kiss her. Her pulse accelerated even as a tiny portion of her conscience protested.

"You shouldn't," she whispered, brushing his lowering lips with hers.

"I know."

But still he kissed her, seducing her mouth with such expertise her legs went numb. Dance? All she could do was cling to his jacket to stay upright.

His tongue swept inside, teasing, tantalizing, tormenting until Stacy joined him in a sensual tango that completely destroyed what few defenses she might have maintained. The air around them tingled, pulsating with an almost palpable passion.

If ever a man could kiss a woman to orgasm, it would be Nic. Already, moisture pooled between Stacy's thighs and he hadn't even moved his hands from her back.

They parted briefly, gasping, and Stacy noticed they were now in the main room of the gardener's cottage. Had that been the tingling she'd felt?

She stared at Nic, her chest heaving as she struggled for breath. She wanted him. Lord help her, she wanted him. And the answering glow in his eyes indicated he wanted her, too.

Swallowing, she moistened her lips, intending to speak, to break the spell, but he claimed her mouth again with such tender seduction she willingly responded. His lips were soft yet firm, giving yet taking, weapons in their own right.

He slid one hand over the curve of her hip, then lifted it to cup her breast and thumb her taut peak. Stacy moaned, her body arching in response. It had been so long. Her hips rocked of their own accord, seeking his solid length. Dear Lord, had it ever felt this good?

Using both hands now, he kneaded her breasts, gently, brushing her nipples to shoot fire through her veins even while his mouth continued to meld with hers, to promise a lovemaking she wanted more desperately with every moment.

As he released her lips, he slid the spaghetti straps of her gown off her shoulders so that it fell, catching at the curve of her hips. If anything, her breasts swelled even more beneath his gaze, a gaze that told her without words he found her attractive, sexy, desirable.

He bent to draw one peak into the heat of his mouth, using his talented tongue to increase her passion. Stacy gripped his head, whether to push him away or draw him close, she wasn't sure. Any semblance of coherent thought fled, her body quickly reduced to fiery desire. Nothing in her past had been this fierce, this perfect.

When he finally lifted his head, she ran her hand over his cheek, drinking in his handsome features, his passionate eyes. "Nic."

He brushed his lips over hers. "Anna."

The single name cooled Stacy's desire as quickly as if he'd doused her with ice water. She stiffened and pushed away from him, tugging the dress back into place, rational thought finally regaining a tiny bit of control.

Nic stared at her. "What is it?"

"You called me Anna." She spat out the words. "But I'm not Anna, am I? I'm just someone who's convenient."

Horror crossed his face as the light dimmed in his eyes, turning quickly to concern. "No. Titania has put a spell on me. I can feel it. It's responsible for this attraction between us. I'm—"

She extended a hand to forestall his words. She didn't want his damned apology. She wanted him. Blast him—even though he'd called her by his dead wife's name, she still wanted him. "Don't say it."

Edging toward the door, she watched guilt ease into his eyes, the same guilt that nagged at the edges of her fading pleasure. "Just . . . just good night."

She rushed outside, surprised to find it still daylight, and ran toward the house. Dear Lord, she was an idiot. She knew . . . *knew* the man was destined for her sister, yet he only had to kiss her, and she acted like a love-starved teenager. No, worse than that: a love-starved, oversexed teenager.

Pausing by the back door of the house, she allowed herself to glance back into the depths of the gardens. On top of that, she was falling in love with him.

She hurried to her room and changed quickly into jeans and a T-shirt, then paused to slide her hand over the dress's silky material where it lay on the bed. For a while, a short while, she'd been able to escape, to have fun, to share laughter with a wonderful man, to nearly share what promised to be awesome lovemaking.

Stacy released her breath in a shudder. Well, back to the real world.

Dianna caught her before she made it to her office. "Where have you been all afternoon?"

"Out." Stacy met her sister's accusing gaze with no emotion.

"But I needed you. I needed to know what to do. Kevin is angry with me and—"

Stacy shook her head. "You have to learn to live without me, Di. I'm not always going to be here." Especially once Nic took Dianna away. Of course, then, he'd solve all her problems with a simple swish of his magic.

The panic that filled Dianna's features almost made Stacy laugh. "Of course, you'll be here. This is your home, too." She clutched Stacy's arm. "Look, I'm sorry about before. You know I didn't mean it."

"I know." Dianna erupted into anger without thought but recovered just as quickly. "Still, I have my own life to live." Who knew what the future held? Stacy felt less and less certain every day.

Dianna grabbed Stacy's arm. "That's not funny. I need

you, Stace. Promise me you'll always be here."

Stacy hugged her sister. "I can't promise that, and you know it. You're twenty-two now, Di, and plenty able to take care of yourself."

"But if you leave, then Kevin will be in charge, and he hates me."

"No, he doesn't." Stacy smiled. "He loves you and will do what's best for you and your career." If Dianna even continued to have a career once she fell in love with Nic. "Besides, you might not always want to sing."

"Not sing?" Dianna looked at her with the same incredulity as if Stacy had suggested she cut off her head. "I'll always want to sing."

"What if you could live forever? Wouldn't that get boring?" Stacy could think of a hundred or more things she wanted to experience. Seeing Paris had only whet her appetite. Now the thought of visiting London, Athens, Rome, Berlin, Tokyo, Moscow, Sydney stretched before her as a possibility. Someday.

"I can't see growing tired of singing. Besides, I'm not going to live forever, so it's a stupid question." Dianna produced her brightest smile guaranteed to get her way. "Please, Stace, make it better with Kev for me."

Stacy started to agree, then bit back the words. In the past she had run interference for the highly volatile Dianna, but no more. If Dianna belonged to Nic, perhaps it was better she and Kevin were fighting. "No, Di. You're going to have to apologize by yourself."

"But he's the one who's wrong."

"Maybe." Stacy eased her arm from her sister's hold. "Maybe not."

The phone ringing in the office provided the excuse she needed. "I have to get that." Ignoring the distress on Dianna's face, Stacy entered her office and shut the door. She closed her eyes as she drew in a deep breath. Was she doing the right thing?

Part of her cried out to say to hell with Dianna and claim Nic for herself. The part influenced by Titania, no doubt. No, she knew what she had to do.

She lifted the receiver on the fourth ring. "Stacy Fielding."

"Miss Fielding, it's Bob Edwards again. From the Pepsi Center." His voice sounded as if he'd been kicked in the chest. "You're not going to believe this . . ."

Stacy smiled wryly. He'd be surprised at what she'd believe.

After verifying that Dianna's Denver concert was indeed on again due to an honest-to-goodness miracle that no one could explain, Stacy headed for the living room. She had to do this now while she still had the courage. She didn't want to lose these feelings for Nic, but she had to before she messed up everything.

She faced Titania's portrait, studying the woman's beauty. Though the woman was beautiful, Stacy saw more than the surface loveliness now. There was a tightness around the queen's full lips, a hardness in her gaze.

As Stacy stared, she noticed a slight flicker of light traveling around the portrait, disappearing as Stacy blinked. Did that mean Titania was listening?

"You're very beautiful." She grimaced at hearing her words out loud, but they needed to be said. If she didn't speak for Nic now, she was afraid she never would. "You have power, everything you want. So why are you being so mean to Nic? All he wants is his Anna, his true love. Does that threaten you?"

Something sparked in the portrait's eyes, and Stacy stepped back, trepidation rising. "Leave him alone. He deserves happiness, and I intend to do whatever it takes to ensure he ends up with his Anna."

The portrait exploded. That was the only way Stacy could describe the rush of light and energy that knocked her to her butt. As she stared, six balls of light erupted from the portrait, then skittered into the dark corners of the room. She heard giggling, a high-pitched sound, then a crash as a vase sailed off a nearby table.

"What the hell?" Stacy jumped to her feet, her heart pounding. She scanned the room and was rewarded by a glimpse of movement from the corner of her eye. She followed the movement out of the room, through the back door left swinging open, and into the gardens.

What was going on here?

She could hear the noise of something crashing through the shrubbery, hear that odd giggling, yet could see nothing. This was definitely something magical, but what?

Nic.

Nic would know.

She hurried toward the cottage and caught him on the path. His first glance held heat and self-condemnation, reminding Stacy of what they'd briefly shared. Despite the awareness that tingled through her body, she rushed into a recitation of events.

"Something happened. I was talking to Titania. In the portrait. I told her to leave you alone. That I would help you get your Anna and—"

"You told her that?" Nic searched her face, his gaze intent. "After what I did to you?"

"You . . . you said it was because of a spell." Stacy clenched her fists, resisting the urge to touch him. Titania mixed one potent spell, that was for sure.

"Yes," he agreed, but he didn't sound happy about it.

"Anyhow, something popped out of the portrait. Six flashes of light. Then there was giggling. And a vase broke. And something came out here. At least, I think something did. The back door was open." Stacy paused for breath. "What is it?"

Nic frowned, his eyes narrowing with suspicion. "It can't be."

"What? Can't be what?"

Giggling erupted nearby, and flowers suddenly flew into the air, torn ruthlessly from their stems. Nic and Stacy turned to look, and Nic's jaw tightened. "I'm afraid it is."

"What?" Why did he look so grim? "Is it bad?"

"It can be." He watched the flower shreds fly for a moment, then placed his hand on Stacy's shoulder. His gaze held pity.

"You've got pixies."

"Pixies?" Stacy frowned. "But I always thought pixies were supposed to be fun little sprites."

"Well, they're little and fun-loving." Nic stepped toward the flying flowers. "They're also malicious and more than willing to go wherever Titania sends them."

"What do they do?" Had the queen of the Fae sent killers into the house?

"Mischief, mostly, but it can be pretty destructive mischief. Like the garden." Nic indicated the flower heads soaring into the air.

Her garden. Stacy ran forward, waving her arms. "Leave them alone. Now."

The flower shower stopped as the giggling resumed. By the time she reached that area, all that remained were shredded stems and decapitated lilies. Her heart sank. All that beauty destroyed.

"What can we do to stop them?"

"Don't worry." Nic rested his hand on her shoulder as he joined her. "I can fix it."

The giggling resumed a short distance away, and bushes rustled as if someone was dancing inside them.

Stacy curled her hands into fists. This had to quit.

"Let me try a removal spell first. That's easiest." Nic lifted his hands. "I banish you, pixies. Return to the place from which you came."

Lightning crackled from his fingers, and a flash burst in the area of the bush. For a brief moment there was silence, then the laughter resumed and pansy tops flew into the air.

Nic sighed. "I half expected as much. Titania has a protection spell on them."

"We can't get rid of them?" Stacy shuddered. The studio contained expensive equipment. If they got in there . . .

"Not all at once. If we can catch them and I can touch them, then I should be able to send them back."

His dry tone warned her. "Why do I think that's not going to be easy?"

"Because it's not. As a mortal, you won't even be able to see them. They're small and fast."

"Well, I can hear this one." She dashed toward the giggling and dove in. She caught a brief glimpse of movement, even felt something slide through her grip, but ended up face first in the soil.

Spitting out dirt, she climbed to her knees. "Almost had him."

Nic extended a hand and pulled her to her feet, humor dancing in his eyes, his lips twitching. "A valiant attempt."

He was teasing her. Stacy glared at him, and he ran his finger over her nose, then held it up to show the dirt. "I'll catch them, Stacy. Don't worry."

"Don't worry," she muttered. "Easy for you to say."

Something hard replaced the humor. "I'll get them, Stacy." The coolness of his voice sent a shiver along Stacy's spine. Though he could be caring and tender, she suspected he could be quite ruthless if necessary. He gave her a smile that didn't quite reach his eyes. "Go in and clean up. I'll handle this one."

She stalked off, and Nic grimaced, unable to shake the impending sense of doom. Pixies. What had Stacy said to infuriate Titania so?

He blew out his breath and stepped toward the quivering bushes. This was not going to be pleasant. Dealing with pixies never was.

By the time he managed to capture the tiny creature, Nic was coated with dirt and sported a small but painful bite on his hand. He dangled the pixie in the air away from him, avoiding the swinging hands and feet and the very sharp teeth.

"What are you supposed to do here?" he demanded.

The pixie only giggled, a sound guaranteed to drive Nic crazy in a short period of time. *By the Stones, I hate pixies.*

"Why did Titania send you?"

It smiled, revealing its tiny but wicked teeth. "Have to play. Have to stay. Queen says."

That didn't tell him anything. "Sorry, chum, you're not staying." Nic muttered a few words that sent the pixie back into the magical realm. Of course, Titania could just as easily send it back. With reinforcements.

With a sigh, Nic transported himself into the living room. From the distant sounds, everyone was in the kitchen. He faced Titania's portrait.

"Why the pixies?" he asked, not bothering to control his frustration. The last thing he needed now was pixies on the loose. He had enough problems trying to woo his wife. "What purpose do they serve?"

She didn't appear, but her voice floated from the portrait. "For fun, of course. They are such delightful creatures."

"Delightful isn't the word I would use." Nic crossed

his arms. "What did Stacy say to you? She scared you, didn't she, oh mighty Queen?"

"Nothing frightens me." The eyes in the portrait flared.

"Then why pixies?" He produced a mocking smile. "Sounds like panic to me."

"I am merely sending you a reminder, my dear Nic."

"A reminder? Of what? I know what I'm doing. And I'd make far better progress without your interference."

"You don't appear to be doing well from what I've seen." The smile in the portrait broadened. "The pixies are merely . . . catalysts."

"What?" What was she up to now? Not another change in their deal.

"Each time you kiss Dianna Fielding I'll remove a pixie. Simple, isn't it?"

Nic scowled. He didn't mind kissing Dianna at all. Only it wasn't as easy as he'd assumed. Her response hadn't been what he'd hoped for. Did Titania hope to force him into kissing Dianna too soon and frighten her away?

"Or not so simple." The light in the portrait faded along with Titania's mocking laughter.

Nic glanced toward the kitchen. He could go in there now, grab Dianna, and kiss her several times, but that wouldn't help him achieve his final purpose. He wanted to win her love.

Earlier today he'd made some progress. She'd responded to him. Only he hadn't felt a response in return. It had been Stacy's kiss that had ignited his desire, dancing with her that felt right, making love to her what he wanted so badly. He still ached with it.

Stones. Titania and her spell were driving him crazy. He had to win Dianna and stay away from Stacy before he lost all control.

And with it, Anna and his freedom.

• • •

"Try it again, Dianna." Stacy and Kevin spoke at the same time, then grinned at each other.

Dianna didn't share the amusement. "Very funny." She paced away from them and lifted the sheet music. "I'm ready."

Stacy launched into the accompaniment, a lively tune Dianna had insisted be included in her tour, even though it hadn't been recorded yet. Hell, Stacy had only written it days before Dianna left for her recording session.

It was a definite Dianna Fielding song: toe-tapping and fun, with words of great love and romance. All of it far from what Stacy currently felt.

But Dianna did it justice, her clear voice carrying the melody, letting loose on the chorus. Except for . . .

"There." Stacy stopped. "You did it again, Di. Here, listen. Those are triplets."

"I know what they are." Di gave Stacy a how-dumb-do-you-think-I-am look. "I'm putting my spin on them."

"Your spin is throwing everything else off." The way Di dragged out the triplets made the rest of the chorus go off-kilter.

"Then fix it."

Kevin waved the music at Dianna. "No, you fix it. It flows best the way Stacy wrote it, so sing it that way."

"But it's not *my* way."

"Your way is lazy."

Stacy flinched. The tension between Kevin and Dianna had been evident all morning, but this was the first time it had broken into the open.

"Oh, so now I'm lazy?" Dianna slammed the music down on a table. "Last night I was just selfish. It makes me wonder why you'd ever want to marry me."

His expression was stony. "I'm beginning to wonder myself."

Stacy started to speak, then bit her tongue. Perhaps this was for the best. Then Dianna would be available for Nic.

But she still hated to see it. She'd always thought Kevin and Dianna perfect for each other.

"Um, look, why don't we try this later?" Stacy said finally, breaking into the thick silence.

"That sounds like a good idea," Kevin replied.

"Of course you'd think so. You think everything Stacy does is perfect." Dianna stormed for the doorway. "Why don't you marry *her?"*

"Maybe I will," Kevin yelled after her, then grimaced and shook his head as she disappeared. "God, that was childish. Why I do let her do that to me?"

Stacy turned on the piano bench to face him. "Because you love her?"

"Must be." He gave her a self-deprecating smile and sat on the bench beside her. "She can push all my buttons—good and bad."

"How bad is it between you?" Stacy didn't hesitate to ask. She'd been a sounding board for both of them from the beginning.

"Bad," he admitted. "She's begging to go away for a weekend, and you know we can't do that, especially with this new song and routine to put together. The band arrives next week, and we're on the road in less than two after that."

"Dianna's never been one to be cooped up for long." Her sister required people around—preferably ones who adored her. "It's hard for her. And she *is* working hard."

"So are you. So am I. Everyone here is working hard, but she thinks she's better than the rest of us." Kevin sighed. "She's spoiled. You know it as well as I, and we're both guilty of letting her become that way."

Stacy grimaced. After their parents had died, it had been easier to give in to Dianna, especially with her rising fame and the chaos of trying to manage a career along with raising a sister. "True, but she has a good heart."

"I know that. Otherwise I never would have fallen in

love with her. It's those glimpses of who she is when out of the spotlight that keep me going."

"We're all stressed out right now." Boy, wasn't that the truth. "She'll be better once she's on the road. That always energizes her."

Kevin grinned. "All we have to do is survive until then." He wrapped his arm around Stacy's shoulders and gave her a hug. "Thank God one of us keeps a clear head around here."

"Not always." *And not much lately.* "It's just my turn." Stacy rested her head against his shoulder, secure in their friendship. "I do have to ask one thing, though, Kev."

He leaned his head against hers. "Ask away."

"Can you be both manager and husband to Dianna? Won't one influence the other?" If he was angry, he had the potential to hurt her sister's career.

"It's not going to be easy. I know that. But I think I can handle it. I know the business, and I love her. You're her sister. You've managed."

Stacy hesitated a moment before continuing. This was difficult to ask, but she needed to know. "But what if it came down to the marriage or the career? Which would you choose?"

He didn't answer right away, and Stacy's heart sank. Was it Dianna's career that he loved more than Dianna?

"I'd like to hear the answer to that myself."

Kevin and Stacy jerked upright as Dianna appeared in the doorway to the music room. "Which would you work harder to save, Kev? Our marriage or my career?"

He rose slowly. "Our marriage, of course."

"Took you a moment though, didn't it?" Sparks flared in Dianna's eyes. "Is it the pop star, successful, wealthy Dianna Fielding you want, or the spoiled, lazy Dianna Fielding?"

"Neither." He made his way across the room. "I want the woman I fell in love with. A woman who doesn't believe all her promo, who has the most incredible voice I've ever heard, a woman who doesn't think she has to come on to every man she meets, a woman who loves me as much as I love her. That's the woman I want."

Stacy's chest ached with his words. She remembered those earlier days, too. Had they all changed so much since then?

"And what if she doesn't exist anymore?" Dianna snapped.

"Then we'll both be sorry." He reached out to touch her, but she turned away.

"Yeah, I guess we will." She rushed away for a second time, ignoring Kevin's call to stop.

He slammed his fist against the doorframe. "Damn." Glancing over his shoulder, he looked at Stacy. "You sure ask great questions, Stace."

"I had to know." She could almost feel his pain.

"Well, now we all know. For whatever good that does." He left, his shoulders slumped, and Stacy closed her eyes for a moment.

She'd handled that well. Now everyone was pissed.

Swinging back around to face the piano, she sighed. What should she do for an encore?

She let her fingers find the tune, plucking the notes out of her troubled emotions, easing the ache and loneliness that filled her. Slowly, a song took form, becoming a part of her, capturing some of her angst.

Stacy paused only to snare some blank staff paper and a pencil. Perhaps now was time she started creating her own music.

And her own life.

Nic brushed the soil from his knees as he stood. With the help of Lily and the other pillywiggins, the sections of the garden destroyed by the pixie would be like new within two days. At least he could accomplish that much.

From the brief flickers of light he'd spotted in the house windows last night, he could tell the remaining pixies had been active as well. He either had to capture them or kiss Dianna enough times to make them disappear. He knew which method he preferred.

The only remaining question was how to achieve it.

As if in answer, Dianna ran down the path, nearly colliding with him. He caught her shoulders to steady her, noticing the dampness in her eyes.

"What's wrong?"

"Oh, everything." Her bottom lip quivered. "Stacy and Kevin hate me. They want to control my life. They want me to be this . . . this perfect somebody that I'm not. And I think . . . I think my sister is trying to steal my boyfriend."

Her voice broke, and she fell against Nic's chest, burying her face in his shirt. He wrapped his arms around her, unsure whether the sudden clenching in his gut came from her closeness or her words. "You're perfect just the way you are."

She sniffed. "You're the only one who thinks so."

"I'm sure Stacy doesn't hate you." Stacy adored her sister.

"Well, maybe not hate me. But she's always telling me to do this, do that, do it her way. What about my way? The faeries in my tours were her idea, not mine. The songs I sing are hers, not mine. I wouldn't be surprised if she picked out Kevin for me to marry."

"I doubt that." Her description didn't fit the Stacy he knew. Or thought he knew. But then, how well did he really know either sister?

"I think she wants Kevin for herself."

Again, his stomach rolled. "What makes you say that?"

"I went into the music room, and they were cuddling on the piano bench like long-lost lovers. I bet they've been fooling around behind my back." She sniffed again, then rubbed her nose with the back of her hand.

Her description made Nic catch his breath. Cuddling like long-lost lovers? Fooling around? No, he wouldn't . . . couldn't believe that.

Yet, wasn't that what he wanted—to match up Stacy and Kevin?

That was his plan. He didn't have to like it, but it was his plan.

Dianna was in his arms. He should be thinking of that, not Stacy. He tightened his hold on Dianna. She fit exactly as Anna had. "How about I take you on a vacation?"

"A vacation?" She looked up at him, her eyes red-rimmed, tear tracks staining her cheeks, and still looking beautiful. "Where?"

"Wherever you want to go." Though he'd probably have to use mortal methods of transport . . . until he could tell her the truth.

Dianna gave him a brilliant smile. "There are so many places: Rome, Athens, Paris, London, Tokyo."

"We can go to them all." The sooner he could take her away from Kevin, the sooner she'd realize she loved him.

"You'd really do that for me?"

"In a moment." He caressed her face. "You're important to me, Dianna."

She sighed and snuggled against him again. "I like you."

He grinned. It was working.

"But I can't go."

What? "Why not?"

"Kevin is right, blast him. I have a tour leaving in a few weeks. I have too much to do to get ready."

"Give up your tour." Nic didn't relish the idea of his woman touring the country surrounded by raving groupies. "We'll travel, have fun, see the world."

"Give it up?" Dianna pulled away from him, her expression shocked. "Are you crazy? This is my dream come true. This is what I've always wanted since I was child, what I've worked for. I'm not about to give it up. For anyone."

"I didn't realize it meant that much to you." If she truly desired it, he wouldn't stop her. Besides, once she learned to love him again, she'd probably change her mind. Knowing he was magic and that they were both immortal was bound to change her priorities.

"It does. But . . ." She smiled again, a come-hither gleam in her eyes. "Nothing says I can't have a day to play."

He returned her smile even as he noted how different it was from the honest warmth of Stacy's. "Then let's play." He bowed and motioned with his arm down the path.

Dianna linked her arm through his and pulled him with her. "I haven't been downtown in ages. Or to Mountain Village."

Nic accompanied her willingly but couldn't resist a glance back at the main house. What would Stacy say when she discovered her sister was gone? He magically sent a message to her office. Once Stacy knew Dianna was with him, she wouldn't worry.

He wasn't about to lose this perfect opportunity. By the time he and Dianna returned, she'd be head over heels in love with him.

He was Fae. How could he fail?

Conjuring up a car and driving into Telluride's narrow downtown was easy compared to Dianna deciding where she wanted to stop. She finally had Nic park near the New Sheridan Hotel on Colorado Avenue and led him toward a tiny jewelry store nestled between the large, Victorian-style buildings.

He grimaced. She didn't need to buy jewelry. He could create whatever she wanted: diamonds, opals, emeralds. But he couldn't tell her that. Not yet anyhow.

While she exclaimed over the intricate rings in a showcase, Nic stared out the store window, more impressed with the exquisite architecture and nearby mountain peaks. He enjoyed the sense of history here—recent history compared to his life span, yet carefully preserved in this small town.

"What do you think of this one, Nic?" Dianna held out her hand to display a large ruby ringed with diamonds.

He answered her honestly. "Your beauty doesn't need any adornment."

She beamed at him. "You're quite the charmer, aren't you?" But she returned the ring to the display, so perhaps she understood his point.

Back on the sidewalk, Nic waved a hand to indicate the surrounding area. "What can you tell me about this town, the history here?"

"Not much, I'm afraid." Dianna shrugged. "Stace is the history buff in the family. Doesn't interest me at all. I prefer the here and now."

"You know nothing about Telluride?" He found that hard to believe. Anna had always loved learning about places. Though he had to remember, Dianna would not be exactly Anna. Her upbringing hadn't been the same, which meant there had to be some differences.

"It was a mining town that almost went bust until someone brought in skiing. I know that much." Dianna linked her arm through his and steered him down the street. "And there are lots of festivals during the summer. The Film Festival is my favorite."

"Why did you decide to live in Telluride?" Perhaps her answer would offer some insight into this woman.

"Stacy wanted to stay in Colorado, as we were both born and raised in Denver, and Telluride is the up-and-coming place to be for stars. I wanted the exposure, and Stacy wanted to make sure I could be protected from my adoring fans." The dryness in Dianna's voice made Nic glance at her.

"Do you need protection?"

"I suppose. I had one stalker who lurked outside our house in Denver several years ago. He even tried to break in once. Freaked Stacy out, so we moved here not too long after that."

"Do you always do what Stacy wants?" He'd known Stacy held some influence over her younger sister, but he hadn't thought it was this strong.

"I used to." Dianna pressed her lips together. "But I think it's about time I started making my own decisions—about what to sing, what to wear, how to act."

"Whom to love," Nic added.

She paused and looked up at him. "Yes, that, too." Tilting her head sideways, she studied him. "You're a very handsome man, Nic."

"Thank you." Attractiveness was part of being Fae, a part of him he'd long ago dismissed as unimportant.

"And I like the way people look at me when I'm with you." She snuggled closer as they resumed walking. "I'm used to them recognizing me, but I see admiration and sometimes envy in their eyes when they look at you."

To be honest, he hadn't noticed anyone else. "I only see you."

She laughed. "I *do* like you." Tugging on his arm, she pulled him toward a building at the base of a mountain. "Come on. Let's take the gondola to Mountain Village. I haven't been there in ages."

His spirits lifted. If she liked him, love couldn't be far behind. Though he could have transported them across the mountain in seconds, he boarded the gondola that would take them up over the peak and down the other side to the companion town of Mountain Village.

Dianna stood by the side, watching the trees shrink beneath them through the window, the gondola swinging slightly as it climbed the mountain. Nic slid his arm around her shoulders, holding her next to him. "Don't lose your balance," he said when she glanced at him.

Her gaze held both admiration and a challenge. "Thank you."

He was never one to back away from a challenge. "I'm going to kiss you, Dianna," he said, pulling her closer.

"Are you?" Mischief danced in her eyes.

"Most definitely." He touched her hair, running his hand along the silky length, the sensation so familiar it made him ache.

"I've never been kissed in a gondola before."

She didn't try to turn away as he lowered his head toward hers. "Then it's time you were," he murmured.

His lips were a breath away from hers when a young female voice shattered the moment.

"You're Dianna Fielding."

Nic lifted his head to see a young teenage girl, probably all of twelve, staring adoringly at Dianna. Dianna stepped away from him and smiled at the girl.

"Yes, I am."

"Can I . . . can I have your autograph?"

"Of course." Dianna took the tourist leaflet from the girl. "What's your name?"

"Kim."

Kim's timid approach apparently broke the ice, for one after another of the gondola's occupants came over to talk to Dianna, request an autograph, or stare in awe.

And Dianna loved it. Nic watched, a dry smile on his lips. Dianna glowed in this element, surrounded by those who adored her. If anything, she became more beautiful, more alive.

A young boy stumbled forward, flushing pink to the tips of his ears, unable to do more than stare at his feet as he stammered out an autograph request. Dianna smiled and accepted the torn scrap of paper.

"Who are you?" she asked softly.

"Carl," he whispered.

"Do you live in Telluride, Carl?"

He shook his head. "We're on vacation."

"Do you like it so far?"

"It's okay." He ventured a glance at her, and Dianna gave him a warm smile. "I liked the waterfall."

"I like that, too." She passed him back his paper, then bent forward and placed a light kiss on his cheek. "Have a great vacation, Carl."

Nic basked in the warmth that filled him. That was his Anna. Giving, kind, thoughtful of others.

By the time they reached Mountain Village, she'd charmed nearly all their fellow travelers and willingly posed for photographs before waving good-bye and leaving on Nic's arm.

"You were good with them," Nic said.

"They're my fans. I'd be nothing without them." She pointed toward an outdoor café up the street. "Let's eat. I'm starving."

Starving, yet she only ordered a salad and mineral water. Nic shook his head with a smile. No matter how many centuries he lived, he'd never understand women.

Then again, that was what made them so interesting.

"How did you get started singing?" he asked while they waited for their meal.

"If you've read any of a hundred interviews, you'd know."

"I haven't." He'd only read enough to learn where to find her. "And I'd like to hear it from you."

"I'd always sang." Dianna sipped from her water before continuing. "In choir, at school, at church, everywhere I could. Folks always told me I had a voice too big for the rest of me." She smiled, her eyes dreamy. "So I started singing at weddings and special occasions."

"How did you get into selling your music?" Many youngsters had talent, but few went on to the stardom Dianna had achieved.

"When I was thirteen, my parents paid for me to record some songs as a demo, so I used the songs Stacy had written for me."

"Didn't she sing, too?" To write songs, Stacy had to understand music. Why had Dianna gone on to fame and not Stacy?

"She preferred to play the piano and would often accompany me when I went places. She can sing, but she doesn't, not for other folks." Dianna gave him a small smile. "Her voice isn't like mine."

"Instead, she wrote your songs?"

"Uh-huh. Most of them were similar to what was popular right then. So I recorded them, and we sent the demo to Talent Records, who signed me. One of those songs went on to become a top ten." Dianna made a flippant gesture with her hand. "The rest is history."

"Has Stacy been the only one to write your music?"

"Most of them. Kevin has written a couple for me." Her smile grew sad. "He first told me he loved me in a song."

Nic leapt in to divert that subject. "What did your parents think when you became famous?"

"Oh, they were thrilled, but they still treated me like a child." She grimaced. "I had to empty garbage and vacuum. Mom insisted it kept me grounded, though I managed to get out of most of it after she and Dad died. Stacy isn't nearly as strict."

Nic hesitated. "What happened to your parents?" He had to know. Their loss had to have affected the person Dianna was today.

Dianna drew idle designs on the tablecloth. "They were killed in a car accident the day after my sixteenth birthday. I was just starting to make some really good money and had signed a new contract only a couple of weeks earlier." She grimaced. "Happy Birthday to me." Her dry tone held an underlying layer of hurt.

"Then Stacy raised you?"

"Yeah. The first couple of years were rough. We had enough money to get by, but Stacy took over as my manager and had to learn a lot about the business end of things that Mom and Dad had always handled. Plus she insisted I finish high school and get my diploma. I wasn't very happy with her at the time. I didn't see why I needed a diploma when I was doing fine by singing."

Nic pushed a little, sensing she wanted to say more. "But now?"

Dianna shrugged. "She was right. Of course. As always."

"Always?" No mortal was perfect.

"It sure seems that way. Everywhere I go, I get people telling me how lucky I am to have a sister who does so much for me, who's guided my career so well." Dianna waved her hand in the air. "What about me? I work hard, too."

"And in return you get the adoring fans your sister never does."

Dianna blinked. "Hey, you're right. I never thought about that."

"And she does love you. Her decisions aren't made to harm you." Nic paused. Why was he defending Stacy? Didn't he want to separate Dianna from Stacy and Kevin?

"I know. I love her, too. Most of the time." Dianna grimaced. "She's not always awful. She did let me choose my costumes for this tour."

Nic grinned. "That's good."

"I was able to select the songs for my new album, too. She and Kev made suggestions, but I had the final say. Well, the producer did, really."

Their food arrived, and Dianna picked at her salad, her ravenous hunger apparently gone. The silence stretched until she finally met Nic's gaze.

His gut clenched. Her previously playful air had given way to guilt. Stones. That wasn't what he wanted.

"You know, I may be a spoiled brat after all." Dianna stabbed her fork into the lettuce. "Stacy has always tried to include me in decisions. I usually choose not to get involved. All I want to do is sing. That isn't such a bad thing, is it?" She looked to Nic for confirmation.

"Not at all. Someone in demand has to surround herself with people she can trust to make the right decisions." He'd done so in the past when he'd been the famous Nic Stone.

"When Stacy hired Kevin to help her, I was so resentful at first. I didn't see why we needed anyone else." Dianna pounded a cucumber slice to pulp. "But from the first moment we met, I knew. I knew he was the one for me."

Just what Nic needed to hear. He grimaced. "First impressions aren't—"

"You know, Nic. I do have a lot to do." Dianna pushed her salad away. "I'd like to go home now."

"Are you sure?" This conversation had definitely taken a wrong turn somewhere. "I haven't seen much of Mountain Village yet."

"Another time perhaps."

He grimaced but nodded. So much for convincing Dianna to fall in love with him today. Titania would be thrilled.

They made their return in silence, though Dianna did smile and chat with fans who recognized her. Nic debated on transporting them away somewhere, on holding Dianna captive until she recognized him as the man she needed.

Only the passion was missing, and that bothered him most of all. From the first moment he'd met Anna, he'd wanted her. But though he found Dianna beautiful and desirable, he lacked that burning passion to claim her.

It had to be Titania's spell influencing him, transferring the passion he should feel for Dianna to Stacy. Yet knowing that didn't help him fight it.

As he walked Dianna up to the main house, he paused and caught her face between his hands. "I never did get my kiss." He kept his tone light but determined. A kiss could ignite the passion. At the very least it could get rid of a pixie.

He bent forward, but Dianna pulled free, then pressed a kiss to his cheek. "Thank you, Nic, for being there. I won't forget it."

Nic sighed as he watched her dash into the house. Oh, yeah. That made him feel better.

He wanted a kiss. He wanted passion. He wanted his Anna.

Now he had to think of another way to get her.

• • •

Stacy heard Dianna's footsteps in the hallway and called out to her. "That you, Di?"

She pushed away from the piano and stood, then jumped as the lid slammed down. Again.

Followed by that damned giggling.

Again.

"Blasted pixies," she muttered.

She scanned the music room as she had the last time this happened but saw nothing. Except a piano that was going to desperately need tuning if this continued.

"It's me." Dianna appeared in the doorway, her expression contrite.

Stacy bit back the first angry words that wanted to emerge. "Where have you been?"

"With Nic. We went to town."

"I . . . see." Apparently Nic was using Kevin and Dianna's spat to his advantage. "And you couldn't be bothered to let me know where you'd gone? Did you think I wouldn't worry?"

"Oh, come on, Stace. I'm a grown woman now."

"So when it came time to go over the routine Jermaine developed for this new song and I couldn't find you, I shouldn't have worried?" She hadn't, at first, figuring Dianna was sulking somewhere on the estate, then had found the note Nic had left for her. Though that hadn't made her feel any better.

"No. I can take care of myself."

"That's good to know." Stacy advanced on her sister. " 'Cause you're going to have to work hard tomorrow to catch up. Your backup dancers have the new steps down already."

Dianna glanced at her watch. "It's still early enough. I'll run through it a couple of times now."

"Sorry." Stacy shook her head. "Once they had it down

pat, there was no use in keeping them around if you weren't going to show."

"Oh." Dianna hesitated, then grimaced. "I'm sorry, Stace."

Stacy shrugged. Actually, it had been nice to have some extra time of her own. She'd spent the last hour or so working on her new song.

"Where's Kevin?" Dianna asked.

Uh-oh. Stacy touched Dianna's shoulder. "He's in Denver."

"Denver?"

"We needed some details finalized there for your opening night, and he thought it best you had some time apart right now." Dianna's eyes reflected her shock. "He didn't know you'd taken off when he left."

"Jeez, I blew it, didn't I?" Her voice wavered, and Stacy hugged her.

"We're all on edge right now," she said. "We always are before a tour. It'll be all right."

Dianna sniffed once, then nodded. "What did you do this afternoon then?"

"I started writing a new song." Remembering how the music had flowed made Stacy smile. "I like it."

Dianna produced a slight smile. "A weepy ballad?"

"Of course." The difference in their musical tastes had long been a running joke.

"Can I hear it?"

"Not yet." The music was still too raw, too emotional. "It's not ready."

"Soon?"

Stacy smiled. "Soon." She squeezed Dianna's shoulder. "In the meantime, it's just us. Why don't I order a pizza and make popcorn and we can watch sappy movies that make us cry all evening?"

"I'd love it."

Much later, snuggled on the couch with Dianna, a bowl

of popcorn between them, Stacy felt herself relax. It had been ages since she and Di had shared any sister time, and though she hadn't consciously realized it, she'd missed it.

They giggled and cried over a romantic comedy and wrapped their arms around each other as they staggered up to bed at an indecently late hour. Stacy expected to fall asleep the moment her head hit the pillow. Instead, an hour later, she was still wide awake, staring at the ceiling, listening to pixies bang around downstairs.

"This is ridiculous." A soak in the hot tub would make her sleepy. She padded down to the huge bathroom designed around a large Jacuzzi tub. Though she didn't spend nearly as much time in here as Kevin and Dianna, she did enjoy it on occasion.

Minutes later, sunk deep in the tub with the jets pulsating against her tight muscles, she sighed and leaned her head back against the edge. Ah, yes, this was what she needed. Just ease those troubles away. Forget all about Dianna and Kevin and Nic. Especially Nic.

Was he part of the reason why she was still awake at oh-dark-thirty? In the dim light she could admit to the pangs of jealousy she'd felt when Dianna had said she'd been with Nic. Jealousy she had no right to feel.

But after that wonderful night in Paris, how could she not?

Stacy closed her eyes. Forget about it. All of it.

She had to.

She'd almost fallen asleep when she heard the distant high-pitched giggling she'd come to dread. Jerking upright, she caught a glimpse of the bathroom door closing. Dear Lord, what now?

After drying herself off, she reached for her nightgown and froze. It was gone. Pixies, no doubt.

"Very funny," she muttered. She tucked the towel around her, grateful for the large bath sheet. Kevin was gone. Her room was only a couple doors down the hall. This wasn't a problem.

Or so she thought until she tried the door handle. Locked.

How could it be? The door locked from the inside. But no matter how many times she twisted the knob or fiddled with the lock, the door remained firmly shut.

She rested her forehead against the door with a groan, only to have giggling begin out in the hallway. "This is not funny," she snapped. The laughter only increased.

Great. Other homes had termites. Not hers. Hers had to have pixies.

Stacy tried kicking the door open but only succeeded in hurting her foot. Damn. It had seemed like a good idea to have solid wood doors when they'd built the place.

Pounding on the door, she called for her sister. "Dianna. Di."

Of course, Di's room was at the far end of the hall, and she tended to sleep like the dead. "Di!"

Who else could help? Nic? He was in the cottage. He'd never hear her. But anything was worth a try.

"Nic." She hammered harder. "Anyone? Help!"

Abruptly, the door disappeared, and she staggered forward. Nic caught her shoulders before she hit him.

Her pulse increased tenfold as he left his hands on her bare skin. "How did you know?"

"I heard you call me."

"Clear in the cottage?"

"I think I can hear you, no matter where I am." His voice grew husky as his gaze dropped to her sagging towel.

Stacy's throat went dry as she met his gaze. Fire burned deep in the dark depths, stirring an answering blaze within her.

Oh, Lord. What now?

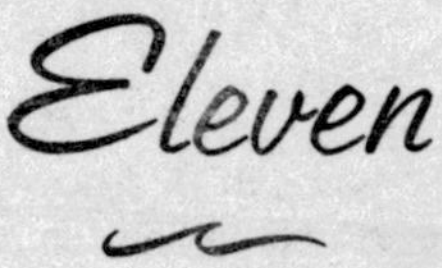

"The . . . the pixies were having fun," Stacy murmured, forcing words through her tight throat. "They locked me in."

"They do that." Even as he spoke, Nic lifted one hand to smooth her damp hair away from her face.

Stacy leaned into his palm, her senses stirring, the fire deep inside her flaring to life. She shouldn't. But that didn't stop her from raising her lips as he bent closer.

He brushed her mouth softly, as if sampling. Once, then twice until Stacy moaned, unable to stand it any longer. She pulled him forward and seized his lips, demanding the passion. A passion he readily supplied, no longer gentle, but hungry, devouring her mouth with an urgency she strained to meet.

Yes, this was what she wanted, what she needed. Her desire flared to life, and she wrapped her arms around his neck, unheeding as the towel came untucked until her bare nipples peaked against his muscular chest.

"Stacy," he murmured against her mouth, before he dipped to nibble a path down her neck.

She tilted her head to give him better access, her rapid

pulse increasing as he placed his lips against that point in her throat. Raising one hand, he cupped her breast while he stroked the long line of her back with the other.

"N . . . Nic." Her breath came in gasps, her desire rising to a fever pitch. "I . . . I want you."

"I—"

"Stace, that you?"

Dianna's sleepy voice drifted down the hall, and Stacy stiffened. In the next instant she found herself in her bedroom, naked . . . and alone. Damn him. Couldn't he have come here with her? This way might be for the best, but it sure didn't feel like it at the moment.

Her body still trembled with the passion Nic had triggered, and she pulled the comforter off her bed to wrap around her as tears stung her eyes. Why did she do this to herself?

"I want him," she murmured. It wasn't right, but she wanted him more than any man she'd ever met. He made her feel truly alive, as if she'd waited all her life for him.

And he belonged to her sister.

Somehow . . . some way, she had to avoid him, get over these irrational feelings.

Stacy tumbled onto her bed and curled into a ball. Yeah, easier said than done.

Nic paced the garden paths, the flagstones dimly lit by the full moon, his long strides covering territory that led nowhere. He was trying to escape but couldn't. He had to stop himself. Somehow.

Despite his good intentions, he couldn't stay away from Stacy. Then, when he was with her, he had to touch her, to feel her smooth skin beneath his palm, her soft lips beneath his.

Stones. He had to stop this, had to fight Titania's spell before he lost Anna forever. But it was difficult—far more difficult than he'd expected.

He'd heard Stacy's cry for help as if she'd been standing next to him, and he only needed an instant to reach her, to remove the magically locked door. Then to see her so close, her curly hair damp, her fair skin glistening, her curves barely hidden by the towel . . . No Fae could be expected to resist that.

And he hadn't.

If Dianna hadn't interrupted them, shaken him from his mindless passion . . .

He fell to his knees in a small grove and lifted his hands to the moon illuminating the sky. "I call upon the powers of nature to help me, to guide me in winning my lady. Give me the strength of will to resist all spells, to follow only the true love of my heart."

A cold wind, fresh from the snowcapped peaks, tossed his hair and stirred the leaves on the surrounding trees. But it held no answers, no magic to solve his inner torment.

Nic bowed his head. His body still shuddered with the ache of desire, his palms still tingled with the sensation of Stacy's heated skin and the fullness of her breast, and his erection remained rock hard. He longed for satisfaction, to bury himself within Stacy's welcoming warmth.

Clenching his fists, he shook his head. No. That could not be allowed to happen. He had to remain strong, to focus on what truly mattered.

Anna.

If he foolishly gave his love to the wrong woman, he would not only lose the greatest love of his vast long life but his very freedom for the rest of eternity. He ground his teeth together. He could win Anna. He *would* win Anna.

He had no choice.

Nic dabbled at the scenery. In all actuality, it was completed, but this pretense at working allowed him to stay and watch Dianna as she practiced.

For the past two days, her rehearsals had been exuberant, vital, with an energy he hadn't realized was missing until it appeared. Apparently her trip into town had helped her, if not him.

He never tired of watching her perform the moves of her dance routines or of hearing her fantastic voice belt out the songs. Her obvious talent appeared more focused. He liked to think he'd had something to do with that.

However, she barely spoke to him, giving him a brief smile in passing but no more. Evidently he'd moved too fast, frightened her away. Stones.

He responded in kind; warm, friendly, but no more. He could pull back and take his time, lure her in slowly if that was what it took. At her next break, he noticed her water bottle was empty and produced another one, which he presented to her.

"Thanks," she murmured, downing half the contents in one swallow.

"You look great out there."

"Thank you." She met his gaze with a grin. "It was past time I got into it, don't you think?"

"I didn't think you were bad before," he admitted. "But now it's even better. Your trip to town must have helped."

"It did." She touched his arm briefly. "Thank you for being there and understanding."

He lifted his lips in a half smile. "That's what friends are for."

Dianna nodded. "I'd like to consider you my friend, Nic."

"Always." He'd been Anna's friend as well as her lover. It was as good a start as any.

A tingling at the back of his neck told him Stacy had appeared in the studio. He'd managed to avoid being near her or talking to her, but he couldn't stop noticing her presence. His traitorous body reacted the moment she entered a room.

"I have a ton of good wishes for you, Di," Stacy called. Dianna brushed past Nic, and he turned to see Stacy waving a sheaf of papers in the air. "And a very special one from Mr. Gallagher at Talent Records. He says your new album is going to be the best yet."

"All right!" Shooting her first into the air, Dianna bounded from the stage to her sister's side and snagged the papers. Her smile grew broader as she read them.

"It's going to be a great tour, little sis," Stacy said, squeezing Dianna's shoulder.

"You betcha, big sis." Dianna leaned against Stacy for a moment, then resumed reading.

Something had happened between them. The earlier antagonism was gone. The love was more open. He took a step toward them, wanting to share in that love, then paused. Bad idea. He needed to stay as far from Stacy as possible. He had enough mental sense to realize that, even if his body thought otherwise.

"I think it's going to be an excellent tour." Kevin stepped from the shadows, eliciting a cry of surprise from Dianna. "You look great, and you nailed those triplets."

Dianna ran toward him. "When did you get back?"

"A little while ago. I wanted to watch without you knowing I was here. It's awesome, Di. Absolutely awesome."

She paused in front of him, catching herself before she flung her arms around his neck. "I'm sorry, Kev. I—"

He smiled and ran his finger down her nose. "My fault as well."

"God, I've missed you." Dianna leapt at him, encircling his neck with her arms and his waist with her legs, then claimed his lips.

Nic grimaced. Now there was the passion that had thus far eluded him and Dianna. How could he earn that for himself? Only one solution presented itself. He would have to get rid of Kevin Montgomery.

When Kevin and Dianna parted, Kevin grinned at Stacy over Dianna's shoulder. "Okay if we take off for a little while?"

Stacy raised her eyebrow but nodded. "Go ahead." She turned to face the folks on stage. "Take an hour, everyone."

Kevin and Dianna left first, followed slowly by the others, until the stage was empty. Except for Nic. He'd told himself to leave, but his rebellious feet hadn't obeyed.

Glancing up at him, Stacy shrugged. "I'm sorry."

"Not your fault." She had no more control over Dianna's silly attachment to Kevin than he did. He crossed to the edge of the stage but didn't go down to the floor beside her. He didn't dare. "I'll come up with something."

"They'll be leaving on tour in two weeks," she added, concern in her eyes.

Just what he needed. A deadline. "Can you get rid of Montgomery?"

"Kevin? I doubt it, not this close to the opening."

"I see." Nic frowned. He might be forced to resort to some magic after all.

Stacy rushed toward the stage, apparently reading his mind. "Don't you dare harm Kevin. You promised me: no magic."

"I promised no magic on Dianna. Everything else is fair game. Besides, I won't hurt him." Nic didn't meet her gaze, unable to shake the sudden surge of guilt. "He might like some time on a tropical isle."

"No. I won't let you do that to him."

Nic drew up to his full height. Guilt be damned. He'd had enough setbacks, and now Stacy was fighting him. "Are you challenging me? You, a mere mortal?"

She blinked. "Mere mortal? If that's what you think of us, why are you even interested in Dianna?"

"I love her." The love he'd shared with Anna had been beyond anything—mortal or Fae.

"Then win her fairly. No trickery. No magic."

Nic met her defiant gaze. "You can't stop me." Even as he spoke, he knew she could. All it would take was a word, a look. She held more power over him than he liked to admit.

"I can try." Stacy didn't back away, and his admiration rose reluctantly. Surely she, more than anyone, had some idea of what he could do if he chose.

"You could," he said. "But it wouldn't do you any good." Stones. He wanted to shake her.

He wanted to kiss her.

Only one thing left to do.

He transported himself away. Far away from Stacy Fielding.

Stacy sighed as Nic disappeared, and she whirled on her heel. How dare he threaten Kevin. Just because things weren't going his way, Nic had to go all macho. Well, she wasn't going to let him get away with it.

Though she had no idea of how she'd stop him.

Perhaps he was only making idle threats. Or maybe she really needed to think of a way to send Kevin elsewhere for a few days. He'd already gone to Denver. Nothing else needed doing at this point.

She retreated to the music room, her sanctuary over the past few days, where she could lose herself in the passion and depth of her ballad. The melody was set now, and she almost had the words finished. Then what?

She'd never written songs for anyone but Dianna, never attempted to send them elsewhere. Stacy straightened her shoulders. If she was going to have a life of her own, then it was past time she did so. She'd never know if she could succeed if she didn't try.

And she knew exactly where to start.

Donovan Reeves sang exactly this kind of music. She

loved listening to his easy tenor voice sing ballads of lost love and heartache, songs that called to her, touched the ache inside her.

She'd send this song to him and see if he was interested in singing it. Whether he wanted it or not, she would have taken that first step toward independence.

Stacy played the tune on the piano as her thoughts continued to spin. Strange, she'd always thought it was Dianna who needed to grow up, to be independent, but she was finally realizing she needed it as well. She'd always been there for Di, but Di had always been there for her, too.

It was past time both the Fielding sisters grew up.

The abrupt clanging of pots in the kitchen caught Stacy's attention. What was that? Dianna didn't usually cook, and Stacy doubted she'd be anywhere near the kitchen at this point, anyway. Not with the way she and Kevin had looked at each other when they left the studio.

Leaving the piano, she headed for the kitchen. The noise continued, increasing in volume as she grew closer.

She froze in the doorway. "Dear Lord." Pots and pans, usually hung on hooks over the center island, were flying across the room, tossed by invisible hands.

Pixies.

"Stop it right now," she ordered, marching into the room. A pot flew at her, and she ducked, pressing against the island. "Stop."

The destruction continued. Why had she even expected them to obey? Hearing a drawer open, she crawled on her knees around the island, then gasped to find herself face-to-body with a small, six-inch creature: a combination of man and Cabbage Patch doll. He had pointed ears and wild hair that had obviously never seen a comb, but his face was round, his eyes large, his mouth oversized. He grinned at her to reveal pointed teeth, and she swallowed. He wore what appeared to be a tunic and slacks, but his feet were bare with only four toes. His small hands only had four fingers as well, but he used them to yank the silverware drawer from its slot, spilling the utensils all over the floor.

"Hey, stop that." Stacy jumped forward to keep the creature from grabbing another drawer, only to have him leap into the air, giggling the entire time.

She scrambled to her feet just as the cupboard door swung open and dishware flew out, the plates becoming deadly flying saucers before smashing into bits on the ceramic floor. "Dammit. This isn't funny." She rushed forward to slam the door shut, only to have a pot ricochet off her temple.

With a cry of pain, she slid into a sitting position on the floor, her hand pressed against her forehead. Damn, that hurt. Her eyes stung with unshed tears, while the sounds of dishes shattering rang around her.

She wasn't going to be able to stop them. Not alone. She needed Nic's help. Why did fate constantly throw them together? Clenching her fists, she called for him. "Nic, help." With luck, he hadn't been lying when he said he could hear her anywhere.

Evidently not, for he appeared beside her a moment later, only to have a mixing bowl bounce off his shoulder. He dropped to his knees and touched Stacy's shoulder. "Are you all right?"

How could he sound so concerned now and so hateful only a half hour ago? "More or less." She met his gaze. "The pixies are loose."

He nodded. "Two, at least. Stay down. I'll get them."

As he stood, another wave of dishes flew from the cupboard, and he was forced to weave and bob to avoid them. As he dove for one of the creatures, the spice rack fell on him, and he slid across the floor into the cupboard with a groan. "Stones."

Stacy bit back a grin. He wasn't having any better luck in stopping the pixies than she had.

As he climbed to his feet, a large soup pot soared toward him, and he dodged, only to have it bounce on the floor near Stacy. She sat upright, her heart pounding. It wasn't much safer down here.

She rose to one knee, then paused, spotting a pixie—the same one or another—opening a lower cupboard. Without hesitation, she snagged the soup pot and flung it over the creature. From the way the heavy kettle rocked and the sounds from within—a form of pixie cursing perhaps—she knew she'd succeeded.

Stacy jumped to her feet. "I got one."

Even as she spoke and Nic turned toward her, a bag of flour flew toward the ceiling where it exploded, showering Stacy, Nic, and the kitchen in a shower of white. She wiped at her eyes, opening them in time to see Nic diving toward her.

"Look out." He toppled them both to the floor, knocking the breath from her lungs, his body pinning hers, as the entire contents of the knife block flew through the air. Right where she'd been standing.

Stacy gulped once she could inhale again. These pixies had progressed from malicious to downright dangerous. "Thanks," she whispered.

Nic nodded, his gaze intense, as he brushed back a few stray locks of her hair to reveal the growing bump on her temple. "I can heal that." He pressed a couple of fingers gently to the bump.

Stacy winced. "Ow." But the pain was momentary, followed by a soothing heat until the throbbing ache was gone.

"Better?" he asked.

That depended on his definition of better. The heat had continued through her body, but it had nothing to do with healing and everything to do with Nic's body pressed along hers. Against her will, her breasts swelled as her breathing grew rough.

She stared at him, unable to reply, only to have the flare of passion in his gaze answer her. He stared at her, his obvious erection hard against her leg, adding to her inability to move, to breathe, to think. She could only watch as he dipped toward her, his aim unerring.

Yet he had only brushed her lips with tantalizing promise when Stacy realized it had grown quiet. Very quiet.

Evidently Nic sensed it, too, for he raised his head, then tensed, his gaze focused on the doorway. Stacy twisted her head around to look, then groaned.

Dianna and Kevin stood there, their expressions clearly shocked. "I've heard of rough sex before, but I never expected it from you, Stacy," Kevin said, his censure clear.

Stacy pushed Nic off her and scrambled to her feet. To be caught kissing Nic could be explained, but the total destruction of the kitchen was more difficult. "This isn't what it looks like."

"No?" Kevin tightened his arm around Dianna's shoulders. "Then perhaps you can explain."

Explain? Stacy glanced at Nic. The moment she mentioned pixies, they'd think she was crazy. "I . . . I can't."

"Can't or won't? I thought better of you than that. Come on, Di. You don't need to see this."

But Dianna hesitated. "Are you all right, Stacy?"

"I'm okay." Bruised, covered with flour, and a little more than excited and ashamed, but fine. "Go ahead. I need to clean up this mess."

They left, and she brushed at the flour coating her clothing, aware her nipples were still sensitive. That wasn't helping. She finally looked at Nic to find him watching her, his gaze veiled.

He gave a dry twist of his lips. "My apologies."

Stacy shrugged. She'd called him in to help. Neither of them had expected to end up together on the floor. Yet she couldn't stop the heat from flooding her cheeks.

The rattling of the kettle caught her attention. "Hey, it's still there." She placed her foot on it. "I actually caught one."

"Did you?" Nic looked stunned. "You saw it?"

"Not very attractive, is it?"

"Mortals usually can't see pixies."

Again, Stacy shrugged. "Must come from hanging out with you. Do you want it or not?"

"I want it." Brushing flour from himself, he knelt beside the kettle. "Raise the pot slowly."

Stacy did. As soon as a limb appeared beneath, Nic grabbed it and lifted the pixie into the air. The high-pitched cursing continued, but Nic ignored it, muttering a few words until the creature vanished.

"Good." He dusted his hands together, then held them up over the demolished kitchen. He murmured more words—another spell?—and a burst of light flashed from his hands.

Stacy blinked and staggered back, then looked around in amazement. No sign of the pixies' destruction remained. Even the broken dishes were restored to the cupboards, whole once again. She turned in a circle, surveying the room, then grinned at Nic.

"Boy, you're good. Can I keep you?" She froze, realizing what she'd said as Nic's features hardened.

"I'll be around." For the second time that afternoon, he disappeared.

Stacy sighed and pushed her fingers through her hair, relieved to find herself flour-free. Now to face the music—Kevin and Dianna.

Dianna had resumed practice when Stacy entered the studio. Thank goodness. It allowed Stacy to slide in unseen until she stood by Kevin. He glanced over at her, his gaze cool, then returned to watching Dianna.

"It's . . . it's hard to explain, Kevin," Stacy said. She couldn't conceive a believable excuse for that mess in the kitchen. Or the way they'd found her and Nic.

"I imagine it is." Kevin didn't bother to look at her.

"Besides that, I don't have to explain. This is my house." She let anger color her voice. "Regardless of what happened, I'm entitled to a life as much as you or Dianna, which should be none of your damned business."

He hesitated, then nodded. "Point taken." He turned to face her. "Can I ask what is between you and Nic Stone?"

"We . . . we're friends. That's all." No matter how much she wished it could be different.

Kevin raised one eyebrow. "Friends?"

"Friends. He . . . he's in love with someone else." Her chest ached.

"I don't trust him. I don't like the way he's treating you or the way he looks at Di."

Oh, great. Now she had to deal with macho madness. "Well, I trust him, and that's what matters."

Kevin eyed her, his doubt clear. "Evidently, he's made you believe that."

"I know my mind." It was her emotions she couldn't control. Focusing elsewhere, Stacy watched Dianna execute her dance steps precisely. "She missed you a lot."

"I missed her, too. Our fighting seemed so stupid once I had a chance to step away from it." Kevin smiled. "I love her so much."

Stacy had to force an answering smile. Poor Kevin. Poor Nic. One of them was destined to be very disappointed. "And everything went well in Denver?"

"Aside from all the confusion over whether there was really a fire in the Center or not, yeah, it went fine." He shook his head. "You have to wonder about them. They insisted there had been a fire, but no one could find any sign of one. Weird."

Stacy bit back a smile. "Yeah, pretty weird."

The routine finished, and Dianna started toward them. "Oh, I need to warn you about something," Kevin said quickly.

His tone made her stomach drop. "What?"

"I sort of promised Dianna a party instead of us going away for a weekend."

"A party?" Panic raised its ugly head. "When?"

"Isn't it wonderful, Stace?" Dianna ran to throw her arms around Kevin.

Stacy glanced at Kevin, who gave her a weak smile. "Is what wonderful?"

"The party we're going to throw. A kickoff party for my tour. Kevin says we can invite everyone." She stole a kiss from his lips.

"Oh, he did?" Stacy aimed an accusing gaze at Kevin, and he shifted uneasily.

"It will be a great promotional move," he added.

"And when are we throwing this party?" Stacy asked, the dread muscling in beside the panic.

"Next weekend." Dianna must have seen the expression on Stacy's face, for she released Kevin and came to hug Stacy. "It won't be a problem, will it?"

"Oh, no." Stacy had put together parties at the house before. Just housecleaning to arrange, caterers to commission, invitations to be sent, details to arrange. Still, Stacy returned Dianna's hug, unable to resist her sister's enthusiasm. Well, she definitely wouldn't be bored.

"You can even invite Nic, if you want to." When Stacy jerked in surprise, Dianna drew back. "You do like him, don't you? I mean, I thought . . ."

Stacy resisted the urge to laugh. "Oh, sure. I'll invite him." *Boy, talk about things getting screwed up.*

"He doesn't need to be there," Kevin said.

Fighting back angry words, Stacy frowned. "I can invite whomever I want, too."

Kevin scowled. "The man has far too much freedom around here, especially for a house with two single women."

Dianna kissed Kevin's cheek. "But you're here most of the time, too, so why worry? Nic's sweet."

Her words didn't help change Kevin's mind. That was certain. If anything, he glowered even more. "I'll talk to him."

"That won't help, Kevin." Stacy already knew who'd come out the winner in a confrontation between Kevin and Nic. And it wasn't Kevin. "Let things be."

When he didn't reply, Stacy tugged at her sister's hand. "Come and tell me more of what you want for this party."

They left the studio, Dianna rambling off excited plans, but Stacy barely heard her. How could she convince Kevin that Nic wasn't dangerous?

Nic wanted to get rid of Kevin, and Kevin wanted to get rid of Nic.

Lovely.

• • •

"What's this?" A gaily wrapped package sat in front of the cottage door, and Nic picked it up as he entered. Tearing it open only took moments, and he eyed the faery figurine with a grimace. This poor Fae with its twisted countenance looked like it suffered from one of Titania's more unpleasant spells. Who would send him this?

A card remained in the wrapping, and he read it, his spirits brightening as he noticed Dianna's signature.

"Nic—just a little token of my appreciation for all your work on the scenery. Thank you. Dianna."

From Dianna? Perhaps he was winning her. Nic studied the figurine a moment longer, then placed it on his dining room table.

He took two steps, then paused. Why had he come here? For a moment he forgot, then remembered. To escape the scene at the house, of course. Recalling how Stacy had felt against him, her lips open to his, made him harden. If they hadn't been interrupted . . .

By Kevin and Dianna, no less. That wasn't likely to help his chances. He needed to take action. To lure Dianna to him. Stacy might be a pleasant diversion, but Dianna was who he wanted, needed.

His Anna.

With a roar, Nic stalked outside. What could he do? The woman who belonged with him continued to cling to a miserable mortal.

This had to end.

Nic roamed the garden paths in a futile attempt to ease the frustration eating at him. How would he ever get Dianna to see him as her future lover for all time? Especially when he found himself more with Stacy and unable to keep from kissing her when they were together?

Nothing throughout his entire centuries of existence had been as difficult as this. How could he deal with these two women: one his wife, his lover, the woman he wanted for the rest of eternity, and the other a woman who triggered his libido by simply existing? Too bad he couldn't merge them into one woman.

He paused by a large spruce, considering the idea, then instantly discarded it. Stacy and Dianna were unique individuals, which was part of what made them so intriguing. Resting his forehead against the tree, he sighed. He had to do something, find some way to end this torment.

The only question was what?

"Hey, you. Stone."

Nic glanced around to see Kevin approaching and grimaced. Kevin Montgomery was far from his favorite person, and judging from the anger blazing in the man's eyes, Nic was probably not Kevin's, either. "Me?" Nic played innocent, though he had no doubt Kevin was after him for whatever reason.

"Yes." Kevin paused beside him. "I want to talk to you about your behavior."

Nic raised an eyebrow. "My behavior?" His behavior had been exemplary compared to what he could do if he chose. Most Fae were not willing to be as patient as Nic.

"You are an employee here, nothing more."

Oh really? Nic remained silent, curious now.

When Nic didn't respond, Kevin continued. "Which means you are to have nothing to do with either of the Fielding sisters."

Nic narrowed his eyes but kept his voice even. "I don't see how that's possible. Stacy is the one who hired me."

"If that scene in the kitchen is an example of how you're treating her, I'm surprised she hasn't fired you."

Grinning, Nic shook his head. Just recalling Stacy's body beneath his brought images of long, slow lovemaking. "Ah, the scene in the kitchen. I kissed her."

"And you had to wrestle her to the ground and destroy the room to do so?" Fury vibrated in Kevin's words, and he clenched his hands by his side.

"No. That was the pixies." Let Montgomery make of that what he would.

"Pixies?" Kevin snorted. "Very funny."

"It's the truth. I was helping Stacy get rid of them."

"Enough." Kevin's disgust was evident. "Just stay away from Stacy. She's under enough stress without having to fend you off."

"I can't." As Nic replied, the truth of those simple words made his gut ache. Try as he might, something about Stacy beckoned him, lured him. Titania's spell, of course, and perhaps, something more.

"You will." Kevin stood slightly taller than Nic and glared at him. "And you'll avoid Dianna as well."

For a moment, Nic didn't respond, anger tightening his throat. This mortal had no control over what Nic did or did not do. "Dianna is going to belong to me," he said coldly. The sooner Montgomery faced the truth, the better they'd both be.

"The hell she is." Kevin raised his fist. "That's it. You're fired. Get out of here. Pack your things and leave."

"Stacy hired me. Only Stacy can fire me." And even that didn't mean Nic would go.

"She will."

Nic grinned. "Don't be so sure about that." What would Kevin say if he knew sweet Stacy was helping undermine his engagement to her sister?

Kevin launched into a tirade, his hands waving, but Nic tuned out the words. He didn't have to deal with this nonsense. This man was a hindrance who stood between Nic and what he wanted. Things would be better all around if he simply ceased to exist.

An idea rose, slowly taking shape in Nic's mind as he watched Kevin rant. A slow smile took shape.

Why not?

• • •

Later, Nic located Dianna in the kitchen and paused just inside the doorway. "Come to dinner with me tonight." He made it an order. All he needed was an evening with her, filled with fine dining, wooing, and lovemaking. Then she'd be his.

Dianna glanced over her shoulder at him in surprise. "Nic? Sorry. I have plans."

Closing the distance between them, he noticed the scent of steak broiling and spotted the pan of sautéed vegetables in front of her. "You're cooking?" The words blurted out before he thought. For some reason he'd assumed she never cooked.

"I can, you know." Dianna appeared more amused than insulted. "Stacy made sure of that. Besides, I want everything to be perfect." She turned back to stirring the vegetables.

"For whom?" Nic asked the question, though he knew the answer.

"Kevin." Dianna's smile held enough warmth to bump Nic's pulse up a notch and irritate him at the same time. "I'm making us a candlelight dinner."

"I could give you a candlelight dinner that you didn't have to cook." *Anywhere in the world.* Nic touched her shoulder. "You could relax."

"I want to do this." Dianna met his gaze, her own clear and honest. "I was so horrible to Kev before he left." Her grin held mischief and heat. "I intend to make it up to him."

Nic caressed her shoulder. That heat should belong to him. "What if he doesn't show?"

"Not show?" She tossed her head. "Of course he'll show. Kevin wants to be with me as much as I want to be with him."

Running his finger over the back of her neck, Nic bit back a smile. "If he doesn't, you'll know where to find me."

Dianna ducked away from his touch. "Yeah." Her brush-off answer clearly indicated she had no plans to find him, but Nic only nodded.

She could find herself changing her mind in the near future. Leaning over her shoulder, he sniffed. "Smells good. I can't wait to try it."

"You're not going to try it." Dianna bumped her hip against him, one of the few times she'd touched him. He was making progress, whether she realized it or not. "Now go away, Nic. I'm busy."

"Remember, I'm available if you need me."

"Go, Nic."

He sauntered from the kitchen, heading for the cottage. After a certain amount of time, she'd realize Kevin wasn't going to show up. Then she'd come to him.

And he'd be waiting.

"Have you seen Kevin?"

Stacy looked up from her computer as Dianna burst into the office. "Kevin? Not for quite a while."

"We had a dinner date, and I can't find him anywhere."

"He's here somewhere. Did you check the studio, his room?"

"I've checked everywhere." A note of hysteria rang in Dianna's voice.

Stacy went to hug her sister, resisting a sigh. Di tended to overreact. "Calm down. He's not likely to go far, especially if he made plans for dinner with you."

"He said he'd meet me at seven, and it's nearly eight. He's never been late before."

True. Kevin was as dependable as the sunrise. Especially in regard to Dianna. "I'll help you look. Did you check the grounds?"

"Not yet." Dianna stopped trembling as hope entered her gaze. "You'll find him, right?"

"I'll find him." Poor Dianna had problems finding a

matching sock when it was right in front of her. Kevin had to be here someplace. No doubt he was working on something and had lost track of time. Perhaps he'd gotten involved with the new song he'd talked of writing for Di.

"You looked in the music room, right?" Stacy asked.

"I'll look again." Di darted off, and Stacy headed for the back door.

She doubted Kevin would be in the gardens. It was her territory, and he only strolled there on rare occasions. But she'd look and make Dianna feel better. By the time she returned, he'd probably be here already eating dinner.

Darkness had crept in over the cloud-shrouded mountain peaks, bringing the normal evening chill, but the air still smelled of spring, the blooming pansies and marigolds, and the fresh scent of newly mowed grass. If nothing else, she'd have a nice walk.

Following the paths deeper into the gardens, she ran her hand over the neatly trimmed bushes lining the walk. "Kevin?" The only answer came from crickets playing their nightly song.

She lifted her face to the rising moon, easing away her tensions. Soon Di would be on the road, and life would slow down. Maybe.

She collided with something solid in the path and staggered back. "What the—?" What was that? She stepped away to get a better look in the moonlight and gasped.

"Oh my God." She grabbed a nearby tree trunk to keep her knees from buckling. "Oh . . . my . . . God." It couldn't be. Yet . . . What else could it be?

Standing tall in the middle of the path was a life-size statue of Kevin, hands raised, mouth open as if caught in the middle of speaking. Drawing in a deep breath, she reached out to touch it.

Solid.

He was rock.

Her hand trembled as she drew it back. Kevin had been

angry with Nic. He'd said he wanted to talk to the gardener. With his protective nature, he would warn Nic to stay away. But this . . .

No matter how badly Nic wanted Dianna, he knew better than to harm others. He couldn't be allowed to get away with this. Damn him.

She pivoted and raced back toward the cottage. Not bothering to knock, she burst inside to find the main room empty. "Nic Stone, where the hell are you?"

Circling the room, she scanned for some sign of Nic's magic, but everything looked entirely normal except for the weird-looking porcelain figurine in the middle of the dining room table. What was it? A frowning faery? "Nic?"

"You called?" He stepped out of the bathroom, droplets still clinging to his chest—his bare chest. Her gaze dropped lower. Dear Lord, all of him was bare.

Totally. Completely. Wonderfully.

Bare.

Stacy's jaw fell, and she was unable to stop staring. Magnificent. She'd felt his muscles beneath her hands before, but to see them so well laid out . . . He made the statue of David look like a wimp. Nic was well-toned everywhere. Her glance dropped. Very well-toned.

"I—" Her mouth went dry, words fled, thought disappeared. Heat percolated in her blood, triggering the longing deep within her.

His gaze locked on hers, but he didn't move. "Stacy."

She took a step closer, then paused. She'd come for a reason. What was it? Her brain refused to focus on anything other than the sight before her. "I—"

Surely he could hear her heart pounding, the catch in her breathing? Why wouldn't her brain function? Lack of blood perhaps? It had all rushed to the more sensitive parts of her body, leaving her gut aching and her breasts tingling.

His eyes darkened, and he moved toward her. "Stacy." His voice sounded rougher now.

What was she doing? With an effort, Stacy turned her back on him, struggling to recall the anger that had driven her there, anger now boiling with passion. Wait. Now she remembered.

She whirled back to face him, keeping her gaze focused on his, away from the too-appealing physique. "What did you do to Kevin?"

Nic jerked back, his surprise evident. "I merely removed him from the picture for a while."

"Well, you're going to put him back in the picture. Now."

"No." Nic crossed his arms, daring her to defy him. Even naked, he was imposing.

Especially naked.

Stacy hesitated. Now what? She had no way to fight his magic. "Is he all right?"

"He's fine. He'll remember nothing when I revive him. *If* I revive him."

He had to return Kevin to normal. "You're that insecure that you have to turn a mere mortal into stone in order to win your Anna? That's pretty pathetic for someone with magic, isn't it?"

Nic growled, fire blazing deep in his eyes. "Would you like to join him?"

Stacy lifted her chin. Would he actually harm her? Before this, she would have said no, but now . . . He wasn't acting like the Nic she knew. "What is wrong with you, Nic?"

"Nothing is wrong. I'm doing what's necessary."

"Necessary?" She blew out her breath. "Removing Kevin isn't going to bring Dianna to you. You know that." What was he doing? Was he possessed? Her eyes widened. Under a spell?

"Has Titania done something to you?"

"Other than make me want you, drive me crazy with dreams of kissing you, making love to you?" Nic advanced on her. "No, nothing other than that."

Her heart rate tripled, but she backed away, putting the dining room table between them. "Then listen to me. Doing this to Kevin is cowardly, and one thing you're aren't is a coward, Nic."

"Kevin stands between me and my wife."

She'd always suspected Nic could be ruthless, but she'd never seen it before. Her nerves tingled. Fear or something else? "If you can't convince Dianna to leave him, then maybe you're not the right one for her."

He slammed his fist on the table, making the figurine dance across it. "She is my wife!"

Stacy swallowed. This wasn't going well. Something was wrong with him. Definitely wrong. This had to be a spell, but how could she break it? Her last experience with Titania hadn't accomplished anything, but run-amok pixies.

"Nic, you're not yourself." She kept her voice calm, despite the quavering in her stomach. "Think about what you're doing."

"I know exactly what I'm doing. I eliminated Kevin Montgomery and told Dianna to come to me when she couldn't find him."

"Well, she didn't come to you. She came to me." Stacy eyed his fantastic naked form, especially that part growing larger by the moment. "Is that why you chose the clothing-optional dress tonight? You expected Dianna." Di would have freaked if she'd been greeted by a naked Nic.

Or maybe not. God, he was gorgeous.

Stacy shook her head. *Think.*

"She won't be able to resist me. Neither will you." Moving with a speed that startled her, Nic rounded the table and seized Stacy's shoulders. As she opened her mouth to protest, he claimed her lips, his own hard, hot, and hungry. Gone was the sweet seduction she'd associated with him. In its place was fierce passion without restraint. He plunged in, dueling with her tongue, his hands pulling her close enough to feel his every muscle, and the erection growing against her belly.

Part of Stacy wanted to sink into him, to give in to the wild need he aroused. But this kiss was meant to be brutal, and she'd have no part of that, no matter how much her desire disagreed.

She went limp, then pulled free when he released her in shock. Grabbing the closest thing—the ugly statue—she threw it as hard as she could. It bounced off Nic's shoulder, rebounded on the wall, then shattered against the tile floor.

Smoke rose from the splintered pieces, swirled up and around, then disappeared through the ceiling. Stacy turned back to face Nic and found his expression horrified.

"Stacy." He extended his hand, but she ducked away. He winced. "Did I hurt you?"

"N . . . no." She eyed him dubiously. Had that been it? The statue? Had that put the spell on him? "Where did you get that figurine?"

He glanced down at the shattered remains. "Dianna left it for me as a thank you. For painting the scenery."

"I'm afraid not. Di is not one to give gifts for things like that. Trust me." Stacy met his gaze. "It must have come from Titania."

"And touching it, leaving it here gave her power over me." Nic wove his fingers into his hair. "Stones. What did it do to me? What have I done?"

This sounded more like the man she knew. "Kevin." She spoke gently, a reminder.

"Of course." He lifted his hands and sent a lightning bolt out the cottage door. "If the day comes I can't best a mortal, then I don't deserve the lady."

"He'll be all right?"

"A headache, perhaps. Nothing more. His memory will stop at the point where he came to the garden this afternoon."

"Thank you." Knowing Kevin would return to normal eased Stacy's worry. Now she could focus on Nic. "Dianna will learn to love you." Saying the words hurt, but he needed to hear them. "Give her time. Be yourself. How can she not?"

He gave her a wan smile, then pulled her into his embrace. "What would I do without you?"

"I imagine you'll find out," she murmured. After all, he would live forever, while she would grow old and die. And before that, he'd be with her sister.

He pressed a kiss against her forehead, holding her close, his body heat drawing a response from hers. Stacy shuddered. "You know . . ." She had to swallow. "You know you're still undressed." Every inch of her was aware of that.

Nic drew back far enough that she could see the mischief in his eyes. "I can produce clothes." He ran his hand over her side, lingering along the side of her breasts. "Or I can remove yours."

Now Stacy knew what Eve had faced in the Garden of Eden. *Temptation* with a capital *T*. Every cell in her body screamed at her to seize the moment, but a small corner of her mind remained lucid. "Nic, we can't."

He brushed his lips over hers, teasing, making her want more. "We can."

He kissed her again, lingering, tracing the outline of her lips with his tongue, until Stacy moaned and clutched his shoulders. To give in, to explore these feelings he aroused would be so easy, so wonderful.

"Stacy." Dianna's wild cry jerked them apart. It came from the house. "Stacy, come now."

Despite her inner trembling, Stacy managed a tight

smile. "I think Kevin found his way back. He's probably confused." She stepped away from Nic. "I have to go."

He nodded. "Go then." But he held her gaze as she backed to the doorway, the fire banked only slightly, his desire every bit as fierce as her own.

Stacy gripped the door frame, digging her fingernails into the wood, while she battled the urge to return to his arms. With a groan, she threw herself out of the cottage and ran the entire way back to the house.

How much longer could she resist? Reaching the house, she paused. As long as she could. Nic was meant for Dianna, not her. She had to remember these feelings came from Titania's spell, not real emotion.

No matter how much she wished they did.

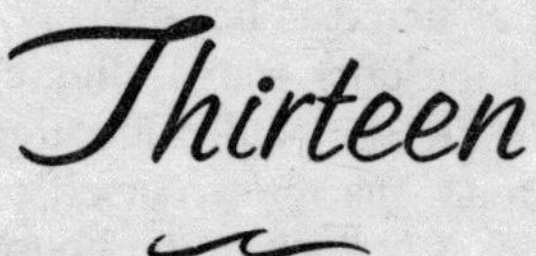

Stacy spent most of the next day in her office, making lists for the party. She had a caterer and cleaning agency she'd used on other occasions, so that wouldn't be too large a problem. The first thing would be to find out who and how many were coming; then she'd have something to work with.

They had given parties before, but never so close to leaving for a tour. But Kevin was right. It would be great publicity. Stacy froze, her pen poised. Especially if Dianna performed part of her program for the attendees. That meant they could invite some media representatives.

She grinned. Okay, it was going to be work, and it was probably well worth it in the long run.

Reaching for her electronic Rolodex, she began a list of attendees. That would be a good place to start. She then searched her E-mails and correspondence until she had a hefty pile of papers at her elbow.

Now to work.

She'd barely begun compiling a list when her computer died, followed by an overly familiar giggling. Placing her hands flat on the desk, she sighed. These pixies were getting old in a hurry.

She moved slowly, conscious of movement out of the corner of her eye. Only one pixie that she could tell. Wrapping her fingers over the edge of the trash can, she waited, immobile. Experience had taught her that these creatures wanted a reaction. What would they do if she didn't give them one?

Her ever-present vase of fresh, fragrant lilacs, a daily gift from Nic, crashed to the floor. She didn't move.

Books toppled off the nearby bookcase. Stacy bit her lip but didn't react.

There. She saw it now, the tiny hands wrapped around the edge of the desk, drawing closer. She tried not to tilt her head while keeping her gaze on the pixie. It crept toward her chair—to hit the seat release, no doubt.

Closer. Closer. Her muscles tensed with anticipation. Wait.

Now.

In one fluid, quick movement, she flipped the trash can over the pixie and placed her foot on the top. The shrieking and rattling from inside made her smile. She was getting good at this.

Only, what did she do with it now? She didn't have Nic's magic. So she had to take it to Nic. Simple.

Yeah, right.

Grabbing a wide book, she righted the can and slapped the book over the top. Curses flew from inside. "Say what you will," she said smugly. "I won this round."

She cradled the can in one arm and held the book down with the other while she made her way to Nic's cottage. Once there, she kicked at the door, only to receive no answer.

Now what?

The can rattled even more fiercely, and the book flew up just enough to hit her chin before dropping back into place. She tightened her hold and worked her jaw. Nothing broken.

Turning, she searched the gardens for some sign of Nic, but other than the birds darting among the trees, she saw no movement. She couldn't just leave the trash can. The pixie would escape for sure. "Nic. Nic, where are you?"

Probably off watching Dianna rehearse. Stacy grimaced. "Nic," she called again.

"Yes?"

She spun around and collided with Nic, who had appeared behind her. "Don't do that." Her pulse went from zero to ninety in one second.

Humor danced in his eyes. "My apologies."

She smiled, then paused, realizing her body was already starting to warm as it usually did in Nic's presence. Especially with the memory of how wonderful he looked naked. Not a good thing.

She thrust the can into his arms. "Here. Another pixie for you to get rid of."

"A pixie?"

Backing away, she nodded, amused at his apparent surprise. "I may get them all yet."

"I . . . I'll take care of it." Nic shook the can and was answered by a string of pixie cursing. His shock gave way to admiration. "Good job, Stace."

"Thanks." She put more distance between them. "By the way, you're invited to a party at the house. Next weekend."

"A party? For what?"

"A kick-off for Dianna's tour."

"When did this come about?"

Stacy glanced at her watch. "Yesterday, before . . . well, you know. Di told me to invite you." That should cheer him. He didn't need to know Di thought he was Stacy's boyfriend.

His answering smile made her catch her breath. Damn the man for looking like that.

"I'll be there," he said.

"Good." She had to rip her gaze away from him; then, coward that she was, she bolted for the house.

By the time she decided to quit for the night, she'd made a significant dent in the preparations. The guest list was done, and a tentative invitation drafted. She'd even cleaned up the pixie's mess.

Stretching, she made her way through the living room. The house was quiet and dark around her. She'd told Dianna and Kevin she'd grab some dinner later, but she hadn't expected it to be this much later. Oh, well, time always flew when she was working.

The moon sliced through a window to illuminate Titania's portrait, and Stacy paused before it. The last time she'd spoken to the Fae queen, she'd been rewarded with pixies. Probably better to keep her mouth shut.

But she found herself staring at the woman, their gazes locking. Stacy raised her chin in an outward show of defiance. She wasn't going to let this witch win, no matter how much mischief the pixies caused.

A glow rippled around the edge of the frame, and Stacy stepped back, half expecting eruptions like before. But nothing happened. Thank God.

Stacy shivered, the back of her neck prickling. Time to go, before Titania did decide to do something Stacy was guaranteed not to like. Pixies were bad enough.

She whirled around, took two steps, then froze, her path blocked by the figure of a man, his face masked in the dark. Her heart jumped into her throat. He stepped into the light, and she released her breath in a whoosh.

"Nic, what are you doing here?"

"I came to see you." His voice was low, husky.

Stacy took a step backward. "Why?" The more time she spent near him, the more her willpower weakened. "You know that's not a good idea."

"I want to show you something." His gaze bored into her, dark, intense.

"Did you . . . did you get rid of the pixie?"

He hesitated, momentary confusion crossing his face, then smiled. "Of course." He extended his hand. "Come with me, Stacy."

"I can't. It's late, and I really want to get to bed."

Nic drew closer, exuding sex appeal in waves, a secretive grin forming. "You will. This won't take long. Trust me." He caught her hand in his, then touched her face with his other hand. "Come, Stacy."

Like she had much chance of resisting him. "Okay."

His smile was broad, seductive, yet somehow different. "Close your eyes and hold on," he said, tightening his grip on her hand.

Stacy's stomach flipped, but she did as he asked, closing her eyes. As she somewhat expected, she felt the familiar tingling that signaled travel somewhere. But where?

The ground beneath her feet was soft, spongy, and the scent in the air held the perfume of at least a million flowers mingled together to create an intoxicating aroma. Where was she?

"Open your eyes."

She did so and inhaled sharply. This was no place she'd ever been or seen. Except perhaps in faery tales.

They stood at the edge of a forest, thick with trees of all shapes and sizes: pines, elms, maples, and many others she couldn't begin to identify. Stretching away from the forest was a vast meadowland dotted with a wide variety of flowers, the colors so brilliant they hurt Stacy's eyes.

In the distance, tall mountain peaks stretched up into the most incredible sky she'd ever seen. It was like a rainbow, no, it *was* a vast, unending rainbow, streaked with bands of color from one end to the other, glowing with light that gave it the appearance of a stained-glass window.

"Where am I?" She had to ask, though she probably knew the answer.

Nic indicated the surrounding area with a sweep of his arm, pride evident. "It's the magical realm, Stacy. My home. Where I belong."

Where he belonged? Stacy frowned. "I thought you hated the magical realm, that you preferred living in . . . with . . . us."

He shrugged. "A few centuries of that can get boring." He squeezed her hand. "Come, I have lots to show you. You will love it."

The vivid green of the grass gave way to dusky mosses growing beneath the trees within the forest. The trees appeared almost alive, dipping their branches toward Stacy as she passed, so that she found herself ducking constantly. "I don't think they want me here," she said, pressing closer to Nic.

"We don't get many mortals here." He released her hand and draped his arm over her shoulders, holding her by his side. "Don't worry. I'll keep you safe."

As they continued walking, music drifted from the trees, evidently from birds she couldn't see, but the notes were so exquisite, the blending so perfect, it made Stacy's chest ache. "That's beautiful." She stopped to listen, closing her eyes to lose herself in the tune. "If I could capture that, write it down." She sighed. "No, it would be impossible."

Nic chuckled. "Nothing is impossible here." While she listened, he rubbed his hands over her neck and shoulders in slow, sensuous strokes. Between the music and his touch, Stacy found herself melting, her resistance draining away.

She leaned against him, lulled by the exquisite melody, the drugging aroma. "I've never experienced anything like this," she murmured.

Nic slid his hands over her shoulders and along her

sides. Stacy drew in a sharp breath, his touch more startling than erotic. He nibbled at her earlobe. "There's much more to come," he whispered.

He held her away from him and took her hand again, desire glowing in his eyes and something else—something she couldn't quite name but that made her hesitate. "Where are we going?" she asked, trying to shake off the hypnotic effect of her surroundings.

His smile held sensual promise. "You'll see."

Her stomach knotted as she walked with him, unable to shake the persistent feeling of something wrong. "Why did you bring me here?"

"So we could be alone. We never have the chance to be alone together, do we?"

"It . . . it's better that we don't." Being alone with Nic led to thoughts of making love and impossible dreams of a future that couldn't be.

"That's there. But here . . ." He paused beside a swiftly flowing stream, also streaked with extreme bands of color. "Here, we can do anything we want. Here, we can be together, Stacy. You and I."

She stared at him, uncertain she was hearing correctly. After fighting their attraction, he now wanted to give in to it? What about Dianna? What about his plans for her?

Holding her hand, he floated them over the stream, then walked beside it to where it widened in a gentle pool, glowing with brilliant color. Creatures similar to fish swam inside, long, lean, with fins but also with facial features. They pooled together, their lips moving, their colors brilliant, vivid: purple, orange, blue, red. If she bent closer, would she hear them talking?

"Would you like to take a swim?" he asked. "The water is warm." He released her hand and pulled off his T-shirt to reveal his muscular chest sprinkled with fine, dark hair.

Stacy's throat went dry. Seeing this much of him

brought back too-vivid memories of what remained covered. "I . . . I don't have a suit."

His eyes gleamed. "Who needs suits?"

This was so unreal. Was she dreaming? Had Nic somehow invaded her sleep to make her deepest desires come true? Stacy pinched herself. "Ow."

Okay, so she wasn't asleep.

Nic approached her at a slow but steady pace. "We have to stop fooling ourselves, Stacy. You want me. I want you. Here we can have each other with no one the wiser."

"But . . . but what about Dianna?"

He shrugged. "I'll get back to her."

"No." Stacy stepped back. "It's not right."

"Right has nothing to do with wanting." Nic touched her shoulders, his gaze holding hers. "I want to touch you everywhere. To kiss you."

Before she could react, he scooped her into his arms. "I intend to make love to you as you have never been loved before." He headed for a small grove of trees forming a ring beside the pool. Inside the ring, one of the trees formed a headboard for a large bed—an invitingly soft bed.

She stared up at Nic. This couldn't be happening. "N . . . Nic?"

"You want me, Stacy. I know you do."

"W . . . wanting isn't the same as having." She'd told herself that a million times.

His smile held more than a touch of satisfaction. "Here, it is."

He started to lower her to the bed, but Stacy twisted in his arms, sudden panic driving her, so that he was forced to deposit her on her feet beside it.

Nic shook his head and chucked her chin like she was a little child. "Stacy, this has been inevitable since we met.

I promise you'll enjoy it. Making love with a Fae is unlike anything you will ever experience."

She was trembling, unable to stop. "Nic, I—"

Lowering his head, he claimed her mouth, his lips and tongue working together with an experienced sensuality to destroy her defenses.

But something was wrong. The desire his kisses usually provoked remained dormant. The touch of his lips was harsher, more calculating.

Oh, dear Lord.

With a gasp, Stacy pushed him away. "You're not Nic."

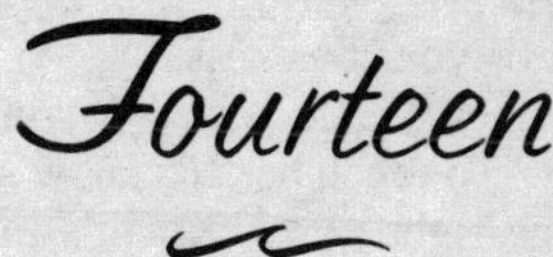

Nic jerked out of a sound sleep, his heart pounding. Had Stacy called him? No, he didn't hear her, yet he couldn't shake the feeling she was in danger.

He transported to her bedroom, risking his fragile hold on control where she was concerned. But the first pink rays of sunrise on her bed showed it still made up. She hadn't slept here last night.

His throat closed. Where was she?

It only took him minutes to check the house and grounds. No sign of her. None. Had she gone somewhere?

Of course. The party. No doubt she had errands to run in preparation for the upcoming party. But would she leave so abruptly? And be gone overnight?

The nagging sensation that he should be doing something wouldn't leave. By the time Kevin and Dianna reported to the studio for rehearsal, Nic had lost all patience.

"Where's Stacy?" he demanded as he confronted them.

"Hiding from you, perhaps," Kevin replied, fire in his gaze. He might not remember being turned into stone, but he still held no fondness for Nic.

"Her bed's not slept in. I can't find her anywhere."

"How would you know her bed's not slept in?" Accusation added chill to Kevin's voice.

Nic sighed. *Stones.* The man thought he was protecting Stacy from him. "I checked. Did she go somewhere on business? An errand?"

"That's none of your business."

"It *is* my business." Nic seized Kevin's shoulders. "I have to find her." To touch her. To know she was all right.

"Let go of me right now." Kevin's eyes burned with fire.

Dianna touched Nic's arm. "What's wrong, Nic?"

Nic released Kevin and faced Dianna. "I have a feeling she's in danger, that she needs me."

"Needs you?" Kevin laughed. "Why would she need you? You're the gardener. You're nothing to her."

Nic grimaced. He was much more than that. "That doesn't matter. I have to find her."

"She should be here," Dianna said, her voice wavering. "She wouldn't go anywhere without telling me."

"Let's check her car first, Di." Kevin softened his voice and wrapped his arm around Dianna.

Nic forced himself to walk with them to the large garage. He could easily transport there, but which was Stacy's car? He'd never seen her drive.

Dianna's whimper after they entered gave him his answer. "Her car's still here," Dianna whispered. "First you disappeared, now Stacy."

Kevin frowned. "She has to be somewhere on the estate."

"I've looked everywhere." Nic clenched his fists. *Some places twice.*

"Then we will look again."

Nic sighed, but he searched again, concentrating on the gardens. Stacy would have gone there if she'd been upset. But why would she be upset? Because of him, no doubt. He had to leave her alone, for both their sakes.

And he would—once he knew she was safe. He criss-crossed every path, peering behind trees and bushes, checking every tucked-away bench. Nothing.

His gut twisted. This wasn't like her. She wouldn't just disappear. Not without a word. Not when there was so much to be done. She was too reliable.

She wouldn't leave. Not voluntarily.

Something was wrong. But what? Why couldn't he find her? All she had to do was call for him, and he'd hear her.

He rejoined Kevin and Dianna in the office, his chest now so tight it hurt to breathe.

"Nothing," he snapped.

Kevin sat in her chair and indicated the papers stacked on the desk. "She was here last night, probably until late, judging from the amount of work she's left. Di and I last saw her around seven. She didn't want any dinner. Said she'd get some later."

"Nice of you to leave her to do all the work." Wasn't Kevin supposed to help her?

Kevin frowned, but concern and guilt flickered in his eyes. "I was to start on the invitations today."

"I think we should call the police." Dianna stood by the desk, her face pale. "She would be here. She's always been here."

"I'll find her before any police will," Nic snapped. All she had to do was call for him.

If she was alive.

A chill stabbed through his veins. She was alive. She had to be. He refused to consider anything else.

"And how's that?" Kevin asked. "You have magical powers or something?"

Nic twisted his lips. "You'd be surprised."

"We have to call. The longer we wait, the worse it might be." Dianna lifted the phone and prepared to punch the numbers, but Kevin took the receiver from her hand.

"Not yet," he said gently. "We'll make one more search of the entire estate front to back. We'd look pretty foolish if we called in the police, and she was napping in the back gazebo, wouldn't we?"

"She's not in the gazebo," Nic said. He'd checked there already.

"I'm just making a point." Kevin stood and pressed Dianna into the chair. "You stay here in case she comes in or calls. Nic and I will search again."

"Then we'll call if you don't find her?" Tears welled in Dianna's eyes.

"Yes, then we'll call." Kevin kissed her, then aimed an authoritative glance at Nic. "Check outside again. Everywhere. I'll look in the house and studio."

Nic sighed, but he returned to the gardens. He had looked everywhere. Stacy wasn't here.

He sank onto the grass and buried his face in his hands. He was Fae. He had magic. Yet it didn't mean anything right now. He'd only felt so helpless once before—when Anna had died in his arms. And the ache currently burning inside him felt remarkably similar.

"Where are you, Stacy?"

He strained to listen, to hear her voice. Only the distant chirping of birds answered him.

"Stones!" He slammed his fist against the ground. There had to be something he could do.

"Is that you, Nic?" Petunia floated down to perch on his knee.

"Of course, it's me. Why wouldn't it be?" He was in no mood for exchanging pleasantries.

"I saw you go into the magical realm last night. With the time difference, I didn't expect you back until later today at the earliest."

Nic stiffened, his pulse skipping a beat. "You saw me?"

"Yes, you and Stacy. You went into Titania's portrait."

"Stones." Nic jumped to his feet, accidentally tossing

Petunia into the air. That explained it. He couldn't sense Stacy because she wasn't even in this realm.

He had to get into the land of the Fae. Now.

Yet Titania wasn't likely to allow him through her portrait, and the entrance from the mortal into the magical realm tended to change positions as time passed. "Where's the portal?"

Petunia straightened her gown and hovered near his face, her displeasure at his rude tossing clearly evident. "I'm not certain I want to tell you."

"Petunia." He sent her a clear note of warning.

"Oh, fine. It's at the top of a mountain. K-something. Twelve. Fourteen." She shrugged. "Something like that."

"K-Twelve." He knew where that was and transported himself there with a thought.

The howling wind blew snow so thick he could barely see, let alone locate the portal. But he would find it. If Titania had lured Stacy into the magical realm, it only meant trouble.

"Hang on, Stacy," he muttered. "I'm coming."

Stacy took another step away from the man who looked so much like Nic. She should have known it wasn't him. There was something in the eyes. Something devious.

"You're not Nic," she repeated.

"No, I'm not." His smile was so different. Why hadn't she seen it at once? "But you can pretend I am." He advanced on her. "Close your eyes and pretend, and we'll make love for hours, days, until you forget about everything."

A lump formed in Stacy's throat. "I don't want to forget about everything."

"Yes, you do. You can satisfy your longing for Nic and give him the opportunity he needs to win your sister." The man's voice held a persuasive note that made her hesitate.

If she was gone, would Nic do better with Dianna?

"See now? Do the reasonable thing." He caught her in his arms, holding her close. He pressed kisses to her face and neck while he ran one hand along her back and cupped her bottom to bring her hips close against the bulge in his pants.

Stacy shuddered and struggled to free herself. "No. You're not Nic."

He caught her chin in his fingers and forced her to meet his gaze. "Relax. Give in to it, Stacy. I can be Nic. I can be all you need."

His features wavered before her, and she blinked, caught by the soothing note of his voice. She swayed forward, and he seized her lips in a fierce kiss before realization dawned. He was using magic on her.

"No." She thrust her knee into his groin and pushed away as he doubled over. Not waiting to see how badly he was hurt, she dashed into the thick trees. She had to get away from him, away from here.

But go where? She had no clue where she was or where to go to escape. Only away from him.

She ran, darting between the trees, pushing herself to go faster when she heard the distant sound of someone . . . something moving through the forest. If he caught her . . . if he used stronger magic . . . She could be trapped forever. Trapped having sex with a man who was only the image of the man she loved.

Oh, Lord. Stacy bent beside a tree, gasping. The man she loved. Now she'd done it: fallen in love with the man destined to be with her sister. Maybe she *should* stay here.

She glanced over her shoulder. But not with him. Not that way.

Drawing air into her aching lungs, she pushed forward. She ran until her legs refused to go another step, and she slid down a tree trunk to the dirt. "What am I going to do?"

Would Nic hear her if she called him from this realm? Should she call him? Knowing what she knew, knowing what she felt? As if things weren't complicated enough.

The colors in the sky never changed, remaining bright, yet she felt as if hours had passed since her arrival. Her legs hurt, her chest burned, her mind whirled. She should rest, but she didn't dare. If he—whoever he was—caught her . . .

Stacy pushed to her feet, but she walked now, staggering through the forest until she came upon a large opening. Two large thrones dominated the clearing, hewn into rock, but no one was around. Music, like that of a flute, drifted on the air from nowhere, from everywhere.

Cautious yet curious, Stacy moved closer. What was this? If she was truly in the faery realm, then the thrones had to belong to the king and queen of the Fae: Oberon and Titania.

"You foolish, mortal girl."

Stacy whirled around, recognizing the woman who appeared behind her at once. Nic's portrait was an excellent portrayal, capturing even the hard glitter of her eyes.

"Titania," she whispered.

"Your Majesty to you." Titania came to stand before Stacy, power radiating off her like a heat lamp. "Why did you run, foolish girl? I was giving you Lenno, one of my best lovers. You would not have been disappointed."

"I don't want one of your best lovers."

"Again, foolish. Fae make extraordinary lovers. You can never have Nic. Why not settle for a substitute?"

"That's not how it works." Nic had told her once that emotions were different in this world. He couldn't have been more right. "Just . . . just let me go home."

Titania drew one finger along Stacy's cheek, her smile bitter. "I'm afraid not. If you want to play cat and mouse with Lenno, please do. I find it amusing." She abruptly cut Stacy's cheek with her nail, and Stacy jerked back.

"But he will find you," Titania continued. She studied the red moisture staining her fingertip. "And with this blood he will bind the spell tighter until you cannot resist. Then he will love you until you forget about Nic, forget about your sister, forget everything except being in his arms."

"No." Stacy backed away, shaking her head. That couldn't happen. She had to get home. "Why are you doing this to me?"

"I have my reasons." She twisted her lips into a semblance of a smile. "Don't you want Nic to find happiness with your sister?"

"I do, but not like this. I don't want to be here."

"Then run." Titania laughed, a sound with no humor. "Run while you can." She glanced back toward the trees. "Lenno is almost here."

Panic gave Stacy new energy, and she rushed into the forest again, darting among the trees that grew larger, thicker, taller, dimming the light from the ever-brilliant sky. She could almost believe it was night now.

She rested against a tree, swiping at the useless tears that fell down her cheeks. How long could she run? How long could she elude this Lenno? He had magic. She had nothing. And if he succeeded . . .

No, she didn't dare consider that. She'd keep going as long as she could. She had no other choice.

Pressing her face against the rough bark, she choked back a sob. "Oh, Nic, where are you?"

"Stacy?" A man appeared between two trees, his features veiled in the darkness.

Stacy froze, alarm filling her throat. She searched the ground for a weapon—a branch, a stone. "Stay away from me."

He came closer, reaching out to her. "Stones, Stacy, are you all right?"

Oh, God, he looked like Nic. He sounded like Nic.

She held out her hand in a futile attempt to keep him away. To her surprise, he stopped. "What's wrong?"

"Are . . . are you really Nic?" Her voice trembled despite her resolve to be strong.

"It's me, Stacy. I swear it." His eyes held only concern, not the lust she'd seen earlier.

But could she trust herself? What if this was the spell strengthened?

"I've been worried about you. Dianna, Kevin, all of us."

She stared at him. He sounded so much like Nic: caring, warm. But was it him? "I . . . I want to go home."

"I want to take you home. Away from here." He glanced into the trees. "The magical realm is no place for mortals." He lifted his hands as if to hold her. "Stace?"

Oh, God, she needed to know, but there was only one way to tell for sure. Could she afford that risk? What if she was wrong?

She swallowed. "Kiss me, Nic."

The corner of his lips quirked upward. "With pleasure." He rested his hands on her shoulders, not restraining her, yet with enough pressure to bring her to him so he could brush her lips with his own. Soft, feather kisses that teased, tantalized, before he groaned. "Stones, Stacy, what you do to me."

His kiss deepened, and Stacy felt the answering swell of passion from deep inside her. She flung her arms around his neck. "It *is* you!"

He brushed her hair with a frown, then wrapped her tight in his embrace. "We're getting out of here. Now."

She experienced tingling, saw a brief flurry of snow, then found herself standing in the middle of the garden path. Her garden path. Home. She was home.

With a sob, she buried her face against Nic's shoulder. He even smelled like himself. She should have noticed that at once.

"What happened, Stacy?" He spoke quietly, stroking her hair, letting the tension ease out of her. "I knew something was wrong, but I couldn't find you. I never dreamed you'd be in the magical realm."

She drew in a deep breath and met his gaze, his deep gaze so filled with warmth. This was the man she loved. "I . . . I met a man by Titania's portrait. He looked like you, sounded like you. He said he had something to show me, and next thing I knew, we were in the magical realm."

Nic's gaze grew hard, his jaw rigid. "Then what?"

She had to turn away in order to continue. "He . . . he took me into the woods and said it was our chance to be alone, to . . . to make love."

She heard Nic's sharp inhale but didn't dare look at him. "I . . . I was tempted, but when he kissed me, I knew it wasn't you. I ran."

"By the Stones." Anger vibrated in Nic's voice. "Do you know who it was?"

"His name is Lenno. Titania told me."

"You met Titania?" Nic pulled her around to face him, then cradled her cheeks between his palms and forced her to meet his eyes. "Are you truly all right? Where did you get that scratch?"

She forced a wan smile. "I'm fine. Titania scratched me. She told me once he made love to me, I'd forget you, forget Dianna, forget everything. That it was a spell so you'd be free to win Dianna."

Nic closed his eyes for a moment. "It's not worth that, not worth losing you."

While his eyes were closed, she drank in his features. She knew this face so well. How could she have been fooled by an imposter? "How did you find me?"

He opened his eyes and touched the scratch on her cheek, healing it beneath his fingertip. "Petunia, one of the Fae here in the garden. She told me she'd seen you leave with me, and since it couldn't have been me, I knew where to go. And once there, all I needed was to hear you call my name."

"And you came."

"I'll always be there, Stacy. Always."

She shook her head. "No, you won't. Once you're with Dianna, it'll be different. I . . . I'll have my own life."

His slight hesitation indicated he understood, and Stacy drew away from him. "I need to find Dianna. She'll be worried. I've been gone for hours."

"More than that." Nic caught her arm. "The police are involved now. You need to know what you're going to tell them."

"Police?" Dianna had called them in that quickly? "But I haven't been gone that long."

Nic hesitated, his head tilted as if sniffing the wind. "It's been almost two days, Stacy."

"What?" She swayed, the ground unsteady beneath her feet, and Nic pulled her close again.

"Time is different between the two realms. It moves much faster here. Hours there can be days here."

Dianna would be frantic. "I have to go then." Stacy paused. "But what do I say? They'll lock me up if I tell them I was in faeryland."

Nic stared over her head toward the back of the gardens. "Do you ever go out that gate in the rear? Along that path?"

"Not often. It gets pretty dangerous along that gorge where the path is rocky. Oh." His meaning became clear. "Oh. I could tell them I fell into the gorge and just got out."

"That you hit your head and were unconscious for a while. Here." Nic touched her forehead, and she experienced a slight burning. "This will look worse than it feels."

She touched her head with tentative fingers to feel a

ragged cut along her temple, yet no pain accompanied it. "That'll work."

"And special effects." Nic splayed his fingers toward her, and bloodstains and tears appeared on her shirt. "Go on now."

She took two steps but looked back. "What about you? Aren't you coming?"

"I'll be there, but it may be a day or so. First I need to return to the magical realm." His expression grew grim, his eyes hard, reminding her how ruthless he could be. "I'm going to ensure this never happens again."

Fifteen

Nic waited for Stacy to enter the house, then transported himself back into the magical realm. Titania could not be allowed to get away with this. If Stacy had succumbed to the lust of a Fae spell, she could have been lost for all time.

He would have lost her.

Nic paused en route to the central grove and drew in a deep breath. Stacy didn't deserve it. Nor did Dianna.

But Titania, being Titania, gave no thought to anyone else. She did as she pleased, no matter who paid the price. Was it any wonder he preferred living among mortals?

Music drifted on the air, triggering memories of dances centuries before in the Fae grove, of a pleasant life before mortals became so interesting and Titania so controlling. That time was long past.

Yet the scene that greeted him upon arrival could have been stolen from that previous era. Fae danced—with or without partners—around the circle, and the members of the queen's court attended Titania, who sat regally on her throne, while Oberon, who rarely sat on his throne, stood by a tree, engaged in conversation with no less than three attractive pillywiggins. In the dim shadows of the trees ringing the grove, Fae shared their bodies with no sense of commitment, only a longing for pleasure, however fleeting.

At one point centuries ago, he had lived like that, but now that he knew love, he could never return to this frivolous, pointless way of life. Feeling emotions—even pain—far surpassed anything he could find here.

He approached Titania's throne, weaving through the dancers, until he reached a point where he could kneel and wait to be recognized. Fury churned his insides, but protocol must be observed. To anger Titania immediately would only cause more problems. Problems that could potentially create more difficulties for Stacy.

"Nic." Her voice rang out over the music and the chatter, dominating the clearing. "What a surprise. Have you admitted defeat and come to give yourself to me?"

She'd spoken to him. That was close enough acknowledgment. Nic rose to his feet and faced her, not bothering to hide the anger in his gaze. "Never."

Her false smile faded. "Then what brings you here? I could swear you said you never wanted to set foot here again." She raised her voice. "Don't you prefer living among those foolish mortals?" Her derisive laughter drew accompaniment from the others in the grove.

"You know why I'm here." Nic took one step closer. "And you are never to try to harm Stacy or Dianna again."

"Harm?" Titania raised one beautifully arched eyebrow. "The woman would not have been harmed. She would have known ecstasy most mortal women never experience."

"You know well what would have resulted from that, too. That isn't what Stacy wants. She has a life, a sister she loves. You have no right to take that away from her."

Sparks glittered in Titania's eyes. "That woman is ruining your chances with Dianna. I was only trying to help."

"I don't need your help." Besides, Titania never did anything unless it helped herself. So, why would she try to remove Stacy, when Dianna was the one he needed? He scowled. Of course. Titania was not subtle with her trickery "I know what you're trying to do, and it won't work."

"Oh, really?" Titania turned her back on him and studied her fingernails. "And what is that?"

"You think by doing these things to Stacy that I'll think she's Anna and forget about Dianna."

"Would I do a thing like that?"

"Without hesitation." He glared at her back. "You've already put a spell on Stacy and me to make us want each other."

"Did I?" Titania turned back to face him, her smile tight, her eyes glowing with satisfaction. "That must create problems, when you're trying to seduce the other sister."

"I will get my Anna. I have no doubts."

"Don't you?" Titania approached and ran her hand over his shoulder and down his arm. "You should have. You're failing abysmally in wooing Dianna Fielding. The way you're going, she'll be married to that mortal of hers, and you will lose her. This time forever."

Nic's stomach knotted. There was too much truth in her words. He'd been spending far more time with Stacy than Dianna. That had to stop. "That is my problem. Not yours."

"It will be my reward when you make the wrong choice." Titania leaned forward and kissed him, her touch cool, reminding him more of an ice cube than a person. "But I can wait."

He tried not to show his distaste as a shudder ran through his body. To make the wrong choice and end up with Titania . . . He couldn't allow that to happen. Clenching his fists, he met her gaze. "I want to see Lenno."

A glimmer of interest filled her eyes. No doubt the restrained violence in his voice promised her a show. She would get one, all right. "Lenno. Come here."

Lenno drifted forward from among the dancers, wearing his own face now, that of a handsome blond, his eyes filled with lazy interest. Titania had chosen him well for this scheme. Lenno was well-known for his sexual appetite. To bed a mortal would have been merely a game to him.

"I almost had her convinced I was you," Lenno said, coming to stand beside Nic. "In another few moments, I would have had her naked and buried myself inside her. She promised to be a pleasant experience."

Nic didn't think. He reacted by plowing his fist into Lenno's face, knocking the Fae onto the ground with blood trickling from the corner of his mouth. Lenno brought his hand to his face, obviously shocked. Physical violence did not usually occur among the Fae. The normal punishments were much more creative.

Nic flexed his hand. It had felt strangely satisfying. Perhaps Nic was becoming more like the mortals than he knew.

"If you ever come near Stacy again, I will destroy you." Nic bit out the words.

"Fae cannot kill one another," Titania said from behind him.

"There are fates worse than death." Nic glanced back at her. "You are well aware of that."

"Do you threaten me as well?" Her voice grew cold.

"I pledge my protection to Stacy and Dianna. Make of that what you will." He bowed his head. "Your Majesty." Turning his back on the queen, he stalked from the clearing.

"I am not finished with you," Titania said.

"But I am finished with you." Nic kept walking, half expecting a lightning bolt in his back.

"You will be very sorry for your words when you are at my command." Her voice promised much suffering.

"I will never be at your command." He would win his Anna. The alternative was unthinkable.

As soon as he cleared the grove, he transported back to the mortal realm. Hours would have passed during the minutes he was with Titania, and he needed to see Stacy, to know she was truly all right. He could weave a protection spell around her to prevent any further magic by other Fae to affect her.

And Dianna. He could no longer afford to be subtle in his attempts to woo her. He would weave a protection spell for her as well, then charm her. When he applied his Fae charm, no mortal woman could resist him.

Dianna . . . Anna would soon be madly in love with him.

"Stacy, you're alive." Dianna ran toward Stacy the moment Stacy entered the living room, nearly knocking her over with her exuberant hug.

Kevin followed close behind. "Are you all right?"

"I've been better. Shaky mostly." Which was the truth. Her heart still raced with the realization of how close she'd come to losing everything.

"What happened?" Dianna asked. She released Stacy from a hug, but held her hand.

Stacy hesitated. Better not to tell the truth. As if they'd believe her. "Stupidity."

"I'd like to hear this, too."

Stacy looked past Kevin in surprise to see a young man approaching. He wore a suit, complete with tie, his dark brown hair cleanly cut over the ears and collar, and walked with brisk steps. Attractive, not much older than Kevin.

The palm computer he held and the bulge along his side beneath the jacket indicating a weapon gave him away. Police.

Kevin stood aside to allow the man to join them. "Stacy, this is Detective Morrow. He's been heading the team looking for you."

"You called the police?" She frowned. Yes, Nic had said that, but she'd been too dazed to pay close attention.

"You've been missing for two days." Dianna squeezed Stacy's hand. "Of course we called the police."

"It . . . it didn't feel that long." Her body clock said she'd only been gone a few hours.

"Are you all right, Miss Fielding? Do you need medical attention?" The detective studied her, his gaze intent, finally focusing on the injury mark Nic had created on her forehead.

"I . . . I'm fine." Would a doctor be able to tell the mark was nothing? "I would like to sit down though."

"Of course. How thoughtless of me." Detective Morrow took her elbow and led her to a nearby couch. Dianna and Kevin immediately sat on either side of her with Dianna again taking her hand.

The detective knelt before Stacy and brushed back her hair to examine the fake injury closer. "That looks bad. You should have a doctor look at it. It may need stitches."

"I . . . I will." Stacy managed a slight smile. She'd never lied to a police officer before. Hell, she rarely lied to anyone.

He nodded, his face grim, and moved to a nearby chair. Concern lingered in his eyes, and Stacy looked away. His kindness made the lies she had to tell even more difficult. "Are you able to tell me what happened?" he asked.

"It's stupid, really." She thought back to where her strange adventure had started. "I . . . I worked late but was too tense to go to sleep, so I went for a walk. The moon was full, so everything was fairly bright. I decided to go out the back gate on that path along the cliffs."

Dianna gasped. "You tell me to stay away from there, but you go?"

Stacy grimaced. "I told you it was stupid. I was just wandering, thinking of all the things that had to be done." Things that still had to be done. She turned to Kevin. "Did you find my lists? Did you get the invitations out?"

"I started." He squeezed her other hand. "But finding you was more important."

Closing her eyes, she sighed. Even more to get done in less time.

"Please continue, Miss Fielding."

"I'm sorry." She drew in a deep breath and rushed through the rest of her story. "I slipped, on . . . on loose pebbles, I think, and fell." She pulled her hand free from Kevin and motioned toward the mark on her forehead. "I hit my head. I guess I was unconscious for a while. When . . . when I woke up, I was on a ledge. I called, but no one heard me. When I finally felt strong enough, I climbed up the cliff and came home."

Now she was glad her clothes were torn and dirty from her frantic race through the forest. And the addition of magical blood completed the illusion. "I had no idea it had been that long."

The detective gave her a warm smile. "Losing consciousness can do that to you, but you should definitely see a doctor to ensure there is no further damage."

"Yes, of course." Though a doctor wasn't going to find anything wrong with her except for a rapid pulse. "I'm sorry you were bothered." She looked at Dianna. "I'm sorry I scared you."

Dianna's smile was tremulous, but love shone in her eyes. "Just don't do it again."

Stacy grinned. Now who sounded like the older sister? "Trust me, I won't." She cast a quick glance at Titania's portrait. She was never going near that again.

The detective made some notations on his palm computer, then stood. "This will be an easy one to close. I prefer missing persons with happy endings." He gave a business card to Stacy. "Call me if you think of anything else I need to know."

Stacy rose to her feet. "Thank you, Detective." Kevin and Dianna joined her in escorting him to the door.

He paused just outside the door and extended his hand. Stacy placed hers in his. "And be careful, Miss Fielding." Humor danced in his eyes, competing with the seriousness of his expression.

"I will." She eased her hand out of his hold, surprised to find herself smiling in return.

After he left, Dianna enveloped her in another hug. "I was so afraid I'd lost you."

"I'm not that easy to get rid of." Stacy squeezed her sister in return. She could have lost this—her sister, her life—all over her misguided love for Nic. No more.

Kevin brushed past them. "I'm calling Matthew and asking him to come by."

Matthew was a doctor who lived nearby and a ski friend of Kevin's. "That's not necessary," Stacy said, breaking away from Dianna.

"Oh yes, it is." Kevin wore his implacable face as he headed for the kitchen phone.

She sighed. Arguing would be futile. Instead, she followed Kevin. "What about the party? We need to get all the invitations out now."

"I can do it."

"We'll both have to do it at this point." And make all the arrangements.

"Let's see what Matthew has to say first."

Fortunately, at least in Kevin's opinion, Matthew was free and arrived at the house in record time. In his mid-thirties, good-looking, and happily married with two children he adored, Matthew kept up a running banter as he examined Stacy. As she expected, he found nothing.

"You're lucky." He packed his medical bag. "I'd expect at least some sign of a concussion, but there's nothing. And you don't need stitches. That butterfly bandage should do it."

"I guess I have a hard head."

"However, I want to see you tomorrow at the medical center for a CAT scan. Just to be safe."

Stacy groaned. "Matthew, I have a million things to do."

"You can spare an hour." Matthew grinned at Dianna. "Make her come, Di."

"She'll be there." The determination in Dianna's voice didn't bode well.

Great. Stacy sighed. Another hour or so wasted when she already had too much to do.

Kevin showed Matthew out, the conversation dissolving into men talk. Dianna put her hand on Stacy's arm. "Now you're going to take a long bath, pop a couple of aspirin, and go to bed."

Stacy laughed. "When did you get your medical degree?"

"I mean it."

"I'll compromise. I'll take the bath and aspirin, but I need to get some work done before I turn in." She needed to see how much Kevin had completed in preparation for the party. Her internal clock was off anyhow. The clock said seven at night, but it felt more like five in the morning.

"The party isn't that important, Stace."

Stacy raised her eyebrows. Dianna was saying a party wasn't important? Stacy grinned and placed a quick kiss on Dianna's cheek. "Sure it is. You're going to perform for our guests."

Before Dianna could respond, Stacy raced upstairs to stand in the shower until the hot water ran out. When she made her way to the office, dressed in clean jeans and T-shirt, over an hour had passed.

Kevin sat at the desk, hanging up the phone as she arrived. He turned to smile at her. "I knew you'd be here, so I've been busy." He pulled the side chair up for her. "I've made several phone calls, and nearly everyone has said they can make it."

Smiling, Stacy slid into place by the desk and examined the list of names she'd compiled earlier. He had been busy. Only about ten remained to be invited. "That *is* good. We can call the rest in the morning."

"Actually, I've already faxed invitations to all of them, but I can call to confirm tomorrow." Kevin produced a satisfied grin, and Stacy laughed. She should have known he'd be on top of things. "Want to discuss the menu?" he added.

After two hours of intense discussions, Stacy could no longer hold back a yawn. Kevin pushed back the papers. "That's enough for tonight."

"Sounds good." Stacy pushed back her chair. "I'm surprised Di hasn't been in to bug us by now."

"She turned in early. She hasn't slept much the past couple of nights."

Guilt washed over Stacy. If she hadn't allowed her attraction to Nic to get her into trouble, she could have avoided that. "I'm sorry."

Kevin put his arm around her shoulders as they made their way upstairs. "Not your fault. Accidents happen. What counts is that you're not hurt, and you're home."

"You're right." She didn't want to consider the alternative. Pausing at her room, she opened the door, then turned back to Kevin. "I'm glad you were here to watch over Dianna."

"Yeah, me, too." He dropped his arm but hesitated. "You know, Stacy, almost losing you made me realize how much I care about you, too. You're pretty special."

Warmth oozed through Stacy. Too bad he hadn't said that two years ago. Perhaps then she'd be engaged to him instead of Dianna. Now it didn't matter. She struggled to keep her voice light. "Bet you say that to all your bosses."

"No." He produced a slow smile and touched her hair. "Just all my future sisters-in-law." Leaning forward, he kissed her.

They'd exchanged friendly kisses in the past, but this went a moment past that, not into the world of lust, but enough to let Stacy know he meant every word he said. When he drew back, Kevin produced a half smile.

"Stay safe, okay?"

She nodded and gave him a light kiss in return—a sister to a beloved brother. "I promise."

Entering her bedroom, Stacy closed the door, then leaned against it, her head whirling. "Wow." Who would have expected that reaction from Kevin?

Nic found the house dark and quiet on his return. Just as well. He could perform the protection spells on Dianna and Stacy with neither of them being aware of it.

He made his way to Dianna's room first, then paused beside her bed. So beautiful. He ran his hand over her long blonde hair, and she stirred slightly.

"Sweet Anna," he murmured.

With a few quiet words and a brush of magic, he created a protection spell around Dianna to keep her safe from any of Titania's other crazy ideas. Dianna sighed in her sleep, her lashes fanned against her cheeks, her lips parted slightly.

An invitation, surely? Nic touched his lips to hers, caressing, seducing, longing to feel the passion Anna always created within him. He heard a distant pop—a pixie disappearing, perhaps—but experienced none of the familiar lust. Where was the fire?

He deepened the kiss, touching his tongue to her lips,

and Dianna moaned, the sound enticing but still not triggering the response he wanted. She murmured against his mouth, and he drew back to listen. Did she remember him now?

"Kevin?"

His blood went cold. She thought he was that weak Kevin? Weren't his kisses more potent? His touch more appealing?

She stirred again, her lashes fluttering. "Kev, that you?"

Stones. Nic stood and transported into Stacy's room. Though the room was still bathed in darkness, the door stood open, allowing light from the hallway to filter in, framing Stacy where she stood facing Kevin.

They were muttering pleasantries—good nights, no doubt. He drew back further into the shadows. He could wait.

His jaw dropped when Kevin abruptly kissed Stacy, really kissed her. Nic had seen them exchange friendly pecks before, but this went beyond that. His hands curled into fists before he was aware of it. Hitting Lenno before had given him some satisfaction. Perhaps he would try it again.

He took a step forward, then drew in a deep breath as Stacy bestowed another brief kiss on Kevin. What was going on?

Stacy entered the room, closed the door, then leaned against it. "Wow."

"Stealing your sister's fiancé, are you?" The words erupted from Nic before he thought.

She jumped and flicked on the lights. "Nic?"

"What was that?" He motioned toward the door as he crossed the room to face her, his gut churning.

"What?" She turned toward the door, then nodded. "Oh. That was Kevin letting me know he does care about me. Nothing major."

He growled. "It looked major to me."

Stacy hesitated. "Why should you care? I would think you'd want me to get Kevin away from Dianna."

Why did he care? He should be pleased, but the tightening of his stomach said otherwise. Stones. What was this? "I can manage to win Dianna on my own." If he said that enough times, it had to be true.

"Fine, then go win her." Stacy went to brush past him, but he caught her arm, pulling her against him.

She flattened her hands against his chest as she met his gaze, her eyes wide. "Nic . . ."

"I need to put a protection spell on you." He felt the increase in her pulse mirroring his own, his blood warming. "So Titania can't harm you."

"Okay." Her whisper came out husky, stirring his desire.

He quickly murmured the spell, then listened to the fire in his gut instead of to his head and kissed her. The passion he'd hoped to find with Dianna burst into life with just a brief touch of Stacy's lips, enticing him to delve deeper.

Her desire responded to his, her breasts swelling, her tongue mating with his until thought became impossible and overwhelming need took control. He swung her into his arms, then carried her to the bed and pressed her into the soft mattress. Burying his fingers in her hair, he kissed her again, her lips meeting his in perfect harmony.

"Stacy." He could only whisper her name.

"Nic." Stacy slid her arms around his neck, holding him closer, heat radiating from within her. She met him kiss for kiss, demanding as well as giving, seducing as well as being seduced.

He needed her. Nothing else made sense but that.

Cupping her breast, he caressed it, the softness filling his palm. Her nipple grew rigid beneath her T-shirt, and she gasped when he brushed his thumb over it, her hips rocking in response.

More. He needed more. Without a thought he removed her clothing, then bent to draw her breast into his mouth, to tease it as thoroughly as her mouth until her moans increased and heat poured from her in waves. Heat that fueled his inner fire.

He ran his hand over her smooth skin from her slender neck, over her pebbled peak and belly to the curls of her mound. Dipping into her moistness, he caressed her more until her body tensed, then jerked with the force of her response.

Yes. This was what he sought.

Stacy's breath came in gasps as he made his way back to her lips. Her hands ran through his hair, then over his back. "Is this . . . is this part of the spell?"

He smiled. Only the one she had over him.

By the Stones! He jerked back. Titania's magic still worked against him. No protection spell could remove the insidious lust for Stacy that Titania had already placed within him, a lust that could destroy him.

"The wrong spell," he murmured, leaning his forehead against hers. Drawing back, he stole one more kiss, one more taste of her sweetness, then bowed his head. "I'm sorry."

To stay was dangerous, too dangerous.

So, with infinite regret, he left.

Nic approached Dianna during the first morning break. He had to take action. She was due to leave in less than two weeks, and he didn't dare wait any longer. Now, while Kevin and Stacy were working in the office, offered the perfect opportunity. Dianna's rehearsal was light today, merely a running through the schedule of her program, so she was smiling when he approached.

"What do you think?" she asked.

"You're going to be wonderful." He touched her arm and produced his most charming smile. "Walk with me?"

Her hesitation was brief. "Of course."

He led her onto a garden path, still clinging to her arm, radiating the sensuality natural to all Fae. His senses knew when her pulse quickened and her body temperature rose. "Do you believe in soul mates, Dianna?"

"One right person for everyone? Yes."

"How about one right person for all time?"

"Isn't that the same thing?"

"Yes and no." He paused and faced her. How much could he reveal? Should he reveal? "What if you could live forever?"

"What do you mean?"

"Can you imagine living with Kevin forever?" Surely she'd realize how unsuited they were for each other.

"I hadn't thought about that."

Nic leaned closer, holding her gaze with his, smiling as her pupils dilated. The Fae charm was working. Now to plant new thoughts in her mind. "I don't think Kevin is the one for you."

"But I love him."

"Do you? Or is he just convenient? What if by allowing Kevin to sidetrack you, you miss your soul mate?" He bent to whisper in her ear. "What if you're missing the greatest love of your life?"

Pulling back, he paused, his mouth just a breath away from hers. "Do you want to take that chance?"

Her eyes grew wide. "I . . . I . . ."

He brushed his lips over hers, concentrating on creating an aura of sensuality. "What if there is someone else, Dianna?" He kissed her again with more force, using his tongue to seduce her mouth into opening for him. Where was the response? The fire? By now Stacy would have melted in his arms, turned his blood into lava.

"Dianna," he murmured, willing her to respond.

Slowly, tentatively, she did, her lips moving against his, her arms coming up around his neck. Excellent.

A distant pop indicated the loss of another pixie. Odd that he should remain focused enough to notice that. He should be delirious with passion by now.

Heightening his Fae aura, he kissed Dianna with all the passion he could muster, and she responded, but it wasn't the same. Though the man in him quickened, the heat was missing. Had Titania done something to affect that as well? That wouldn't surprise him. She had meddled in this from the beginning.

"Nic." Dianna pushed against his chest, and surprised, he released her. "This . . . this isn't right."

"Are you sure of that? Maybe what you have with Kevin isn't right. Maybe you're about to lose out on the one man meant only for you."

Confusion flickered in Dianna's eyes, but she backed away. "I . . . I don't know." A sob emerged. "I don't know."

Nic caught her shoulder and ran his hand over her hair. "It's all right, Dianna. Just think about it. Let your heart guide you."

If she let herself feel, she'd realize she was meant to be with Nic. Maybe she'd even remember something of their previous life together.

"I have to go." She bolted like a frightened doe, and Nic let her go.

His Fae sensuality had worked, but not enough. He needed to discover what kind of spell Titania had put on him and remove it. Otherwise, this seduction would never work.

He grimaced. He'd never before had difficulty discovering passion with Anna. Just looking at her would trigger it. Touching her would drive him to the brink.

Yes, he definitely needed to remove Titania's spell. Then his next encounter with Dianna would be much better.

"Okay, how many then?" Stacy peered over Kevin's shoulder as he hung up the telephone.

"That makes forty-three. Everyone is coming except for Fred Larson from *The Reviewer*. He has other plans."

"Considering the short notice, I'd call that excellent. I'll pass that on to Lola at the caterers." This party might come together yet.

Kevin pushed away from the desk. "I'll go see about getting the studio ready so Dianna can do a short presentation." Standing, he glanced at Stacy. "What did she say when you told her you wanted her to perform?"

Stacy grinned. "I didn't wait for an answer."

"Smart woman." Kevin started for the door. "Though I'm sure it won't be a problem. Dianna loves to perform."

Dianna raced into the room, gasping for breath, her eyes wide, and Stacy jumped to her feet as Kevin grabbed Dianna's shoulders to steady her. "What's wrong?" he asked.

She jerked herself free. "Don't touch me."

Frowning, Stacy came to hug Dianna. "What happened? Are you all right?"

"I'm okay. I . . . I don't know what to do." Her pupils were dilated, and she trembled within Stacy's arms.

"Do about what?"

"About Kevin." Dianna lowered her voice. "Do I really love him?"

"Di." Kevin stepped toward her, his concern evident, and she shrank closer to Stacy. "I love you."

"But . . . but do I love you? Really?" Dianna peeked around at him, her eyes watering. "Enough for eternity?"

Stacy lifted Dianna's chin so she could peer into her sister's face. She appeared to be hypnotized with her dilated, unfocused eyes. This was Nic's doing. Damn him. He'd promised her no magic.

"You need some rest, Di. Let me take you upstairs." She glanced at Kevin. "Later."

"Is she all right?" he asked, his hands clenching and unclenching.

"She will be." A cold lump formed in Stacy's stomach as she led Dianna upstairs to her bedroom and tucked her into bed with a sleeping pill. She perched on the edge of Dianna's bed, smoothing her sister's hair until Dianna's even breathing indicated she'd finally fallen asleep.

Stacy rose slowly, her jaw clenched. No matter how badly Nic was doing in wooing Dianna, he had no call to resort to magic. He'd just lost any help from Stacy. In fact, he'd lost his welcome here entirely.

What did it matter if he didn't find his Anna right now? If she was immortal like he was, he could wait a hundred years for her.

She found Kevin waiting outside Dianna's room, his face pinched. "Is she all right? What happened to her?"

"Last-minute jitters." Stacy said the first excuse that came to mind. "She's been working a lot lately. I think we just need to let her rest for now."

"Can I stay with her?"

Stacy nodded. "But don't wake her."

"I won't. I only want to be with her." Kevin entered the bedroom, and Stacy rushed for Nic's cottage.

The door was open. Good. She didn't bother knocking but stormed inside to find him at the dining room table, poring over some kind of old scroll. Apparently, he didn't even know she was there.

Well, he would.

She stalked over to the table and slammed her palms on the top, bringing Nic's head up with a jerk. "Stacy."

He looked surprised to see her. Did he not expect her to defend her sister?

"You promised me: no magic." Stacy leaned toward him. Was he under another spell? "You agreed to win Dianna as a normal man."

"I didn't use magic." He glanced away. "Exactly."

"It sure as hell looks like magic to me. Di is ripped apart, so confused she doesn't know if she's coming or going. Believe me, confusion has never been a problem for her. Di knows what she wants and goes for it. Always." Stacy stabbed her finger against his chest. "What did you do to her?"

Sparks appeared in Nic's eyes. "I only enhanced my charm, my Fae sex appeal. That isn't magic."

"Isn't it? Sounds a hell of a lot like a Lenno to me."

Nic rose, sparks firing in his eyes, bringing him uncomfortably near, and Stacy jumped back to put some distance between them. Even angry, she was far too aware of him.

"It's not the same thing at all."

"You tried to seduce Di. Sounds like the same thing to me."

"She belongs with me."

"Not now, she doesn't." Stacy lifted her chin, meeting his fiery gaze.

"What does that mean?" His voice came out with a growl.

"It means you're done here. Take off. Go back to your magic land, anywhere but here." The thought of never seeing him again made her heart skip a beat, but it was best. For all of them.

"You can't be serious." Nic stepped closer, forcing her to look up at him.

Stacy fought the urge to take a step back. "I'm very serious. You've endangered my sister. I will not allow that. Just because you can't win her love as a normal man does not mean you can use trickery. Of any kind."

"She's my Anna."

"And if she is, she's immortal, right? Go away, let her have her happiness with Kevin. You can always come back in a hundred years after he's dead and start over. Maybe you'll have learned some tact by then."

Nic seized her shoulders. "I have no intention of waiting any longer for my wife. It's been far too long already."

His touch triggered heat in her blood as always, but Stacy struggled to ignore it. "Give it up, Nic. Whatever you're doing isn't working. Maybe you and your Anna just aren't meant to be."

"Don't say that." He shook her once, then released her, horror on his face. "Stones, Stacy, I'm sorry."

Stacy backed away from him. He'd startled her more than harmed her, but she wasn't about to give him another opportunity. "Go away, Nic. Remove whatever spell you put on Di and go away."

"There is no spell. The effect will wear off in an hour or so." Nic held himself rigid, his dark gaze burning into hers.

"Then leave. Now."

"You're making a mistake."

"No, you've already made one."

"You can't protect Dianna from making her own choices. She belongs with me."

"Then she'll make that choice without magical influence." While Di needed to stand on her own, she had no chance against someone like Nic. She probably had no clue what even happened to her.

Nic crossed over to Stacy, then stopped in front of her, not touching her, but close enough that he only had to move a finger to do so. He radiated sensuality. Was he trying to use his magic on her now?

His gaze fell to her mouth, and Stacy's throat went dry. "Go." Her voice came out raspy. "Don't pull your Fae charm on me."

His face went stony hard, then he stepped back, bowed, and disappeared.

Stacy released her breath in a whoosh. If he hadn't obeyed, what would she have done? Broken another figurine? More than likely, given in . . . again . . . to the seduction of his lips. At least what he'd done to Dianna wasn't a spell, more a desperate act by a desperate man. Was winning Anna that important?

She sighed. Of course it was. He'd loved her completely, still loved her.

As she returned to the house, her steps dragged. She'd sent him away, and already she felt the loss. But this was for the best. Dianna didn't need her loyalties torn, and Stacy didn't need to love another man who only wanted her sister.

She didn't need to, but she already did. She swallowed the lump in her throat. She would get over him. In time.

Maybe.

She joined Kevin by Dianna's bedside until her sister awakened shortly after noon. Dianna blinked once, twice, then focused on Stacy perched on the edge of the bed. "Stace?"

"How are you feeling, little sis?" Stacy touched Dianna's hand, relieved it no longer felt cold.

"Fine." Dianna frowned. "I was pretty out of it earlier, wasn't I?"

"You were."

"It was the weirdest thing. I was talking to Nic, and he asked me some questions, and before I knew it, I was doubting whether Kevin was right for me." Dianna slid into a sitting position and spotted Kevin on the chair beside the bed. She held out her arms to him, and he bounded up to embrace her. "I love you," she murmured. "I should never doubt that."

"Thank God." Kevin kissed her, then hugged her tight again. "I'd die if I lost you."

"You'll never lose me."

Stacy left the room, grinning. They weren't likely to miss her.

The phone was ringing when she entered the office, and she snagged the receiver. "Stacy Fielding."

"Miss Fielding, it's Detective Morrow. I wanted to see how you were feeling." She recognized his voice at once: deep, intriguing, sexy.

Stacy blinked. She hadn't expected to hear from him again. "I'm fine. Thank you, Detective."

"Good. I'm glad."

Silence lingered for a moment until Stacy spoke up. "Is there something else?"

"Well, actually, yes." He hesitated. "I'd like to see you again."

"Are there some papers I have to sign or something?"

"Huh? No. I wanted to see you again, off-duty. Coffee, perhaps?"

Stacy took the receiver away from her ear and looked at it. He was asking her for a date? Well, why not? He seemed nice enough, and perhaps he'd help her forget Nic. Not likely, but the detective wouldn't be a bad diversion for a day . . . or so. And she certainly deserved a short break from the pile of work on her desk.

"Miss Fielding?"

Hearing him speak, she returned the receiver to her ear. "I think if we're going to have coffee together, you'd better call me Stacy."

His rough chuckle vibrated along the connection. "Call me Xander."

"Xander?"

"Short for Alexander. How about tomorrow? I can pick you up."

"Why don't I meet you? It's out of your way to drive up here. Do you know where Sarah Lynn's Coffee Shop is?"

"I only visit it daily." She sensed his smile. "Sounds great. I have a late shift tomorrow. About nine in the morning okay?"

"That sounds great. I'll be there."

"Thanks, Stacy. See you then."

"Bye." Stacy hung up the phone but continued to stare at it. Who would have ever expected that? She hadn't been on a real date in forever.

Unless she counted her trip to Paris with Nic. Memories rushed in, and she drew in a deep breath. No, that had been just two friends seeing the sights.

And so much more. Her chest ached.

Nic was gone. Forever.

Tears pricked at her eyes, but she blinked them back, furious at herself. He'd never offered love, only stolen kisses. He'd made it plain all along he wanted Dianna, yet she still fell in love with him.

She must be a glutton for punishment. Then why did she agree to have coffee with Detect—Xander?

A salve to her ego, perhaps. Nothing would probably come of it, but sitting across from an attractive man and having a cup of coffee was a change of pace.

She called Lola next and made final changes to the menu for the party, passing on the latest attendance count—give or take five to twenty. Somehow Dianna's parties had a way of growing larger than planned.

The phone rang as soon as she hung up, and she sighed before answering it. Now what?

"Stacy Fielding, where are you?"

She grinned, recognizing Matthew's voice. "Hey, Matthew."

"You were supposed to come in for a CAT scan today, remember?"

"I'm fine. Really. Not even a headache."

"Doesn't matter. I want to be sure. I'll be here at the med center for another couple of hours. I expect to see you soon."

"Very well." She knew better than to argue. "I'll leave right away." But it would be a wasted trip. He wouldn't find anything, especially since she hadn't actually hit her head.

She told Kevin and Dianna where she was going, then headed for the garage. Her car sat in the middle: a gold Saturn purchased years ago, before she and Dianna had decided they were wealthy. It drove like a charm, so why trade it in when she adored it?

As she opened the car door, she heard the distant sound of giggling, and her heart rose to her throat. Pixies. Damn. What were they doing here? Half expecting something to be thrown at her head, Stacy circled the car, kicking the tires, looking for anything obvious. All appeared fine.

It was only after she raised the garage door that she noticed the huge puddle of oil on the floor nearby. Obviously, the pixies had emptied every can of oil in the place. Wonderful.

She managed to avoid the puddle as she backed out and made her way off the estate onto the twisting road to town. She drove with care. Despite the guardrails along the road and the spectacular views, the drop-offs were intimidating.

Approaching the first scary curve, she pressed the brakes to slow down but felt little response. She pushed harder, her knuckles white on the steering wheel, until the pedal hit the floor and finally the brakes engaged, slowing her enough to round the corner.

Her heart pounded in her chest. This wasn't good. She tried to pull over on a nonexistent shoulder, only this time the brakes failed completely. No matter how hard she stomped, the car continued.

In a desperate attempt, she yanked on the emergency brake. No response.

Dear Lord, the pixies!

Her concentration focused on the road, she negotiated the hairpin curves as the car continued to pick up speed. Gravity was not always a good thing.

She squealed going around a curve, coming dangerously close to the rail. Her chest closed so tight, she could barely breathe. What could she do? With cliffs up one side and a drop-off on the other, she had no real choice.

Perhaps if she maneuvered close to the inside cliff, then jumped out. Dangerous, but better than remaining inside with a rapid loss of control.

She pulled on the door handle to ease it open, but it wouldn't budge. "What?" She pushed against it with no success. She was trapped in a runaway tomb.

What to do? What to do? Would Nic come if she called him? She'd sent him away.

Given a choice, hitting the cliff had to be preferable to falling a few hundred feet. That would slow her. *If it doesn't kill me.*

She gripped the steering wheel so tight her hands ached. The next curve approached far too soon. She wasn't going to make this one.

Jerking the wheel, she smashed her car into the cliff, only to have it rebound off, spin across the road, and crash through the guardrail, sailing into the air. She screamed. "Nic!"

The car plummeted down, slicing off treetops, her stomach rising to her throat. She closed her eyes. This was it.

She was going to die.

Seventeen

She braced herself for the crash, every muscle tense, then abruptly stopped moving and opened her eyes to find herself in Nic's arms on the edge of the road. She met his gaze just as the distant crash of her car reverberated through the air.

His face was pale, but she felt certain hers was whiter. She didn't speak. She couldn't. An explosion sounded, and she buried her face in his neck, her body trembling. That could have been her.

For several minutes, neither of them spoke as Nic nuzzled her hair, holding her tight. Finally, her shaking eased, and she could look at him. "I . . . I thought you left."

His smile was warm. "I'm not easy to get rid of."

"Thank God. Thank *you.*"

"What happened?"

"The pixies, I think. I heard them in the garage when I left. My brakes went out, even the emergency. And the door wouldn't open." Her voice broke on a sob, and she shuddered again as she recalled that horrible feeling of shooting off the road into space.

Nic held her tight. "You're fine now. I won't let anything happen to you."

"I was so mean to you." Only a few hours earlier, she'd told him to leave. Yet he'd still saved her.

He grimaced. "You were protecting your sister. I understood."

"You didn't act like it at the time." *Though who wouldn't respond in anger with someone yelling at him?*

"I've had time to think since then. You're right. Dianna has to love me for me, just as Anna did. I won't use magic or Fae charm or anything but my good nature to win her."

"Your good nature can be pretty potent all on its own," Stacy said, then wished she could retract the words as heat crawled into her cheeks.

Naturally, Nic noticed and grinned. "You think so?"

She squirmed, too aware he still held her in his arms as her body responded to that devastating smile. "You can put me down now."

"Are you sure you can stand?" His eyes twinkled.

"I'm sure." Not one hundred percent, but if she remained in this close proximity, her knees would definitely give out.

He lowered her feet to the ground but continued to hold her arms until she stood upright. "Okay?"

"Okay." He released her, and Stacy drew in a deep breath, then turned and made her way to the edge of the road. Far down below, a fire burned while the remnants of her car were scattered over the cliff, a door dangling from the top of a tree. "My poor car."

Nic joined her. "That's easily fixed." After some muttered words and a flash of lightning, her car appeared on the road behind her, intact once again, while the fire below disappeared.

That did it. Stacy's knees gave out, and she sat on the ground with a plop. "That . . . that's amazing. Is it really okay, even the brakes?"

"It's perfect, better than new, especially the brakes."

Nic reached down and pulled her to her feet once again. "Where were you headed?"

"The medical center." She grimaced. "Matthew wants to take pictures of my head after my *accident.*"

Nic grinned. "Would you like some company?"

"Actually, I'd like you to drive. I'm not sure I'm up to it right now." Stacy started toward the car, then paused to glance at him. "You can drive, can't you?"

"I can drive. It's come in handy a time or two." Nic went around the car and held open the passenger door for her. "My lady."

Stacy took her seat inside with trepidation. Everything looked the same, better even. The stain on the floor mat was gone. Nic slid behind the steering wheel and started the engine. She gulped, seizing the armrest, when he put the car into gear.

"It's all right," he said.

"I know." But some part of her brain wasn't quite ready to accept that yet. Her muscles tensed as they approached every curve, but the car slowed as needed, and Nic eased around them without difficulty. Only when Nic pulled into the medical center parking lot did she relax.

Nic came around and held out his hand to help her out. "All right if I come with you?"

Placing her hand in his, she nodded. "Very all right." Her insides were still pretty shaky. If Matthew insisted on taking a blood pressure check, he would be in for a surprise.

She had Matthew paged, and he joined her a few minutes later. "About time," he said with a smile. "Come this way, and I'll have you in and out before you know it."

Stacy glanced back at Nic, hating herself for her insecurities but not willing to fight them right now. "Will you wait?"

His smile held more than casual promise. "I'll be here."

As Matthew pledged, the procedure went fairly quickly. Afterward, he escorted her back to the waiting area. "I didn't see anything unusual right off the top, but I'll examine the scan in detail and let you know," he said.

"I told you it was nothing." They entered the room, and Nic came immediately to join them.

"Of course." Matthew grinned. "What else should I expect from a woman with a head obviously as hard as a rock and the health of an ox?"

Stacy wrinkled her nose. "An ox? Just because I don't get sick?"

"You never get sick. During the entire time I've known you, you haven't had so much as a cold. I figure I'm going to get information while I have the chance so I can write you up for the scientific journal."

She laughed as Nic said, "She doesn't stand still long enough for germs to catch her."

"That could be true." Matthew extended his hand. "I'm Matthew Beltane, Stacy's neighbor and doctor when necessary, which isn't often."

Nic grasped Matthew's hand. "Nic Stone. I'm the gardener."

"You're the one keeping that place looking so good?" Matthew continued sotto voce, "How much to steal you away?"

"There isn't enough money in the world." Nic rested his hand on Stacy's shoulder. "Ready to go?"

"Yes. Thanks, Matthew." She took a step, then hesitated. "We're having a party on Saturday to kick off Dianna's tour. Want to come? You and Ginger? About six or so?" Dianna usually invited a dozen extra, so why couldn't Stacy throw out an extra invitation or two? At least with Matthew and his wife she could discuss something other than the music industry.

"I'll check with Ginger and let you know, but it sounds

like fun. Thanks." Matthew waved them off, and soon Nic had the car on the road again.

"Do you need to stop anywhere else?"

"Actually, yes." She might as well get as many errands done as possible. "There's a florist close to downtown—The Village Green. Do you mind?"

"Your wish is my command."

They had to park a couple of blocks away, but Stacy didn't mind. She always enjoyed walking through downtown and soaking up the wonderful Victorian ambiance.

"Dianna told me this was originally a mining town, but she didn't have much more information than that," Nic said.

Stacy smiled. "History was never Di's favorite subject. Me, I eat it up. Especially the strange stuff. For instance, some folks say Telluride is named for tellurium, a gold-bearing ore, but I like the other theory better."

"What's that?"

"I guess this place used to be a hell-raiser in its younger days, so they say Telluride came from 'to hell you ride.' Sounds more fun, doesn't it?"

Nic laughed. "How rowdy was this place?"

"Butch Cassidy robbed his first bank here." Stacy loved the stories about the town. "Have you heard of him?"

"I've heard of him." Nic dropped a casual arm around her shoulders, and heat rushed through her body. "I've lived among mortals long enough to learn some things."

"Here's the florist." Stacy used that opportunity to slip out from under his arm. As much as she enjoyed it, she maintained control much better when Nic wasn't touching her.

Finalizing the arrangements for flowers to be delivered for the party only took a few minutes, then Nic and Stacy emerged back outside into the warm sunshine and cool breeze.

"Is that it?" Nic asked.

"I think so." No doubt she'd remember another errand after she returned home.

"Then I'm buying you a drink. You're still paler than I like." Nic touched her arm. "Where would you recommend?"

Stacy glanced at her watch. Just past three. Where could they go? "I know. Fly Me to the Moon Saloon isn't too far away."

"Lead the way."

The saloon was nearly empty, the large dance floor quiet. They had no trouble finding a small table and placed their order. "During the weekend, this place really rocks," Stacy said. "It's a bit quieter during the week."

"Good. I'm after quiet right now." He stared at Stacy across the table, his dark eyes revealing nothing of his thoughts.

She shifted in her seat, too aware of his knee brushing hers beneath the table.

"I'm going to have to do something about those pixies," he said. "I thought we'd gotten rid of most of them."

"I had hoped. Didn't you say they weren't intentionally harmful? Surely they knew what would happen if they messed with my brakes." And if they did something to her brakes, what was to stop them from doing the same to Dianna or Kevin's cars?

"They have been acting out of the norm, more vicious. Titania's doing, I'm certain."

Their drinks arrived, and Stacy waited for their server to leave before continuing. "Why? Does she hate me that much?"

"I think it's more that she knows I like you that much." Nic took Stacy's hand in his, and she inhaled sharply. His touch set off too many internal alarms. Coupled with his words, she wasn't doing as good a job as she liked in remaining neutral.

"Titania doesn't want me to have Anna," he added.

"She also doesn't want me to find anyone else, either. She wants me at her beck and call, to be her—what's the expression—her boy toy."

Stacy shuddered at the thought. She'd only dealt with Titania for a few minutes, and that had been more than enough for a lifetime. With the way the Fae queen toyed with other people's lives, Nic's existence would be miserable. She squeezed his hand. "Then we won't let that happen."

"The only way to prevent it is to win Anna over, to tell her I love her and hear that she loves me. Otherwise Titania wins." Nic sighed and ran his finger over the middle of Stacy's palm until she was ready to leap out of her chair and onto him.

She tried to pull her hand away, but he only tightened his hold. "Tell me what to do, Stacy," he murmured.

"Me?" How could she possibly know? Nic met her gaze, his expression somber. He meant it. "I . . . I don't know. Have you kissed her?"

"Several times. It hasn't worked."

Stacy flinched. The thought of Nic kissing Dianna made her stomach whirl. "You tried Fae charm, and that didn't work."

"It didn't?" Dismay filled his features. "I had hoped she'd reconsider her attraction to Kevin."

"She loves Kevin. I'm sorry, but she does." Stacy squeezed Nic's hand, wanting to take away his obvious pain.

"There must be something I can do, something I've overlooked."

Stacy hesitated. She knew what made her agree to help him. "Why don't you tell her the truth? About Anna. About yourself. About what happened."

"Only as a last resort. I don't want her pity. I want her love."

Whereas he could have Stacy's love without even trying.

She looked away and drank heavily of her wine. Her heart ached, and she wanted to run away and hide. It wasn't *her* love he wanted.

"Then I don't know. I'm sorry." She managed to ease her hand free and wrapped both her palms around her glass. The wine helped, loosening her tight muscles. "What if . . . what if you don't win Dianna at this time? What if you have to wait a few years?"

Bleak despair filled his eyes. "I can do that if I have to, but it already feels like I've been eons without her. She was my best friend as well as my lover. We liked the same things. We could talk for hours. We had fun together." A slow smile spread over his lips. "Both in and out of bed."

Stacy fought down a blush, recalling only too well how entertaining he could be in bed. If she'd kept her mouth shut, she might have experienced the ecstasy she longed for.

With a gulp, she finished her wine. "I think we ought to head back. I have a lot to do yet for the party."

"Isn't Kevin supposed to be helping?"

"He is, but right now he's more concerned with Dianna. She frightened us both this morning." Stacy aimed an accusing glance at Nic, and he grimaced.

"Point taken. Come on then. I'll drive."

The glass of wine definitely helped during the drive home, making her mellow and more than a bit sleepy. Stacy settled against the passenger seat and closed her eyes. Only for a moment.

The next thing she knew, she felt the light touch of lips against hers, a soft caress that hinted at tantalizing pleasures. One brush, then another. With a groan, Stacy lifted her hand to the face over hers and opened her eyes.

Nic's gaze met hers, fire flickering in the depths.

"You're home, Sleeping Beauty," he whispered, his voice husky.

"I . . ." Stacy kept her palm against his cheek, absorbing the warmth and unique scent that was Nic. She longed for more, to lose herself in him.

But she couldn't.

She dropped her hand and her gaze. "Thank you, Nic."

Taking the hint, he moved back so she could exit the car. "Do you plan to tell Dianna what happened with the car?" he asked.

"No. It would only worry her, and everything turned out okay, thank goodness." Not being dead at the bottom of the cliff was a *good thing.*

"I'll check out all the cars before I leave."

"Leave?" Stacy grabbed his arm, then realized he still intended to abide by her earlier order. "No, stay. Please." After all, he promised no more magic to sway Dianna.

"I'm still going to do what I have to," he reminded her. "I have to win Dianna."

"I know. It'll be all right." It had to be.

He nodded and went to turn away, but Stacy stayed him for a moment and pressed a brief kiss to his cheek. "Thank you, Nic. For being there."

His gaze smoldered as he gave her a warm smile. "I'm glad I was."

Stacy swayed toward him, then jerked herself back. Time to go. Now. She ran toward the house, then paused at the door and glanced back. Nic stood in the same place, watching her, and her heart skipped several beats.

Oh, hell. Why was everything such a mess?

Coffee. Oh, jeez, how could she have forgotten her date with Xander? Stacy rushed toward the coffee shop. The trip down the mountain had been harrowing at best, with memories of the previous day slipping in far too often, but she'd made it. Only ten minutes late.

Would he still be there?

She paused in the doorway, searching the room, then released her breath when she saw him approaching. He wore casual clothes today, which made him even more appealing. The close-fitting T-shirt did nothing to hide his excellent physique, and his blue jeans molded to muscular thighs and a damned cute butt. "I'm sorry I'm late," she said before he had a chance to speak. "I was busy and almost forgot."

"It happens." Xander smiled and motioned with his hand. "I have a booth back here."

Several twisted stir straws dotted the table, a sign that perhaps her delay had bothered him a little, but he quickly brushed them aside as he sat across from her. "I'll go get our order. What do you prefer?"

"I love the café au lait. No sugar."

"Anything to eat?"

Stacy glanced at the nearby display case, then wished she hadn't. A huge blueberry muffin sat in there calling her name. "A blueberry muffin?"

"Got it. Be right back." Xander went to the counter to get their order, giving her time to study him.

He was appealing, but she immediately recognized why. In build and appearance, he was a lot like Nic. True, Xander's hair was darker and shorter, but his sculpted cheekbones and dazzling smile were very reminiscent of Nic. Not to mention the very attractive tush.

Xander returned with the coffee and muffins and settled in across from her. "I'm glad you agreed to come," he said, stirring sugar into his coffee. "I wasn't sure you would."

"Why not?" He couldn't know about her attraction to Nic. No one knew that but her.

"You and your sister live a bit differently than a local cop. I thought maybe . . . well . . . it doesn't matter anyhow."

He'd assumed she'd be too much a snob to date a cop. Stacy smiled as she held up her cup. "You thought wrong."

"I've seen you around town for the past couple of years now. You always caught my eye, but I never worked up the courage to actually call. Then, after meeting you, well, I figured I'd give it a try." Humor danced in his gray eyes. "And you know, that was harder to do than to face an armed robber."

Stacy laughed. "And here the worst I've done is stomp on a spider."

"I haven't dated much, I'm afraid. Usually I'm pretty much wrapped up in my work."

"Telluride isn't that dangerous a place." Murders here were pretty rare.

"Say that when ski season begins." He grinned. "I also volunteer on the mountain rescue teams and ski patrols, so that keeps me busy when I'm not on duty."

"I'm surprised you have any free time. Have you had to rescue many people?"

"More than I'd like. Some folks go off hiking and get hurt or lost. Others try rock climbing and get stuck. It's always a race to see who's going to win—me or the mountain." He met her gaze. "That's why I was so glad you came through okay. Though how mountain rescue missed you in the gorge is still surprising. I know they searched that area."

"I . . . I was near some bushes. Maybe they hid me." Stacy picked at her muffin. They were treading dangerously near the lies she preferred to forget. Lying was not something she did easily or often.

"Maybe." He accepted her lame explanation easily enough, and her tense muscles relaxed. "Then there are the ones who come for the festivals. Talk about crazy." Xander went on, and their conversation moved into the first date territory of preferred movies, books read, and favorite musicians.

"What do you think about Dianna?" Stacy had to ask, though she hated to do it. She liked him. But she'd know from his answer whether his interest was actually in her or her sister.

Xander shrugged. "She's talented enough, but I prefer the blues or ballads. Donovan Reeves is who I listen to most."

"You're kidding. I adore Donovan. I have everything he's ever done. I could listen to him for hours." And she had. "I just sent him a new song I wrote."

"Something you wrote?" Xander looked interested and slightly surprised, and Stacy nodded.

"Not everything I do is like what Dianna sings. I have other songs inside me, too." Songs that would soon have a chance to emerge.

"That's great." Xander paused, glanced into his coffee, then back up. "Maybe you'll sing it for me sometime."

She hadn't sung it for anyone yet. The emotions were still too near the surface. "Maybe." His interest appeared genuine, and she hesitated only a moment before continuing. "We're having a party at the house on Saturday to kick off Dianna's tour. Would you like to come?"

He frowned. "Are you sure I'd fit in?"

"Nobody fits in with this crowd." Stacy grinned. "But I'd appreciate the company."

"I'd like to come. What time should I be there?"

She shrugged. "I expect some people to arrive around midafternoon, and it'll go all night."

"Great. I have early shift that day. I'll come up afterward."

"Which reminds me." Stacy glanced at her watch and grimaced. "I have really enjoyed this, but I have to get back to work. My to-do list is miles long."

"I'm glad you could stay as long as you did." Xander

walked with her outside, then paused beside her car to take her hand in his. "I'm looking forward to seeing you again, Stacy." He placed a gentle kiss on her cheek, then dropped her hand and opened her door. "Drive safely."

"Oh, I will." He could bet on that.

But her mind did wander on the drive home. She liked Xander Morrow. Maybe he could help her survive Nic and Dianna. He was charming and enjoyed many of the same things she did. Even better, he looked so much like Nic, she was immediately attracted.

In fact, she only saw one problem.

He wasn't Nic.

Nic pored over the ancient scroll, looking for some hint of the spell Titania had used on him and Stacy. If he could remove it, his pursuit of Dianna would go much more smoothly.

It wasn't that he didn't like Stacy. Stones knew, he liked her—a lot. But he could scarcely stand to be in the same room with her without wanting to make love to her. Her kisses and touch drove all reason from his mind and made Dianna appear pitiful in comparison.

That would never do. He had to eliminate the spell that befuddled him and made him lust for the wrong woman. Simple magic, such as transporting, could be done with a thought, but to remove a spell of this sort required a precise counterspell.

Wait. There. Was that it? Nic read through the ancient script twice. Yes, a spell of lusting with instructions on removal. He was saved.

He gathered the necessary ingredients and went to stand in the moonlight. A shadow passed a window in the main house, and he hesitated. What would happen to his relationship with Stacy after he removed the spell? Would he detest her or merely see her as a friend?

He wanted to remain friends. They shared more than

simple lust. She made him laugh, made him feel, even when she was angry with him. Yes, he'd ensure they remained friends.

Somehow.

The time had come. He could no longer wait. Mixing the flower pollens together with Fae magic, he offered it up to the moon, reciting the few words that would remove the spell. The bowl vanished from his hands with a clap of thunder.

It was done.

Nic touched his chest. He didn't feel any different. Had it worked? Watching the light dance in a spiral to the moon, he nodded. It had worked.

Now he could win Dianna.

Eighteen

Stacy made a final walk through the house. The first guests were expected at any moment, and she couldn't shake that feeling of something having been left undone.

In the kitchen, the caterers worked to display everything in a decorative manner. Several of them were remaining to act as servers. Stacy had planned to have them serve hors d'oeuvres for the first two or three hours, then set up a buffet for later in the evening. A bar had been set up in the corner of the garden just beside the patio off the living room.

The flowers had been delivered, the majestic centerpieces designed to mimic musical notes, and Stacy had brought in more from her garden to place in vases around the rooms, creating an enticing fragrance.

Kevin's state-of-the-art sound system had been placed in the seldom-used living room, and all the furniture had been pushed to the walls to provide room for dancing. Sometimes it happened, sometimes it didn't. Though with Dianna's exuberant mood of late, Stacy expected something to happen.

Everything shone from the ceiling to the floor, expertly

polished by a cleaning crew who had left only that morning. The four extra guestrooms were ready for those few who needed a place to stay. Thank goodness they had the space. Though she'd made reservations in Telluride for most of the out-of-town guests, some—like Leonard Gallagher, owner of Talent Records—insisted on the comforts of home.

Stacy had just finished putting packets together for all the guests, along with special gifts to commemorate Dianna's tour, and she hurried to place them on a table in the foyer. As far as she could tell, everything looked ready. She'd realize what she'd forgotten when it was needed, no doubt.

Kevin had taken the responsibility for the program Dianna would perform, but Stacy wandered out to the studio. Just to be sure.

The stage bustled with activity as Jermaine shouted out last minute orders to the dancers. The backdrops hung in place, so vibrant, Stacy expected them to be real. After visiting the magical realm, she could understand why Nic made his colors so bright.

Nic.

She paused. She hadn't seen him in the past few days and had even managed not to think about him on a few rare occasions. But he'd been invited to this party. Would he show?

Of course he would. Dianna would be there.

Her sister ran toward her and linked her arm through Stacy's. "Come on. We need to change. They'll be here soon."

"I was just checking."

"Everything here is fine. Believe me. Kevin's been a maniac lately." Dianna grimaced, but her eyes held warmth. "I'm going to amaze them."

"I don't doubt that a bit." On stage, Dianna became a

true presence. She could probably sing "Three Blind Mice" and still stun her audience.

They hurried upstairs into their separate rooms. Stacy pulled a gown out of the closet. Dianna had selected it, insisting it would make Stacy look sexy. Stacy preferred the simpler gown Nic had created for her, but that one held too many memories. Better to go with this.

The color was right for a change, a deep gold that complemented her hair, but the gown was strapless, dipping low enough to reveal significant cleavage. Dianna rarely considered that aspect as she had much less cleavage to worry about, but Stacy hated to feel so exposed. Still, it was the style.

The gown hugged her figure, then flared at the hips and dropped to the floor with a slit riding up one leg well past her knee. Very sexy.

Stacy applied her makeup first and gave up trying to make her hair behave. The short curls had minds of their own. At least, none of them were standing up straight. She should be thankful for that.

Now the dress.

She shimmied into it, twisting to zip it up, then examined her reflection in the mirror critically. Way too much cleavage for damned sure, but other than that, it looked good. Her curves were rounder than Dianna's, but not extraordinarily so.

Why was she worrying, anyway? No one even saw her when she stood next to Dianna.

She slid into comfortable sandals with a low heel. Dianna didn't mind wearing the high-heeled spikes for hours at a time, but Stacy went for comfort every time.

Finished, she went to rap on Dianna's door. "Ready yet?"

"You're ready?" Dianna's wail drifted out. "I can't make my hair behave. Help me, Stace."

Going inside, Stacy found Dianna seated before her

makeup mirror, her hair hanging loose with clips in it here and there. "What are you trying to do?"

"I knew I should have asked Sue to help with my hair. She does such a great job on the road."

Stacy sighed. "What do you want?" They'd been down this road before. Dianna tended to forget who had done her hair during those first few years before she achieved her current success.

"Something to make me look beautiful, like a princess." Dianna frowned at her reflection.

Stacy placed a kiss on the top of her sister's head. "You always look beautiful, but let me give it a try. Curling iron?"

"Here."

"Okay then."

Another hour passed before Dianna was ready, but Stacy had to admit she did look beautiful. The bulk of her blonde hair was piled on her head inside a diamond-encrusted tiara, but several curled ringlets hung around her face, drawing the eye to her perfect features. Her makeup emphasized her blue eyes and full lips, giving her a polished look of youth.

The vivid red dress clung to her like a second skin, the front dropping even lower than Stacy's, revealing so much that they used double-sided tape to ensure things stayed in place. The hem came up high, barely covering her bottom, which necessitated the matching panties beneath. And of course, she wore sandals with high spikes that made her legs look gorgeous.

Stacy sighed. Beside Dianna, she always felt like a sack of potatoes.

"Ready to go?" Stacy asked.

"I'll be down shortly."

Naturally. Dianna liked to make an entrance. Stacy went first to the sound of voices below. Guests had already arrived. Thank goodness Kevin had acted as host, getting them drinks and keeping a conversation going, but he sent Stacy a grateful look as she appeared.

With a practiced smile, she set to work, greeting everyone and ensuring they felt at ease. As other guests arrived, it grew easier. The music business was surprisingly well connected, and everyone knew everyone else.

Kevin made it his business to schmooze with the press representatives they'd invited in order to get them excited about Dianna's upcoming new release and tour. Stacy had everyone else.

She felt Nic arrive, the back of her neck growing warm, but she couldn't turn to look for him until several minutes later. By then he'd vanished in the growing crowd. Just as well. Being near him was too distracting.

When silence fell over the crowd, she knew Dianna had decided to make her appearance. She turned to see her sister enter the living room, a brilliant smile on her face, most definitely on and ready to play to the audience.

As she made her way through the guests, she greeted them all, pausing to chat briefly before moving on. And they all melted beneath her charm and beauty. As usual.

Stacy shook her head. Why did she ever worry about these things? As long as Dianna showed up, everything was fine.

Taking advantage of Dianna's appearance, Stacy stole away to check on the kitchen and the bar. Everyone was eating and drinking. A good sign. And the chatter was growing louder. Another good sign.

Best of all, she hadn't seen nor heard from the last remaining pixie since yesterday. Maybe it would behave today.

She emerged to find all the rooms filled with people. Time to mingle. Leonard Gallagher, the owner of Talent Records, captured her arm as she passed by.

"Stacy, you're looking good."

Funny how his gaze dropped to her chest when he said

that. Stacy forced a smile. "Good to see you, Leonard."

"What's this I hear about you turning everything over to Montgomery?"

"That's right. After this tour, the job is his. I'm moving on."

"On to where? You have nowhere to go." Leonard shook his head. "You're making a mistake, Stacy."

"I don't think so. Dianna needs to branch out in other directions, directions I can't take her. Kevin can."

Leonard narrowed his eyes. "Is he talking to other companies? We have a contract, you know."

"I'm well aware of that, and so is Kevin." Stacy met Leonard's gaze. "As you know, it expires after one more album from Dianna."

"We want to see how this new one goes before we commit any further."

This from the man who sent a telegram telling Dianna this was her best album yet. Stacy gave him a smile and eased away. "So do we."

A drink. She really, really needed a drink. She hated dealing with Leonard and others like him. Let Kevin handle the crap. He actually enjoyed it. She just wanted to write music.

Arriving at the bar, she bumped—literally—into Matthew and Ginger, and they exchanged hugs all around.

"Quite a crowd here," Matthew said.

"You're telling me." Good thing she'd planned for more. "These things always seem to get out of control."

"Not if I know you." Ginger touched her glass to Stacy's. "You've prepared for everything, and I am proclaiming it a major success."

"Wait until you've seen Dianna sing. Then it'll be a success." Stacy searched the crowd for a sign of a server. "Have you had something to eat? Everything I saw looked truly decadent."

"It is," Matthew said. "Haven't you had any?"

"Not yet. But I will." Clutching her wineglass, she dove into the crowd again, then found herself caught in the movement toward the studio as Kevin announced Dianna's upcoming performance.

She bumped into someone as she bent to sip her drink and looked up to apologize. Nic.

Her throat went dry as she smiled. "Nic. Hi. I wondered if you were here."

"Is it always like this?" Though polite, he seemed distant, and Stacy frowned.

"Sometimes it's worse." She touched his arm. "Is something wrong?"

His gaze held no heat. "I removed the spell on us."

"Oh." Then why did her insides still quiver at his nearness, her heart pound in her chest? His Fae charm? "That . . . that's good."

"Yes." He drew his arm away and melted into the crowd, leaving Stacy staring after him. Her stomach felt like lead. Maybe he'd broken the spell as far as he was concerned, but she still felt the same.

At least now she didn't have to worry about fending off his kisses. That was a good thing. Wasn't it?

"Stacy."

Hearing her name, she turned to see Xander approaching, a welcoming smile on his face that she returned. "Did you just get here?" she asked.

"A little while ago. I haven't been able to find you." He linked his arm through hers. "And I'm not letting you get away now that I have."

"Works for me." His approval helped after her encounter with Nic.

"You look wonderful." His gaze covered her from head to toe. "Though I may have to arrest you."

"For what? Indecent exposure?"

He grinned. "No, inciting a police officer to heart palpitations." He placed his hand over his heart. "I'm not sure how much I can take."

She laughed and steered him toward the studio. "Wait until you see Dianna perform."

By the time they reached the studio, the only seats left open were in the back. Stacy didn't mind. She'd seen the show plenty of times. "I'm sorry you can't see better," she told Xander as they settled into seats.

"That's all right. I didn't come to see her." The look he gave Stacy boosted her ego at least fifty percent. Of course, he hadn't seen Dianna perform yet, either.

The lights dimmed, and the music started, the pounding rock beat of Dianna's first major hit had Stacy tapping her toe. No doubt one of the reasons it became a hit. The lights came up to reveal Dianna on the stage in the middle of her dancers, clad in an outfit that made Stacy feel completely covered. Well, Stacy had said Dianna could have more input on her costumes. With luck, Kevin would learn from that mistake.

The music changed, merging into one of Dianna's new tunes. After a few dance steps, she erupted into song. That was the only way to explain it, for the guests jerked back in their seats as if caught in a power blast, then leaned forward for more. Yep, that was the Dianna she knew and loved.

Within moments, everyone was enthralled, caught in the spell that was Dianna's voice. Stacy took the opportunity to study the setting, the movements, the lights, noting where slight changes were needed. But overall, everything was going wonderfully.

Stacy examined the guests, smiling at their reactions, from open-jawed admiration to dollar signs in the eyes. She spotted Nic standing by the wall, his gaze intent on Dianna, his expression openly admiring. Stacy's stomach clenched, and she closed her eyes.

"Are you all right?" Xander touched her arm, and she glanced at him to find his gaze concerned.

"I'm okay. It's . . . just getting warm in here."

"Let's step outside then." Xander rose, his hand at her elbow.

"But the show . . ."

He shrugged. "Not my style, I'm afraid. Come on."

As they emerged, Stacy had to admit the fresh air felt good against her face. "Good choice," she admitted.

"Yeah, you look better already. Besides . . ." He gave her a warm smile. "This gives me an opportunity to be alone with you out of that crowd."

Stacy looked at him in amazement. "You do believe in being direct, don't you?"

"I told you I didn't date much." But mischief glittered in his eyes. "Have I frightened you off?"

"Not yet." In fact, she rather liked his style. Blunt but not aggressively so. She could handle this.

They sauntered along the path with no particular destination in mind. "Do you go with your sister on her tour?" Xander asked.

"Not this time. Kevin gets that duty."

"So you'll have a lot of free time while she's gone?"

"I hope so. I need to build myself a new career."

"A new career? I thought you wrote songs."

"All the songs that I've had performed were for Dianna. I hope to sell some to other singers."

Xander grinned. "Like Donovan Reeves?"

"Exactly like Donovan Reeves." Stacy shrugged. "But I haven't heard anything yet."

"How about letting me hear this new song? I promise to love it. Really."

Xander's enthusiasm made her laugh. "Okay, this way." She led him to the music room, where he insisted on sitting beside her on the piano bench. "Fine, but if I knock you off, it's your problem."

"Hey, I'm tough. I've had training."

Stacy placed her hands on the piano keys, then hesitated. She didn't enjoy the performing nearly as much as Dianna. There was a reason why Dianna was out front and Stacy stayed behind the scenes writing the music.

Xander nudged her. "Come on. I know it's great."

Shaking her head, Stacy tapped her foot, then launched into the song. She didn't sing with it. The words were still too close to her heart, but she could put the feeling into the notes, losing herself in the music.

When she finished, silence reigned for a moment, then Xander spoke, his voice a whisper: "Wow."

She turned to glance at him, then jumped as a single person clapped methodically from the doorway. They both twisted around, and Stacy inhaled sharply.

Nic.

"Outstanding, Stace." He leaned against the doorway, his gaze dark and intent as usual. "Why haven't I heard anything like this from you before?"

"It's my music. It's personal." Her chest grew tight.

"I see." His lips quirked in a dry smile. "Sorry to bother you."

He left as quietly as he appeared, and Stacy struck a dischord on the piano.

Xander cleared his throat. "Can I ask who that was?"

"Nic, our gardener."

"A friend?"

"Used to be." Now she didn't know what he was. She glanced at Xander and found a wariness in his gaze. Forcing a smile, she tried to change the subject. "Did you like it?"

He hesitated, then followed her lead. "It was great. Honest. Are there words to go with it?"

"Yeah. I'm just not ready to sing them for an audience yet."

"Because it's personal."

Stacy nodded. "You're pretty quick."

"That would explain my surprisingly slow rise among the ranks." Xander grinned, then looked over his shoulder. "I hear voices in the distance."

"The show must be over. Back to work." Stacy went to stand, but Xander caught her hand, holding her in place.

He opened his mouth to speak, then closed it again, before starting again. "Don't you dare desert me."

She had the feeling he intended to say something different, but she answered with a smile, "Come along, then. How would you like to meet Preston Winters, the renowned reviewer of musical releases?"

They both rose. "Should I be impressed?" Xander asked.

"Very. He'll be disappointed, otherwise." After dragging Xander through the gauntlet of speaking to everyone and checking on the food and drink, Stacy reached the living room to discover the dancing had started, spilling out onto the patio as guests moved to the beat of an up-and-coming artist from Talent Records. Stacy nodded. Trust Kevin to see to the details.

As she expected, Dianna was in the middle of the dance area, changing partners with regularity as one song progressed into another. Stacy caught Kevin's eye across the room, and he returned a wry smile. Chances that he'd get to dance with his fiancée tonight were slim.

"Good thing you don't have any neighbors near," Xander said into Stacy's ear.

"Why is that?"

"We'd be getting a call for disturbing the peace for sure. I think they're even louder than before."

"They are. More booze."

"I hope you don't let them drive anytime soon."

"They won't. I hired some cabs to take folks to their hotels."

Xander nodded. "You think of everything."

"No, but I try."

They watched in companionable silence until Xander's watch beeped. He quieted it with a grimace. "Time to turn into a pumpkin. I have the early shift tomorrow."

"On Sunday?"

"I told you it was a more than full-time job." He hesitated. "I hate to leave you here with this crowd, though."

Stacy laughed. "I've dealt with them many times over the years, Xander. I'm safe."

"That's what you think. They've lured you into a false sense of trust." The melodrama in his voice hinted at his teasing.

"Come on," she said. "I'll walk you out."

Once on the front stoop, they paused. "I'm glad you came," she added. Xander's presence had made Nic's coolness a little easier to take.

"Believe it or not, so am I." Xander took both her hands in his. "Can I call you?"

She hesitated. Was it fair to lead him on when Nic still owned her heart? Yet he didn't want it. Maybe someone else could win it one day. Someone like Xander. "You have the number."

"Great." He grinned at her. "I'm going to kiss you now."

"Are you?"

"Damn straight." Still holding her hands, he stole a lingering kiss—a kiss that said he'd had more than a little experience at this. As he drew back, he quirked one eyebrow in query.

She smiled. "And you said you didn't date much."

"I don't, but I practice every chance I get." He released her hands, a twinkle in his eyes. "Good night, Stacy."

"Good night." Stacy watched him drive away, then shook her head. Damn, but she liked him. Unfortunately, his kiss hadn't made her think a single lusty thought other than to compare it with Nic's seductive kisses.

She returned to the living room. The rhythmic beat of rock had given way to a more mellow sound: another Talent Records artist, of course. Slow dancing, obviously. Would Kevin get a chance to dance with Dianna now?

Dianna was dancing, all right. With Nic. She had one hand pressed against his chest, the other arm wrapped around his neck. If they danced any closer, they'd combust. Nic murmured something to her, his gaze capturing hers, and Dianna laughed, a melodic, full sound that carried well.

With a slight moan, Stacy sank against the wall, the pain sharp and abrupt. Realization finally hit. This was what it would be like when Nic won Dianna. This was what Stacy would have to live with, face on a regular basis.

She couldn't do it. She couldn't. Rationalizing them being together was one thing; seeing it before her was another.

"They're a fine-looking couple, aren't they?" Leonard paused by Stacy.

"What?"

"Dianna and that guy. They look right together."

Too right. "I guess." Stacy wrapped her arms around herself and nearly doubled over from the clenching in her stomach.

"You going to be sick?" Leonard asked, more curious than concerned.

"I might be." Stacy fled, unable to stand another moment. With the way her gut churned, she might very well be ill.

She stumbled upstairs to the relative peace and quiet and splashed cold water on her face in her bathroom. When Anthony had betrayed her, she'd been hurt and angry, her pride damaged more than her heart, but now . . . now she wanted to curl up and die. This kind of pain cut to the soul.

"What am I going to do?" she whispered. *Leave, of course.* As much as she loved this house and the gardens, she couldn't remain here where she'd see Dianna and Nic in their bliss together. It would be torture.

She sank onto the edge of her bed and buried her face in her hands. The distant sounds of the party drifted in, but another noise blended with it, one she couldn't place. She looked up, frowning. What the hell was that?

Crossing to her bedroom door, Stacy opened it and stepped out. There. It was coming from further up the hallway. The Jacuzzi.

As she neared the room, the noise became identifiable. Water. Running water. Was someone using the Jacuzzi?

She rapped on the door but received no answer. The knob turned easily, and she pulled the door open. "Oh my God."

Water poured out of the room, nearly knocking her over as it flooded the hall. The tap on the Jacuzzi was turned on full as well as the faucet in the sink.

Unheeding of her dress, Stacy waded in to turn them off, but the handles wouldn't budge, no matter how hard she struggled. She next tugged on the plug wedged into the drain. Again with no success. Damn and double damn.

She went back to the door and tried to close it again, but the constant flow of water prohibited that. She kicked at the door, then whirled around as water poured from Dianna's bedroom. "What the hell?"

The situation was the same in Dianna's bathroom, the tub and sink flooding with unstoppable water. This was not good. She slapped her palm against the wall. Now what?

Nineteen

Hearing a noise in her room, Stacy raced down there to see a pixie turning the faucets of her sink. The tub was already filling rapidly. "You are dead meat," she cried. She snatched a towel off the rod and threw it over the creature, managing to catch it by surprise.

She grabbed hold, then found herself thrown against the wall by the pixie's struggle. "Oh, no, you don't." This one was not getting away.

Anger lent her strength as they wrestled, the creature in the towel fighting with more power than she'd expected for something only six inches tall. But finally it quit struggling, resorting to what had to be a string of curses. Well, names couldn't hurt her.

Water was already starting down the staircase when she made her way downstairs, the squirming bundle in her arms. She found Nic in the living room, no longer dancing but standing near Dianna, one of her many admirers.

"Good Lord, what happened to you?" Michael Raymond, an executive at Talent Records, asked as he spotted her. As one, the guests turned to look, and Stacy examined herself.

The dress was ruined, water-soaked, and the slit reached nearly waist high now. Her hair was wet and helter-skelter, and no doubt she wore some of the bath salts that had gone sailing during her struggle with the pixie. Her first instinct was to flee, but she held her head high and waited for Nic to meet her gaze.

"I need your help, Nic." She struggled to keep the panic out of her voice. "Now." As he came toward her, she smiled weakly at the crowd. "Nothing to worry about. Just a small plumbing problem."

She led Nic to the staircase and thrust the towel-wrapped pixie into his arms. "Get rid of this first."

He muttered the spell to send the creature back to the magical realm while climbing the stairs, now more a waterfall than a staircase. "I take it the small plumbing problem isn't so small?"

"It plugged the sinks and tubs and turned the water on full in every bathroom. I can't turn anything off or get the plugs out."

Nic nodded and moved to the center of the upstairs hallway and held out his hands. Closing his eyes, he moved his hands from side to side, lightning forming around them like a halo.

Stacy swallowed. Lightning and standing in three inches of water didn't seem like they went together well, but if Nic felt safe, who was she to argue?

Clapping his hands caused an equivalent thunderclap and burst of light that knocked Stacy to the floor. She blinked, bringing things back into focus, then gaped at Nic. The water was gone. Completely. With no sign it had ever existed.

"How do you *do* that?"

He gave her a crooked grin as he extended his hand to help her up. "Eye of newt, hair of dog . . ."

"Yeah, right." Stacy surveyed all the bathrooms to ensure the faucets were off. The rooms looked undamaged, back to normal. She returned to Nic with a smile. "You're a handy guy to have around."

"So I've been told." His gaze met hers, his eyes dark and unreadable. What was he thinking?

Stacy's throat went dry, the internal quavering starting as it always did when she spent more than thirty seconds in Nic's company. "Thank you. You . . . you probably want to get back to Dianna now. I need to change."

This dress was ruined for all time. She turned to go, but he caught her hand to stop her.

"Wait." He rested his hands on her shoulders, his palms triggering sparks throughout her veins.

"I . . ." She licked her dry lips, and his gaze dropped to her mouth. Something flickered in his eyes, something hot and unidentifiable; then he looked away and ran his hands over her hair, over her shoulders, and down her sides. By the time he finished, Stacy wanted to jump out of her skin from the heat and tingling he'd caused.

"There," he murmured, returning one hand to her hair. "You're better now, too."

She glanced down. The dress was restored to pristine condition, along with the rest of her. Her smile held more than a little warmth. "Thank you, Nic. You're amazing."

"I bet you say that to all the men."

She blinked. Was he teasing her? "Not all."

His expression grew somber, and he cupped her chin in his hand. "We need to talk, Stacy. Soon."

"Talk? About what?" Earlier, she could have sworn he never wanted to talk to her again.

"The man you were with tonight for one thing."

"Xander?" She jerked away from Nic's touch. "What's wrong with him?"

"I just don't think it's wise for you to involve yourself with him."

If Nic had shown some emotion while saying those words, she might have received them a little better. As it was, her temper flared. She couldn't have Nic, and now he was telling her she couldn't even consider the next best thing. "Too damn bad. I like Xander." She hesitated, then decided to go for broke. "What's the matter? Jealous?"

Flames did flare in Nic's gaze then, and he stepped toward her. "You—"

"Everything okay up here?" Dianna appeared on the staircase and looked from one to the other.

"Fine," Stacy snapped.

"Good." Dianna beckoned at Nic. "Come on. You promised to show me that new dance step."

Nic honored Dianna with his heart-stopping smile. "Sure." He left with her, not even bothering with a backward glance at Stacy.

Her eyes watered, her heart ached. Her first instinct was to run to her room and hide, but she couldn't. Not with a house full of guests downstairs.

Holding her head high, she returned to mingle again. No one mentioned her previous appearance. Of course, no one probably cared.

She made nice, polite conversation, dulling the pain in her chest with several glasses of wine, which only created more pain in her head. But she didn't care. Not now. She just wanted to survive the rest of this evening.

Dawn was peeking over the horizon, the first pink rays of sunshine stretching over the mountains, when the final guest left. Others were bedded down upstairs.

Finally.

Kevin walked Dianna upstairs, while Stacy made one last check of the premises to ensure no one was passed out anywhere. The place was a mess. Thank goodness, they had the cleaners returning tomorrow.

She should be sleepy, but her mind continued to whirl amidst the pounding. Her last glass of wine was ebbing, and the emotional ache returned, more painful than anything physical. No, she wasn't going to sleep anytime soon.

Snagging a bottle of wine from the bar, she wandered into the garden, sipping at it. Maybe she could get drunk enough to pass out with no memories, no dreams, no shattered hopes.

Her life was falling apart. She loved the man destined for her sister, and he had the nerve to warn her away from the only other man she might like. She was losing control—of everything: her life, her sister, her music, her emotions.

By the time she sank on a bench in the middle of the gardens, the bottle was half empty, but she didn't feel drunk. Just a little light-headed and not nearly as numb as she wanted to feel. Tears streaked down her cheeks as she went into a poor, pitiful-me routine, blaming everyone but herself for her recent misfortunes.

It was all Titania's fault, she finally decided. The Fae queen had ruined her life. She had made Stacy fall in love with Nic.

She hiccuped and took another swallow from the bottle. It was just damned unfair.

"What are you doing here?"

To her credit, she didn't jump when Nic appeared before her. She merely glanced up at him and frowned. He was a little fuzzy around the edges. "It's all Titania's fault," she informed him.

A slight smile framed his lips. "It usually is." He eased beside her on the bench and took the bottle from her hand. "I think you've had enough of this."

"Not nearly enough. I can still feel the pain." She blinked, trying to bring him into focus.

"Pain?" He touched her shoulder. "Are you hurt? Why didn't you say so?"

"Not that kind of pain." She placed her hand over her heart. "This kind of pain."

"Oh. I see." He hesitated. "Can I help?"

"No." He wasn't about to give up his Anna. "Yes." She changed her mind just as quickly. "Can you hold me?"

"I can do that." Nic wrapped his arm around her shoulders and pulled her close. "Better?"

"A little." She sniffed and swiped at the tears on her cheeks. "My life is a mess."

He grinned. "No, it's not."

"Trust me. It is." She rested her head against his shoulder, closing her eyes to keep the nearby pansies from spinning. It didn't help much. Now her head spun as well.

"I think you need a vacation," he murmured.

"What's that?" She hadn't taken a vacation in ages, unless she counted the traveling she did with Dianna.

"Where would you go if you could go anywhere, do anything?" His voice was soft, intoxicating, and Stacy sighed, snuggling deeper against him.

"I'd run away where no one could find me." She'd had this fantasy several times. "A deserted tropical island where I could be all by myself and run naked if I wanted to." The details of food and shelter were always fuzzy, but the escaping part remained clear.

"A deserted tropical island, eh?"

"Course I doubt if there is one anymore. Every place is filled."

"Don't be too sure of that." Humor lingered in his voice as he pulled her onto his lap, stroking her shoulder and arm. "You've worked hard. Kevin and Dianna wouldn't miss you if you took a break for a couple of days."

"Yes, they would. They always do." Stacy rested her head against his chest now, listening to the rhythmic pounding of his heart. "They'd call the police again." She smiled. "Maybe Xander would come."

"No Xander." Nic's voice grew cold for a moment, then softened again. "Just close your eyes, Stace. Rest. You've earned it."

"No, I haven't. I've failed at everything: Dianna, my songs, love." Fresh tears welled.

"That's the wine talking, not you." Nic wrapped her tight in his arms. "Come, Stacy. Close your eyes. Let go of the tension. Rest."

Rest. He made it sound so easy. Stacy tried to open her eyes, but the blurry colors and swaying of the flowers had her snapping them shut again. She breathed in Nic's masculine scent, a mixture of outdoors and wood. As long as she was with Nic, she was good.

"You're special, Nic," she said without thinking.

"So are you." She thought she felt him place a kiss on her head.

She yawned. "Nic, I . . ." Her control gone, the words threatened to escape. "I . . ."

"Sleep now." He touched her face with gentle fingers and she sighed.

And slept.

Stacy stretched, sliding her legs against the bottom sheet. She had no blanket, yet she wasn't cold. The temperature was warm, hot even. Had summer decided to come to the mountains?

Cracking her eyes open against the sunlight, she groaned. Dear Lord, her head hurt. She closed her eyes again, then frowned as the little she had seen finally reached the functional part of her brain.

She wasn't in her bed.

Forcing her eyes open, she studied her surroundings. She appeared to be in a one-room cottage, the bed tucked against the side with a wicker dresser and chair nearby. A small table with two chairs sat in the middle, a large red hibiscus floating in a bowl on the top. Tucked along one wall was a small shelf loaded with paperback books—enough to last for weeks.

Two doors opened into this room. One with a solid

door—the bathroom, perhaps? The other obviously led outside, for she could see daylight through the hanging bamboo curtain.

Bamboo?

What the hell?

Stacy swung into a sitting position, then slapped her hand to her forehead as the room swayed and hammers pounded from inside. What made her think she could use that brain?

After a moment's hesitation, she stood and gasped. Her evening gown was gone. In its place, she wore some kind of nightgown, if it could be called that. It was barely large enough to cover the important parts and then so sheer, she wondered, *Why bother?*

What was going on here?

The smell of fresh coffee teased her nose, and she homed in on that at once. A pot of coffee sat on a warmer on the table, a large mug beside it. That table had been empty a second ago. She'd swear to it.

But coffee was coffee. She staggered over and poured a full mug, then sipped, feeling the caffeine kicking her brain cells awake. Two aspirin sat beside the mug, and she grinned. Nic was involved in this. She'd bet on it.

She swallowed the aspirin, then looked around for clothing. No matter how warm the air, she wasn't going exploring in this gown. Her other choices didn't turn out to be much better: a dark jade green bikini and a pair of faded blue jean shorts. She hadn't worn a bikini in like . . . ever.

But it fit as if tailored for her, covering enough to be decent, but she tugged on the shorts over the bottom anyway. They were cut so short they barely served their purpose, but at least she felt a little more clothed.

The bathroom contained everything she needed from toothbrush and toothpaste to a shower and shampoo.

Pushing aside the bamboo curtain, she stepped outside. Whoa.

Ocean stretched as far as she see, the edge of the beach only a few yards away from the cottage, lined with white sand and littered with shells. A single reclining lawn chair sat on the beach, a closed beach umbrella beside it.

She staggered to the water and waded in past her ankles, then stood there as the waves slapped against her. Her headache was fading, enabling her to recall bits of her conversation with Nic. Parts of it were hazy, but she remembered the word *vacation,* and this place summed up her dream vacation perfectly.

Alone on a tropical island—no phone, no fax, no computer. Best of all, no people.

Heaven on earth.

If only she could stay. But Dianna would worry about her, especially with her departure less than a week away. True, all the details were covered, but something always broke loose at the last minute.

Always.

Stacy sighed and lifted her face to the tropical sun. Somehow Nic had done it—found her a place in paradise. Maybe he didn't hate her after all. Too bad she couldn't accept the gift.

Turning back to face the cottage, she called his name. He materialized in front of her at once, so sudden and so close that she gasped and staggered back.

"You called?" He wore a wicked grin, humor dancing in his eyes.

"Never, ever do that to a woman with a hangover." She pushed him playfully. "You could be shot for that."

"But what a way to go."

Stacy looked at him in surprise to find his gaze lingering on her exposed and not-quite-as-exposed curves, a hunger she well understood filling his features. Her throat went dry, but she managed to force words free. "This is lovely, but I can't stay here. Dianna will worry."

He shook his head. "It's all taken care of. I gave Dianna your note saying you needed a couple of days to recuperate, and she understood completely."

"My note?" She hadn't written a note.

Nic only raised an eyebrow in response. Of course, he could probably replicate her handwriting without difficulty.

"And she understood?"

"Kevin took charge. He assured her everything was well in hand and that he could handle it. I think he's thrilled you left for awhile. It gives him a chance to shine." Nic rolled his eyes. "Probably taking credit for all the work you've done."

"Kevin helped." She didn't care who took credit for what. The fact that she had two days to spend here loomed before her like a gigantic Christmas gift. "So I can stay here? Really? And no one will worry?"

"You need it, Stace. You were a wreck last night." Nic wound one of her curls around his finger, studying it instead of meeting her gaze.

She gulped, wishing she could recall more of what transpired. "What did I say?"

He grinned. "Nothing I'll hold against you." His gaze darkened. "Or maybe I will." He wrapped his arms around her, cupping her bottom as he pulled her close, her body meshing with his.

Her eyes widened. "N . . . Nic. I thought you didn't like me anymore."

"I tried not to." He brushed her lips, and her pulse launched into a rumba beat. "I removed the spell. I know I did. And I promised myself I'd concentrate on Dianna, that you and I could be friends."

"And we can't be?" That thought hurt almost as much as knowing he belonged to Dianna.

"No." He studied her face. "There are . . . passions between us that I can't escape. I tried to fight it, to deny they existed, but that doesn't make it less true."

"I know." Despite the building fire in her stomach, Stacy pushed herself free and walked away from him. "When you and Dianna get married, I plan to leave, to find a place of my own."

"Stacy—" He didn't sound happy.

"I need to make a new life for myself. It's past time." She kept her back to him and stared over the constant waves.

"Not if it includes Detective Morrow."

The finality of his tone made her whirl around. "And why not?"

"Because it's not real." Concern filled his eyes.

"Not real?" Her chest tightened. "You mean he's Fae? Titania sent him?"

"No, he's mortal, but I could see the spell around him. He's been enchanted, probably to seduce you."

"No," she whispered. She closed her eyes for a moment. Didn't it figure? "I should have known. Why would a good-looking, intelligent man be interested in me?"

"Stop that." Nic crossed to her, unheeding of the waves drenching his pant legs, and seized her shoulders. "Don't belittle yourself like that."

"Excuse me. I've never yet met a man who didn't prefer my sister to me."

"Then they're fools." He cupped her face between his hands. "Do you consider me good-looking?"

"Too much so," she whispered. Devastatingly so.

"And intelligent?"

She could smile at that. "On occasion."

"Well, then." He bent and claimed her lips, his kiss both caressing and demanding.

She knew his touch now and responded at once, the banked desire breaking free. Her lips and tongue dueled with his, seducing, mating, sharing. Her body leapt to life even as she struggled to maintain some control.

With effort, she broke the kiss, though her breathing remained unsteady as she stared at him. "But you belong to Dianna, too."

He released her, closing his eyes, his struggle obvious. Turning away, he walked back to the beach. "You have two days here. Food will be provided for you. If you desire anything, you have only to ask for it."

Stacy stepped toward him, then stopped, clenching her fists at her side. Her heart hammered against her ribs; desire burned in her blood. "But what if what I desire is you?" she whispered.

She hadn't spoken loud enough for him to hear, but Nic spun back to face her, fire blazing in his eyes. "Ask me to stay, Stacy," he murmured.

Their gazes locked. She shouldn't do it. It would be wrong.

She didn't care.

"Stay."

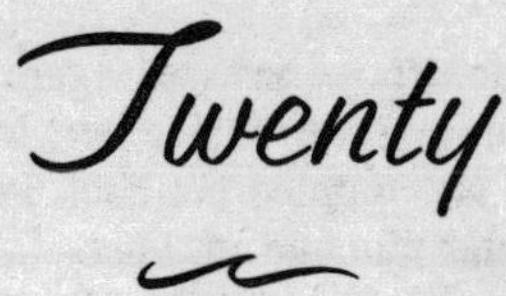

Twenty

Time froze while Nic remained immobile. Stacy didn't dare move. Would he stay?

Between one heartbeat and the next, he crossed to her and pulled her into his arms, his mouth claiming hers. This kiss held no gentleness, no sweet seduction.

Hunger, savage and wild, surrounded Nic, feeding the rampant need within Stacy.

Yes, this was what she wanted, needed.

"By the Stones, I need you, Stacy." He held her head, his fingers entwined in her curls, as he ravaged her mouth, his lips and tongue demanding a response that Stacy gave only too willingly. She craved him like an addict craved a drug long withheld.

Using his free hand, he cupped her bottom and pulled her against his very solid erection. So near and yet so far. She rubbed along that hard length, longing to be free of clothing, her insides clenching, wanting.

She gasped as he left her mouth and blazed a trail along her throat, sending her pulse into overdrive when he nipped at her earlobe. "Nic." His name came out a sob. Frantic desire drove her.

She clawed at his shirt, wanting it gone, wanting her hands on his bare flesh—and just like that, it vanished, along with the rest of their clothing. Their flesh seared where they touched, the heat radiating from their bodies almost palpable.

His erection, free now, pressed against her thigh, and she squirmed, wanting him inside her. Now.

With a growl, Nic toppled her back into the sand, then seized her hips and plunged into her.

Stacy cried out. He fit perfectly—hard, filling her completely. She answered his wild thrusts with her own, her hands clawing his back, her head thrown back. A savagery she hadn't known she possessed emerged, demanding as much from Nic as he did from her.

The fire within her blazed higher, the knot of need growing tighter with each pounding thrust. Yes. Yes. More. This was what she wanted, needed, craved beyond life itself.

"Nic, yes." Her body arched as she exploded, the force of her orgasm rippling through her. For a moment she couldn't move, all energy drained, but Nic didn't pause, only slowed his pace until her passion flared again.

Holding her hips, he plunged deeper, harder, regaining his earlier ferocity as she met him thrust for thrust, the spiral of desire building once more. Lord, she was going to die. No one woman could endure such exquisite pleasure.

She erupted again, a scream ripping from her throat, her entire body arching in spasms. Now Nic joined her in the explosion with a primal growl as he dove deep and remained there, pulsing inside her.

"Oh, God," Stacy whispered when she finally had enough breath to speak. Nothing in her experience had prepared her for this, and she knew with certainty nothing could compare.

Nic rolled onto his back, pulling her on top of him, his

chest heaving with his gasps. "By the Stones, Stacy, you have possessed me."

"Me?" She dropped her head to his shoulder. "I think I've been done in by Fae lovemaking. I can't move." Her bones had turned to water.

He ran his hand over her back, tracing the contour of her spine, then flattening his palm over her buttocks. "That's fine."

She rose up, her palms against his muscular chest, to stare into his eyes. Passion still blazed, momentarily subdued, but behind it was something else: an emotion she couldn't define. "I've never . . . I didn't know I could be like that."

Nic smiled and stole a kiss. "I did. You've given off an aura of passion from the moment I met you."

"An aura of passion. I like that." She smoothed his hair away from his face. "Does making love to a faery make me your love slave now?"

"One can hope." Mischief sparked in his eyes.

She was willing to believe it, despite his teasing. Though exhausted, she already hoped for more. And more after that. Not willing to give that away, she gave him a smug grin. "Of course, you might be too worn out to need a love slave."

"Worn out?" He rolled, tossing her into the sand, then claimed a kiss from her lips that reeked of passion. "We Fae are well known for our endurance."

She sighed. *One can hope.* She raised her arms to encircle his neck, only to bring up a handful of sand that she sprinkled over his back.

"Hey." Nic twisted to remove it, then rose to his knees. "A bit sandy, are we?"

"Well, it does scratch."

"I can take care of that."

Her images of a Jacuzzi soak disappeared as he lifted her into his arms and ran into the surf. When the water reached his waist, he tossed her into the waves. She sank at first, then kicked her way up, sputtering. "It's cold."

"You'll get used to it."

She tried to splash him, but he darted to one side, amazingly agile despite the water's resistance. An instant later, she was splashed from the side. "I'll get you for that."

They cavorted like children, teasing and splashing, diving to capture legs, with an abandon Stacy hadn't felt in years, if ever. When exhaustion set in, she waded toward the shore, her nipples pebbling as the air hit them, capturing Nic's heated gaze.

He smiled slowly, spiking her blood temperature, but she cleared her throat. "You wanted to run around naked," he said.

"I could still use a towel."

He produced one in his hands and approached her with deliberate steps, adding a shiver to Stacy that came from more than cold. Wrapping her in the towel, he used the ends to dry her face, her arms, lingering over her breasts, her stomach, and the junction of her thighs. When his fingers slid free of the towel to delve inside her, she inhaled sharply.

"That's not going to get me dry," she murmured.

"Good." He swung her into his arms, towel and all, and headed for the cottage. "Before was rather . . . wild."

She chuckled. That was an understatement.

"I intend to make long, slow love to you this time."

"Oh, God."

Much, much later, Nic sat across from Stacy at the small table, enjoying the way she devoured the shrimp and lobster supper with enthusiasm. Besides that, he liked watching her.

She looked up and caught him. "What?" she asked. "Good sex makes me hungry."

"Then eat up. You'll need your strength." He grinned

as her cheeks grew pink. Even after intimate exploration of each other's bodies, she could still blush. He liked that, too.

Making love to Stacy had been even more than he'd expected. He'd shared his body with women throughout his centuries among the mortals and pleasured them well, but few—only one, in fact—had given him equal pleasure in return: Anna.

And now Stacy.

She'd dressed in the bikini again, insisting she couldn't eat naked. Which was just as well. He was having enough difficulty keeping his hands off her.

Now he could fantasize about how he'd remove her bikini after dinner, prolonging the ecstasy of loving her again. He hardened at once and shifted into a more comfortable position on the chair. Maybe he should focus on his meal, or they wouldn't get to eat at all.

Stacy had barely finished when she jumped up. "The sun is setting."

He glanced at the door and back. "And?"

"Part of my fantasy is walking on the beach while watching the sun set. If I don't hurry, I'll miss it." She dashed for the door. "Go ahead and eat."

By the time he made it to the door, she was already wading in the water, her face tilted toward where the sun dipped into the watery horizon. If she had a fantasy, he was going to be part of it.

He joined her, wrapping his arm around her waist, tucking her close to him. She fit surprisingly well, despite being taller than Anna, almost better, in fact. Frowning, he shook his head. *No, not better than Anna.*

"Isn't it magnificent?" she asked, watching the horizon blaze with color.

The sunset paled beside her. Her curls flew about her head in wild disarray, another sign of the passion she'd kept hidden from everyone. Everyone but him. Her eyes glowed, reflecting the sunlight. Her entire face was illuminated, the expression of a well-satisfied woman. An expression he used to know well.

Before the night was over, she'd be even more satisfied. He squeezed her waist, and she gifted him with a radiant smile before returning her attention to the sunset.

The end came swiftly, the sun producing a thin sliver of intense brilliance, then disappearing behind the horizon, the light fading quickly.

They stood in silence for several moments until the stars appeared in the darkening sky, brighter and more vivid than she'd ever seen, even in the mountains. Stacy sighed and leaned her head against him. "That was wonderful."

"Do you always have such enthusiasm for simple things?" He found it contagious. During the centuries, he'd seen more sunsets than he could count, but with Stacy he'd actually experienced it.

"It's the simple things that make life worth living," she murmured.

She tugged him into motion, and they walked along the beach, the darkness of night wrapping them in a world of their own. For the first time since Anna had died in his arms, he felt at peace.

"Nic?" The hesitant note in Stacy's voice sent a chill over his skin. He'd been dreading this.

"Don't say it."

"I can't avoid it. We still have to go back. There's still Di—"

"No." Nic swung her around and kissed her roughly. "This is now. That is then." He didn't want this time ruined by what had to be. If he stopped to think . . . "No."

"But—"

"No." He seized her lips, pouring the passion she stirred in him into the kiss. This was what mattered. Here. Now. Teasing her mouth with his tongue, he obtained the response he sought as Stacy moaned and wrapped her arms around his neck, kissing him back with equal fervor.

He slid his hands over her hot, silky skin, pulling her close to move in a seductive dance.

"There's no music," she whispered.

With a flick of his hand, a soft ballad drifted on the air. "Now there is."

They swayed more than danced as he tasted her lips, her throat, her shoulders. Her taste, her scent were uniquely her own. And he would never forget them.

Her breasts swelled, straining the confines of her bikini top. He didn't want her to be uncomfortable. But rather than use magic, he unhooked the top behind her back and let it fall to the sand. He groaned. Better. Her taut peaks rubbed his chest, stirring his desire higher.

He eased her to the sand, remembering to provide a blanket this time, and kissed her again. Her lips could seduce a man all on their own: soft, sensual, pliable, and responsive. The more he kissed her, the more he wanted.

Deepening the kiss, he caressed her breast, drinking her moan as he teased the nipple even tighter. Her breasts were perfect, full enough to fill a man's hand completely, and sensitive enough to drive her crazy.

Stacy ran her hands over his sides and to his thighs, holding him close. He had worn shorts for dinner but made them vanish with a thought. His erection jutted free, hardening more as she touched him.

Not yet. He eased away and drew her breast into his mouth, nibbling on the rigid peak until she writhed, her breathing raspy. Her fingernails dug into his shoulders, flexing as she moved, her hips sliding against his.

Soon. Soon. But not yet.

After loving her other breast, he dipped lower, using his tongue to bring her first orgasm.

But not her last.

He found her mouth again, stealing a burning kiss that

left them both gasping. "What you do to me, Stacy."

Her eyes sparkled in the darkness. "I'm only just beginning." She pushed him back on the blanket and placed kisses over his chest, biting at his hard nipples, eliciting a groan of pleasure.

Her hands roamed over him as well, locating his erection and caressing it as her lips burned a path lower, over his stomach, to his thighs. He arched back when she took him in her mouth, the pleasure so intense he fought for control. He'd never lost control before and didn't intend to start now.

But her mouth and tongue drew him dangerously near the edge until he flipped her back with a roar and buried himself deep within her moist heat. By the Stones, he could spend eternity here.

Her muscles contracted around him as yet another orgasm rippled through her body. He clenched his teeth at the overwhelming ecstasy. Not yet. Not yet.

He moved slowly this time, building her desire to match the fever pitch of his own, until slowly wasn't enough, until their simultaneous cries of pleasure pierced the night.

Collapsing, he rolled to his side, holding Stacy tight in his arms. Their ragged breathing mingled with the crashing waves until Stacy lifted her head from his chest. "You are definitely the stud. That's seven times in one day."

He chuckled. "You're counting?"

"Just curious. You did say the Fae had endurance." He caught the spark of humor in her eyes.

"Shall we go for an even dozen then?"

She gasped. "That's impossible."

With a grin, he pressed her back into the blanket again. "Nothing is impossible."

And he intended to prove it.

Stacy fought against waking up, warm and comfortable within Nic's embrace, but the daylight filtering through the cottage curtain couldn't be ignored. With a small murmur of displeasure, she opened her eyes and propped up on one elbow to watch Nic still sleeping beside her.

He should be exhausted. A dozen. Who'd believe it? She stretched. She would. Her body felt well used, but pleasantly so. Morning hadn't been more than an hour away when they had finally lapsed into slumber, their limbs entangled.

An odd sense of déjà vu swept over her as she studied Nic's face. He grew no beard, but his long, dangerously dark lashes made up for it, softening his sculpted features. His hair fell across his forehead, and she brushed it back, unable to keep from touching him, from loving him.

After this, how could she return home and pretend nothing had changed? How could she stand to see Nic and Dianna together? She had satisfied her desire, for now, but it would never be enough.

And she had yet to pay the penalty.

With a start, she realized Nic's eyes were open, and he was smiling at her, melting her insides without even trying.

"Good morning," she murmured, then glanced toward the door. "Actually, it may be closer to afternoon."

He reached up to toy with one of her curls, wrapping it around his finger. "Sleep well?"

"Wonderfully. Exhaustion will do that."

His smile broadened. "I thought it was the company."

Stacy bent to kiss him, needing that contact at least once more. "Maybe that, too."

As she went to draw back, Nic wound his fingers into her hair and pulled her lips to his, working his sensual magic with a gentle kiss. Passion flared at once so that when he caressed her breast, she was ready, willing, and eager.

Breaking the kiss, she met his gaze, desire burning deep.

He produced a mischievous smile. "How about a baker's dozen?"

Her laugh disappeared in his hungry kiss. That sounded just fine to her.

By the time they finally tumbled from the bed, afternoon had indeed taken control. Ignoring the luscious brunch Nic produced for them, Stacy wandered outside to stare at the sea with its constant movement and changing colors. Just like life: never the same, never what you expected.

She sensed Nic behind her before he rested his hands on her shoulders. "We have to go back today," she said, the ache in her chest intensifying at the thought.

"We could stay. Just one more day."

Part of her wanted to seize those extra hours. With an effort, she dragged responsible Stacy into place. "We can't. I need to be there. You need . . . Anna."

He dropped his hands from her shoulders. "Do you regret this?"

"No." No matter how much pain came after, she would have this memory for the rest of her life. She turned to face him. "No one can regret happiness like this."

"Stacy." His voice was husky as he touched her cheek.

"Take us home, Nic." She closed her eyes, steeling her resolve. "Now."

A moment later, she found herself in the music room, Nic by her side. He wandered over to touch the piano. "Can I ask one last thing?"

He could ask anything, and she'd agree. "What?"

"Sing your song for me. The one you played for Xander."

That? Now? Oh, God. "I don't know that I can right now."

He didn't say anything, but waited. Stacy approached the piano. Who deserved to hear if not Nic?

She settled on the bench, placed her hands on the keys,

then froze. "I can't." The emotions were too near the surface.

"You can."

Closing her eyes, she drew in a deep breath and began. The notes gathered strength as she played, the mood of the music weaving its own magical web. When it came time to sing, she didn't hesitate but launched into a tale of love found, then lost, of love unending, of love wandering through time, always out of reach. Her voice wasn't as full or exciting as Dianna's, but it was adequate.

Tears rolled down her cheeks, but she continued, caught in the passion and pain, of a love that would never be. She finished, the last note wavering around a sob, only to be greeted by silence.

She glanced up at Nic and found his eyes damp. He opened his mouth to speak, but Kevin's voice reached them first.

"That is incredible, Stace." He came into the room. "You're right. Dianna could never sing that, but whoever does is going to make a mint."

Stacy turned to give him a slight smile. "Thanks."

"I didn't hear you get back. Did you have a good vacation?"

"It was . . . wonderful." She stood, not daring to look at Nic.

"Good, you deserved it." Kevin hugged her as Dianna burst in. She ran over and threw her arms around Stacy.

"You're home. Finally."

"Yes, I'm home."

Back in the world of reality.

And lost love.

Twenty-one

Stacy buried herself in work, finding it the easiest way to keep her mind off Nic. Not that it worked, but staying busy helped. In fact, she hadn't even seen him in the two days since she'd returned from her fantasy vacation.

Sometimes she tried to tell herself it had only been a dream. Then perhaps the ache in her chest wouldn't hurt so much. But alone in her bed at night, she relived every moment, every touch, and usually ended up crying herself to sleep.

Fortunately, she had enough to keep her mind from wandering today. Kevin was off at the studio, overseeing the packing and transport of the stage scenery and props. They would be trucked to Denver in preparation for Dianna's opening night—only two days away.

Propping her chin on her hand, Stacy stared at the vase of fresh lilacs that still appeared every day, blooming and fragrant, though the bushes outside had along ago ceased producing. What would happen when Dianna left? Would Nic go with her? Stacy sighed. That would be best. She couldn't see Nic and not want him.

The jangle of the phone made her jump. With a grimace, she lifted the receiver. "Stacy Fielding."

"Stacy, it's Xander."

Her spirits rose, then fell. She honestly liked him, but she'd never love him. She'd given her heart. Not only that, he was bewitched to like her. "Hi."

"Believe it or not, I have Friday night off and wondered if you'd like to go to dinner?"

Part of her was tempted to accept just to escape the tension surrounding the house, but she had a good excuse. "I can't. Dianna's tour opens that night in Denver, and I plan to be there."

"Of course. How about another time? I'm sure they'll give me another day off sometime this millenium."

She had to smile. "I'm sorry, Xander, but I don't think we should see each other anymore."

"Did I do something?" She could hear the puzzlement in his voice.

"No, it's me. I . . . I'm just not ready for a relationship right now."

"Then we'll be friends. Friends can have dinner together."

"Xander . . ."

"You'll discover I can be very tenacious when there's something I want."

Only because you're under a spell. Stacy sat upright. "Can you hold for a minute?"

"Sure. It'll give me time to think of ways to get you to agree."

Shaking her head, she put him on hold and ran into the living room to face Titania's portrait. "I know what you're doing with Xander, and I want it to stop right now. It's unfair to him. I'm not going to fall in love with him, so just give it up."

The frame glowed bright, and Stacy stepped back. *Please, no more pixies.* Instead, Titania's voice flowed from it. "Very well."

Stacy waited for something to occur, but the light only faded. "Thank you."

She rushed back to the phone. "Still there?"

"Yeah." He sounded strange.

"Are you all right?"

"I think so. Just got a killer of a headache all of a sudden."

"I'm sorry."

"About the headache or the fact that you're dumping me?"

"Both."

"Nothing I can say will change your mind?"

"I'm afraid not."

He sighed. "Well, then, best of luck. I'll see you around." He hung up, not sounding nearly as disappointed as he had earlier. With luck, he'd find himself wondering what he ever saw in her now that Titania no longer controlled him.

This messing with magic was no fun.

Though, to be honest, she couldn't imagine Nic without it. His magic was as much a part of him as his hair color. Yet he wanted Dianna to love him as a mortal.

He wasn't a mortal. He never would be. What if Dianna fell in love with the mortal but didn't want the faery?

Stacy frowned. He had to tell Dianna the truth.

And someone had to tell him that.

With a resigned sigh, she headed for the studio.

Nic leaned against a wall, watching Dianna give orders to the packers, who ignored her and went to Kevin instead. She was not having a good day. Organization was definitely not her strong suit.

Over the past couple days, he'd managed to develop an easy bantering relationship with her, but it was still far from the passion he'd shared with Stacy. Nic winced. No, he would not think of that. He had to win Dianna before she left on tour, and he was fast running out of time.

"Come, rest a moment." He snagged her arm as she came near. "Let Kevin handle it. That's what you pay him for, isn't it?"

Dianna pursed her lips as she considered that idea. "I guess I do." She sat on a table near him. "I hate this waiting. I want to open tonight and know now whether they're going to love me or hate me."

"They'll love you, of course. Who wouldn't?" Nic kept his Fae charm banked but produced his most winning smile.

She laughed. "You are so good for my ego, Nic. Want to come on tour with me?"

"I would like that." He intended to stay near her one way or another.

Her surprise told him she hadn't meant the invitation. Too late now.

"I . . . ah . . . we'll see what we can do." Dianna studied him, her gaze lingering on his shoulders and chest. "But aren't you needed here for the gardens?"

"They'll be fine." With the help of the pillywiggins and some simple spells, he could keep the gardens in shape without his presence.

"What about Stacy?"

He struggled to keep any expression from his face. "What about her?"

"I thought you two had something going. Though lately you've just plain ignored her." Dianna gave him a mischievous smile. "Did you have a fight?"

He'd had to ignore Stacy. If he came near her, he'd want to kiss her, make love to her. "There is noth—" He couldn't lie. There was something there, only it was with the wrong woman. "We haven't had a fight."

"You are a strange man, Nic."

"So I've been told." Possibly because he wasn't just a man.

"Nic."

He started as Stacy called his name. Turning, he watched her approach, each step closer adding a beat to his pulse. He swallowed to ease the lump in his throat. "Yes?"

"Can I speak to you for a moment?" She walked away, leaving him to follow her to the back of the studio.

He paused a safe distance away, clenching his fists at his side, fighting the urge to touch her. "What is it? I thought we got rid of all the pixies."

"It's you and Dianna." Stacy didn't look at him as she spoke. "You have to tell her the truth. About you and Anna. About what you are."

"I don't—"

She met his gaze then. "You have to. Your magic is part of who you are. You're asking her to love someone she doesn't really know. That's not fair."

"Life seldom is." Yet she had a point. Though Anna had been attracted to him before she knew he was Fae, he'd told her the truth once he fell in love with her. And she'd still loved him.

"Tell me about it." Stacy stared past his shoulder at the activity on stage, but he caught a glimmer of the hurt in her eyes. Hurt he'd caused.

He reached for her, unable to stop himself, but Stacy backed away, her eyes wide.

"You're right," he said, holding himself back. "I'll tell her."

She bowed her head. "Thank you." She hurried away to join Kevin on the stage, where he stood before the large scenery being dismantled.

Okay, he would tell Dianna. Maybe that would make her memory return. Maybe that would convince her she loved him.

So, why wasn't he more excited?

He returned to where Dianna sat. She gave him an impish look. "What was that about? Hmmm?"

"Just a question she had. Nothing important." He'd survived the encounter. Future ones had to be better, easier. He concentrated on Dianna. "Do you believe in reincarnation?"

She shrugged. "Sure. I guess so."

"Do you think you've lived before?"

Her laugh held the sound of bells. "I like to think I was Cleopatra. Or Judy Garland."

"You—"

"Stacy, look out!"

Hearing Kevin's cry, Nic whirled around. Kevin had apparently walked away, leaving Stacy alone in front of the massive backdrop, which fell steadily toward her. She'd be crushed.

"Stacy." Without thinking, Nic flung out his hand, slowing the fall, allowing Kevin to snatch Stacy out of harm's way and the workers to restrain the scenery. Nic's heart filled his throat, and he took a step toward where Kevin held Stacy in his arms.

Nic forced himself to a halt. If he went over there, if he touched her, he'd never let go. Stacy met his gaze over Kevin's shoulder and gave him a wan smile, acknowledging his intervention.

Kevin led her off the stage. "Come on. You need a drink. Hell, I need a drink." He shook his head. "That was the weirdest thing."

As they left, Nic battled his conflicting emotions. He wanted to rush after them, hold Stacy, kiss her senseless, yet he belonged with Anna . . . Dianna.

Remembering Dianna, he turned and saw her still seated on the table, her face pale and eyes wide. Other than that, she'd given no reaction to her sister's near injury. "What's wrong with you?" He snapped at her, his pent-up frustrations making him careless. "Don't you care about your sister? She could have been killed."

"I . . ." Dianna stared up at him, then flung herself in his arms, trembling.

He embraced her, the feeling so reminiscent of holding Anna, yet overshadowed by the vivid memory of Stacy against him. "Are you all right?"

"I . . . I don't know what I'd do if anything happened to Stacy." She lifted her gaze to his, needing reassurance, and he took the advantage, bending to kiss her softly.

"She'll be fine." He said the words as much to reassure himself as her.

Dianna only clung tighter. "Hold me." Fear filled her voice. For her sister? Of being alone? He wasn't sure which.

"Let's walk, Dianna." He eased her arms from his neck and took her hand in his. "We need to talk."

As they roamed the garden paths, Dianna silent beside him, Nic had to clear his throat twice before he began. "I'm going to tell you something unbelievable," he said finally. "But every word is true."

That brought her gaze to his, curiosity evident.

He hesitated. Where to start? "I was married once before to a woman named Anna who looked exactly like you. I loved her totally. But she died. Only now she's been reborn. As you."

"Me?" Dianna shook her head. "That's crazy. You're only a few years older than me. How could I be your reborn wife?"

"I'm much older than I look." He grimaced. "In fact, I'm timeless. I've existed since the beginning of life and will continue until the end of it, I imagine."

Wariness entered her eyes now.

"Dianna, I'm Fae. A faery, if you will."

"A faery?" She laughed. "Shouldn't you have wings?"

"Not necessarily." He stayed solemn, willing her to believe him. "But I do have magic. Ask for anything, and it's yours."

"Sure. How about that ring from the jewelry store?"

In an instant, he had the ruby ringed with diamonds on his palm and held it out to her.

"Oh my God." Dianna stepped back, then stared at him. "How did you do that?"

"Magic."

She shook her head. "It's a trick of some kind."

He sighed. "What do I have to do to prove it to you, Dianna?"

With a swish of his arm, he changed the nearby pansies into birds that flew into the air around them. Dianna gasped, her eyes wide. "That . . . that's impossible."

"Not for me."

Disbelief lingered in her gaze. What did he have to do? Take her to the top of Palmyra Peak? He grinned, then took her hands in his. "I'm Fae, Dianna. Believe it."

Her cry of alarm coincided with the tightening of her grip on him. "What are you doing?"

"Flying." He'd used magic to float them several feet above the ground.

"I'll fall."

"No, you won't. I control the magic." He eased them gently back to the path. "I'm telling you the truth. I swear it."

She tugged her hands from his, but awe filled her gaze now. "It's true. I don't know how, but it's true."

"I used the name Nic Stone years ago when I was an artist. I painted the portrait of Anna in your living room. She was my wife."

Dianna gaped at him, but she didn't run away, so he continued. "I wanted her to be immortal as I am, but the spell that gave her that life also brought about her death so she could be reborn as an immortal. As you."

"How . . . how do you know it's me?" she whispered.

"You look so much like her. And she liked to sing, though her voice was nothing like yours." Nic approached her, holding her gaze.

"But wouldn't I remember something? Know you?"

"When you were reborn, you lost those memories." He held her shoulders. "But you loved me once." Loved him more.

"Let me convince you, Dianna." He claimed her lips, demanding a response, but what he received was tentative at best, with no fire, no passion. He could have been kissing his sister.

He pulled her closer, deepening the kiss, trying to force the reaction he needed. Pleasant. Nothing more. This wasn't working. Wasn't going to work.

"Dianna."

They jerked apart at Kevin's exclamation. He stood on the path, a short distance away, Stacy by his side. Shocked dismay filled both their faces. Stacy met Nic's gaze, her hurt evident, then looked away.

Kevin, however, stormed toward them. "What the hell is going on here?" Not giving them a chance to answer, he whirled on Dianna. "I trusted you. I loved you. I guess I should know in this business that doesn't mean anything."

"Kevin." Dianna's voice broke on a sob. "It's—"

"I don't want to hear it. We're finished. I'll see the job through until Stacy can find a replacement." He glared at her. "I suppose it's good I discovered your faithlessness now instead of after we were married."

He stalked away, his back rigid, despite Dianna's protests. She burst into heartrending sobs and raced away down the opposite path, leaving Nic standing there. He hadn't had a chance to utter one word.

Feeling a touch on his arm, he turned to see Stacy beside him, tears in her eyes. "She's at her most vulnerable now, Nic. Go to her. You'll win her for sure."

She dropped her hand and headed back for the house, her steps heavy.

Nic remained in the center of the junction, then looked in the direction Dianna had taken. In her present state, he could convince her she loved him, but he still faced one major problem. He didn't love *her*. A dozen kisses weren't going to change that.

Stones, what a mess.

Through her rebirth, his Anna had changed into a person who no longer filled him with passion, whose beauty remained, but little else. Dianna was not the Anna he'd once loved. No matter how hard he tried, he couldn't force something he didn't feel. He'd lost her.

Despite his despair, he held onto the light within him. For he did love . . . the wrong woman.

Drawing in a fortifying breath, he took the path after Kevin and found the man wandering aimlessly. "Kevin."

He turned to face Nic, a single tear track on his cheek, his grief pouring off him in waves. "What do you want?"

"You're making a mistake. I kissed Dianna. She didn't kiss me."

Kevin narrowed his eyes. "That's not how it looked to me."

"Believe me, if she was responding, I didn't notice."

Before Nic could react, Kevin smashed his fist into Nic's jaw, sending him staggering backward. He brought his hand up to his jaw in surprise. That hurt.

"I deserved that," he said. "Want to have another go at it?"

Angry fire blazed in Kevin's eyes. "Pack your things. You're fired. I want you out of here." Not waiting to see if Nic obeyed, he pushed past him and hurried back down the path toward Dianna.

Not to worry. Once Nic spoke to Stacy, he'd be gone forever. Titania would have won.

He grimaced, then winced, touching his jaw. Though

he could heal it, he left the wound. The pain reminded him of his stupidity.

Glancing after Kevin, he nodded. Kevin and Dianna would be all right. Their love was real—like he'd once shared with Anna, like he felt for Stacy.

He loved her. He could continue to deny it, but that wouldn't make it any less real. Only she stirred his passion, made him live. And she deserved to know that. Even if saying the words put him in Titania's power.

Straightening his shoulders, he hurried to the house and found Stacy in the music room, staring at the papers in her hand. "Stacy."

She turned toward him, her expression wary. Her gaze flew to his jaw. "What happened to you? Where's Dianna?"

Nic touched his jaw. "Kevin gifted me with this. I imagine he's with Dianna now."

Her wariness gave way to surprise. "What?"

Nic came to face her and motioned toward the papers. The longer he delayed saying the words, the more time he had with her. "What's that?"

She handed them to him. "A contract from Donovan Reeves. He wants my ballad."

"Of course he does." Only a fool would turn down a song with that much potential. Nic spotted the name on the contract and raised one eyebrow. "Anastasia Fielding?"

Stacy winced. "That's my legal name. I never use it. I have no idea what my parents were thinking when they named me that."

"I like it." Nic set the papers on the piano and took her hands. "And I love you."

Her shock made him grin. She immediately placed her fingers over his mouth. "Don't say that." She cast a worried glance toward the living room.

Taking her hand, he placed a kiss in her palm. "I have

to say it. It's true. I can't keep fooling myself. Dianna may be my Anna reborn, but you're the one I love; you're the one I want."

"Nic." Her eyes spoke for her when her trembling voice failed, stating her love just as clearly.

With a groan, he pulled her tight and kissed her, savoring her taste, the feel of her in his arms, the fire she ignited within him. If this was to be his last kiss, he would enjoy every moment. He expected Titania to jerk him into the magical realm at any second.

But now . . . now was Stacy, responding with equal passion, clenching his shirt with her fists as if to never let him go. His wonderful, beautiful, loving Stacy.

Finally ending the kiss, he stared at her, memorizing every feature. "I love you," he murmured, his voice husky.

Though her eyes watered, she gave him a brave smile. "I love you more."

His gut clenched. "What?"

A blood-curdling scream startled them both. Nic whirled to see Titania in the doorway, and his throat went dry. Time to go.

Before he could move, Stacy darted between him and Titania. "You can't have him." Her fierceness gave him a sad smile. She had no chance against the powerful faery.

"How did you know?" Titania screamed the words, her hair and eyes wild.

"Know what?" He'd never seen her like this. Always she'd maintained total control.

Her hand shook as she pointed it at him. "You are never to enter the magical realm again. Ever."

"With pleasure." Though puzzled, he agreed. He had no desire to return there.

She thrust down her arms by her sides and vanished amidst a brilliant flash of light and a rumble of thunder that shook the house.

Stacy turned to him, her expression as stunned as he felt. "What was that? Why didn't she take you?"

Why, indeed? Nic recalled Stacy's earlier words and grabbed her shoulders. "What did you say earlier? Before Titania's appearance?"

"I love you more." She frowned and placed her hand on his chest. "What's wrong?"

"Why did you say that?"

"Because it's true." As he continued to stare at her, she hesitated. "Because it felt like the right thing to say."

Nic's head whirled. Could it be? It would explain Titania's last fit of rage, her attempts to remove Stacy from the picture. He grabbed the contract again. "Anastasia." Of course.

"What about it?"

"Anastasia means *reborn.*" He met her gaze, realized when she grasped his meaning.

"Does that mean . . . ?" Her eyes grew wide. "Nic, am I Anna?"

He gathered her in his arms and swung her around. "By the Stones, I've been ten times a fool. I should have trusted my heart and not my eyes."

"Are you sure?"

Nic kissed her fiercely. "I'm positive. If I was wrong, Titania would have dragged me away."

"But the spell . . . ?"

He considered that. "I know I removed a spell, and once I did, I convinced myself to concentrate on Dianna, but the appeal she'd once held was gone. Titania's spell was to make me see Dianna as Anna. Only my subconscious, my heart, kept leading me to you."

Dropping to one knee, he kept hold of Stacy's hand. "Marry me? Be with me for all of eternity?"

Stacy's slow smile answered him before she spoke. "I think I can do that."

His heart overflowing, he rose and pulled her close. "Soon."

"Very soon." Stacy nipped at his chin. "We're going to have to tell Kevin all this, you know."

Nic hesitated, then nodded. The man deserved that much. He caressed her cheek. How could he have not seen it? Anna had been more than her appearance, she'd been all the things that made him love her. The same things that made him love Stacy. "Anna . . . Stacy, I love you. Now and forever."

Stacy grinned at him, her eyes twinkling. "I love you more."

Dear Reader,

I hope you enjoy my latest adventure with the Fae. I had wanted to write Nic's story after he appeared in *Prince of Charming*, but the only woman right for him was his wife, Anna. How could I create a romance when the couple was already together? Easy. Split them up and change the rules. I'm sure you'll figure out who Anna really is long before Nic does, but hey, sometimes men have very one-track minds.

My next Fae romance features the two children you met in *Buttercup Baby*: Rose, the faery daughter of Rand and Ariel Thayer, and Brandon, the mortal son of Robin and Kate Goodfellow. Some of you have asked for this story, and it promises to be fun.

Rose takes her magic for granted, much to Brand's chagrin. He's always wanted magic. He's even become a renowned magician, and to see Rose abuse her power angers him. So what happens when he tricks Rose into betting she can get along without her magic? Chaos, of course.

I love to hear from my readers. You can e-mail me at **karen@karenafox.com** or write me at P.O. Box 31541, Colorado Springs, CO 80931-1541.

Karen Fox

Contents

About this Book

KEY TO SYMBOLS

- map reference to the maps found in the What to See section
- address or location
- telephone number
- opening times
- restaurant or café on premises or near by
- nearest underground train station
- nearest bus/tram route
- nearest overground train station
- ferry crossings and boat excursions
- travel by air
- tourist information
- facilities for visitors with disabilities
- admission charge
- other places of interest near by
- other practical information
- ➤ indicates the page where you will find a fuller description

This book is divided into five sections to cover the most important aspects of your visit to Tunisia.

An introduction to Tunisia by the author.
Tunisia's Features
Essence of Tunisia
The Shaping of Tunisia
Peace and Quiet
Tunisia's Famous

The author's choice of the Top Ten places to see in Tunisia, each with practical information.

The five main areas of Tunisia, each with its own brief introduction and an alphabetical listing of the main attractions.
Practical information
Snippets of 'Did you know…' information
3 suggested walks
4 suggested tours
2 features

Detailed listings of the best places to eat, stay, shop, take the children and be entertained.

A highly visual section containing essential travel information.

Maps
All map references are to the individual maps found in the What to See section of this guide.

For example, El Jem has the reference 28C5 – indicating the page on which the map is located and the grid square in which the amphitheatre is to be found. A list of the maps that have been used in this travel guide can be found in the index.

Prices
Where appropriate, an indication of the cost of an establishment is given by **£** signs:
£££ denotes higher prices, **££** denotes average prices, while **£** denotes lower charges.

Star Ratings
Most of the places described in this book have been given a separate rating:

✪✪✪	Do not miss
✪✪	Highly recommended
✪	Worth seeing

Tunisia

by Peter Lilley

After working as a local newspaper journalist and radio reporter, Peter Lilley became a full-time travel writer in 1983. He first visited Tunisia three years later and has made regular trips ever since. Specialising in North Africa and the Far East, he has contributed to many newspapers and magazines and is an almost weekly contributor to the *Travel Trade Gazette*.

Above: *camels arriving at the Festival du Sahara, Douz*

AA Publishing

Above: *local women shopping in the market at Houmt Souq*

Find out more about AA Publishing and the wide range of travel publications and services the AA provides by visiting our web site at www.theAA.com/bookshop

Written by Peter Lilley

First published 2000
Reprinted Feb and Aug 2000; Feb 2001; May 2002; April 2003
Reprinted 2004. Information verified and updated.
Reprinted Jul and Dec 2004
Reprinted Feb 2005.

Published by AA Publishing, a trading name of Automobile Association Developments Limited, whose registered office is Southwood East, Apollo Rise, Farnborough, Hampshire GU14 0JW. Registered number 1878835.

A CIP catalogue record for this book is available from the British Library.

A02559

Colour separation: Chroma Graphics (Overseas) Pte Ltd, Singapore
Printed and bound in Italy by Printer Trento S.r.l.

Viewing Tunisia

Above: *an ancient mosque above the abandoned village of Douiret*
Right: *sweet-smelling jasmine offered in Hammamet*

Peter Lilley's Tunisia

Flying Visits
There is no need to visit Tunisia for a full week or a fortnight. Easy access from Europe has increased the popularity of three- and four-night short breaks. Tunis, with more than enough attractions to interest the short-stay visitor, is a popular destination, and twinning Tunis with Hammamet makes for an exciting city/beach combination – a tonic at any time of year.

Inset: *a* médina *door studded with patterns and symbols*
Below: *men intent on a game of draughts*

Tunisia has rapidly become accepted as a mainstream Mediterranean holiday destination but it still attracts a lot of first-time visitors. In unfamiliar surroundings there is always the temptation to be cautious, trusting that the land and its people will reveal themselves in their own time: with Tunisia the secret is to immerse oneself in the culture from the moment of arrival.

If there's a choice, pick one of the early summer months and go to one of the major centres such as Tunis, Sousse or Sfax. Drop the bags and venture straight out into the streets in the late afternoon, the most magical time of day. Tunisians are at their most animated and convivial in the early evening, having been up since sunrise or soon after, and there is an infectious gaiety in the air, a sense that whatever fortunes have been won or lost, the day is over. On every street corner and scrap of rough ground, boys kick footballs and in the smoky bars and cafés this is the time for coffee, cards, chatter and *chichas* with perhaps a bottle of Celtia, Tunisia's only beer.

In the mysterious *médinas*, where skinny cats slink into every corner and there is the feeling that a thousand secrets lurk behind every studded door, shops and stalls in the *souqs* and surrounding streets spring to life to serve the homeward bound with the freshest food. Chickens are butchered to order, fish are only minutes out of the sea, bread is baked on the spot and stacks of colourful vegetables are haggled over with shouts and handshakes.

Tunisia's Features

A tradtional Bedouin band tunes up for a desert festival

Geography

• Tunisia is the northernmost country in Africa; it lies just 80km southwest of Sicily. It measures 750km from north to south but only 150km from west to east, making it slightly larger than the US state of Florida.

• The northern and eastern coastlines are bordered by the Mediterranean, while much of the southern half of the country is within the Sahara Desert.

Climate

• Summers are hot and dry. In July and August daytime temperatures on the east coast average 30°C with 12 hours of sunshine; in the desert it can reach 45°C.

• In the north, winters are mild but quite wet with occasional snow.

• Daytime temperatures in the south average 20°C but fall rapidly at night to near freezing.

People

• Tunisia has a population of just over nine million.

• More than half the population is under 18 and more than 30 per cent under 14.

• About 98 per cent of the population are Muslim with tiny Christian and Jewish minorities.

•Tunisian women enjoy considerable freedom when compared with other Muslim countries, though many older women still choose to wear the veil.

Language

• Arabic is the official language but almost everyone speaks some French.

• It is rare to find English or German spoken outside the main beach resorts.

The Berbers
The Berbers have been found in various parts of North Africa since *c*2000 BC and are generally considered to be the original Tunisians. A few centres of Berber culture survive in southern Tunisia where the people still speak the Berber language and are noted for their colourful dress, beautiful jewellery and weavings, and intricate woodcarving.

Essence of Tunisia

It would be easy to get the impression that Tunisia's only attraction is the beach resorts, and thousands of foreign visitors are drawn each year by the enticing combination of sandy beaches and sunny skies. The country also has some of the most beautiful hotels in the Mediterranean, whitewashed palaces surrounded by well-tended and spacious gardens awash with bougainvillaea. But there is much more. Even the shortest journey outside the main tourist centres reveals a fascinating and totally different culture with the quietly pervasive impact of Islam and its graceful architecture, many archaeological treasures, vivid landscapes and an exciting and varied cuisine.

Inset: *a jetskier at Zarzis beach*
Below: *visitors take to the 'ship of the desert'*

THE 10 ESSENTIALS

If you only have a short time to visit Tunisia, be sure not to leave the country without having sampled some of the essentials:

- **Buy a piece of pottery** such as an ashtray or vase, large plates or bowls. Blue and white are the traditional colours while fish decorations add extra value. Nabeul (➤ 52) and Guellala (➤ 79) are the major centres but pottery is on sale almost everywhere.
- **Eat a *brik***. This unusual egg dish is popular as a starter at lunch or dinner, but take care, it is not the easiest thing to handle!
- **Haggle** for souvenirs in a bustling *souq* especially in Tunis (➤ 35), Sousse (➤ 62) or Sfax (➤ 73). Start the bidding at around half the price you would really be prepared to pay.
- **Go to sleep** with a sweet-smelling sprig of jasmine on your pillow. Women wear garlands of the flower around their necks while men sometimes tuck one behind their ear.
- **Take a close look** at a traditional Tunisian door. Usually brightly painted, they are made of solid wood and decorated with black metal studs.
- **Ride a camel** at sunset in Douz (➤ 83), the gateway to the Sahara Desert.
- **Eat *baklava***, a honey-laced pastry filled with crushed nuts, at one of the many *pâtisseries*.
- **Listen to the *muezzin*** calling the Muslim faithful to prayer five times a day. Many mosques are closed to non-Muslims but outside prayer hours you may be able to approach as far as the door for a glimpse.
- **Visit a traditional *hammam*** (Turkish bath) and relax for an hour or two to experience one of Tunisia's great unsung pleasures.
- **Take home fresh dates**, extra virgin olive oil and a jar of fiery hot *harissa* paste.

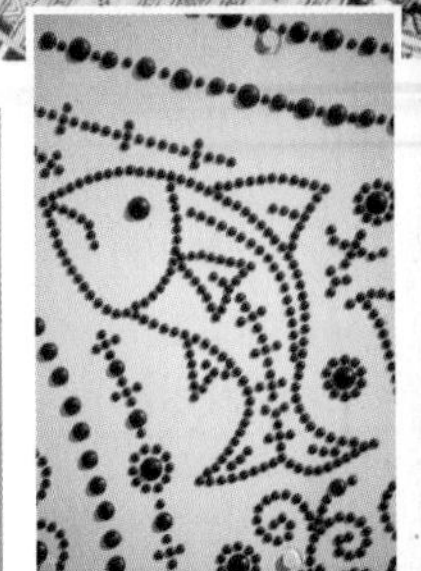

Fish are a favourite motif for use in decorative work

The Shaping of Tunisia

c2000 BC
Berbers settle in Tunisia interbreeding with black Africans from south of the Sahara and blue-eyed, blond-haired immigrants from the north.

1100 BC
Phoenician traders establish trading posts along Tunisia's Mediterranean coastline including Sousse, Bizerte and Utica.

814 BC
The Phoenicians build the walled city of Carthage and rule a vast commercial empire for the next seven centuries.

Dido, Queen of Carthage, inspects the progress of work during the rebuilding of her city

146 BC
A long and violent struggle ends with the destruction of Carthage by the Romans.

44 BC
After defeating Pompey at the battle of Thapsus near Mahdia, Julius Caesar rebuilds Carthage. Over the next 400 years it becomes a major administrative centre and the third largest city of the Roman Empire.

AD 423
Carthage is destroyed by the Vandals, a Germanic tribe which has already pillaged its way through France and Spain, desecrating religious images.

533
Byzantines restore the port of Carthage and create a series of massive fortresses and magnificent churches.

647
Following the death of the Prophet Mohammed in 632, Arab armies arrive from the east killing the Byzantine Prefect Gregory at Sbeitla in 647 and imposing Islam on the population.

797
Ibrahim ibn al Aghlab puts down a revolt and founds a dynasty. The Aghlabids build the Grande Mosquée de Sidi Oqba at Kairouan and the Grande Mosquée at Sousse, and introduce a sophisticated irrigation system, planting thousands of citrus trees.

909–1229
The Fatmids, Zirids, Almohads and Almoravids take turns at control.

1230–1574
The Hafsids make Tunis the capital and establish international trade in

gold, ostrich feathers, ebony, ivory and precious oils during a relatively long period of stability. This is followed by a century of decline.

1574
After a power struggle between the Ottoman Turks and Spanish Hapsburgs Tunis comes under the control of the Ottoman Empire, which appoints a ruling *pasha* who relies on a network of local *beys* (provincial governors) to enforce laws and collect taxes.

1704–1881
Hussein ibn Ali Turki takes control. Under the Husaynids the economy prospers as the *bey*s exercise their monopoly to generate a vibrant trade in agricultural products.

1878
The Ottoman Empire is divided up at the Congress of Berlin and France announces it has a claim on Tunisia. Later it invades the country and in 1883 declares Tunisia a French protectorate.

1934
Radical lawyer Habib Bourguiba (➤ 14) forms the Neo-Destour Party.

1938
Anti-French demonstrators are killed by troops in Tunis. Bourguiba is arrested and imprisoned in France.

1956
Tunisia gains independence from France and a year later declares itself a republic with Habib Bourguiba as its first president.

1987
President Bourguiba is removed from office by his prime minister, the former army general Zine el-Abidine Ben Ali.

1988
Tunisia forms the Union du Grand Maghreb (Arab Maghreb Union) with Morocco, Algeria, Libya and Mauritania to help counter the impact of the European Union.

1991
President Ben Ali condemns the Iraqi invasion of Kuwait, but does not send troops to join the US-led Desert Shield force against Iraq.

1995
Tunisia signs an association agreement with the European Union which will lead to free trade with the EU after 12 years.

2000
Habib Bourguiba dies.

Habib Bourguiba, depicted with his dog, is commemorated by this statue in the public gardens in central Tabarka

Peace & Quiet

It is easy to get away from it all in Tunisia, since there is only one major city and much of the rest of the country is sparsely populated. The country has only a handful of national parks and municipal gardens, but there are few restrictions on wandering in the countryside.

The Coastline

The Roman historian Pliny the Elder (AD 23–79) described the Tunisian coastline as being one of the finest in the world, and nearly 2,000 years later he would probably still hold the same view. Tourist resorts have developed along some of the finest stretches of beach, but with more than 1,100km of coastline available, much of the rest remains completely unspoilt.

Quieter beaches include Raf Raf Plage, a glorious crescent-shaped stretch of fine white sand 38km east of Bizerte facing the small rocky island of Pilau, which is good for snorkelling and underwater fishing. The beach is partly bordered by the small village of Raf Raf and by dunes and pinewoods. Near by is the isolated beach of Sidi Ali el Mekki, where a small number of cafés and a few straw huts for camping are the only facilities. To the west of Bizerte, Rass Engelah is overlooked by a picturesque Moorish lighthouse.

The area around Tabarka has been dubbed the 'Coral Coast' (➤ 43) and the waters are so crystal clear that it offers excellent diving.

The beach at Raf Raf is popular with day trippers from Bizerte and Tunis

The Desert

The Sahara Desert covers nearly the whole of southern Tunisia and the popular image of shifting sands sweeping across a relentlessly barren landscape is an accurate description of the landscape found in the Grand Erg Oriental. Only suitable for four-wheel-drive vehicles and then only when accompanied by skilled drivers and guides, most holidaymakers are content to experience a less harsh version of the desert.

Wind-furrowed sand dunes near Douz

This can be found in the area around Tunisia's two great *chotts* (salt lakes), Chott el Jerid (▶ 82) and Chott el Gharsa (▶ 87), which sit below sea level and are fringed by beautiful oases. Only a few kilometres outside the main desert centres of Nefta (▶ 85) and Tozeur (▶ 87) one can be driving on a totally empty road. Get out and walk around and the silence is almost deafening. Douz (▶ 83) is one of the best places to go for a camel ride into the desert.

DID YOU KNOW?

Arabs have more than a hundred different words to describe a camel. A familiar sight in the southern half of the country, the so-called 'ship of the desert' is an extraordinary animal which can survive for months without water and when it does finally get the chance for a drink it can consume up to 130 litres in one go. Talk about quenching your thirst!

Flora and Fauna

Tunisia was once home to an exotic array of wildlife, including lions and elephants, which has long since disappeared. Today the largest animal existing in any number is the wild boar which is found in the forests around Tabarka (▶ 43) where there are also jackals, porcupines and mongooses. Wild animals in the desert region include foxes, snakes, horned vipers and scorpions – so it is best not to walk around barefoot!

More than two hundred different species of bird have been recorded in Tunisia. Jebel Ichkeul National Park (▶ 19, Top Ten) is a stopping-off point in the spring and autumn migration seasons between Europe and Africa.

Prickly pears are known here as Barbary figs

Tunisia's Famous

Below: *Habib Bourguiba strove for independence from French rule, and instituted education for all*

Habib Bourguiba (1903–2000)

Habib Bourguiba became the republic's first president and is widely known as the father of modern Tunisia. He was born in Monastir in 1903 and educated at the elite Sadiki College in Tunis, and in Paris where he studied law. Bourguiba's political career did not begin until 1932 when, back in Tunis, he started a newspaper, *L'Action Tunisienne*. Two years later he founded the populist Neo-Destour Party which was committed to independence from France. Six months after its foundation the party was declared illegal and for the first of many times over the next two decades Bourguiba was arrested and imprisoned.

Immediately after World War II Bourguiba travelled to many world capitals highlighting Tunisia's plight, gaining considerable support. In 1955 he accepted a French plan for an autonomous state and on 20 March 1956 the country gained independence. The following year the new republic was established and Bourguiba became its first president. He governed for 31 years, until removed from office by the current president Zine el-Abidine Ben Ali. He was sometimes criticised for his autocratic style but his achievements included forging a strong national identity, providing for universal education and elevating the role of women in Tunisian society.

Ibn Khaldun (1332–1406)
Ibn Khaldun, the Tunis-born philosopher and politician, spent four years writing a massive volume on North African history but made a greater impact with *Muqaddima*, a brief introduction to the history of the world. Khaldun is thought to be the first person to write about cyclical patterns in history and the nature and development of society, which now form some of the basic principles of modern-day sociology.

Hannibal (247–182 BC)

Hannibal, although born in Spain, is considered an honorary Tunisian as his birth took place on Carthaginian territory. His most famous exploit occurred during the second Punic war when he invaded Italy from the north after crossing the Alps with an army of 40,000 men and 300 elephants. Support from Carthage collapsed just as Rome seemed to be within his grasp and he was recalled home. In 202 BC Hannibal was defeated by the Roman general Scipio Africanus at the battle of Zama near Le Kef. Forced into exile in Syria and later to (what is now) Turkey, he committed suicide by poison to avoid capture by the Romans.

Right: *after crossing the Alps with his elephants, Hannibal descends into Italy*

Top Ten

Above: *parts of Ksar Ouled Soltane are over 400 years old*
Right: *Tunisia's most famous mosaic depicts Virgil, Clio and Melpomene*

1
Dougga

28B5

110km southwest of Tunis

Daily 7–7 (8:30–5:30 in winter)

Small café (£) near the entrance serving drinks and light snacks in summer, drinks only in winter

Hourly daytime services from Tunis to Le Kef which stop at Nouvelle Dougga 3km from the site. Difficult to reach the site without a car. Taxis available from Tebersouk

Cheap

Summer plays and concerts in Dougga's theatre. Times and dates variable

Dougga is a splendid monument to Roman precision building, with many columns still standing

Tunisia's best-preserved and most spectacular Roman ruins have a dramatic setting on a hillside with wide views of the surrounding countryside.

The Roman town of Dougga was built on the site of the ancient settlement of Thugga, which had become the seat of the Numidian king Massinissa in the 2nd century BC. Dougga prospered under Roman rule and at its peak is thought to have had a population of between 5,000 and 10,000 people. In the early 1950s residents were moved to the nearby purpose-built village of Nouvelle Dougga.

Fervent archaeologists will find Dougga worth a full day's visit, and even those with a limited interest need to allow at least two hours just to see the main buildings. It is advisable – particularly in summer – to arrive as early as possible to avoid the crowds and intense midday heat.

Dougga's star attraction is the well-preserved Capitol built in AD 166 and dedicated to Jupiter, Juno and Minerva. The Roman Theatre, cut into the hillside, is the most complete of any in Tunisia and is still used by a summer touring company. There is a magnificent view over the surrounding wheat fields and olive groves from the impressive Temple of Saturn, dedicated to the sun god Baal Hammon. The centrepiece of the nearby Plaza of the Winds is a compass-like wind-indicator inscribed with the names of the 12 Roman winds. The house of Trifolium is thought to have been the town's brothel; the latrines immediately beside it suggest that this most private of functions was a sociable experience – a dozen seats are set in a horseshoe-shaped row.

2
El Jem

The amphitheatre at El Jem is one of the Roman Empire's greatest legacies to Tunisia.

El Jem is only slightly smaller than the Colosseum in Rome, but it is better preserved and much more imposing, though situated incongruously at the end of a street of modern houses. If it were near a major European holiday destination there is little doubt it would be packed solid with visitors year-round, so try to see it soon before the crowds get there. Early morning is good for taking photographs and dusk is particularly atmospheric.

There is very open access; a few areas have been roped off but only to protect visitors from dangerous drops. Pleasingly, there are no signs or notices inside the amphitheatre, making it easier to imagine the colourful festivals or the bloody dawn-to-dusk gladiatorial contests that were held here. The gladiators – often simply petty thieves, debtors or prisoners – would be pitted against each other or against wild animals to fight to the death.

Built between AD 230 and 238 in the busy market town of Thysdrus, the amphitheatre could seat crowds of more than 30,000. Measuring 149m long by 124m wide, even today it would be considered an impressive building achievement but without modern equipment it is an awesome feat of engineering. In the absence of suitable materials locally, blocks of sandstone were transported from quarries 30km away while water was carried 15km through an underground aqueduct.

El Jem archaeological museum has some attractive 3rd-century mosaics on display.

28C5

70km south of Sousse

Daily 7–7 (8–5 in winter)

Café (£) directly opposite entrance to the amphitheatre

On the main line south to Sfax and north to Sousse and Tunis

None

Moderate

International Festival of Symphonic Music in July

Archaeological Museum

1km south of the amphitheatre on the road to Sfax

7–7 (8–5 in winter)

Included in price of ticket to amphitheatre

The Roman amphitheatre at El Jem could hold 30,000

3
Iles Kerkennah

A watchtower built in the 16th century for surveying the islands

The cluster of seven islands 20km off the coast of Sfax has been called 'The Last Paradise' and would appeal to anyone trying to get away from it all.

28C4

20km east of Sfax

La Sirène (££) on the beachfront in Remla (► 96)

Regular ferry services to Sfax from Sidi Youssef. The journey takes about an hour with at least four services a day in winter and departures every two hours in summer

Buses meet all ferries and all stop in Remla

None

Once a place of exile for the Carthaginian general Hannibal and Tunisia's former president Habib Bourguiba (► 14), there are two main inhabited islands, Chergui and Gharbi, joined together by a causeway. The islands are reached by ferry from Sfax, arriving at Sidi Youssef on the south-western tip of the islands, with a single main road running 35km north to the fishing village of El Attaia.

Fishing remains the main source of income for most of the 15,000 islanders. Strings of clay pots for catching squid can be seen on many quaysides; palm fronds are used to channel fish into waiting nets. Although tourism now supplements the islands' economy it remains very low-key and recent plans by the Tunisian government to transform Iles Kerkennah into a massive purpose-built resort area appear to have been dropped. The small west coast tourist zone of Sidi Frej consists of a handful of modest hotels.

Borj el-Hissar, an old fort 3km north of Sidi Frej, was built by the Spanish in the 16th century; it is surrounded by Roman ruins and has the remains of several mosaics. Remla, the biggest settlement, has a few shops and cafés and one hotel, the Jazira (► 104). With its shallow waters and long stretches of empty sandy beaches, the area is well-suited to walking and cycling.

4
Jebel Ichkeul National Park

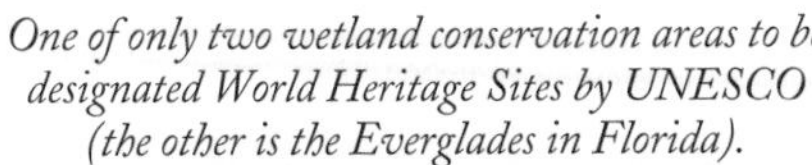

One of only two wetland conservation areas to be designated World Heritage Sites by UNESCO (the other is the Everglades in Florida).

Telescopes enable visitors to view the birdlife of Lake Ichkeul

Jebel Ichkeul is the most important bird sanctuary in North Africa and provides a vital stopping point for birds migrating between Europe and Africa. If you visit at dawn or dusk from October to February, thousands of waterfowl can be spotted on the lake.

Rarer birds on the lake include the marbled teal and the purple gallinule, one of Tunisia's most colourful birds. Looking rather like an oversized moorhen, it has a bright red beak and gleaming purple-blue plumage. Sandpipers, stints and stilts are regularly found on the shores of Lac d'Ichkeul and Moussier's redstarts which are indigenous to North Africa can be spotted in the scrub. The park is also home to many animals including water buffalo, wild boar, jackals, otters and porcupines.

The park is a tranquil and uplifting place to visit at any time of the year; there are some picnic tables and several walking trails. Poppies and wild chrysanthemums bloom in the fields around the lake, and from the car park a steep climb leads to a small **Eco-Museum** which details the area's flora and fauna and explains the ecological importance of the lake. It also has a collection of stuffed birds.

There is nowhere to stay in the park and camping is not permitted, but it is easily accessible from Tunis.

28B6

30km southwest of Bizerte

Daily 7–6

Bring your own picnic, tables provided

No public transport; hire car essential

None

Inexpensive

Eco-Museum

9–12, 1:30–4:30

None

Cheap

5
Kairouan

28B5

70km west of Sousse

Sabra (£), avenue de la République – good value set menus. Fairouz (£–££) just north of the *souqs* on rue des Tailleurs – worth paying extra for

Bus station on the main route between Tunis and the south

Place des Bassins des Aglabides 77 231 897 Sat–Thu 8–6, Fri 8–1. Multiple entry ticket provides access to most of the city's major attractions

Mouled Festival to celebrate the Prophet Muhammad's birthday, June

Grande Mosquée de Sidi Oqba

Boulevard Ibrahim ibn Aghlab (main gate on Boulevard Brahim ben Lagheb)

7:30–2 (8–2:30 in winter). Closes noon on Fri

Cheap

None

Kairouan is Tunisia's holiest city, with more than 50 mosques within the médina.

Kairouan is the fourth most important city in the Islamic world after Mecca, Médina and Jerusalem. The **Grande Mosquée de Sidi Oqba** (Great Mosque) is the star attraction here; the existing building was constructed by the Aghlabids in AD 863. Non-Muslims are forbidden to enter the prayer hall with its 400 marble pillars, many of which were recovered from the ruins of Carthage and El Jem, but visitors may be allowed to take a look through one of the 17 heavy cedar wood doors at one of the world's oldest pulpits decorated with 250 carved wood panels. Entry may also be permitted to the 128-step staircase – made from Christian tombstones – to the top of the square minaret for a superb panorama of the city.

The Mosquée des Trois Portes (Mosque of the Three Doors) also dates from the 9th century and features three arched doorways providing separate entrances for men, women and children.

The Zaouia de Sidi Sahab (Shrine of the Companion) on avenue de la République is the burial place of Abou Zamaa el-Balaoui, a friend of the Prophet. It is sometimes known as the Barber's Mosque as el-Balaoui always wore a medallion containing three hairs from the Prophet's beard. The original mausoleum dates back to the 7th century but tiled archways, antechambers and beautiful floral mosaics were added at the end of the 17th century.

The Bassins des Aglabides (Aghlabid Pools), ten minutes' walk to the east, were part of an elaborate 9th century water system which collected rain from the Tell Plateau via a 35km aqueduct.

Footwear is removed before entering the prayer hall of the Zaouia de Sidi Sahab

6
Ksar Ouled Soltane

28C3

22km east of Tataouine

All day

Hôtel les Ghorfas (£), 6km west of Metameur; Hôtel Ksar Hadada (£)

Three buses a day from Tataouine

Free

Ksar Hallouf (☎ 75 647037). Ruins of 12th-century *ksar* 8km west

The exterior steps of the ksour *look less than safe*

One of the enduring legacies of the Berber culture, ksour *originally served as fortified grain stores.*

Built from mud and stone, *ksour* (singular '*ksar*') are a familiar sight in southern Tunisia especially around Tataouine. In the hostile desert climate there might only be a good crop once every few years making it essential to defend supplies from attack by other tribes. Cool conditions inside the *ksour's* claustrophobic, barrel-vaulted rooms (known as *ghorfas*) meant that grain could be kept for several years without deteriorating. It was typical for *ksour* to be clustered together around a courtyard and to be linked by internal steps and passageways. Usually three or four stories high, some of the *ksour* at Ouled Soltane have precarious-looking outside steps.

The earliest surviving *ksour* are up to 800 years old but Ksar Ouled Soltane is among the best-known because it is particularly well preserved. Buildings in the first courtyard are more than 400 years old while the second complex dates from around 1850. Situated some way off the beaten track – nearly a three-hour drive from Jerba – like many of Tunisia's most impressive sights it remains largely undiscovered by tourists and it is not unusual to find you are the only visitor. One of the most rewarding times to visit is on Friday afternoons, when the courtyard becomes a meeting point for the local community.

A visit to Ouled Soltane is often combined with trips to other *ksour* in the area including the 13th-century Ksar Hallouf near Zammour, part of which has been converted into a very simple hotel with primitive toilet facilities. Better quality accommodation and lunches are available at the *ksour* in Metameur, 6km west of Medenine, and also at Ksar Haddada.

7
Musée du Bardo, Tunis

Tunisia's national museum houses archaeological treasures from all over the country but is known principally for its impressive collection of mosaics.

The Musée du Bardo is housed in a former palace of the Husaynid *beys* (provincial governors). It is arranged in sections covering the Carthaginian, Roman, early Christian and Islamic eras. The undoubted highlight is the Roman section, where entire walls and floors are paved with mosaics from the 2nd century BC to the 7th century AD, many almost intact. The 3rd-century mosaic of the poet Virgil writing the *Aeneid* attended by two muses, found in a villa in Sousse (► 60), and the giant Triumph of Neptune mosaic are among the most exceptional exhibits. Another captivating 3rd-century work which was found at Dougga (► 16, Top Ten) is the mosaic of Ulysses and his sailors resisting the songs of three sirens trying to lure their vessel on to the rocks. The mosaic of Perseus rescuing Andromeda from the clutches of a sea monster was taken from an underground villa at Bulla Regia (► 42). Many of the smaller mosaics feature common themes including hunting and farming scenes, Greek and Roman gods, the sea, battles and family life. Animals, birds and fish are also widely depicted. Apart from the mosaics there are dozens of statues, stelae and sarcophagi from the Carthaginian and Roman periods, including a priceless terracotta statue of the sun god Baal Hammon sitting on a throne and wearing a feathered head-dress. There is also a spectacular collection of bronze and marble figures, which were recovered from the wreck of a ship which came to grief off the coast of Mahdia in the first century BC.

32A2 (arrowed)

Route de Bizerte, Quartier Le Bardo, 6km from city centre

71 513842, Fax 71 514050.

Tue–Sun 9–6; 9:30–4:30 in winter. Closed Mon

Small café on ground floor (£)

Line 4 from Tunis city centre

3 from avenue Habib Bourguiba

Few

Moderate

Above left: *the* Triumph of Neptune *mosaic*
Above: *the magnificent decorated doorway to the Musée du Bardo*

8
Qasr el-Aïn, Nefta

28A4

Avenue des Sources

All day

Drinks at Café Maure el Khazen (£) and Café-Bar La Corbeille (£) which both overlook the site

Up to six buses a day from Tozeur. Also daily services from Nefta to Kairouan and Sfax

Tozeur–Nefta Airport 23km

Free

Avenue Habib Bourguiba ☎ 76 457236

Qasr el-Aïn, or the Corbeille, is the smaller of two oases in the desert town of Nefta; it is dramatically situated in a giant bowl-shaped depression.

Measuring almost 1km wide and up to 40m deep, the massive crater at Qasr el-Aïn is filled with hundreds of palm trees and is watered by 152 natural springs, many of them warm and sulphurous. The springs also supply a large bathing pool at the westerly end of the Corbeille (French for 'basket') which is very popular in summer, generally used by women and girls in the morning and men and boys in the afternoon.

The best view of the Corbeille is from a terrace directly above the bathing pool where there are a couple of cafés and no shortage of persistent but not very knowledgeable guides. It is best to hire a guide from the tourist office. Early evening is a good time to be there, when the palm grove is bathed in a warm glow. The maze of trees can be explored on foot or by donkey following several well-worn paths. Part of the area has been divided into gardens which have belonged to the same families for centuries.

The Corbeille is not quite as attractive as it once was. Some of the wells have run dry amid controversy that the town's modern tourist hotels are taking too much water for their swimming pools. Some of the palm trees have also suffered from fire and floods.

Nefta's main oasis lies in the southern part of town on the opposite side of avenue Habib Bourguiba. Covering more than 10 sq km, hundreds of thousands of palm trees here are watered by 200 springs.

Bunches of ripening fruit hang from a date palm in the Corbeille

9

Sidi Bou Saïd

Sidi Bou Saïd is invariably described as Tunisia's prettiest village and is almost a compulsory stop on any excursion from Tunisia's beach resorts.

Sidi Bou Saïd somehow manages to avoid being a total tourist trap and a blatant distortion of a real Tunisian village. It retains considerable charm and beauty and is always a pleasant place to while away a few of hours. Situated northeast of Tunis and connected by regular metro services, the hilltop village is known for its cobbled streets and whitewashed houses with blue window grilles and studded doors. Its focal point is the main square, place Sidi Bou Saïd, which is lined with cafés and souvenir shops.

The village's history goes back to the 9th century when a fortified monastery was built here as part of a chain of coastal defences aimed at deterring Christian invaders. In the 13th century a community began to form around the tomb of a holy man – Sidi Bou Saïd – whose life is still celebrated during a festival each August. In the late 19th century wealthy French expatriates began buying houses in the village. In 1912 an English baron with the unlikely name of Rodolphe d'Erlanger spent ten years building an exquisite cliffside villa and gardens here – Ennejma Ezzahra. Laws were passed to protect the village and to order that the only colours that could be used in external decoration would be the now ubiquitous bright blue and white. D'Erlanger's palatial home has become Le Centre des Musiques Arabes et Mediterranéennes (Centre for Arab and Mediterranean Music) where concerts are held and there is a fascinating collection of musical instruments.

28B6

20km northeast of Tunis.

Mint tea and coffee at Café des Nattes (£) and Café Sidi Chabanne (£) (► 92)

TGM metro services from Tunis every 20 mins. Journey time 30 mins. 15 min uphill walk from the station to the centre of the village

None

Celebration of the life of Sidi Bou Saïd in August

Le Centre des Musiques Arabes et Mediterranéennes

Ennejma Ezzahra

Tue–Sun, 9–12, 2–7 (2–5 only in winter). Closed Mon

Concerts in July and December

Blue doors, flowers and dazzling white walls in Sidi Bou Saïd

10 Thermes d'Antonin (Antonine Baths)

Once the biggest Roman baths in the Empire and Carthage's best-preserved site.

37C2

Avenue des Thermes d'Antonin

Daily 8–7 (8:30–5:30 in winter). Closed on public holidays

Drinks at Café des Nattes or Café Sidi Chabanne, Sidi Bou Saïd (➤ 92)

Regular TGM metro services from Tunis to Carthage–Hannibal station

None

Cheap (ticket will also provide entry to other Carthage ruins and the Musée National de Carthage)

Above: *a section of the great bathhouse complex*

The site is entered from the top of a colourful garden which slopes gently down to the sea following the pattern of the original Roman streets. Close to the entrance are the remains of a *schola* which was a kind of after-school boys' club for the sons of wealthy Romans, with an unusual mosaic showing children doing physical exercises. The ruins of the Byzantine Basilica of Douimes are marked by three rows of double pillars and a mosaic floor.

Visitors are not allowed to enter the baths, but can study them from a viewing platform. A white marble model shows what the baths would have been like when they were in daily use and a couple of pillars have been repositioned to give an idea of the original height.

Work on the baths began during the reign of the Roman Emperor Hadrian (AD 76–138) who spent a considerable amount of time touring his vast empire and promoting urban life. When the baths were completed, under Antoninus Pius, they were the largest outside Rome. Heat was provided by an underground system of furnaces and there was a series of hot rooms of varying temperatures, a cold plunge pool and a Roman 'whirlpool', (without the bubbles of course).

The baths are surrounded by an archaeological park with a number of Punic tombs, and the site borders the presidential palace, the official residence of the Tunisian leader, President Ben Ali.

What to See

Above: *scarlet national flags of Tunisia outside the Palais du Congrès*
Right: *an Arab horseman at the Festival of the Sahara, Douz*

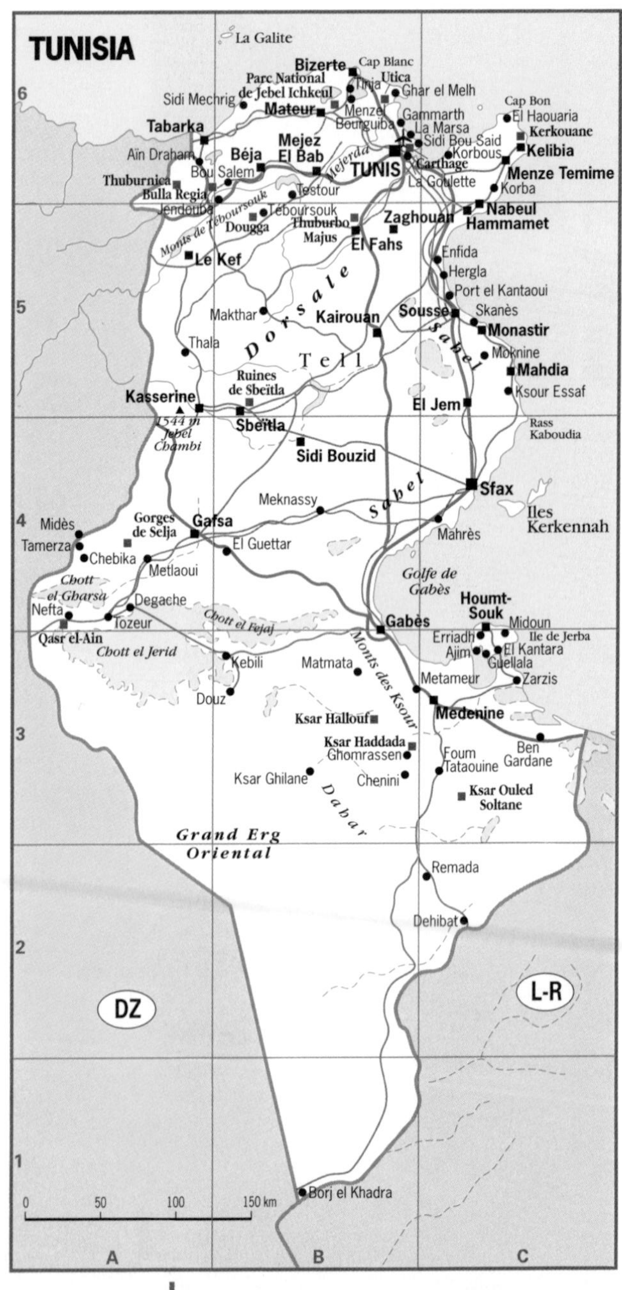
TUNISIA
La Galite
Bizerte
Cap Blanc
Parc National de Jebel Ichkeul
Tinja
Utica
Ghar el Melh
Sidi Mechrig
Mateur
Menzel Bourguiba
Gammarth
Cap Bon
El Haouaria
Kerkouane
Kelibia
Tabarka
La Marsa
Sidi Bou Said
Korbous
Aïn Draham
Béja
Mejez El Bab
Mejerda
TUNIS
Carthage
Menze Temime
Thuburnica
Bou Salem
Bulla Regia
Jendouba
Testour
La Goulette
Korba
Nabeul
Hammamet
Monts de Téboursouk
Téboursouk
Dougga
Thuburbo Majus
El Fahs
Zaghouan
Le Kef
Enfida
Hergla
Port el Kantaoui
Dorsale
Makthar
Kairouan
Sousse
Skanès
Monastir
Sahel
Thala
Tell
Moknine
Mahdia
Ruines de Sbeïtla
Ksour Essaf
Kasserine
El Jem
1544 m Jebel Chambi
Sbeïtla
Rass Kaboudia
Sidi Bouzid
Sfax
Meknassy
Sahel
Iles Kerkennah
Midès
Gorges de Selja
Gafsa
Mahrès
Tamerza
Chebika
El Guettar
Metlaoui
Chott el Gharsa
Golfe de Gabès
Degache
Houmt-Souk
Nefta
Tozeur
Chott el Fejaj
Gabès
Midoun
Qasr el-Ain
Erriadh
Ile de Jerba
Chott el Jerid
Kebili
Matmata
Monts des Ksour
Ajim
El Kantara
Guellala
Douz
Metameur
Zarzis
Medenine
Ksar Hallouf
Ksar Haddada
Ghomrassen
Ben Gardane
Foum Tataouine
Ksar Ghilane
Chenini
Dabar
Ksar Ouled Soltane
Grand Erg Oriental
Remada
Dehibat
DZ
L-R
Borj el Khadra
0
50
100
150 km
6
5
4
3
2
1
A
B
C

Tunis & the North

Although northern Tunisia is home to nearly a quarter of the population, thousands of holiday-makers bypass this area altogether and head straight for the east coast beach resorts. This is a pity as the capital is here and the surrounding countryside and coastline are enormously varied.

Tunis has more than enough attractions to warrant a few nights' stay or, at the very least, a full day's excursion. For more than 3,000 years, Tunis has been among the great cities of the Mediterranean and it still has plenty to offer. It would also provide a convenient base for independent travellers, with dozens of quiet beaches and some of the country's finest archaeological sites within easy reach.

Tabarka is emerging as Tunisia's northern flagship resort, while the charming old port town of Bizerte is still debating whether it really wants to entice international tourists or is quite content to remain a sleepy backwater.

'Around Carthage, immobile waves glistened as the moon spread its beams on the gulf surrounded by mountains and on the Lake of Tunis.'

GUSTAVE FLAUBERT,
1821–80

Tunis

28B6
66km southeast of Bizerte, 120km northwest of Sousse
1 avenue Moham V 71 341077 8:30–1, 3–5.45 Mon–Thu, 8:30–1:30 Fri, Sat

Tunis started life as a small garrison town, defended by the high walls of its *médina*. Its expansion into a wealthy trading city was sparked by the Arab invasion of Tunisia in the 7th century, though it was another 600 years before Tunis became the capital.

Today the city is the undisputed focal point of the nation. It is home to one in ten of the population and forms the epicentre of political, cultural and social life. The city combines a vibrant, atmospheric old town of narrow lanes and covered *souqs* with the more European-style Ville Nouvelle characterised by tree-lined avenues and elegant colonnaded, balconied buildings.

What to See in Tunis

33C2
Café at Hotel Africa (£) (➤ 101), 50 avenue Habib Bourguiba; Le Baghdad (££–£££) (➤ 92)
5, 8, 35, 50
Line 1, Tunis Marine

Cathédrale de St Vincente de Paul
33C2
Avenue Habib Bourguiba
8.30–11.30, 3–6PM. Daily service at 6.30PM and Sundays at 9 and 11AM
Free (donations accepted)

Above: the Avenue imparts something of a French air to the city

AVENUE HABIB BOURGUIBA ✪

The 'Champs Elysées' of Tunis, avenue Habib Bourguiba is the capital's best-known and most prestigious thoroughfare, but like its more famous sister it is not quite as elegant as one might have imagined. Apart from a few grand buildings there is a mishmash of banks, *bureaux de change*, *pâtisseries*, cinemas, car rental agents and hotels, including Hotel Africa – the street's most prominent landmark and a popular meeting place (➤ 101).

Avenue Habib Bourguiba begins at the foot of avenue de France close to the main entrance to the *médina*. Where the streets run together is the **Cathédrale de St Vincente de Paul**, a Catholic church built in 1882. Just across the road is the Ambassade de France (French Embassy) from where the Protectorate was governed between 1881 and the granting of independence in 1956. Further east is the art nouveau-style Theatre Municipal which has recently been refurbished and is regularly used for concerts.

JEMAA EZ ZITOUNA ✪✪

Jemaa ez Zitouna (the Great Mosque) covers an area of more than 5,000 sq m and is the largest mosque in Tunis, dwarfing the surrounding alleyways. It has been at the spiritual heart of Tunis for over 1,000 years and is the only mosque in the city which can be visited by non-Muslims, though access is restricted to a viewing enclosure overlooking the polished marble courtyard.

Jemaa ez Zitouna (literally Mosque of the Olive Tree) dates mostly from the middle of the 9th century, though it has been modified many times since, and was inspired by the slightly larger Grande Mosquée de Sidi Oqba (Great Mosque) in Kairouan (► 20, Top Ten). Its outer wall is built of stone taken from Roman Carthage. The courtyard is flanked on three sides by simple arcades and on the fourth by a prayer hall supported by 184 columns.

During the 13th and 14th centuries the mosque became an important Islamic university attracting students from all over the Arab world. It continued to flourish until the 1950s when the teaching faculty was closed on the orders of President Bourguiba in a bid to reduce religious influence in the country. The mosque and its 500-year-old library, containing one of the world's greatest collections of Arab literature, had its teaching status restored by in 1987 by President Ben Ali.

32B2
Rue Jemaa ez Zitouna
8AM–12. Closed Fri
Café ez Zitouna (£), rue Jemaa ez Zitouna
1
Habib Thameur
None
Cheap

The square minaret of Jemaa ez Zitouna can be seen from rooftop terraces in the souq

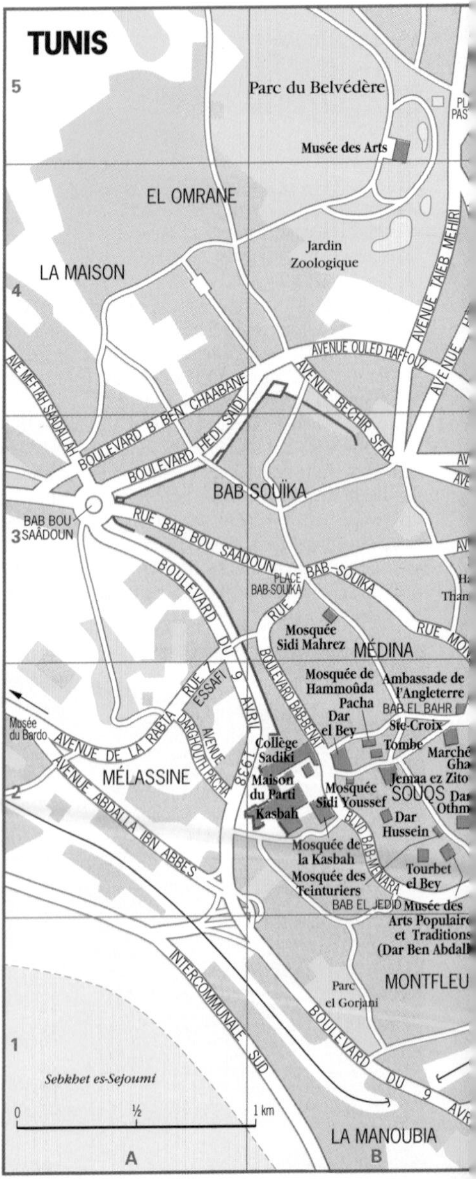

TUNIS

Parc du Belvédère
Musée des Arts
EL OMRANE
Jardin Zoologique
LA MAISON
AVENUE TAIEB MEHIRI
AVENUE OULED HAFFOUZ
AVE MEFTAH SADALLAH
BOULEVARD B. BEN CHAABANE
AVENUE BECHIR SFAR
BOULEVARD HEDI SAIDI
BAB SOUÏKA
BAB BOU SAÂDOUN
RUE BAB BOU SAÂDOUN
BOULEVARD DU 9 AVRIL 1938
PLACE BAB-SOUÏKA
BAB-SOUÏKA
RUE
Mosquée Sidi Mahrez
MÉDINA
BOULEVARD BAB BENAT
Mosquée de Hammoûda Pacha
Ambassade de l'Angleterre
BAB EL BAHR
Dar el Bey
Ste-Croix
Tombe
RUE Z. ESSAFI
AVENUE DARGHOUTH PACHA
Musée du Bardo
AVENUE DE LA RABTA
Collège Sadiki
MÉLASSINE
Maison du Parti
Mosquée Sidi Youssef
SOUQS
Jemaa ez Zitouna
Kasbah
Dar Hussein
AVENUE ABDALLA IBN ABBES
Mosquée de la Kasbah
BLVD BAB-MENARA
Mosquée des Teinturiers
Tourbet el Bey
BAB EL JEDID
Musée des Arts Populaires et Traditions (Dar Ben Abdallah)
INTERCOMMUNALE SUD
MONTFLEURY
Parc el Gorjani
BOULEVARD DU 9 AVRIL
Sebkhet es-Sejoumi
0 ½ 1 km
LA MANOUBIA
A B
5 4 3 2 1

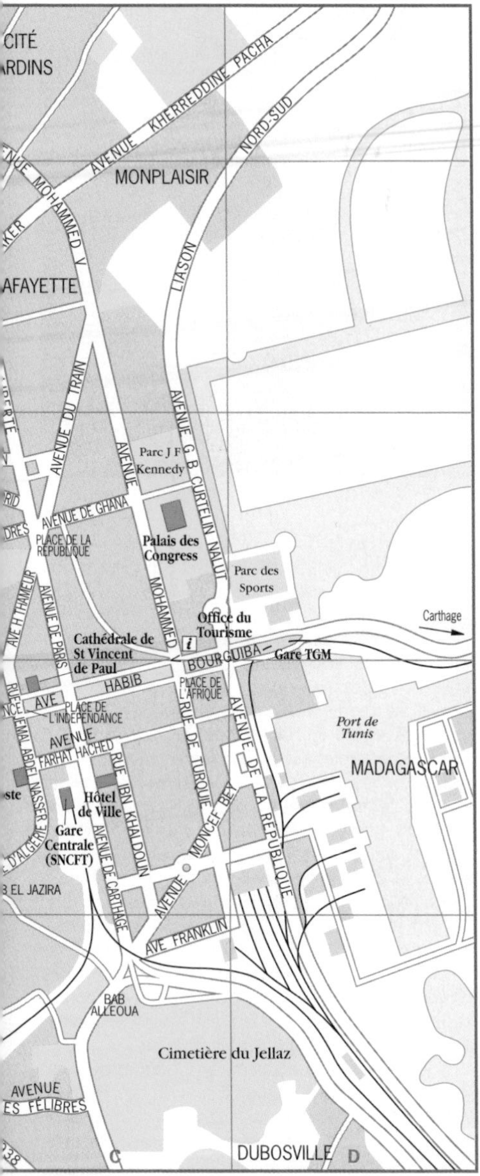

CITÉ
ARDINS
AVENUE KHERREDDINE PACHA
NORD-SUD
AVENUE MOHAMMED V
MONPLAISIR
LIASON
AFAYETTE
AVENUE DU TRAIN
AVENUE G. B. CURTELIN NALUT
Parc J F Kennedy
AVENUE
AVENUE DE GHANA
PLACE DE LA RÉPUBLIQUE
Palais des Congress
MOHAMMED
Parc des Sports
AVE H THAMEUR
AVENUE DE PARIS
Office du Tourisme
Carthage
Cathédrale de St Vincent de Paul
BOURGUIBA
Gare TGM
HABIB
PLACE DE L'AFRIQUE
AVE
PLACE DE L'INDÉPENDANCE
RUE DE TURQUIE
AVENUE DE LA RÉPUBLIQUE
Port de Tunis
AVENUE FARHAT HACHED
RUE JEMAL ABDEL NASSER
MADAGASCAR
RUE IBN KHALDOUN
AVENUE MONCEF BEY
Hôtel de Ville
Gare Centrale (SNCFT)
D'ALGÉRIE
AVENUE DE CARTHAGE
AVENUE
B EL JAZIRA
AVE FRANKLIN
BAB ALLEOUA
Cimetière du Jellaz
AVENUE DES FÉLIBRES
C
DUBOSVILLE
D

Right: *sacks of spices and bundles of dried herbs give a particular scent to the* souq

Bab el Bahr
32B3
Place de la Victoire
1
Habib Thameur
Plenty of choice
Difficult

Mosquée de Hammoûda Pacha
32B2

Mosquée Sidi Youssef
32B2

Dar Othman
32B2

Tourbet el Bey
32B2

MÉDINA ✪✪✪

The medieval part of Tunis is listed by UNESCO as a World Heritage Site. It dates back to the 7th century and remained the commercial centre of the city until the establishment of the French Protectorate in 1881, after which it began to decline. Start by exploring the narrow alleys at the **Bab el Bahr** (also known as the Sea Gate or Porte de France) on place de la Victoire. The arched gateway passes through the old city wall and dates from 1848.

The **Mosquée de Hammoûda Pacha** with its thin Turkish-style minaret, built in 1655 to honour an Italian who had converted to Islam, and the **Mosquée Sidi Youssef** with an octagonal minaret, the oldest of its type in the city, are closed to non-Muslims. There is a good view of Sidi Youssef from the rooftop of the Musée des Turcs, an antique shop in the Souq et-Trouk. **Dar Othman** was a palace built for Othman Dey, who ruled Tunisia from 1598 to 1610, and has a pretty courtyard garden with cypress and lemon trees. The rue des Libraires contains three small 18th-century *medresa* (theological schools) at numbers 11, 27 and on the corner of the street. **Tourbet el Bey** in rue Tourbet el Bey is a royal mausoleum built in the late 18th century for the Husaynid princes.

A stroll around the northern part of the *médina* will reveal the small community which still lives here much as it has for centuries. Narrow streets, with traditional wooden, nail-studded doors and grilled windows, seem to keep their secrets to themselves.

MUSÉE DES ARTS POPULAIRES ET TRADITIONS ✪✪

The Museum of Popular Arts and Traditions occupies a late 18th-century palace, the Dar Ben Abdallah. The ornate entrance leads into a marble courtyard with a fountain, showing the visitor a tantalising example of the largely hidden side of the old city. In many ways the building itself is more interesting than the exhibition rooms which show upper class urban life in Tunis in the 19th century.

- 32B2
- Impasse Ben Abdallah, off rue Sidi Kacem
- 71 256195
- Tue–Sun 9:30–4:30
- Plenty of choice
- 1
- Habib Thameur
- None
- Moderate

MUSÉE DU BARDO (➤ 23, TOP TEN)

PARC DU BELVÉDÈRE ✪

The Belvedere Park was laid out by the French as an exclusive enclave for the families of the ruling classes. Today, with so few green open spaces in the city, the park is a popular place to escape the summer heat. An elegant 18th-century pavilion (or *koubba*) is half-way up the hill and from the top there is a good view of the city. There is also a small **zoo** (➤ 110).

- 32B5
- Avenue Taieb Mehiri
- Open access but avoid at night
- Couple of cafés serving drinks
- 5, 5c, 5d
- Palestine
- Free
- Concerts in summer

Zoo

- 9:00–7:00 (to 4:00 in winter)
- Café
- Cheap

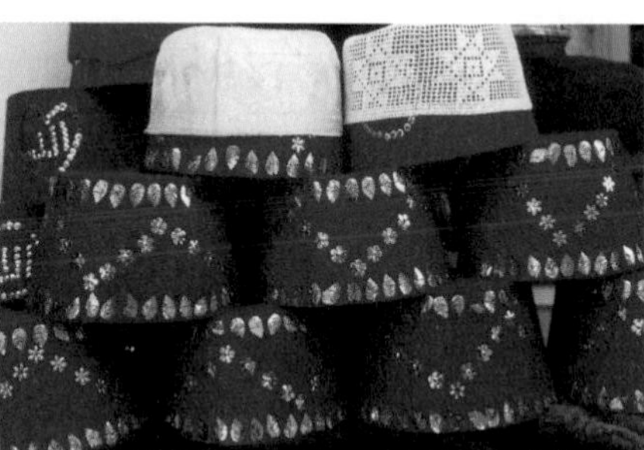

Left: *traditional Tunisian woollen hats on sale in the Souq des Chechias*

SOUQS

Shopping in the *souqs* (markets) is one of the biggest attractions of the *médina* for many. The myriad tiny alleys provide endless opportunities for hunting down bargains and haggling. Originally each *souq* specialised in a single trade and amongst the oldest is the 13th-century Souq el Attarine (the perfume-makers' market) which still sells scents and essential oils. The Souq des Etoffes sells fabric and clothes; search out the Souq du Cuivre (coppersmiths), the Souq des Babouches (slippers), and the Souq el-Kebabjia (silk). The Souq et-Trouk (market of the Turks) was one of the city's finest when it opened in 1630, and the Souq el-Berka was one of the largest slave markets in the Mediterranean.

- 32B2
- Throughout the *médina*
- Mostly closed on Sun
- M'Rabet Café (£), Souq et-Trouk
- 1
- Habib Thameur

28B6
15–20km northeast of Tunis
Daily 8:30–5:30 in winter, 8–7 in summer
Café des Nattes at Sidi Bou Saïd (► 25)
TGM every 20 mins, stopping at six stations in Carthage: Salammbo, Byrsa, Dermech, Hannibal, Presidential and Amilcar
Moderate
Carthage International Festival Jun, Jul

The elegant façade of the National Museum

Carthage

Carthage is one of the best known of Tunisia's archaeological sites, though its impact is lessened by the way the surviving treasures are scattered over a large area in a suburb of the capital.

Founded in 814 BC by the Phoenicians, by the fourth century BC Carthage had become the centre of their vast maritime empire. In 146 BC it was destroyed by the Romans who – only 25 years later – began rebuilding on the same site. It became the third largest city of the Roman Empire before it was destroyed by the Arabs in AD 692, ending its heyday.

A complete tour will take all day; it is probably less overwhelming to make a couple of shorter trips. The Musée National de Carthage (► right) is worth a visit for an overview of the site and to see some of the magnificent treasures, dating back to the city's earliest days.

What to See in Carthage

37A2
Carthage–Hannibal TGM station

Cathédrale de St Louis
Byrsa Hill
Concerts are held here throughout the year

BYRSA HILL ✪✪

It is possible to see the whole of the site from the summit of Byrsa Hill. This was the heart of the city under Punic rule and is the best place to start a tour. The **Cathédrale de St Louis** built here in 1890 is dedicated to the French king who died in 1279 while trying to lay siege to Tunis. The cathedral has been restored as a cultural centre for Arab music and is now known as the Acropolium.

37B4
Rue Roosevelt
Carthage–Presidential
None

CIMETIÈRE ✪

The American War Cemetery commemorates the 6,564 Americans who died in North Africa during World War II. There are 2,840 neatly tended graves and a Wall of Remembrance naming those who were never found.

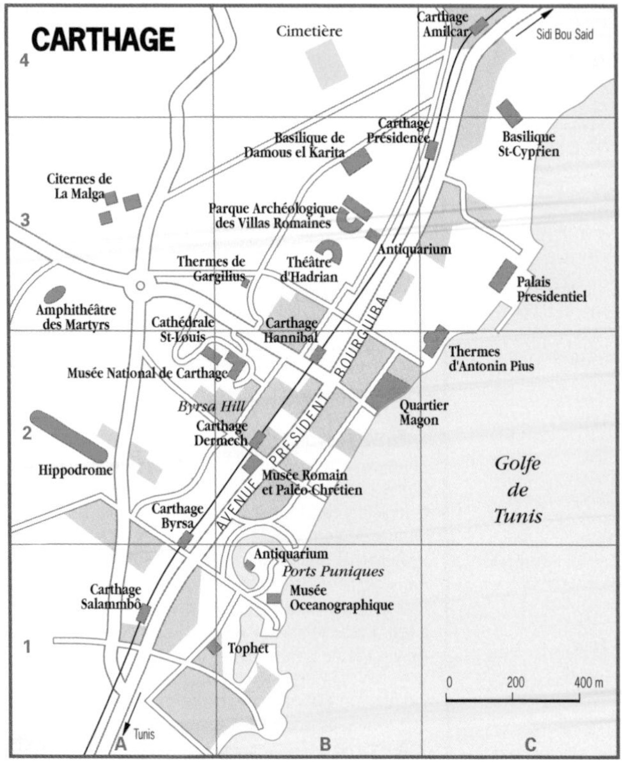

LES PORTS PUNIQUES ✪

In the second century the twin Punic Ports provided berths for more than 200 naval ships but today it is almost impossible to imagine such a sight. The ports have shrunk to little more than ponds and the only way of making any sense of how they operated is to visit the small **Antiquarium** on the edge of the harbour to look at a scale model left behind by a British excavation team. It shows the ports as one giant shipyard surrounded by several slipways. The nearby **Musée Oceanographique** (Oceanographic Museum) has been modernised, with some interactive displays bringing a bit of life to an otherwise dull collection of fish and nauticalia.

37B1
Rue Hannibal
Carthage–Salammbo

Antiquarium
By the harbour
Opening times vary
Free

Musée Oceanographique
Avenue 2 Mars
71 730548
7–7. Closed Mon
Cheap

MUSÉE NATIONAL DE CARTHAGE ✪✪✪

The National Museum of Carthage houses collections of sculpture, statues, masks and mosaics. On the ground floor are Carthaginian, Roman and Christian remains, while the first-floor has incense burners and plates found inside Punic graves as well as glass, ceramics and amphorae.

37B2
71 730036
Near the cathedral
8–7 (8:30–5:30 in winter)
Demech or Hannibal
Moderate

37B2
Daily 8–7 (8:30–5:30 in winter)
Carthage–Byrsa or Carthage–Dermech
Cheap

MUSÉE ROMAIN ET PALÉO-CHRÉTIEN

The small Roman and Palaeo-Christian Museum is located at the crossroads of two ancient Roman streets over a still-intact Roman cistern. Excavations are still going on and exhibits include two peacock mosaics and a 5th-century marble statue of Ganymede.

37B2
Avenue de la République
Carthage–Hannibal
None

QUARTIER MAGON

Located close to the Thermes d'Antonin (► 26, Top Ten), the Magon Quarter has been turned into an archaeological park. There are two small exhibition rooms and a display of mosaic pavements.

37B3
Avenue 7 Novembre
Carthage–Hannibal
None
Cheap
Carthage International Festival in the summer

THÉÂTRE D'HADRIAN

There is little or nothing left of the original Theatre of Hadrian built in the early 2nd century, but it has now been completely restored and is very popular as a venue for concerts and plays during the annual Carthage International Festival. Just beyond the theatre is the Parc Archéologique des Villas Romaines (the Archaeological Park of Roman Villas), a collection of columns, statues and a few mosaics but most acknowledged for its setting with views over the Bay of Tunis.

THERMES D'ANTONIN (► 26, TOP TEN)

37B1
Avenue Farhat Hached
Daily 9–7 (9–5 in winter)
Carthage–Salammbo
None
Cheap

TOPHET

It is hard to imagine this quiet, overgrown garden was used for child sacrifice. Excavations have unearthed more than 20,000 urns containing the ashes of boys aged between two and 12, sacrificed by Carthaginians in the 8th century BC. The remains were cremated as an offering to the sun god Baal Hammon and Tanit, the moon goddess.

Right: *memorial stones at Tophet serve as reminders of a cruel 8th-century ritual*

What to See Around Tunis

GAMMARTH ✪✪

Once a quiet seaside village, Gammarth is now a full-scale resort overrun with expensive hotels and restaurants. In the 1950s the beaches gained notoriety for attracting European nudists and became known locally as the Baies des Singes (Bay of Monkeys). Raoued Plage, beyond Gammarth, is a fine stretch of sand and is packed with families during the summer months.

Above the beaches, on the Hauts des Gammarth, is Jebel Khawi (Hollow Mountain), where there is a French military cemetery for more than 4,000 Frenchmen killed during World War II.

- 28B6
- 20km northeast of Tunis
- Good choice (£–£££)
- 20b from Jardin Thameur in Tunis city centre
- Few

Above: *climb Gammarth Heights for a view along the coast to Carthage*

LA GOULETTE ✪✪

Despite its rundown houses, crumbling *kasbah* and general air of neglect, La Goulette is very popular for its excellent fish restaurants attracting crowds from the city on summer weekends. Once a pirates' stronghold and home to a large Jewish community, La Goulette ('the gullet') is at the mouth of the Tunis canal and is still a major cargo and ferry port. The *kasbah*, built in 1535, was used as a dungeon for prisoners waiting to be taken to the *médina* in Tunis to be sold as slaves.

- 28B6
- 15km northeast of Tunis
- Restaurant Lucullus (£££)
  - place 7 Novembre
  - 71 737310
- TGM from Tunis Marine
- Tunis–Carthage Airport 10km. Internal flights to Jerba and Tozeur
- Few

LA MARSA ✪✪✪

La Marsa is the most upmarket beachfront suburb on the Bay of Tunis. With a palm tree-lined corniche and a long sandy beach it is a popular weekend retreat for residents of Tunis and a permanent home for the well-heeled. Two of the town's finest residences belong to the ambassadors of Britain and France.

- 28B6
- 15km northeast of Tunis
- Several (££–£££) around the metro station
- Regular TGM from Tunis
- Airport 12km
- Few

SIDI BOU SAÎD (► 25, TOP TEN)

The pretty French colonial church in the centre of Béja

What to See in the North

BÉJA 

28B6
110km west of Tunis
Restaurant La Belle Epoque (£), avenue de France
Up to to seven trains a day to and from Tunis
Frequent services from Tunis
Few

Once among the richest and most important towns of the Maghreb, Béja has lost much of its allure and influence. Formerly a Roman garrison, the town was destroyed by the Vandals in the fifth century and again in the tenth and 11th centuries. Since then it has become an important agricultural centre.

The key attraction here is the *médina*; locally handwoven blankets are sold in Souq en-Nehasach and rue el-Attarine is the food and spice market. The Byzantine *kasbah* is used by the military and is not open to the public. There are Colonial and Commonwealth war cemeteries out beyond the station.

BIZERTE 

28B6
66km northwest of Tunis
Le Bonheur (£), 31 rue Thaalbi (➤ 92). Le Sport Nautique (£££), boulevard Habib Bougatfa (➤ 92)
Station on rue de Rinja
To Tunis every half-hour from Quai Tarik Ibn Zaid
rue de Constantinople ☎ 72 432897
Few
Bizerte Festival Jul/Aug

Bizerte is the largest town on the north coast with a picturesque old port and bustling *médina*. It has only slowly begun to embrace tourism with the building of several hotels along the route de la Corniche but it is easily visited on a day trip from Tunis, less than an hour's drive away.

Bizerte has been a major port since the Phoenicians built a canal linking the inland Lac de Bizerte (Lake Bizerte) with the open sea, creating one of the finest harbours in the western Mediterranean. Known then as Hippo Zarytus, it was renamed Bizerte in 678 after being captured by the Arabs. In the 16th century – under Turkish rule – Bizerte became a pirates' den. The French made it their principal

naval base in the late 19th century and it has remained a military centre with young men in uniform a common sight on the town's streets.

The Vieux Port (Old Port), surrounded by shops and cafés and dotted with colourful fishing boats, is the heart of the town. At the mouth of the harbour is the ***kasbah***, which despite its Byzantine appearance dates mainly from the 17th century. In places the walls are up to 10m high and 11m thick, and within is a maze of narrow, winding passageways. Facing the *kasbah* is the smaller Sidi el-Hanni fortress, which has been turned into a small but dull **Musée Oceanographique** (Oceanographic Museum), featuring a motley collection of local fish.

West of the *kasbah* is the *médina*, which was heavily bombed during World War II. Closed to non-Muslims, the 17th-century Grande Mosquée (Great Mosque) with its octagonal minaret is best viewed from rue des Armuriers in the street behind or, better still, from the opposite side of the harbour. The **Zaouia de Sidi Mokhtar** houses the local branch of the Association de Sauvegarde de la Médina, which seeks to preserve and restore the area. Displays include a map of the town showing how it looked in 1881. North of the *médina* the **Fort d'Espagne** (Spanish Fort, which was actually built by the Turks in the 1570s) offers an excellent view over Bizerte. The main beach runs for 5km alongside the route de la Corniche to Cap Bizerte.

Kasbah
- North of the Old Harbour
- Tue–Sun 9–12:30, 2:30–6 in winter (2:30–8 in summer)
- Cheap

Musée Oceanographique
- Avenue Habib Bourguiba
- Tues–Sun 9–12:30, 2:30–6 in winter (to 8 summer)
- Cheap

Zaouia de Sidi Mokhtar
- Place Lahedine Bouchoucha
- Exhibitions
- Free

Fort d'Espagne
- Boulevard Hassan en Nouri
- Cheap

Colourful small fishing boats moored at the Old Port of Bizerte

- 28A6
- 60km south of Tabarka, 9km north of Jendouba
- 78 630554
- Daily 8–7 (8:30–5:30 in winter)
- Nearest cafés and restaurants at Jendouba
- To Jendouba from Tunis or Bizerte (around 4 hours) and then taxi or ***louage*** (shared taxi)
- Cheap

Above: *the monumental ruins of the Memmian Baths*
Opposite: *a good view of Tabarka from the Genoese fort across the bay*

BULLA REGIA ✪✪✪

This Roman site is as remarkable as Dougga but, because it is less well known, it is never overrun with visitors, making it much more atmospheric. Neolithic tombs at the site suggest Bulla Regia was inhabited long before the Romans and it was certainly the capital of one of the short-lived Numidian kingdoms. After it was annexed by Emperor Hadrian in the 2nd century it became one of the wealthiest Roman cities in North Africa.

The rich wheat and olive merchants of the town used to escape the summer heat by retreating to underground villas. Some of these were paved with beautiful mosaics and though some of the best have been moved to the Musée du Bardo in Tunis (► 23, Top Ten), others remain, undisturbed for centuries. These include the mosaic of Venus and a cupid riding on dolphins at the Maison d'Amphitrite (House of Amphitrite); and a mosaic of fishermen at the Maison de la Pêche (House of Fishing), the oldest surviving villa. La Maison de la Chasse (House of the Hunt) has an elegant colonnaded courtyard and a sophisticated private baths complex.

Bulla Regia's two most impressive public buildings are a small and beautifully-preserved theatre with special seating reserved for its most important citizens, and the imposing Memmian Baths close to the site entrance. The market square and forum are flanked by the ruins of two temples, to Isis and Apollo whose priceless collection of statues are also now at the Musée du Bardo. There is a small museum at the entrance to the site.

DID YOU KNOW?

The main road between Tunis and Bulla Regia largely follows the Mejerda Valley, which became a bloody battlefield during World War II. Hundreds of lives were lost when British and American troops clashed with the Germans at Mejez el Bab, about 40km east of Béja.

DOUGGA (➤ 16, TOP TEN)

JEBEL ICHKEUL NATIONAL PARK (➤ 19, TOP TEN)

TABARKA ✪✪✪

Tabarka is Tunisia's flagship resort on the north coast. During the late 1980s and early 1990s the Tunisian government invested heavily in the town, building an international airport nearby. It is used regularly only in summer, bringing in mainly German and Italian holidaymakers. Nestled beneath the Kroumirie Mountains which are still covered with cork oaks, pine and eucalyptus, the town is not without charm, offering a long, unspoilt stretch of sandy beach to the east of the centre and to the west, a series of small rocky coves. The area is developing a reputation as a watersports centre with quality facilities for sailing, diving and windsurfing. Tunnels Reef (20 minutes by boat from Tabarka) is an extraordinary complex of tunnels, caves, caverns and gullies. Tabarka also has an 18-hole golf course.

The town began life as a Phoenician settlement and prospered in Roman times as a trading port. Modern-day Tabarka was largely designed by the French, who also built the causeway connecting the island of Tabarka to the mainland. The focal point of the town is avenue Habib Bourguiba where most of the shops and restaurants are to be found. The old port has been expanded into a luxury marina, Porto Corallo, and across the water is a 16th-century Genoese fort which is being prepared to house a small archaeological collection. The **Musée du Liège** (Cork Museum) 2km outside town on the Ain Draham road explains the industry and sells souvenirs.

28A6

175km from Tunis

Hôtel Andalous (£), avenue Habib Bourguiba (➤ 92)

Up to six buses daily to Tunis

Tabarka Airport, 14km east of town

Rue de Bizerte 78 671491 Mon–Thu 8:30–1 and 3–5:45. Fri, Sat 8:30–1:30. Closed Mon

Few

Université de l'Été is a festival of music, comedy and debates held in July. The annual Fête du Corail (Coral Festival), also held in July, is largely for tourists

Musée du Liège

2km out of town towards Aïn Draham

Tue–Sun, 7–1, 3–6 (8–12, 2–5 winter)

None

Free

THUBURNICA

- 28A6
- 180km west of Tunis
- Open access
- At Ghardimaou
- To Ghardimaou and then taxi
- None
- Free

Way out west, only 15km from the Algerian border, the Roman remains at Thuburnica are not exceptional and the journey is only for the really adventurous. The most intact remnant of the town is the beautiful Roman bridge crossing the bed of a river which carries the run-off from the surrounding hills in winter. This is still used to reach the ruins of the town itself. Visitors who know what they are looking for will see the remains of a couple of temples, a triumphal arch and parts of a two-storey mausoleum. At the top of the hill is a small Byzantine fort.

UTICA

- 28B6
- 30km southeast of Bizerte
- Daily 8–7 (8:30–5:30 in winter)
- Picnic tables provided
- Regular bus services between Tunis and Bizerte; get off at the turning about 2km from the site
- None
- Cheap

Equidistant between Tunis and Bizerte, Utica is now 10km from the sea though in Roman times it was an important port and the capital of the province of Africa. Much of the old Roman city lies buried under the deep mud of the Mejerda river which has been silting up for the past thousand years. The most intact part of the Roman remains is around La Maison de la Cascade (the House of the Waterfall) which obviously belonged to a very wealthy private citizen. The courtyard fountain, which gave its name to the house, still has remarkable mosaics.

The ruins of Utica's once-massive public baths complex still give an idea of how impressive they must once have been. Just in front of the entrance to the site there is a small museum containing pottery and other objects found at the baths.

The site of Utica's public baths was huge, and much remains intact

Tunis to Jebel Ichkeul

An absorbing full-day itinerary which combines an unspoilt nature reserve and Roman ruins with one of the most striking and atmospheric towns in the country.

Head northwest out of Tunis on the A7 Tabarka road, through Jedeida to Mateur. Turn right towards Tinja and Menzel Bourguiba, following the signs to Lac Ichkeul.

The road becomes a track near the entrance to the park and at the gate visitors are asked to sign an official form (in French) promising to treat the countryside with respect.

From the gate, it is another 3km to the car park for the Eco Museum and the starting point for various walks (► 19). Leave the park following signs for Bizerte. After 15km, take the turning to Menzel Bourguiba, the former French garrison town of Ferryville.

The town was founded at the end of the 19th century to house European immigrants. Once nicknamed 'Little Paris', it has lost much of its charm but is worth a short stop on the way.

Return to the main Mateur–Bizerte road at the village of Tinja.

Fishermen can usually be seen battling to stop eel and mullet finding a way through the mesh of nets from Jebel Ichkeul to the open sea.

Head 20km north to Bizerte (► 40), the largest town on the north coast. Leave Bizerte on the A8 Tunis road. After 30km, there is a sign to the old Roman city of Utica (► 44). From Utica it is another 30km back to the centre of Tunis.

Distance
180km

Time
8 hours including several stops

Start/end point
Tunis
28B6

Lunch
Le Sport Nautique (£££)
Boulevard Habib Bogatfa, Bizerte
72 431495

An atmospheric view of Lac d'Ichkeul, the heart of the Jebel Ichkeul National Park

Cap Bon

Standing slightly apart from the rest of the country, the peninsula which ends at Cap Bon is the most productive in Tunisia. With a year-round mild climate, it is known as the Garden of Tunisia; there are citrus and olive groves, and vineyards – although this is a Muslim country there is a long tradition of wine-making, and a wine festival at Grombalia during the autumn grape harvest.

On old maps of Tunisia, the town of Nabeul is given as the focal point of the region. It remains the largest town and seat of local government, but in recent years it has been eclipsed by the relentless expansion of near-neighbour Hammamet – the most cosmopolitan resort in Tunisia and a firm favourite with package holidaymakers from all over Europe. In contrast, on Cap Bon's northern coast there are many small villages and long stretches of deserted beach without a hotel in sight.

'The earliest navigators rounded Cap Bon and the glorious prospect of the Gulf of Tunis was unfolded before their eyes, the emerald waters being separated from the golden sand by a delicate edging of white surf'

A. MACCALLUM SCOTT,
Tunis. A Medley of Races Under the French Flag (1921)

Original columns and mosaic floors at the winter baths of Thuburbo Majus

Hammamet

28C5
60 km southeast of Tunis
To Tunis and Nabeul
One train a day between Tunis and Hammamet
Avenue Habib Bourguiba
72 280423

Tunisia's largest resort has been attracting package holidaymakers since the 1960s. Less than an hour's drive from Tunis–Carthage airport and only slightly more than that from Monastir–Skanès airport (the main arrival point for charter flights), Hammamet is geared up to year-round tourism and is equally popular with families and couples.

Easy-going and lively and with a good choice of restaurants, Hammamet's first hotels were built in the town centre close to the *médina* (► 49) but later developments stretch along the coast almost as far as Nabeul (► 52), making the most of some of the best beaches in the country.

The swimming pool of Sebastian's Villa, framed by whitewashed arches

What to See in Hammamet

CENTRE INTERNATIONAL CULTUREL

Avenue des Nationes Unies
72 280065
8:30–6 (9–5 in winter)
None
Cheap
Festival of the Arts, Jul, Aug

Built by millionaire George Sebastian in the 1920s, Sebastian's Villa has been described as 'the most beautiful in the world' (ostensibly by Frank Lloyd Wright, and he should know). Guests have included Winston Churchill, Anthony Eden and the artist Paul Klee; Rommel used it as his headquarters during World War II. It is now used to stage an annual cultural festival each July and August and is also a venue for conferences and art exhibitions.

DAR HAMMAMET

The *médina*
72 281206
8:30–7:30
None
Moderate

A small museum in the *médina* (► 49), filled with traditional costumes and a selection of bridal dowries from various parts of the country. The jewellery and embroidery are particularly impressive. There is a fine view of the modern town and the old *médina* from the rooftop terrace.

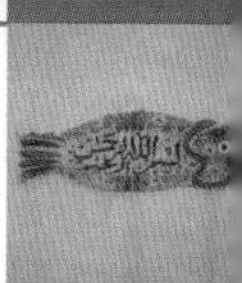

Hammamet's médina *is an atmospheric place to wander and shop*

KASBAH ✪✪

First built in the 15th century but heavily modified and restored since, the Kasbah is the best place to begin a tour of the *médina* (► below). The fort is Hammamet's most conspicuous landmark and is entered by way of a colossal ramp. There are steep steps up to the ramparts, from where there are fine views over the white domes and terraces of the *médina* and the surrounding coastline.

- The *médina*
- 8AM–9PM (8:30–6 in winter)
- On the ramparts, the Café Turk (£)
- None
- Cheap

MÉDINA ✪✪✪

Much smaller than the *médinas* of Tunis (► 34), Sousse (► 62) and Sfax (► 73), but not without its charms, Hammamet's old town nestles around the Kasbah and Grande Mosquée (Great Mosque). It was built between 1463 and 1474 on the site of a 9th-century settlement. Although the streets closest to the *médina* walls are lined with souvenir shops there is a residential area which remains almost completely unspoilt. Wander through the narrow alleys – it's almost impossible to get lost. The studs on the doors are all individually designed and many incorporate the good luck symbols of fish and the hand of Fatima (the daughter of the Prophet Muhammed).

Immediately in front of the *médina* there is a market, and to the east is an ancient Muslim cemetery.

- Café Sidi Bou Hdid, at the foot of the *kasbah* (► 94)
- None

PUPPUT ✪

Hammamet's only archaeological site consists of a couple of large Roman villas and a bath house paved with some fine mosaic floors. There are also 4th-century Christian tomb mosaics displayed on a perimeter wall. The ruins are all from the 2nd to the 4th centuries, when Pupput was a prosperous port.

- 6km south of the town centre
- 9–1, 3–7 (to 5:30 in winter)
- No public transport
- Cheap

The Ghar el Kebir caves near El Haouaria

What to See in the Cap Bon region

EL HAOUARIA

Just outside the village of El Haouaria are the spectacular Grottes Romaines (Roman Caves). On the seafront directly opposite the island of Zembra, there are 24 caves which were quarried for the soft orange limestone used by Carthaginian, Roman and Byzantine builders and sculptors. La Grotte des Chauves-Souris (Cave of the Bats), 4km from the town, is home to thousands of bats.

- 28C6
- 14km northwest of Kerkouane
- Hotel Épervier (£–££)
  - rue Hedi Chaker
  - 72 297017
- Festival of falconry (Jun)

KÉLIBIA

Kélibia is a busy working town with a picturesque fishing port, still unspoilt by tourism and a good base for exploring the Cap Bon region. Overlooking the town is the giant Fort of Kélibia which was built in the 6th century. The ramparts offer excellent views over the harbour, coastline and surrounding countryside. Kélibia's main beach is 2km north of the town at Mansourah.

- 28C6
- 68km northeast of Hammamet
- Restaurant Anis (£)
  - avenue Erriadh
  - 72 295777

KERKOUANE

Dating from the 4th century BC, Kerkouane is a remarkable survival of a purely Punic town. It was destroyed in 236 BC and unearthed in 1952; it is now listed as a UNESCO World Heritage Site. Many of the houses had private bathrooms. The little museum has some beautiful jewellery, funerary statues and pottery.

- 28C6
- 9km north of Kélibia
- 02 294033
- Tue–Sun 9–7 (9–4:30 in winter)
- Bus from Kélibia or taxi
- None
- Inexpensive

KORBOUS 

A small spa town where people have come to 'take the waters' since Roman times. There are five springs including the hot and sulphurous Aïn el-Atrous (goat spring), said to be good for skin complaints and rheumatism. Women regularly slide down the nearby Zarziha Rock as a cure for infertility.

- 28C6
- 48km east of Tunis
- Several cafés (£) and Résidence des Thermes has a restaurant (££)
- Bus from Tunis
- None

A Walk Around Nabeul

This leisurely walk offers an easy introduction to Nabeul (▶ 52–3).

Start at the Giant Orange Bowl on avenue Habib Thameur, a monument to the town's ceramic industry. Go past the regional hospital on the left before reaching the junction of avenue Farhat Hached and avenue Habib Bourguiba. Cross into avenue Farhat Hached.

This is a busy shopping street packed with shops and stalls selling everything from jeans and T-shirts to leather bags and suitcases.

Follow the road round to the left and after 150m turn left again into the covered souq. *Walk through to emerge facing one of the elaborate entrances to Nabeul's Grande Mosquée (Great Mosque).*

The lanes of the covered souq *lead to the Great Mosque*

Non-Muslims are barred from entry but walk round to the front for a glimpse of the courtyard. Note also the pretty tiled frontage of the house to the left of the mosque.

Cross the square, turn right into rue Souk el Ghezel and then right again into rue de France. With the Neapolis Center on the left, walk down the street and as you approach place des Martyrs – a formal public square with a fountain – turn left and through the gates of the bustling Marche Central.

The town's market is a riot of colour, sights and smells.

Return to place des Martyrs, turn left back into rue de France. After 250m head right into avenue Hedi Chaker, follow the road for 1km until a right-hand fork leads into rue Mohamed T'Latli and return to the Giant Orange Bowl.

Distance
3km

Time
2 hours allowing for shopping and drinks at the end

Start/end point
Giant Orange Bowl, Nabeul
28C5

Drinks
Café Errachida (£)
Avenue Habib Thameur
All day

NABEUL ✪✪✪

28C5
65km southeast of Tunis
Hourly to Tunis; depart from bus station on avenue Habib Thameur
avenue Taieb Mehiri
72 286800

Neapolis

Opposite Hotel Monia Club, just off the *route Touristique*
8–1, 4–7 (9:30–4.30 in winter). Closed Mon
None
Cheap

Nabeul used to be known simply as Tunisia's pottery town but over the last decade or so it has rapidly developed as a resort in its own right and now has a clutch of large beach-front hotels. The main streets are crammed with pottery shops, souvenir stores and clothing boutiques, and every Friday the heart of the town is blocked off as Nabeul plays host to the so-called Camel Market. Drawing a good deal fewer camels than it does tourists, the event presents more of a chance for a shopping spree than anything else. For non-tourist goods the Marche Central (Central Market, ➤ 51) is much more genuine and well worth a visit.

In Roman times Nabeul's major industry was the manufacture of a pungent fish sauce called *garum* which was made by salting the blood and guts of tuna fish and then leaving it in an airtight container for three or four months. During excavations at Roman **Neapolis** on the outskirts of town during the 1960s several amphorae of the sauce were unearthed – but they appear to have passed their sell-by date. Neapolis is something of a

The Friday market in Nabeul attracts large crowds

disappointment if you have visited any of Tunisia's major archaeological sites – there is not much to see apart from a few pillars, some mosaic fragments and a series of pits thought to be the remains of a fish processing factory.

Nabeul's pottery industry also dates back to Roman times with many of today's designs and popular colours (blue and white, and yellow and green) the same as those used 2,000 years ago. Although pottery can be bought all over Tunisia Nabeul offers one of the biggest selections. Tourists who hate the idea of haggling can shop for pots and plates at two official tourist shops in the town (➤ 109) where all goods have fixed prices. (Even if you like the idea of haggling it is worth calling in at one of the shops just to get an idea of the true cost of items.) Do not be fooled by one or two other shops in the town displaying signs which suggest they too have set prices. It is just a ploy to entice visitors in – you will then find prices become surprisingly flexible.

Nabeul is a thriving centre for the manufacture of bricks and perfume, the suburb of Dar Chaabane specialises in stone carving and the village of Beni Khiar 2km to the east is known for its carpet weaving and wool products.

Exhibits at Nabeul's regional Archaeological Museum, directly opposite the railway station, include sculptures of the Carthaginian moon goddess Tanit unearthed in 1948 from a temple called Thinissut in the hills above Hammamet; some Carthaginian pieces excavated from Kerkouane (➤ 50); a 2,500-year-old statue of a naked man and a collection of Roman domestic pottery. In the courtyard there are a series of mosaics taken from the archaeological site at Neapolis illustrating episodes from Homer's *Iliad*.

The highly decorative Nabeul pottery is produced in many shapes and sizes

Archaeological Museum

✉ 44 avenue Habib Bourguiba

☎ 72 285509

🕘 8–1, 4–7 (9:30–4:30 in winter). Closed Mon

✋ Cheap

28B5
60km southwest of Tunis, 65km west of Hammamet
Daily 8–7 (8:30–5:30 in winter)
From Tunis to El Fahs and then taxi
Inexpensive

Below: *the extensive Roman ruins* , inset: *a relief of Pegasus*

THUBURBO MAJUS

First settled in the 5th century BC, most of the ruins at Thuburbo Majus are from later Roman times when the town was an important trading centre for the region's agricultural produce and probably had a population of around 8,000. Like many of Tunisia's archaeological sites, it is not unusual to have the place almost completely to yourself. With no guides available, even if you have a map, it can be quite difficult to make sense of the sprawling site.

The paved open space at the centre is the forum, which was where political and financial matters were discussed; the temple, built in AD 168, was dedicated to Jupiter, Juno and Minerva; the Winter Baths with their veined pink marble columns are up the hill. The Palaestra of the Petronii was a gymnasium (delineated by a line of columns) where young men took part in boxing or wrestling bouts. Many of the best finds from this site, including a statue of Jupiter and some fine mosaics, are now in the Musée du Bardo in Tunis (➤ 23, Top Ten).

28B5
30km west of Hammamet
Café at Temple des Eaux (£)
Frequent buses from Tunis, Nabeul and Hammamet

ZAGHOUAN

A sleepy, unspoilt agricultural town between Hammamet and Thuburbo Majus, with cobbled streets and tiled roofs. Dating from Roman times, water from Mount Zaghouan was used to supply Carthage by way of a 70km aqueduct, parts of which can still be seen along the Tunis–Zaghouan road. The Temple des Eaux (Temple of the Waters) built by the Emperor Hadrian in 130 is the town's greatest sight.

From Hammamet to Thuburbo Majus

An opportunity to combine spectacular Roman ruins with some unspoilt Tunisian countryside.

Head out of Hammamet on the main road towards Tunis. At the junction with the motorway follow the Zaghouan sign. On the outskirts of Zaghouan (➤ 54) follow signs for 'Centre Ville' turning left at the pharmacy and driving up the steep hill to the old town. Follow signs for Hôtel les Nymphes, turning right at Club de Chasse.

The Temple des Eaux (➤ 54) is surrounded by 12 empty niches which used to hold statues depicting the months of the year.

Turn left following signs to Tunis and El Fahs. After 12 km, immediately after the 'Welcome to El Fahs' sign, turn right and then left following the signs for Thuburbo Majus.

Allow at least an hour to look round the site (➤ 54).

Turn right out of the site, turning left after 1km on to the main Tunis road. Drive through the village of Bir M'Cherga and soon after take the right fork. After 25km, there is a right-hand turning towards Oudna.

As you pass by note the well-preserved remains of the Roman aqueduct, which carried water from Zaghouan to Carthage.

After 6km turn right towards Mornag. Follow signs to Grombalia, crossing a rickety metal bridge only big (and safe) enough for one vehicle at a time. Turn right after 3km and follow signs for Bouficha. Just after the village of Oued Ezzit turn left towards Hamman Jedidi and the road back to Hammamet.

Distance
200km

Time
7–8 hours including stops

Start/end point
Hammamet
28C5

Lunch
Picnic lunch at Thuburbo Majus or beside the Roman aqueduct at Oudna

Jebel Zaghouan stands high above the surrounding country

Food & Drink

Tunisian cuisine is typically North African and is influenced by Islamic traditions as well as by its Berber culture, using powerful spices and plenty of vegetables and fish. The French colonial heritage has produced some excellent wines.

Dried beans and peas of many varieties are a staple part of Tunisian cuisine

Although international food is served in most Tunisian tourist hotels many holidaymakers will want to try at least some local cuisine. The Arabs, Turks and French have all had an influence on the country's cooking. Fish is given pride of place on any menu and restaurant owners compete with each other to display the freshest catch. Bream, grouper, sea bass and red mullet are among the most widely available, while seafood speciality dishes are based on prawns, lobster and squid. Tuna is added to everything – even when you ask for a vegetarian pizza or green salad! Eggs are another staple ingredient which appear unexpectedly in many dishes.

A Typical Tunisian Meal

In all but the cheapest restaurants customers are nearly always welcomed with complimentary *hors d'oeuvres* which may be as simple as a bowl of black olives and some delicious crusty bread. In most places the bread will also be accompanied with a small saucer of fiery red *harissa* paste made from hot chillies (caution is advised).

A very popular starter is the famous *brik*, a unique Tunisian dish which consists of a triangular-shaped envelope of crispy pastry containing a lightly cooked egg and often topped with fresh herbs, prawns or – of course – tuna. It can only really be eaten with the fingers but beware of the yolk making a sudden and undignified escape. Safer starters include *ojja,* which are scrambled eggs mixed with tomatoes, pimentos, peppers and garlic. *Mechouia* consists of diced onions, red peppers and tomatoes mixed with olive oil, grilled and then served with

hard-boiled eggs and tuna. *Chorba* is a spicy soup of tomatoes, onions and *harissa* with tiny grains of pasta.

The obvious main course is *couscous*, a tasty vegetable, meat or fish stew served on a bed of steamed semolina grains, Tunisia's national dish. *Mesfuf* is a sweet *couscous* made with nuts and raisins. *Mechoui* (not to be confused with *mechouia*) is a plate of grilled meat, typically

Makroud, *a sweet and sticky pastry filled with dates, is a Kerouan speciality*

lamb chops with liver and *merguez* sausages generously laced with chilli.

Dessert is often a choice of fresh fruit or very sweet pastries like *baklava* (pastry with nuts and honey) or *kab el ghazal* (a horn-shaped pastry filled with almonds).

What to Drink

Although Tunisia is a Muslim country alcohol is quite freely available in hotels and restaurants in Tunis and the main beach resorts. Bars outside hotels are male-dominated which may make women feel uncomfortable. Although a new German beer, *Berbere*, brewed in Hammamet, is slowly becoming available, most bars still only serve *Celtia*, a pleasant enough lager when served sufficiently cold. Some bars are also starting to serve local table wines by the bottle. The best red is the full-bodied Vieux Magon which is like a powerful shiraz, while the very dry Blanc de Blanc goes well with fish and seafood.

Tunisia's best-known spirits are *Thibarine*, a sweet, aromatic date liqueur and *boukha*, a fig brandy.

Couscous, traditional in Berber cuisine, is now Tunisia's national dish

Central Tunisia

Central Tunisia is a booming holiday region, combining two distinctive landscapes with a trio of colourful cities and a major Roman site. Sfax and Sousse are a delight with their ancient city walls, vibrant *souqs*, fascinating museums and thriving fishing ports. In the Islamic world their importance is overshadowed by Kairouan which is at the heart of the country in every sense. Tunisia's most holy city combines its spiritual role as a national centre for prayer and pilgrimage with the secular demands of its commercial carpet-making industry.

The surrounding richly fertile plain, known as the Sahel, stretches down the central east coast embracing the resorts of Mahdia and Monastir. Its vast numbers of olive trees have been the mainstay of the region's economy since Roman times. In contrast, the western Tell, once forested, is now a hauntingly desolate terrain only suitable for rough grazing. Its main attraction is the isolated Roman ruin of Sbeïtla.

'We quenched our thirst with tea in order to proceed in the dignified manner fitting for discovering such marvels'

PAUL KLEE
Describing his first trip to Kairouan, 1914

Tourists can try their hand at parascending from the water's edge

Sousse

Sousse used to be just an excursion destination for day trippers; now it is a busy holiday centre in its own right. Packed with atmosphere and hundreds of years of history, Tunisia's leading city beach resort offers good quality hotels, a wide choice of affordable restaurants and endless possibilities for shopping.

+ 28C5
✉ 143km from Tunis
Train: From Tunis
Ferry: To Monastir
Bus: Buses to south and north
i 1 avenue Habib Bourguiba ☎ 73 225157
Hours: 7:30AM–7.00PM (8:30–1, 3–5:30 in winter). Morning opening only Fri, Sat. Closed Sun
Restaurant: Plenty of choice (£–£££)

With Carthage (➤ 36) and Utica (➤ 44), Sousse was one of the Phoenicians' three great coastal cities, with the earliest archaeological finds dating from the 6th century BC. In the 7th century AD the city fell to Arab invaders who left it in ruins, but in 790 the foundations for a new city were laid, and many remnants of this time still survive today.

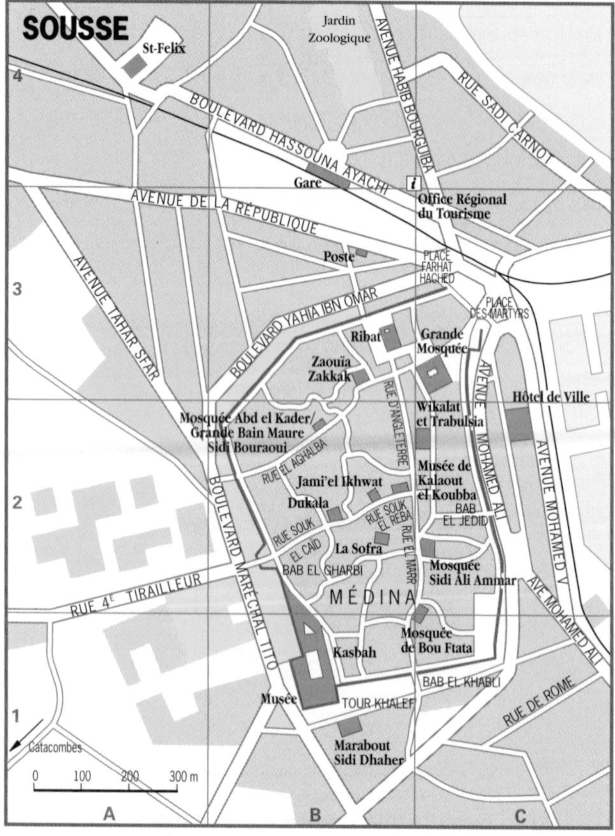

What to See in Sousse

CATACOMBS ✪

The catacombs could be developed into a major tourist attraction but for the moment their appeal is limited. There are purported to be more than 15,000 marble tombs from the 2nd to the 5th centuries spread throughout a 5.5km network of tunnels but currently only one very small section is open to the public.

60A1 (arrowed)
About 1km west of the *médina*, off rue Abdou Hamed el Ghazali
8–12, 3–7 (9–12, 2–6 in winter). Closed Mon
Cheap

GRANDE BAIN MAURE SIDI BOURAOUI

The Sidi Bouraoui Baths is one of the best places to try a traditional *hammam* or *bain maure* (Turkish bath) with lengthy separate sessions for men and women. In a country where not everyone has a private bathroom but where personal hygiene is taken very seriously the *hammam* plays an important role in Tunisian society. For tourists it offers an interesting insight into local culture, is a chance to meet local people and, most importantly, is a healthy, relaxing and pleasurable way to spend two or three hours. The masseur (or for women, a masseuse) uses a coarse glove known as a *tfal* which leaves the skin pink and tingling.

60B2
Rue el Aghlaba (behind Mosquée Abd el Kader).
4AM–3PM for men; 3PM–midnight for women
Cheap

Above: *the beautiful city and historic port of Sousse*

GRANDE MOSQUÉE ✪✪✪

Respectful dress is required for a visit to the Great Mosque, which looks like a fortress with turrets and crenellations. Originally built in 851 by a freed slave called Mudam on the orders of the Aghlabite ruler Abdul Abbas, the internal courtyard has the pleasantly uncomplicated architecture common to many Islamic places of worship, the only decoration being a single line of Koranic inscription. A wide stairway leads to the walls; the minaret and prayer hall are not open to non-Muslims.

60C3
Rue el-Aghlaba
Daily 8–2. Closes early on Fri for noon prayers, and all day Sun
None
Cheap

60B1
Off boulevard Marechal Tito
73 233695
8–12, 4–7 (9–12, 2–6 in winter). Closed Mon and public holidays
None
Moderate

KASBAH SOUSSE MUSEUM ✪✪✪

Situated in the southwest corner of the *médina* (▶ below) the Kasbah Sousse Museum not only offers a superb panoramic view across the city, but has a fine and most interesting collection of mosaics rivalling those at the Musée du Bardo (▶ 23, Top 10). Most of the mosaics date from the 3rd and 4th centuries with the depiction of the Triumph of Bacchus among the most noted. The adjoining courtyard is a pleasant place to sit amongst the palm trees, flowers and bits of marble column and stone tablets.

60B2
Many cafés (£)
None

MÉDINA ✪✪✪

The *médina* is the old heart of Sousse and the area of the city with the greatest appeal. Its 9th-century walls are still largely intact apart from the area around the former sea gate at place des Martyrs, which was destroyed by the Allies during World War II – a testament to the continuing strategic importance of the city.

The *médina*'s biggest attractions are the Grande Mosquée (▶ 61), the *ribat* (▶ 63) and the Kasbah Museum (▶ above). Equally evocative and rewarding, however, is its overall ambience. Despite the increasing impact of tourism, the *médina* has retained a considerable amount of charm and character. The main shopping street runs from east to west from Bab Jedid to Bab el Gharbi. Halfway along, as the thoroughfare changes its name from rue Souq el Reba to rue Souq el Caïd, is a small warren of covered *souqs* selling everything from food and clothes to perfume and jewellery.

52B2
Rue Souq el Reba
9–1, 4–6:30 Mon–Thu, 9–2 Sat, Sun. Closed Fri
None
Cheap

MUSÉE DE KALAOUT EL KOUBBA 

The Museum of Kalaout el Koubba is in one of the most unusual buildings in the *médina* (▶ above) with a striking zigzag decoration on the dome. Dating from around the 11th century and believed to have been either an audience chamber for a neighbouring Fatimid palace or one of the hot rooms of a *hammam*, it has had many uses over the years, most recently as an art gallery and café. Today the museum's displays focus on the traditional life of the *médina* with ceramics, kitchen equipment, musical instruments and national costumes.

Above: *haggling over souvenirs in the rue d'Angleterre in the Médina of Sousse*

The main gate and circular tower of the Byzantine ribat *in Sousse*

RIBAT ✪✪✪

The *ribat* was built early in the 9th century as one of a chain of fortresses stretching along the Mediterranean coast to defend North Africa from European invaders. It was completed by the Aghlabids in 821, incorporating an earlier structure built in 790 which itself was sited on the ruins of a 6th-century Byzantine fortress. The large central courtyard which slopes downwards to a cistern is surrounded by a series of small cells which were used by the warrior-monks as tiny study-bedrooms.

A room above the main gate has four slits in the floor through which boiling olive oil was poured on unwelcome visitors. For many visitors, though, the most interesting part of the *ribat* is the view from the ramparts over the *médina* (▶ 62). There is often a queue to climb the 75 steps to the top of the circular tower for views of the town.

60B3

Rue el Aghlaba

Daily 8–7 (8–5:30 in winter)

None

Moderate

DID YOU KNOW?

If you are in Sousse on a Sunday there is a large open-air market which sprawls endlessly along the Sousse–Sfax road and draws a huge crowd. It is said to be possible to buy anything from a car to a camel – although most people make rather smaller purchases.

From Sousse to El Jem

Distance
160km

Time
Seven hours including stops

Start/end point
Sousse
60C5

Lunch
Scandinavia Corner Cafeteria (£) for sandwiches and snacks
Opposite the entrance to the amphitheatre

This scenic drive includes the tourist town of Monastir (➤ 68) and is ideal for holidaymakers looking for a day trip from Sousse (or Port El Kantaoui, ➤ 70). Starting soon after breakfast is recommended.

Head southwest out of Sousse past the louages station following signs to Sfax and Kairouan. Drive through the suburbs of Zaouiet Sousse and Messadine. Soon after leaving M'Saken join the A1 and head south on a long, straight road flanked by row upon row of olive trees.

It takes just over an hour to get to El Jem (➤ 17, Top Ten) driving at a leisurely pace. It is impossible to miss the amphitheatre which dominates the small town and can be seen clearly from the approach road. Finding somewhere to park may be more difficult. Allow a good 90 minutes for the amphitheatre and a quick walk around town.

At the top of the main street, at the furthest point from the amphitheatre, turn left, taking the Mahdia road out of El Jem. Drive for 10km passing through the village of Telelsa and then turn left at the signpost for Moknine. Reaching a crossroads after about 12km head straight on into the village of El Fhoul, reaching Moknine 16km later. Follow the signs to Monastir 30km further north.

The extravagant mausoleum of Habib Bourguiba, seen from the tower of the ribat in Monastir

The *ribat* and Bourguiba Mausoleum are among Monastir's main tourist attractions (➤ 68–9). The town is also good for souvenir shopping.

Head out of town following signposts for Tunis. Take the A1 north for the easy 20km drive back to Sousse.

What to See in Central Tunisia

EL JEM (➤ 17, TOP TEN)

ILES KERKENNAH (➤ 18, TOP TEN)

KAIROUAN (➤ 20–1, TOP TEN)

LE KEF ✪✪✪

Le Kef – which means 'rock' in Arabic – refers to the town's dramatic setting on a rocky outcrop just below the summit of Jebel Dyr. Considered to be the capital of the Tell region which covers much of Central Tunisia, Le Kef is Tunisia's most significant inland centre after Kairouan. This was a fortress town from 450 BC, and tools have been found in surrounding caves and woodland dating back 50,000 years. In Roman times Le Kef became an important trading post and over the last thousand years it has been involved in numerous border wars and disputes. During World War II it served as headquarters for the Free French.

Aïn el Kef is a spring which may well have been the reason for a town being built here; it has been venerated for centuries and a small shrine still attracts votive offerings. Le Kef has two ***kasbahs*** which are linked by a drawbridge and enclosed by a wall. The older, larger fort was first built in Byzantine times and later remodelled by the Turks; the other was built in the early 19th century. Jemaa el Kebir (Old Mosque) was one of the oldest mosques in Tunisia but is now closed. Next to it the Mosquée de Sidi Bou Makhlouf was built at the beginning of the 17th century and is named after the town's patron. The **Musée Regional des Arts et Traditions Populaires** (Regional Museum of Popular Arts and Traditions) focuses on the culture of the Berber people with displays of clothes, jewellery and household objects.

Below: *the fortifications at Le Kefa*

28A5
170km southwest of Tunis
To Tunis from the Gare Routiere SNT
The Artisanat Dar El Medina (The Association for the Protection of the Medina) acts as an informal tourist office: rue Hedi Chaker
Hotel-Restaurant Venus (££) Junction of rue Farhat Hached and avenue Habib Bourguiba 78 200355

Kasbahs
Daily 7–5. Closed Mon
Free

Musée Regional des Arts et Traditions Populaires
Place Ben Aissa
78 221503
9–1, 4–7 (9:30–4:30 in winter)
Cheap

MAHDIA

Set on a peninsula and still clinging to its old way of life with its weaving industry and thriving fishing port, Mahdia's small *médina* is the most obvious sign of the town's changing fortunes. Nearly every shop and stall is now geared towards tourists since the creation of a burgeoning *zone touristique* 6km west of the town centre, where the best beaches are to be found.

Mahdia's history dates from the 10th century when it was the capital of the Fatimid dynasty. All that remains of the town's fortifications is the Skifa el-Kahla (the Dark Gate), which stands at the entrance to the *médina*. Next to it is the new **Regional Museum of Mahdia**, with archaeological exhibits from Punic, Roman and Fatimid times and a collection of traditional costumes.

Take a walk along the main thoroughfare, the rue Obidallah el Mehdi. At the end of the street there is the peaceful place du Caire where cafés, some with seats shaded by trees and vines, serve refreshments throughout the day. Just beyond the square is the Grande Mosquée (Great Mosque), but do not be fooled by its aged appearance – it was only built in the 1960s and is a replica of the thousand-year-old original. The large fortress which stands on the highest point of the peninsula is the **Borj el Kebir**, a 16th-century Turkish fort which offers excellent views over the town, port and surrounding Muslim cemetery. The port may look familiar: it was used as the setting for the German invasion of Benghazi in the Oscar-winning film *The English Patient*.

28C5
205km from Tunis, 62km from Sousse
Cafés in place du Caire (£)
Three services a day from Tunis from the station on avenue Farhat Hached
Almost hourly buses to Sousse and Sfax
Rue el Moez (just inside the *médina* by the Skifa el-Kahla) 73 681098
Few

Regional Museum of Mahdia
Place de l'Indépendance
9–12, 2–6 (9:30–4:30 in winter). Closed Mon
None
Moderate

Borj el Kebir
Rue du Borj
9–12, 2–6 (9:30–4:30 in winter). Closed Mon
None
Cheap

The entrance to the newly built mosque in Mahdia

A Walk Around Mahdia

This walk can be done at any time of the day but is particularly recommended in the early morning.

Start at the fishing harbour, which is still the focal point of Mahdia despite the onslaught of tourism.

Allow some time to wander around the harbour to watch fishermen unload the catch or repair their nets; call in at the slippery-floored fish maket where traders auction fish straight from the sea.

*Turn right out of the harbour entrance on to the seafront path which leads to the Grande Mosquée (Great Mosque) and Borj el Kebir (**➤ 66**). With the fort on your left, branch off to walk through the cemetery with its simple white gravestones. Follow the path round to the tiny red lighthouse passing the gardens and rocks off to the right which form Cap d'Afrique. Turning the corner of the windswept headland, notice the whitewashed roofs of the* zone touristique *in the distance. Walk back towards Mahdia town along a narrow street of traditional seafront houses.*

You will pass the Artisanat Dar El Médina on the left, which offers information about the *médina* and is located in an attractive house on avenue 7 Novembre.

Turn left up the alleyway running alongside the Hotel Al-Jazira. Follow it around to emerge next to the tourist information centre and the main entrance to the médina. *Stroll down rue Obidallah el Mehdi to the shaded place du Caire and then turn right by the side of Mosquée Mustapha Hamza which leads to a cluster of shops and cafés on rue des Fatmides.*

Distance
4km

Time
Two hours including stops

Start point
Fishing port
28C5

End point
Rue des Fatmides
28C5

Lunch or coffee
Café Sidi Salem (£)
rue du Borj

The old port of Mahdia, protected by the lighthouse on Cap d'Afrique

Monastir

Until the 1960s Monastir was a fairly typical Tunisian town, but it has been transformed into a showpiece tourist resort of pristine streets, elegant turn of the century lampposts and an abundance of greenery. It has an attractive 400-berth marina and an old fishing port. Most of Monastir's tourist hotels are located 6km west of the town centre in the suburb of Skanès near the international airport.

28C5
160km south of Tunis
From Sousse
Frequent departures to Sousse
Rue de l'Indépendance
8:30–1, 3–5:45 Mon–Thu; 8:30–1.30 Fri, Sat. Closed Sun
Also Monastir Airport
73 461205 24 hrs

What to See in Monastir

BOURGUIBA MOSQUÉE ✪✪

In the early years of his presidency, the Republic of Tunisia's first leader Habib Bourguiba built himself an elaborate mausoleum here in the centre of the town of his birth. Instantly recognisable by its twin minarets and golden dome, it has an impressive tree-lined drive leading to the gates; at its foot is a kiosk commemorating those who died fighting for Tunisia's independence. A golden statue of the schoolboy Bourguiba stands in the nearby place du Gouvernorat.

Top end of Sidi el Mazeri Cemetery
Closed to visitors

Above: *the massive* ribat *of Harthema stands above the harbour at Monastir*

MÉDINA ✪

A great chunk of Monastir's *médina* was demolished in the 1960s in the course of a misguided modernisation plan, and with it the Old Town district lost much of its heart. Dedicated to protecting the *médina* from any further development (a somewhat lost cause) is the **Association de Sauvegarde de Médina** (City Safe-Keeping Association). Its centre, built around a whitewashed courtyard shaded by an orange tree, provides a welcome oasis from the surrounding bustle.

Association de Sauvegarde de Médina
Rue du 2 Mars
9–1. 3–7 (9–12, 2–6 in winter). Closed Mon
Special exhibitions occasionally mounted

MUSÉE DES ARTS ET TRADITIONS

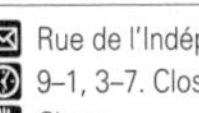

Refurbished in 1996, the stone-floored, somewhat spartan Museum of Arts and Traditions contains a collection of impressive outfits worn by couples on their wedding day – and for many days following the ceremony. In the 18th and 19th centuries it was traditional for the bride's dress to be made by her mother and sisters, which sometimes took several years because of the huge amount of intricate embroidery involved. The men's costumes are much simpler. The costumes are attractively presented in glass-fronted cabinets, with a display of costume jewellery.

Rue de l'Indépendance
9–1, 3–7. Closed Mon
Cheap

RIBAT

Founded in 796, the *ribat* has been reworked and restored so many times that there is little left of the original structure. One surviving section from earliest times is the prayer hall which is now used as a **Museum of Islamic Arts**. Exhibits include fragments of 12th-century weaving, Egyptian fabrics, samples of Islamic writings and a gold jewellery collection from Persia. The Nador tower offers spectacular views over the town centre and corniche.

The *ribat* has provided the backdrop for scenes in several major films including *Jesus of Nazareth* and *The Life of Brian*. Connected to the southern gate is the Grande Mosquée (Great Mosque), built at the same time as the *ribat* and *médina* walls. It is closed to non-Muslims.

Behind the route de la Corniche
73 461272
8–7 (9:30–7 in winter)
Moderate (includes entry to Museum of Islamic Arts)

The Nador tower gives spectacular views over Monastir

- 28C5
- 134km south of Tunis
- Buses to Sousse operate along the main road just outside the entrance to Port El Kantaoui
- The marina 8:30–1, 3–5:45 Mon–Thu. 8:30–1:30 Fri, Sat. Closed Sun
- Les Emirs (£££), The marina 73 240865

Above: *the recently built resort town of El Kantaoui is focused on the marina*

PORT EL KANTAOUI

Port El Kantaoui arouses quite strong feelings between those who love the resort and those who are rather less keen. Purpose-built around a picturesque marina which now draws luxury yachts from all over the world, it opened in 1979 and has been Tunisia's most outstandingly successful tourist centre.

With the look and feel of an elite residential district, it is the sort of development where you would expect to find the homes of top politicians, diplomats or the fabulously wealthy. The only difference is that the residents of this smart enclave are mainly package holidaymakers, often first-time visitors looking for a gentle introduction to Tunisia. Equally popular with families and older couples who like its reassuringly familiar ambience and strong sense of safety, detractors criticise Port El Kantaoui for its artificiality. It's also not unusual to find holidaymakers outnumbering Tunisians ten to one.

Millions of dinars have been poured into landscaping, with palm trees, shrubs and grass borders lining every road and not a tatty bit of paintwork in sight. The resort's hotels are equally sparkling; giant whitewashed palaces with their own terraced gardens awash with bougainvillaea.

DID YOU KNOW?

If you want to get from Port El Kantaoui to Sousse and don't want to take a taxi, you can ride in an open-sided 'Noddy Train' which is very popular with children. It operates hourly daytime services between the two resorts, leaving from the main entrance to the Kantaoui marina in front of the imitation fort.

The early built hotels have the advantage of being closest to the marina and are also generally thought to offer the best quality. Some of the newest accommodation can involve a good ten-minute walk to the shops and restaurants surrounding the harbour. Port El Kantaoui is practically self-sufficient and apart from the obligatory souvenir shops it has banks, a supermarket, hairdressers and a newsagent.

Sailing trips in glass-bottomed cruisers, fishing boats or in an imitation pirate's galleon are available from the marina. There is also a diving club and nearby riding stables have horses and camels for hire. Port El Kantaoui's pride and joy is its beautifully manicured 36-hole championship golf course (➤ 113). There are no membership requirements and while golfers with their own equipment are welcome, those who prefer to travel light can hire everything from clubs to caddies at very reasonable rates. Most hotels will arrange bookings and pre-set tee-times with the club.

The Temple of Jupiter catches the evening sun at Sufetula near Sbeïtla

SBEÏTLA ✪✪

If it were not for its impressive Roman ruins, Sbeïtla would attract very few visitors. Far from any tourist resort, Sbeïtla is the most southerly of Tunisia's major Roman sites. Established at the beginning of the first century on what had been an early Numidian settlement, it was known as Sufetula and reached the height of its prosperity towards the end of the 2nd century. By then it had a population of more than 10,000 people, double the number of people who live in Sbeïtla today.

There is a massive triumphal arch just before the entrance to the archaeological site; other interesting ruins include the much-photographed forum built in 139, the well-preserved baths with their ingenious under-floor heating system and a more modern structure, the 6th-century Basilica of St Vitalis with a beautiful baptismal font covered in mosaics.

- 28C5
- 117km west of Kairouan
- 7–7 (8:30–5:30 in winter)
- Three buses a day to Kairouan from a car park on the southern edge of town, off rue Habib Thameur
- None
- Moderate

28C4
270km southeast of Tunis
Five services a day (four in winter) to El Jem, Sousse and Tunis from the station at the eastern end of avenue Habib Bourguiba.
To Tunis and Sousse
Regular daytime services to Iles Kerkennah
Four Tuninter flights a week to Tunis
Avenue Mohamed H Khefacha (near the ferry port for Kerkennah)
74 211040
7:30–1, 3–5:45 (8:30–1, 3–5:45 in winter)
Socopa Craft Shop
rue Hammadi Taj
74 296826 9–12, 4–7 (9–12, 3–6 in winter)

Above: *the massive defensive walls of the old town of Sfax*

Junction of avenues Habib Bourguiba and Hedi Chaker
74 229744
Tue–Sat, 9:30–4:30
Cheap

Sfax

Tunisia's second city is rarely visited by holiday-makers except perhaps those with a couple of hours to spare while awaiting ferries to Iles Kerkennah (► 18). Although it is mainly an industrial city with factories sprawling along the coastline, the city centre is attractively compact and very underrated. One of the joys of Sfax is being able to wander through its streets and *souqs* without hassle from over-eager traders.

Founded in 849 near the site of a small Roman town, Taparura, Sfax quickly became prosperous by trading in the products of the Sahel's olive trees. Remaining largely independent until the beginning of the 17th century it strongly resisted the imposition of the French Protectorate in 1881 which led to French marines storming the city defacing its mosques and killing several hundred people. Hedi Chaker and Farhat Hached, two of the Tunisia's trade union leaders involved in securing the country's independence and whose names are seen on street signs across the country, both hailed from Sfax.

What to See in Sfax

ARCHAEOLOGICAL MUSEUM

The archaeological collection is housed on the ground floor of the Town Hall, an unmistakable colonial building with a dome and clock tower. Although it only comprises six exhibition rooms there are several items of interest including an unusual 3rd-century Roman mosaic of children wrestling, Christian funerary mosaics and Roman and Muslim tombs. There are also displays of Roman wall paintings, glass and prehistoric tools from Gafsa (► 83).

MÉDINA ✪✪✪

The old town in Sfax has one of the best-preserved and most atmospheric *médinas* in the country. Surrounded by massive stone walls originally built by the Aghlabites in the 9th century, it is a hive of activity with dozens of first-floor workshops for tailors, engravers and furniture-makers. At the heart of a labyrinth of narrow streets and *impasses* is the Grande Mosquée (Great Mosque), which was started in 849 and extensively rebuilt in the 10th century. Closed to non-Muslims, the best view of its celebrated, several-tiered minaret is from place Souk el Djemaa.

Sfax's covered *souqs* run between the Grande Mosquée and rue des Forgerons. Immediately beyond Bab Jebli, the oldest surviving gateway to the *médina*, is a large food market. Go early in the day as the night's fishing catch is unloaded from cold storage vans. An even bigger daily fish market operates opposite the docks on avenue Ali Bach Hamba.

Main entrance on avenue Ali Belhouane
Many cafés (£)
Free

MUSÉE REGIONAL DES ARTS ET TRADITIONS ✪✪

The Regional Museum of Arts and Traditions (also known as the Dar Jallouli museum), is at the heart of the *médina* in a handsome 17th century townhouse, the former home of one of Tunisia's most influential families, and gives an idea of what life would have been like for an upper class family in Sfax in the 19th century. The house itself is just as interesting as the exhibits, with its white paved floors, tiled walls and carved wood ceilings. As well as displays of furniture, traditional costumes and jewellery, there are special sections on calligraphy and painting on glass.

Rue de le Driba
74 211186
9–4:30. Closed Mon
Cheap

Below: *narrow alleyways honeycomb the* médina *in Sfax*

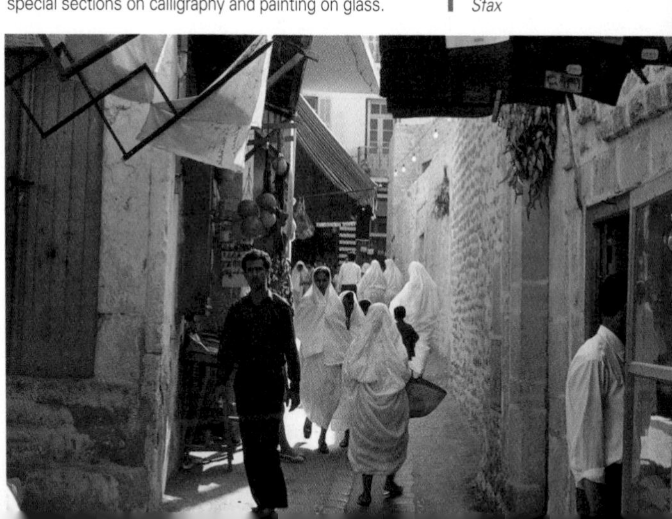

In the Know

If you want to get the real flavour and feel of the country, here are some ideas.

10 Ways to Be a Local

Learn a few words of Arabic – it works wonders and is well worth the effort for the obvious pleasure it brings.
Avoid talking politics or making any criticism of the President, whose photograph appears everywhere.
Eat in a *gorgote* or *rôtisserie* and enjoy the value for money.
Buy a *burnous* – a long woollen coat with a hood which is very useful in the winter when it can turn extremely cold in the north.
Smoke a *chicha* (hookah pipe) while playing a game of cards in a smoky, starkly lit café or bar.
Never switch on your car headlights until it is pitch black assuming that because you know you are on the road everyone else must be able to see you.
Get up at sunrise and consider you are having a late night if you are still out on the town at 10PM.
Don't worry about being under-dressed – even deluxe hotels rarely insist on a jacket and tie.
Be prepared for the incessant ringing of mobile phones; conversations will be conducted at a decibel level which would seem to make their use superfluous.
Don't drive past a hitch-hiker if you have room to pick them up. Car ownership is rare and poor public transport in rural areas means hitch-hiking is common. It adds an extra dimension to a journey, and the gesture will be much appreciated.

10 Good Places to Have Lunch

Restaurant Bon Kif (££–£££) avenue Marbella (off avenue Habib Thameur), Nabeul ☎ 72 222783. Stylish Tunisian restaurant where tourists and locals gather for long, lazy lunches.

Fishing from a small boat is a way of life for many Tunisians

Boys enjoy a game of football in Belvedere Park, Tunis

Dar El Jeld (£££) rue Dar El Jeld, Tunis ☎ 71 260916. Superb Tunisian food in the setting of a sumptuous mansion.
La Daurade (££–£££) The Marina, Port El Kantaoui ☎ 73 244893. Very popular fish restaurant with shaded outside seating.
Le Lido (££) avenue Mohammed V, Sousse ☎ 73 225329. Sit outside opposite the harbour and enjoy fresh fish.
Les Margaritas (££) rue de Hollande, Tunis ☎ 71 240631. There is a theatrical feel about this perennially popular lunchtime venue.
RestoVert (£) avenue de la République, Hammamet. Soups, salads and sandwiches in a friendly café lined with movie posters.
Café Sidi Salem (£) rue du Borj, Mahdia. Sit outside and admire the expansive sea view.
La Sirine (£–££) avenue Assad ibn el Fourat, Hammamet. Everything from *crêpes* to *couscous* at this beach restaurant.
La Sirène (££) Remla beachfront, Iles Kerkennah ☎ 74 281118. Excellent fresh fish in a venue overlooking the sea.
Le Sport Nautique (£££) boulevard Habib Bougatfa, Bizerte ☎ 72 433262. Ideal for a leisurely lunch overlooking the entrance to the harbour.

10 Top Activities

Bathing Most Tunisians visit a *hammam* (Turkish bath) at least once a week.
Cinema-going A very popular pastime, even though most films are dubbed and long films heavily cut.
Cycling No better place than on the flat, uncrowded roads of Iles Kerkennah.
Diving Quality tuition and excellent dive sites in the waters around Tabarka.
Fishing A way of life for many Tunisians; no permit is required to fish from any of the harbours.
Football Tunisians are fanatical about football at all levels with Sunday the big day for local matches.
Four-wheel driving Ideal transport for exploring the desert region.
Golf Very high standards and eight courses to choose from.
Hunting Wild boar is hunted in winter in the forests around Tabarka.
Watersports Try waterskiing, paragliding and windsurfing in all the main beach resorts.

10 Places to Picnic

- Jebel Ichkeul National Park (► 19)
- Thuburbo Majus (► 54)
- Any of the deserted beaches on Iles Kerkennah (► 18)
- Parc du Belvédère, Tunis (► 35)
- The empty roadside near the desert villages of Chebika, Midès and Tamerza (► 82, 85, 86)
- Dougga (► 16)
- Bulla Regia (► 42)
- Carthage (► 26, 36)
- Sbeïtla (► 71)
- Thuburnica (► 44)

A poster advertising an Egyptian film; cinema-going is very popular

Jerba & the South

Apart from Jerba which offers some of the most unspoilt beaches in the Mediterranean and a charming pocket-sized capital, Houmt Souq, the desert region remains a well-kept secret. Covering much of the southern half of the country, it is beginning to attract more attention since the worldwide success of the Oscar-winning movie *The English Patient*, much of which was filmed around the oasis town of Tozeur. European holidaymakers usually prefer to visit the desert region in early spring or late autumn as the summer months can be oppressively hot.

Desert safaris from the east coast beach resorts rarely stay more than two or three nights in the region, with Tozeur the traditional focal point. Popular spots en route include Matmata with its unusual cave dwellings made famous in another big movie, *Star Wars*, and the Gorges de Selja, famous for the rail journey on Le Lezard Rouge (Red Lizard) train.

'I slipped into the orchards and experienced the cheerfulness of the fountains amidst the blossoming trees.'

SIMONE DE BEAUVOIR (1908–86) on seeing the oasis at Gabès.

The dramatic gorge of Midès in the far southwest

Jerba

Thought to be the 'land of the Lotus Eaters', where Ulysses came ashore during his Odyssey, Jerba is the holiday destination of many Tunisians. It is the only beach resort in the country which can claim to be attractive year-round, though it can be quite chilly during the day from November to January with the temperature dropping further at night.

28C3
506km south of Tunis
Two services a day to Sousse, Sfax and Tunis
Up to seven Tuninter flights a day from Jerba to Tunis from Mellita airport
place des Martyrs, Houmt Souq 75 658116

Above: *a shady square in Houmt Souq, the main town on the island of Jerba*

While its population is one of the most cosmopolitan in the country, Jerba society is deeply conservative and – confronted with the demands of foreign tourists – there remains a strong determination to preserve the island's distinct identity. Measuring just 29km wide by 27km long, Jerba is said to have 354 mosques – one for every day of the Islamic year.

What to See in Jerba

AJIM

22km south of Houmt Souq
To Jorf every 30 minutes, 6am –midnight; every 2 hours, midnight–6AM
Cheap for cars; free for foot passengers

Visitors arriving by ferry dock at Ajim. Still an important centre for sponges, which are collected from the seabed by divers, it is also a busy fishing port. In the summer months there can be long queues for the car ferry to Jorf – a two-hour wait is not unusual. Swimming around Ajim is not recommended, as there are often swarms of jellyfish in this area.

EL KANTARA CAUSEWAY

7km long from southeast corner of Ile de Jerba to the mainland
Free

Driving across the El Kantara Causeway is the alternative to taking the ferry to and from the mainland, but it adds around 100km to a journey. The first causeway was built in Carthaginian times and survived until 1551, when it was badly damaged by the Turkish pirate Dragut. Repairs were not made until 1953.

ERRIADH (HARA SEGHIRA) ✪

The only reason for coming here is to see the **El Ghriba Synagogue**, one of the most holy Jewish shrines in North Africa. There has been a strong Jewish presence in Tunisia, and particularly in Jerba, going back many centuries. Jerba's Jews today number around a thousand, many having migrated to Israel, and the synagogue now provides a meeting place for the ageing community. Suitably dressed visitors are welcome to enter the atmospheric synagogue with its bright blue pillars, dark wood panelling, painted tiles and stained glass.

- 8km from Houmt Souq
- Buses from Houmt Souq to Guellala (► below) stop in Erriadh

El Ghriba Synagogue

- 1km from town centre
- Daily. Closed Sat
- None
- Free

Left: *a potter at work in Guellala*

GUELLALA ✪✪

Guellala rivals Nabeul (► 52) as a pottery-producing centre. The clay for the pottery – all of which is handmade – is quarried from hills above the village and out towards nearby Sedouikech. The main street is lined with shops all piled high with pots and plates; there are several workshops and dozens of kilns. Haggle effectively and most pieces are very cheap, though quality varies enormously. Expect to pay more for anything with fish on it and look out for specialities such as camel-shaped water jugs. Guellala is a popular morning stop on coach tours of the island, so the best bargains can usually be negotiated in mid-afternoon when there are fewer people around.

The Mosquée de Guellala (1km out of town on the road to Erriadh) dates from the 15th century. On the same road, nearer El Kantara (► 78) is the crumbling ruin of the Mosquée de Sidi Yati which was built in the tenth century.

- 18km from Houmt Souq, 6km from El Kantara
- Four buses a day from Houmt Souq
- None

28C4
22km northeast of Ajim
Good choice (£–££)
Bus station on avenue Bourguiba
Boulevard de l'Environment 75 650016 and avenue Bourguiba 75 650915

Borj el Kebir

At the seafront end of rue Taieb Mehiri, 700m from the fishing port
8–12, 3–7 (9:30–4:30 in winter). Closed Fri
Cheap

Musée des Arts et Traditions Populaires

Avenue Abdelhamid el-Kadhi
75 650540
8–12, 3–7 (9.30–4.30 in winter). Closed Fri
Moderate

Above: *carpet market*
Opposite, top: *silver brooch from the museum*
Right: *ancient olive tree near Midoun*

HOUMT SOUQ

Houmt Souq, the capital of Jerba, is situated on the island's north coast 6km from the airport at Mellita. It is a charming place to spend few days and makes a good base for excursions to other parts of the island and further afield. Houmt Souq means 'marketplace', and this remains the town's primary purpose despite its now blossoming tourism industry, which has brought the inevitable crop of souvenir shops and European-style restaurants.

The heart of the town is the snug little complex of whitewashed squares and streets surrounding the *souq*, where goods including jewellery, coral and leatherware are sold. There is also a daily fish auction. Mondays and Thursdays are the busiest days when traders come in from all over the island to sell straw baskets and mats.

On the seafront, close to Houmt Souq's busy fishing harbour, is the **Borj el Kebir** (also known as Borj Ghazi Mustapha). There has probably been a fort here since Roman times, but the earliest remains are of a fortress built at the end of the 13th century by the Sicilian Roger de Loria. Most of the existing structure dates from the late 15th and early 16th centuries. In 1560 – when controlled by the Spanish – it was the scene of a famous two-month siege and massacre led by the Turkish pirate Dragut, who stormed the castle and killed all its occupants. The skulls of the defeated Spanish soldiers were dumped in an 11m-high pile close to the port; today a small white monument marks the spot.

Among several interesting mosques (all closed to non-Muslims) is the multi-domed Mosque of the Strangers, the Jami'et-Turuk (the Mosque of the Turks) which has a beautiful minaret and the Zaouia de Sidi Brahim which contains the tomb of a 17th-century saint.

The **Musée des Arts et Traditions Populaires** (Museum of Arts and Popular Traditions) is housed in a former mosque – the Zaouia de Sidi Zitouna. Dedicated to Jerban culture, it has a large collection of costumes and jewellery; a reconstruction of a pottery workshop with some huge jars which were used to store everything from grain to clothing; and another room is filled with antique wooden chests.

MIDOUN ✪✪

Jerba's second biggest town really springs into life on Friday – market day – when streets all around the centre are filled with makeshift stalls, attracting a large crowd of local people and tourists. Try to arrive as early as possible, because it is all but over by lunchtime. Another crowd-puller takes place on Tuesday afternoons, when a mock Berber wedding procession is held for the benefit of visitors.

28C3
16km east of Houmt Souq
Several (£–££)
Frequent from Houmt Souq and the tourist resorts

SIDI MAHREZ ✪✪

Starting at Flamingo Point about 8km east of Houmt Souq and extending as far as Ras Taguermes (marked by a lighthouse), this 10km stretch of coastline is said to be the best beach in Jerba. The *zone touristique* occupies some of this with its cluster of large hotels, but there are quieter areas. Another unspoilt stretch can be found south of Aghir while the wild and rocky west coast is almost totally uninhabited.

28C4
8–18km east of Houmt Souq
Bar snacks at the beach hotels
Bus from Houmt Souq

What to See in the South

28A4
60km northwest of Tozeur
No public transport; join an organised excursion or hire a car

Above: *steep limestone cliffs overlook the palmery at Chebika*

CHEBIKA ✪✪

Chebika is the southernmost of three mountain villages close to the Algerian border which can be visited together on a day trip from Tozeur (▶ 87). The others are Midès (▶ 85) and Tamerza (▶ 86).

Abandoned after serious flooding in 1969, the old village of Chebika is now in ruins, but the villagers are making the most of tourism and still cultivate their gardens. There are guides available to lead you up the mountainside to see the waterfall which feeds the oasis; there is a good view of the salt lake of Chott el Gharsa.

28A3
Kebili is 120km west of Gabès
Small cafés in most oasis towns
Four a day from Gabès

CHOTT EL JERID ✪✪

Chott el Jerid is the most southwesterly of a series of salt lakes lying inland of Gabès (▶ 83). This vast salt lake of shifting colours and mirages covers nearly 5,000sq km. Lifeless in summer, the water evaporates leaving a crust of salt crystals which glisten in the sun, brilliant white interspersed with patches of green, orange and pink, caused by the different chemical constituents of the salts. In winter water collects on either side of the raised causeway built across the Chott from Degache to Kebili (▶ Drive, 90) and life returns to this inland sea. The lake is fringed with small oasis towns, whose economy depends entirely on the cultivation of dates.

Journeys across the Chott used to be hazardous and all the tourist literature tells of a huge caravan wandering off the main route and disappearing through the thin surface. It's still advised not to go off the beaten track.

Opposite: *pomegranates ripen in a lush oasis near Gafsa*

DOUZ ✪✪✪

Douz is right on the edge of the desert as most northerners think of it – the dunes are not quite so impressive here as they are a bit deeper into the Eastern Desert but they are enough for most visitors. Just outside the town near the village of Gleissia is the so-called Great Dune where most tours stop. The town centre is transformed early on a Thursday morning into a frenetic weekly produce market which draws shoppers and traders from a wide area, selling everything from sheep, goats and camels, to dates, spices and beans, as well as clothing and leather goods.

The recently reopened **Douz Museum** explores the history and culture of the southern Jerid with costumes and jewellery, camel harnesses and a Bedouin tent.

28B3
148 km southwest of Gabès
Choice of cafés (£)
To Tunis, Douz and Kebili
Place des Martyrs ☎ 75 470351 8:30–1, 3–5:45 Mon–Thu. 8–1:30 Fri, Sat. Closed Sun. Also route de Zaafrane ☎ 75 470351 8:30–1, 3–5:45 Mon–Thu. 8–1:30 Fri, Sat. Closed Sun
Annual International Festival of the Sahara, Nov or Dec.
Camel treks organised by Douz Voyages ☎ 75 470178; Abdel Moulah Voyages ☎ 75 95484

Douz Museum
Avenue des Martyrs
8:30–1, 3–6 Mon–Sat
Cheap

GABÈS ✪✪

Initially Gabès appears to be a modern industrial city at the crossroads for tours to the interior, but it has more to offer. It was a major Phoenician and Roman port; during the 14th century it was on the main east–west trading route and was a transit stop for Muslim pilgrims en route to Mecca. It was heavily battered in World War II raids and by devastating floods in 1962 but the old town still has atmosphere with its *souq* and mosques, and its huge plantation of date palms is a true oasis.

28B4
405km south of Tunis
Wide choice of restaurants (£–££)
To Sfax, Sousse and Tunis
To Matmata
Avenue Hedi Chaker ☎ 75 270254

GAFSA ✪

A former Berber stronghold and a prosperous Roman town, Gafsa is an important regional centre and phosphate-producing town. Most tourists pass through on their way to the salt lakes and dunes but there is a picturesque *kasbah*, a huge date palm grove and the Piscines Romaines (Roman Pools) with a small museum.

28A4
93km northeast of Tozeur
Good choice (£–££)
To Tunis, Tozeur, Sfax
Place des Piscines Romaines ☎ 76 221664

28A4
16km west of Metlaoui
Le Lézard Rouge
Metlaoui station
76 241920; one departure a day
Expensive

Below: *this ancient underground dwelling at Matmata has been converted into a hotel*

GORGES DE SELJA

This impressive 15km-long gorge stretches from Redeyef to Metlaoui, a thriving phosphate mining town. One of the best ways to see the gorge is from **Le Lézard Rouge** (the Red Lizard): a restored 19th-century train which operates a two-hour round-trip from Metlaoui. Selja itself is halfway along the gorge and is a good place to stop for a walk down into the deepest parts of the gorge. The railway tunnels and bridges were originally built by the French to transport phosphate from the mines to Gafsa (► 83).

KSAR OULED SOLTANE (► 22, TOP TEN)

28B3
43km southwest of Gabès
Up to ten buses a day to Gabès and daily services to Sfax, Sousse and Tunis
Main square 75 230114
Hôtel Marhala 75 230015, Hôtel Sidi Driss 75 230005, Hôtel Berbères 75 230024
By arrangement

MATMATA

One of the best-known villages in Tunisia, mostly due to the opening sequence of the original *Star Wars* movie which featured its troglodyte dwellings. Dating from the fourth century BC, many of the underground houses are still inhabited, providing homes that are cool in summer and warm in winter. Some of the houses can be visited by arrangement with the owners, but it is advisable to arrange a price beforehand or buy some of the craft goods on sale. Three of the traditional dwellings in Old Matmata have been turned into hotels: the Marhala, part of a chain run by the Touring Club de Tunisie; the Hôtel Sidi Driss whose bar also appeared in the film as the setting for the alien jazz club sequence; and Les Berbères – named after the people who have lived here for centuries.

A whitewashed mosque stands alone in the desert near Midès

MIDÈS ✪✪

The oasis village of Midès is in the mountains which border Algeria. Originally a Berber village, Midès became an outpost of the Roman Empire. All but a handful of residents have now left their single room mud brick houses in the original village perched precariously on the sides of the deep gorge, and moved to the new town which has been built on the other side of the palm grove. The oasis itself is, as usual, a place of refuge from the fierce heat of this desert region. The Tunisian government is now helping to restore the old houses as tourist accommodation, and shops that sell local produce and souvenirs to a small but steadily increasing stream of day-trippers.

28A4
75km west of Gafsa
None; join an organised excursion or hire a car

DID YOU KNOW?

Sufism is a devout sect which has been marginalised by Orthodox Islam. Followers seek to achieve a direct relationship with God through spiritual association rather than by learning Koranic texts. They are known for achieving a trance-like state through chanting, dancing and meditation.

NEFTA ✪✪

The main attractions in Nefta are the Qasr El-Aïn (➤ 24, Top Ten) which is set in a deep basin (the Corbeille or 'basket') below the town, and the other oasis which lies just to the south. But Nefta itself is worth exploring too. The best-preserved of Nefta's Old Town districts is Ouled ech Cherif, where the narrow alleyways are often covered and the walls are decorated with traditional patterns created in the brickwork. There are literally dozens of mosques throughout the old quarters with Sidi M'Khareg in one of the most scenic positions overlooking the oasis.

Nefta is a centre of Sufism – a branch of Islam (➤ above) – and the town has over a hundred shrines (or *marabouts*), that make this city the holiest in Tunisia after Kairouan (➤ 20–1) . The Zaouia de Sidi Brahim is the headquarters of an important Sufi order.

28A4
25km west of Tozeur
Hôtel Marhala (£) avenue de l'Environment 76 430027
Six a day to Tozeur. Daily services to Kairouan and Sfax
Tozeur–Nefta airport (23 km) for flights to Tunis and Jerba
Avenue Habib Bourguiba 76 430236
Thursday is market day

QASR EL-AÏN, NEFTA(➤ 24, TOP TEN)

Above: *the mud-brick village of Tamerza is fast dissolving back into the landscape*

28C2
70km south of Tataouine
Daily from Tataouine
Cafés (£) on place de l'Indépendance

REMADA ✪

Remada is Tunisia's southernmost town, beyond which there is nothing but desert, is dominated by the military, due to the proximity of the Libyan border. Centred on a little oasis where the Romans had a small fort, day-to-day life focuses on the shady place de l'Indépendance. Remada's most distinctive sight is on the southern edge of town – a 15-domed mud brick building once used as a slaughterhouse. Borg Bourguiba, 40km southwest of Remada, is where Habib Bourguiba (➤ 14) was held prisoner for a year in the early 1950s.

28A4
85km west of Gafsa
Tamerza Palace Hotel (££) ☎ 76 453844 Fax 76 453722
Two buses a day to Tunis and three a day to Gafsa
Tourist bureau Daily 8–6

TAMERZA ✪✪

Once a Roman military post called Ad Turres, Tamerza later became the seat of a Christian bishop during the Byzantine era. The original village of Tamerza was devastated by catastrophic flooding in 1969 and now lies abandoned. Today visitors walk through its eerily empty streets; it looks strangely beautiful at night when floodlit and viewed from the comfort of the Tamerza Palace Hotel directly opposite. There is a small waterfall and a swimming area known as the Cascades.

28C3
49km south of Medenine
Hôtel Sangho (££)
3km from town on road to Chenini ☎ 75 860102 Fax 75 862177
To Sfax, Sousse and Tunis.
Festival of the Ksour, Apr

TATAOUINE ✪

A good base for exploring the *ksour* or fortified villages (➤ 22, Top Ten). Tataouine is a Berber word meaning 'springs' and historically there was an important camel market here; there is still a busy market every Monday and Thursday held in and around the central *souq* – one of the best places to buy *kilims* (woven rugs) and pottery. Ksar Megabla, 2km south of the town centre, offers good views of the surrounding area.

Traditional brick designs adorn the entrance to the oasis in Tozeur

Tozeur

The area around Tozeur has been inhabited since at least 8000 BC, sited around an oasis on the northern shore of the great salt lake of Chott el Jerid (► 82). The town prospered as a trading post on the route of the great trans-Saharan caravans but today Tozeur is the focal point of Tunisia's ever-expanding desert tourist industry. Until relatively recently Tozeur was merely an overnight stop on desert safaris from the east coast resorts, but it is now an established resort in its own right.

28A4
220km west of Gabès; 450km south of Tunis
Good choice (£–£££) around avenue Bourguiba
To Tunis, Nefta, Gafsa and Kebili
Regular flights to Tunis, Djerba and Monastir
Avenue Abdul Kacem Chebbi 76 450503
Bedouin Festival, Dec

What to See in Tozeur

BELVÉDÈRE

This rocky outcrop offers panoramic views over the palm grove (► 89), the Chott el Jerid (► 82) and the Chott el Gharsa. It is a 20-minute walk from the Dar Cheraït (► below); go early in the morning or at sunset, or at night when the site is floodlit.

3km southwest of the town centre
Open access
None
Free

DAR CHERAÏT MUSEUM

Purpose-built in the style of an upper-class Tunis townhouse, the displays depict scenes from Tunisian life past and present: there is a typical kitchen, a *bey's* bedroom, a wedding scene, a *hammam* and a Bedouin tent. There are displays of costumes, jewellery, ceramics and sacred books; and the work of weavers, cobblers and tailors is also highlighted. A sound-and-light show called 'One Thousand and One Nights' is based (very) loosely on the book of the same name.

Route Touristique
06 452100
8AM–midnight
None
Moderate

A Walk Around Tozeur

Distance
5km

Time
Half a day allowing for visits

Start/end point
Grand Hôtel de l'Oasis
28A4
place des Martyrs
76 452699

Drinks
Cafés (£) on avenue Habib Bourguiba

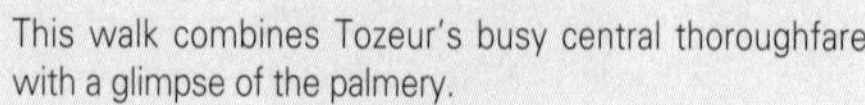

This walk combines Tozeur's busy central thoroughfare with a glimpse of the palmery.

Start at the Grand Hôtel de l'Oasis and walk up avenue Habib Bourguiba.

Tozeur's main street is a curious mix of sleepy desert town catering for the everyday needs of local people and brash tourist centre with dozens of shops selling carpets, pottery and stuffed camels.

At the tiered pottery bowl landmark turn right for a look around Tozeur's covered market hall. Walk past the slim sandstone minaret of Mosquée El Farkous, turning right at the end of avenue Habib Bourguiba. Continue straight ahead at place des Martyrs. Take the second right towards Mosquée Sidi Abdesallem at the far end. Veer left towards a dome-shaped tiled monument in front of the École Primaire ibn Chabbat and walk down the left-hand side of the school. After 200m, at the end of a concrete wall, turn right following the path through a courtyard to the palmery.

Tozeur's palmery (▶ 89) covers around 10sq km, has more than 200,000 palm trees and 200 springs.

After two or three minutes' walk, cross a small stream, turn left out of the palmery and then right following a path leading into the médina. *Take the third turning right, under a double arch. Note the roofs made of dried palm trunks.*

Call in at the Musée des Arts et Traditions Populaires (▶ 89).

Turn right out of the museum. At the end of the street turn left which leads back to avenue Habib Bourguiba.

Tozeur's palmery is a lush oasis of greenery

MUSÉE DES ARTS ET TRADITIONS POPULAIRES (MUSEUM OF ARTS AND POPULAR TRADITIONS) ✪

This museum illustrates traditional life with costumes, pottery and furniture. One of the most interesting exhibits is a collection of manuscripts describing Tozeur's water system. Originally conceived in the 13th century by the town's *imam* (religious leader) Ibn Chabbat, the distribution network was handed down orally from generation to generation until finally committed to paper in 1911.

Rue de Kairouan
8–6 Mon–Sat. 8–2:30 Sun
Cheap

OULED EL HADEF ✪✪✪

Tozeur's Old Town is a web of narrow alleys which have changed little since the 14th century when it was built by the Ouled el Hadef tribe. Its distinctive architecture is considered to be one of the marvels of Islamic art. Unique to Tozeur and neighbouring Nefta (► 85), houses are decorated with geometric motifs (also found on local carpets and shawls). The yellowish bricks are handmade from a mix of local sand and clay, soaked in water, shaped in a wooden frame and left to dry in the sun before being baked in a kiln for three days. The bricks provide excellent insulation against the extremes of the desert climate, swelteringly hot in summer and freezing on winter nights.

North and east of the Hôtel Splendid
Choice of cafés (£)
Free

PALMERY ✪✪✪

Within the oasis at Tozeur are thousands of date palms and hundreds of springs; the oasis is best viewed from the Belvédère (► 87), from a **hot air balloon**, or from a *calèche* (horse-drawn carriage) which you can hire to drive around the palm groves. A popular stop on every tourist circuit is the Paradis, a lush tropical garden which is seen at its best in early spring.

Northeast of the Market Square
Calèches for hire from opposite the Hôtel Karim
Open access
Free
Hot air balloon flights: Aeroasis
avenue Abdul Kacem Chabbi
76 452 361
Fax 76 451 500

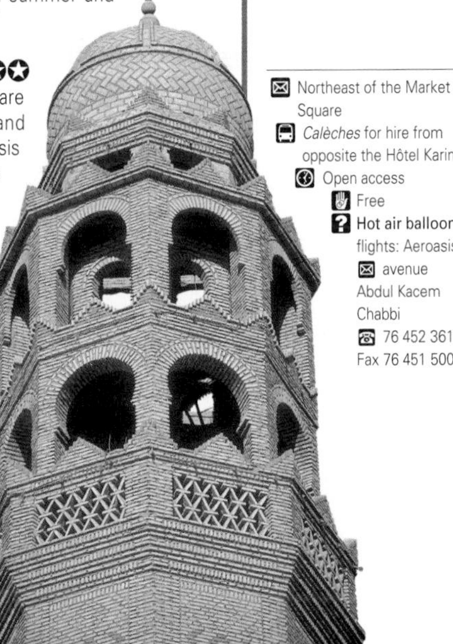

The minaret of the Mosque El Farkous is built of thousands of tiny bricks arranged in geometric designs

Tozeur to Kebili: the road across the Chott

Distance
186km

Time
Allow five hours including time for lunch and a bathe in the Roman pool

Start/end point
Tozeur
 28A4

Lunch
Hôtel l'Oasis dar Kebili
(££–£££)
✉ Zone Touristique de Kebili
☎ 75 491436

A drive along the causeway across the Chott El Jerid which can produce stunning mirages.

Leave Tozeur heading northeast on the GP3. After 8km drive through the village of Bouhel, turn right and 3km later pass through Degache, which marks the start of the 80km-long / 2m-high causeway across the Chott.

The Chott El Jerid (➤ 82) is one of a series of giant salt lakes that divide the north of the country from the true desert landscape of the south. There are no significant landmarks en route; however, look out for the abandoned burnt-out shell of a bus and a handful of isolated huts and stalls selling souvenirs. The terrain can appear to change enormously according to the time of year and the brightness of the sunshine. In winter if there has been quite a lot of rain it is not unusual for the water to look pink on one side of the road and green on the other; this is caused by the natural chemicals in the water.

The first signs of life come as you pass through the village of Souk Lahad, which is worth a short stop. You reach Kebili after another 15km.

Kebili was an important slave-trading town until the 19th century but is now simply a regional transport centre. There is a large palm grove, and just outside town – 1km south on the road to Douz – a Roman bathing pool and *hammam* fed by a 3km-deep borehole.

Leave Kebili, returning to Tozeur along the causeway.

The 90km-long causeway across the Chott el Jerid, the largest salt lake in southern Tunisia

Where To...

Above: *Guellala pottery*
Right: *a character in* A Thousand and One Nights

Tunis & the North

Prices
The restaurants listed in this section have been grouped into three price categories based on a three-course meal per person without drinks.
£ = budget – less than 10D
££ = moderate – 15–25D
£££ = expensive – over 25D

Bizerte

Le Bonheur (£)
Grilled meats, fish and seafood at this simple but convivial local restaurant.
✉ 31 rue Thaalbi ☎ 72 431047 ⌚ Lunch, dinner

L'Eden (££–£££)
Fresh fish and seafood specialities on a flower-adorned terrace 3km from the town centre.
✉ route de la Corniche ☎ 72 439023 ⌚ Lunch, dinner

Le Petit Mousse (££)
In hotel of the same name (► 100). The upstairs dining room offers a long French-inspired menu; in summer grilled fish and pizzas are served outside.
✉ route de la Corniche ☎ 72 432185 ⌚ Lunch, dinner

Le Sport Nautique (£££)
Seafront restaurant near town centre. Ideal for a leisurely lunch, with people-watching thrown in.
✉ boulevard Habib Bougatfa ☎ 72 433262 ⌚ Lunch, dinner

La Goulette

Le Café Vert (££)
The leader among the cluster of mid- to up-market fish restaurants. *Poisson Complet* is the most requested dish.
✉ 68 avenue Franklin Roosevelt ☎ 71 736156 ⌚ Lunch, dinner

Lucullus (££)
This popular fish restaurant features uniformed waiters and tables set with linen tablecloths.
✉ 1 avenue Habib Bourguiba ☎ 71 737310 ⌚ Lunch, dinner

Sidi Bou Saïd

Café des Nattes (£)
Allow time to linger and relax while enjoying a coffee at this atmospheric Moorish café overlooking Sidi Bou Saïd's main street.
✉ place Sidi Bou Saïd ⌚ All day

Café Sidi Chabanne (£)
Sit outside sipping the house speciality – mint tea sprinkled with pinenuts – while admiring the view of the Gulf of Tunis. You will pay well over the odds but, for once, it's worth it.
✉ rue el Hadi Zarrouk ⌚ All day

Tabarka

Hotel Andalous (£)
The three-course set menu here represents good value, and as an added bonus you can have a beer with your meal.
✉ avenue Habib Bourguiba ☎ 78 644 577 ⌚ Lunch, dinner

Tunis

Le Baghdad (££–£££)
A rather formal restaurant with uniformed doorman. The Tunisian specialities are good and there is occasional evening cabaret.
✉ 29 avenue Bourguiba (next to the Carlton Hotel) ☎ 71 259 068 ⌚ Lunch, dinner

Bolero (££)
This eaterie is located in a scruffy alley off rue de Yougoslavie, but is very popular with local residents. The main choice is between grilled meats and seafood – and there is a good value tourist menu.
✉ passage el-Guattar ☎ 71 245 928 ⌚ Lunch, dinner

Café de Paris (£)
Always busy and a convenient meeting place and people-watching spot. One of the few cafés to serve beer.
corner of avenue Habib Bourguiba and avenue de Carthage All day

Café Plantation (£)
Smiling, customer-friendly staff and a pleasant ambience make this a welcome addition to Tunis's café scene.
12–14 rue de Marseille 71 343565 All day

Capitole Restaurant (££)
Long-established, reasonably priced first-floor restaurant with a particularly good tourist menu.
60 avenue Habib Bourguiba 71 256601 Lunch, dinner

Chez Gaston (££)
Good value lunchtime tourist menu and a more extensive *à la carte* selection. Occasional live music.
73 rue de Yougoslavie 71 340417 Lunch, dinner

Chez Nous (££)
Photos of guests such as Edith Piaf and Muhammad Ali line the walls of this intimate French restaurant which offers good *à la carte* and set menus.
5 rue de Marseille 71 243048 Lunch, dinner. Closed Sun and Ramadan

Chez Slah (££)
Serving International, Tunisian and French cuisine in an agreeable setting. The house speciality is seafood fresh from the Gulf of Tunis. Alcohol and beer served and good selection of wine. Popular with locals.
14 Bis rue Pierre de Coubertin 71 258888 Lunch, dinner. Closed Mon

Dar El Jeld (£££)
Said to be the best restaurant in Tunis and it certainly has a grand setting in the former mansion of a fabulously wealthy family. It provides superb Tunisian cooking with gracious service and discreet musical accompaniment. Advance booking recommended.
rue Dar el Jeld 71 560916 Lunch, dinner. Closed Sun

Hollywood Dinners (££)
New movie-theme restaurant with some nice touches like presenting the bill in a metal filmreel case. The staff are welcoming but the food is over-fussy and lacks star quality.
12–14 rue de Marseille 71 343565 Lunch, dinner

La Mamma (£)
Pizzas and pasta as well as a range of Tunisian dishes at this dependable Italian-style restaurant which draws a continual flow of regular customers.
11 rue de Marseille 71 241256 Lunch, dinner

Les Margaritas (££)
Formal restaurant attached to the Hôtel Maison Dorée (► 101). Very popular as a lunchtime venue for local people. The set menu is good value.
rue de Hollande 71 240631 Lunch, dinner. Closed Sun

Grabbing a Sandwich
If you do not feel like having a full meal at lunchtime, drop in at a sandwich bar or pizzeria (both of which can be found all over Tunisia) and ask for a '*cassecroute*'. This is a thick chunk of French bread – usually buttered with fiery *harissa* sauce – then generously filled with lettuce, tomato, egg, tuna, olives and occasionally boiled potatoes or sausage.

Cap Bon

Self-help for Self-caterers
If you are on a self-catering holiday do not expect Tunisian supermarkets to be as well stocked as those in Europe or North America. Many food stores are part of larger shops selling a variety of household goods. The best advice is to shop Tunisian-style and buy food fresh from market stalls.

El Haouaria

L'Épervier (£–££)
Straightforward food at this popular venue busy with tour groups at lunchtime and a local crowd in the evening.
3 avenue Habib Bourguiba 72 297017 Lunch, dinner

Hammamet

Belle Vue (£–££)
Everything from soup and salads to full meals at this busy restaurant.
Centre Commercial, avenue Habib Bourguiba 72 280825 Lunch, dinner

Café Sidi Bou Hdid (£)
Also known as Café des Muriers. An atmospheric domed café which is at its best on warm summer evenings, when customers spill out on to the surrounding ramparts to sip coffee, smoke *chicas* and mull over the events of the day.
Seafront end of the *médina* All day

Le Carrefour (££)
Adjoining a popular bar run by three brothers. Pizza and fish highly recommended.
avenue des Nations Unies (outside the town centre close to the Hotel Miramar ➤ 102) 72 281776 Lunch, dinner

La Casa Doro (£££)
The extensive menu in five languages on boards outside suggests a cheap outlet but this is a place to linger over dinner, enjoying good food and attentive service.
60 avenue Habib Bourguiba 72 260099 Lunch, dinner

Chez Achour (££–£££)
Tucked away in a side street, this restaurant is solidly dependable with a strong local following and outside seating in summer. Fish is the house speciality.
rue Ali Belahouane, off avenue de la République 72 280140 Lunch, dinner

La Pergola (££)
Pleasant location with a large outside terrace awash with greenery. Efficient service and comprehensive menu with everything from soups and salads to grilled meats and fish.
Centre Commercial, avenue Habib Bourguiba 72 280993 Lunch, dinner

Pomodoro (££–£££)
The style of this restaurant is as discreet as its first floor location. A seriously classy but unstuffy place to eat, with courteous staff and excellent food.
avenue Habib Bourguiba 72 281254 Lunch, dinner

Restaurant Barberousse (££)
Hugely popular in the summer months with its roof terrace overlooking the *médina*. Both view and food are good value.
Entrance to the *médina* 72 282037 Lunch, dinner

Restaurant La Brise (£)
With its tiled floor and plastic tablecloths, this is not an ideal choice for dinner, but it is certainly worth considering for lunch, as its food is both wholesome and cheap.
2 avenue de la République 72 280073 Lunch, dinner

Restaurant Chinois (££)
For a change, try this

Chinese restaurant offering all the usual favourites.
Centre Commercial, avenue Habib Bourguiba 72 261937 Lunch, dinner

Restaurant Fatma (££)
Two minutes' walk from the *médina*. The service is pleasant but the food can be indifferent.
Commercial Centre, avenue Habib Bourguiba 72 280756 Lunch, dinner

RestoVert (£)
Cosy movie-themed café with walls lined with film posters. Serves simple food including salads and sandwiches.
avenue de la République All day

La Scala (£££)
The pasta is excellent at this intimate Italian restaurant themed around the La Scala Opera House in Milan. Book in advance.
off avenue des Nations Unies 72 280768 Lunch, dinner. Closed in winter

La Sirene (£–££)
Very casual beachfront restaurant/snack bar with shaded terrace. Wide range of food from pizzas and crêpes to grilled fish and *couscous*.
avenue Assad ibn el Fourat close to Hotel Belle Vue Lunch, dinner

Les Trois Moutons (££–£££)
One of the best restaurants in town, with excellent meat and fish dishes. Offers an extensive menu and a good value set dinner.
Centre Commercial, avenue Habib Bourguiba 72 280981 Lunch, dinner

Kélibia

Anis (£)
Very good value town centre budget restaurant offering Tunisian specialities and pleasant service.
avenue Erriadh 72 295777 Lunch, dinner

Restaurant El-Mansourah (££)
Choose grilled fish and salad with a bottle of the local Muscat de Kélibia, a refreshing medium-dry white wine.
Out beyond Kélibia's fort, at the southern end of Mansourah Beach 72 296321 Lunch, dinner

Nabeul

Café Errachida (£)
A welcoming café specialising in mint tea served with tempting sticky cakes.
avenue Habib Thameur (at the junction with avenue Habib Bourguiba) All day

Restaurant Bon Kif (££–£££)
Attracts as many local diners as it does tourists; ideal for a long, lazy lunch or dinner. Excellent grilled fish and succulent seafood, matched with quietly efficient service and Tunisian décor.
avenue Marbella (off avenue Habib Thameur) 72 222783 Lunch, dinner

Restaurant de l'Olivier (£££)
This restaurant is not cheap, but it offers up-market French cooking in smart surroundings. The wine list includes imported wines as well as some that have been produced locally.
6 avenue Hedi Chaker Lunch, dinner

Time for Tea?
Although mint tea is Tunisia's national drink, standards can vary enormously. Outside the main tourist areas many cafés serve a very sweet lukewarm mixture of gunpowder tea and sugar – often well stewed. For a piping hot glass of freshly-brewed mint tea topped with pinenuts it would be hard to better the Café Sidi Chabanne in Sidi Bou Saïd (► 92).

Central Tunisia

Rôtisseries and Gargottes

Rôtisseries are the cheapest of Tunisia's restaurants. Aimed at working men, they are easily identified by a rotating spit of roasting chickens at the entrance. This is usually the only food served – accompanied by chips and salad. Gargottes offer a wider range of food including *chorba* (spicy soup), kebabs and *merguez* sausages, but still served in very basic surroundings.

Iles Kerkennah

La Sirène (££)

Looks like a glorified beach hut, but serves excellent fresh fish and seafood. Friendly service and good value. In the summer you can sit out on a shaded terrace overlooking the sea and have a beer.

✉ On the beachfront at the end of the road next to Hôtel el-Jazira in Remla ☎ 74 481118 🕐 Lunch, dinner

Le Kef

Vénus (££)

One of the best restaurants in town, offering good value set price meals and an extensive *à la carte* choice.

✉ rue Farhat Hached ☎ 78 200355 🕐 Lunch, dinner

Mahdia

Le Lido (££–£££)

Brightly lit, Le Lido draws a good mix of tourists and locals. Opposite the fishing port, fish *couscous* is a favourite here, as well as grilled fish and seafood.

✉ avenue Farhat Hached ☎ 73 681339 🕐 Lunch, dinner

Restaurant el-Moez (£)

Popular with local people; fish soup and *kammounia* are among the specialities served here.

✉ In a small side street between Skifa el Kahla and rue des Fatmides 🕐 Lunch, dinner

Monastir

La Plage (£)

Dine overlooking the sea at this restauarant close to the fishing port; naturally, fresh fish is the speciality of the house.

✉ place du 3 Août ☎ 73 461124 🕐 Lunch, dinner

Les Remparts (£–££)

Concentrates on pizzas during the day, but offers a more extensive menu in the evenings. Service is a little slow, but if you are sitting outside watching the world go by it does not matter too much.

✉ avenue Habib Bourguiba ☎ 73 460752 🕐 Lunch, dinner

Roi du Couscous (£)

Cheap, cheerful and popular, with outside seating. Some may be deterred by the swarm of cats waiting to be thrown titbits.

✉ place du Gouvernorate 🕐 Lunch, dinner

Port El Kantaoui

La Daurade (££–£££)

Fresh fish tops the menu at this popular venue with outdoor seating in demand at lunch and dinner. Worth booking ahead to secure one of the best tables.

✉ The Marina ☎ 73 244893 🕐 Lunch, dinner

Sfax

Café Diwan (£)

A popular café with a rooftop terrace offering views over the city wall. A quiet, relaxed place to stop for tea or coffee during the day or to mingle with local people in the evenings.

✉ off rue de la Kasbah, next to No 37 🕐 8 till late

Chez Nous (££)

The food here is good, even if the service is somewhat surly. Tunisian specialities include various *ojjas* (egg dishes) and fish *couscous*.

✉ 26 rue Patrice Lumumba ☎ 74 227128 🕐 Lunch, dinner

Le Corail (£££)
Rather formal but no complaints about the food.
39 rue Habib Mazoun 74 210317 Lunch, dinner

La Gondole (£)
Pocket-sized daytime café with a handful of seats and constantly changing flow of customers. Good for coffee and croissants; the window seat is well-placed for people watching.
Taieb M'Hiri 7AM–8PM

Mamma Rosa (£)
Good quality pizza and pasta, friendly staff and attentive service.
55 avenue Farhat Hached 74 225886 Lunch, dinner

Le Printemps (££)
Despite its smart appearance the food and service are a bit disappointing. Stick to the set menu.
55 avenue Habib Bourguiba 74 226973 Lunch, dinner

Sousse

La Calèche (£££)
Aimed squarely at the tourist market but most dishes are quite pricey. Set menu is good value.
rue Remada 73 226489 Lunch, dinner

Hong Kong Restaurant (£££)
Here is an alternative to *briks* and *couscous* but the *à la carte* selection is quite expensive. The set menu is better value.
boulevard de Rabat – opposite El Hana Beach Hotel 73 221366 Lunch, dinner

Le Lido (££)
A restaurant in a great location opposite the port, offering some outside seating. The menu is dominated by excellent fresh fish.
avenue Mohammed V 73 225329 Lunch, dinner

El Pescador (£££)
A very good fish restaurant with seafood pasta among the specialities.
rue de Ribat 73 226260 Lunch, dinner. Closed Mon

Restaurant Les Remparts (££)
This atmospheric restaurant is located next to the Hôtel de Tunis and just inside the walls of the *médina*.
17 rue de l'Église 73 226326 Lunch, dinner

Les Sportifs (££)
A popular venue, endorsed by several European tour operators. Good food and service at value-for-money prices.
avenue Bourguiba 73 224756 Lunch, dinner

Tip Top (££)
Aimed at the holiday market, Tip Top is a deservedly popular choice, offering a warm welcome, cosy ambience and excellent choice of food.
boulevard de la Corniche 73 226158 Lunch, dinner

Restaurant Le Viking (£££)
Centrally placed off avenue Bourguiba, Le Viking can be expensive so it's best to stick to the set menus.
rue de l'Algerie 73 228377 Lunch, dinner

Blowing Bubbles
In most bars there will be several men smoking *chichas* – also known as hookah pipes. This is the most popular way of smoking in Tunisia. Contrary to popular perception, the water pipes are not filled with hashish but with *tombac*, a close relative of tobacco. The *tombac* is placed on top of the pipe and covered with a very hot piece of charcoal. The smoke is then filtered through the water before being inhaled.

Jerba & the South

Tipping and TGV
Waiters do not expect to be tipped in the same way as they do in Europe and North America. In budget restaurants it is acceptable to leave a few coins unless the food and service were exceptional, in which case you may wish to leave more. In tourist restaurants it is more normal to leave ten per cent – but only if the service merits it. Always check to see if service has already been included. TGV is not the service charge but a sales tax.

Gabès

Restaurant el Mazar (£££)
Despite its name this is basically a good French restaurant with Tunisian influences.
39 avenue Farhat Hached 75 272065 Lunch, dinner

Restaurant de l'Oasis (£££)
Generally reckoned to be the top spot in Gabès. The set menu is good value.
17 avenue Farhat Hached 75 270098 Lunch, dinner

Jerba

Aladin (£)
Fish and some interesting seafood dishes at this small, low-priced restaurant.
40 avenue Mohamed Badra, Houmt Souq Lunch, dinner

Baccar (££)
Split-level tourist-oriented restaurant offering all the usual Tunisian specialities including various types of *couscous*.
place Hedi Chaker, Houmt Souq 75 650708 Lunch, dinner

Blue Moon (££–£££)
Stylish and spacious air-conditioned restaurant heavily geared to tourists with a good value set menu and much more expensive *à la carte* selection.
place Hedi Chaker, Houmt Souq 75 650559 Lunch, dinner

Dar Faïza (£)
Good value set price menu in a cosy hotel dining room where it can be hard to find a table in high season.
rue de la République, Houmt Souq 75 650083 Fax 05 651763 Dinner

El Hana (££–£££)
Dine by candlelight with linen napkins and tablecloths at this snug, welcoming little restaurant which feels like someone's front room. The food is very good with exceptional mashed potato dishes.
place Mohamed Ali, Houmt Souq 75 650568 Dinner

La Mamma (£)
You can eat with the locals at this atmospheric and cheap eatery which does a roaring trade in soups and *couscous*.
rue Habib Bourguiba, Houmt Souq All day

Les Palmiers (£)
Come to this friendly restaurant for great value eating. With its colourful menu, pretty tablecloths, pictures on the wall and subtle lighting it is a cut above most Tunisian budget restaurants and worth a visit. No alcohol is permitted.
place d'Algerie, Houmt Souq Lunch, dinner

La Princesse d'Haroun (£££)
Jerba's most famous restaurant. In summer you can eat on the terrace overlooking the harbour. Meat dishes available but seafood starters and grilled fish rule the waves. Smart casual dress preferred.
Opposite the fishing harbour 75 650488 Lunch, dinner

Restaurant de l'Ile (££–£££)
This is a rather formal, serious restaurant, and quite pricey; the set menu represents the best value.

✉ off place Hedi Chaker, Houmt Souq ☎ 75 650651 🕐 Lunch, dinner

Restaurant du Sportif (£–££)
Starkly lit restaurant catering for a mainly local clientele mostly with meat grills and stews.
✉ 147 avenue Habib Bourguiba 🕐 11–9

Restaurant du Sud (££–£££)
Aimed squarely at the tourist trade but with better food than most.
✉ place Sidi Brahim ☎ 75 650479 🕐 Lunch, dinner

Tamerza

Tamerza Palace Hotel (££)
Good for lunch or dinner with agreeable food, attentive service and excellent views of the abandoned village of Tamerza.
✉ Tamerza ☎ 76 485322 Fax 76 485322

Tozeur

La Diamanta (£)
Not a place to linger but perfectly good for a quick lunch or light supper. No alcohol.
✉ avenue Abou El Kacem Chabbi ☎ 76 453867

L'Grand Oasis (££)
The three-course evening buffet is good value but get there early while the food is fresh and hot.
✉ avenue Abou el Kacem Chabbi ☎ 76 452699 🕐 Dinner

Le Palmeraie (£££)
An expensive but pleasant hotel restaurant offering high standards of food and service. A tourist menu is available.
✉ Hotel Palmeraie ☎ 76 452041 🕐 Lunch, dinner

Le Petit Prince (££)
Long-established restaurant which sometimes has evening shows of traditional music and dancing.
✉ off avenue Abou el Kacem Chabbi leading into the palmery ☎ 76 452318 🕐 Dinner

Restaurant de la République (£)
Tucked away in a corner, this cosy little restaurant appeals to local people and tourists. Good, affordable food.
✉ avenue Habib Bourguiba (on the west side at the back of an arcade of shops) 🕐 Lunch, dinner

Restaurant Sheherezad (£££)
Part of the Dar Charait complex. Good food and gracious surroundings.
✉ Zone Touristique ☎ 76 452100 🕐 Dinner

Restaurant du Sud (£)
Basic restaurant very popular with young travellers, serving a range of Tunisian specialities at rock bottom prices.
✉ avenue Farhat Hached (opposite Agil petrol station) ☎ 76 450826 🕐 Lunch, dinner

Le Soleil (£)
Opposite Résidence Warda, the best of Tozeur's budget options with clean surroundings and an extensive menu. Camel-meat *couscous* is available if ordered in advance.
✉ avenue Abou Kacem el Chabbi ☎ 76 554220 🕐 Lunch, dinner

Hot-Headed
Harissa can be a bit of a shock to the system on first acquaintance but many visitors develop such a liking for the fiery hot chilli paste that they take home a jar or two at the end of their trip. Used throughout the countries of the Maghreb for soups, stews and *couscous*, it is made up from ground dried red chilli peppers, garlic, coriander, cumin seeds, sea salt and olive oil.

Tunis & the North

Prices
The hotels listed are grouped into three categories based on one night's double room in high season including breakfast and taxes. All rooms have en suite facilities unless otherwise stated.
£ = budget – under 30D
££ = moderate – 30D-80D
£££ = expensive – over 80D

Bizerte

Bizerta Resort (£££)
Beachfront hotel in the *Zone Touristique* with indoor and outdoor swimming pools and a health club. The bedrooms are equipped with minibars and satellite television.
route de la Corniche 72 436966 Fax 72 422955

Le Petit Mousse (££)
Well-run hotel with an excellent restaurant (► 92). One of its few negative features is that the private beach is just a very narrow strip, close to the road.
route de la Corniche 72 432185 Fax 72 437595

Gammarth

Abou Nawas Gammarth (£££)
Luxury hotel with a Moorish café and Tunisian/Moroccan restaurant convenient for Tunis Airport and the ruins of Carthage.
20km north of Tunis, 10km from the airport 71 741444 Fax 71 740400

La Résidence (£££)
One of Tunisia's newest and most luxurious hotels with a thalassotherapy spa, tennis courts, Mediterranean restaurant and free shuttle service to Tunis city centre.
2km north of Gammarth
71 910101 Fax 71 749888

Sidi Bou Saïd

Dar Said (££)
Small attractive hotel, often recommended as a good choice for honeymooners.
Top of the main street
71 729666 Fax 71 729599

Dar Zarrouk (£££)
A recently renovated former palace, the Dar Zarrouk is right in the heart of Sidi bou Saïd and must be booked well in advance. The courtyard garden is a haven of peace and quiet.
rue el Hadi Zarrouk 71 740591

Sidi Bou Saïd (£££)
This small recently renovated hotel is owned by the Tunisian National Tourist Office to provide hands-on experience for students at the adjacent hotel school. Full of character, it has a swimming pool, tennis courts and – from its sun terrace – an excellent view of Tunis.
avenue Sidi Dhrif (800m north of the village) 71 740411 Fax 71 745129

Tabarka

Abou Nawas Montazah (£££)
This sprawling beachfront hotel boasts tennis courts and a diving centre – but the rooms can be very noisy.
route Touristique 78 673532 Fax 78 673530

Hôtel De France (£)
Fairly basic town centre hotel with shared bathrooms; busy restaurant (► 92) and convivial bar. Habib Bourguiba stayed here in 1952 during his internal exile.
avenue Habib Bourguiba
78 644577

Royal Golf (£££)
Operates as an all-inclusive hotel in the summer with all meals, drinks, activities and entertainment included in the room rate. Aimed principally at tour groups.
route Touristique (2km from town centre) 78 644002 Fax 78 673838

Tunis

Abou Nawas (£££)

Located next to the Palais du Congres and within walking distance of the *médina*, this is one of Tunis's top hotels. It houses a high-class Italian restaurant, a fitness centre and a swimming pool.

✉ **avenue Mohammed V**
☎ **71 350355 Fax 71 352882**

Carlton (££)

A clean, central mid-market hotel, but lacking in a certain warmth both in the starkness of the rooms and the attitude of the staff.

✉ **31 avenue Habib Bourguiba**
☎ **71 330644 Fax 71 338168**

Excel (££)

A centrally located, clean and comfortable hotel, offering in-room television and telephone and a friendly bar.

✉ **35 avenue Habib Bourguiba**
☎ **71 355088 Fax 71 341929**

Hilton (£££)

Located near Parc du Belvédère and aimed at business travellers on expense accounts. Free shuttle services to the city centre and airport.

✉ **avenue de la Ligue Arabe**
☎ **71 728100 Fax 71 782208**

Hotel Africa (£££)

One of the city's major landmarks and meeting points (► 30), L'Africa Méridien is conveniently situated fronting the bustling main thoroughfare, a ten-minute walk from the *médina*. The hotel's facilities are more modern than its drab, ugly exterior might suggest.

✉ **50 avenue Habib Bourguiba**
☎ **71 347477 Fax 71 347432**

Hotel de Russie (£££)

Spotless hotel discreetly located in a back street just off the bustling rue el Jazira.

✉ **18 rue de Russie** ☎ **71 328883 Fax 71 321685**

Maison Dorée (£–££)

A well-maintained budget hotel with luxurious bedding and the atmosphere of a bygone age. The staff are a little formal and unless you particularly like the sound of trams thundering past your window every few minutes ask for a room at the front of the hotel.

✉ **6 rue de Hollande (entrance in rue el Koufa)** ☎ **71 240631 Fax 71 332401**

Majestic (££)

One of the great old-established hotels of Tunis, but now beginning to show its age.

✉ **36 avenue de Paris** ☎ **71 332666 Fax 71 336908**

Médina (£)

Probably the most pleasant of the Old Town hotels with clean double rooms; however, there are no singles or en-suite facilities.

✉ **place de la Victoire** ☎ **71 327497**

Salammbo (£)

Very basic hotel with few en-suite facilities. Reasonably clean, but with an unwelcoming atmosphere.

✉ **6 rue de Grèce** ☎ **71 334252**

Transatlantique (£)

Another fairly basic hotel with large and noisy bedrooms, but attractively tiled lobby and passageways.

✉ **106 rue de Yougoslavie**
☎ **71 334319**

Bargain Beds

Outside the peak summer months the price of beds comes right down, often to half the high season rate. Hotel prices are fixed by the Ministry of Tourism and are usually displayed in hotel reception areas. Always agree on the rate in advance and ask to see the room before making up your mind.

Cap Bon

Tourist Terrain
Tunisia is very fond of its *zone touristiques* (tourist areas) where most big holiday hotels are located. They are often sited along some of the best stretches of beach, but they are usually also several kilometres from the heart of a town and so lack local flavour. They also give the impression that the Tunisian authorities want to keep tourists and local people apart – which rather defeats the object of visiting someone else's country.

Hammamet

Alya (££)
Excellent little place in the heart of Hammamet. The clean, comfortable rooms have en-suite showers with plenty of hot water. Back-facing rooms also have balconies with views across to the *médina*.
✉ 30 rue Ali Belhouane ☎ 72 280218 Fax 72 282365

Aziza (£££)
A family-oriented beachfront hotel which is very popular with tour groups. It includes a health club, tennis courts and disco.
✉ boulevard Assad ibn el Fourat (3km from town centre) ☎ 72 283666 Fax 72 283099

Bel Azur (£££)
A Moorish-style hotel on a small headland with pretty gardens and two sandy beaches. There is a separate children's pool as well as a pizzeria, snack bar and an *à la carte* restaurant.
✉ boulevard Assad ibn el Fourat (2km from town centre) ☎ 72 280544 Fax 72 280275

Belle Vue (££)
The advantage of this hotel is its superb beachfront location just 400m from the *médina*. All rooms are doubles; the hotel includes a billiard room and TV lounge.
✉ boulevard Assad ibn el Fourat ☎ 72 281121 Fax 72 283156

Dar Hayet (£££)
The smallest and most discreet of Hammamet's deluxe hotels. Rooms are all doubles and are plushly decorated with locally produced furnishings; most have sea views. There is a pool, and a small café.
✉ rue de la Corniche ☎ 72 282856 Fax 72 283399

Khella (££)
Town centre hotel within two minutes' walk of several restaurants. Clean and comfortable.
✉ avenue de la République ☎ 72 283900 Fax 72 283704

Miramar (£££)
The hotel is well maintained and sits on a pleasantly uncrowded strip of beach. Shops and restaurants just across the road.
✉ rue de Nevers (4km from the centre) ☎ 72 280344 Fax 72 280586

Les Orangers (£££)
This two-hotel complex is some way out of the town centre. It offers a sandy beach, colourful gardens, a health club and a regular programme of evening entertainment.
✉ rue de Nevers ☎ 72 280457 Fax 72 280144

La Résidence (£££)
One of Hammamet's longest-established tourist hotels and still one of the best. All rooms sleep up to four and have mini-kitchens. There is a rooftop terrace with swimming pool and a private beach; very close to the *médina*.
✉ 72 avenue Habib Bourguiba ☎ 72 280406 Fax 72 280396

Royal Azur (£££)
Every comfort at the best luxury hotel in Hammamet. Most rooms have sea views. Fully equipped spa uses seawater, mud and algae for health/beauty treatments.

boulevard Assad ibn el Fourat (2km from town centre) 72 278500 Fax 72 278999

Sahbi (££)

Sprawling town centre hotel with a carpet bazaar taking up most of the ground and first floors. Spacious bedrooms decorated in Tunisian style.

avenue de la République 72 280807 Fax 72 280134

Shératon (£££)

An extensive resort hotel with rooms built in small clusters in lush gardens. There are six tennis courts, a swimming pool and children's play area.

route Touristique Hammamet Sud (6km from town centre) 72 226555 Fax 72 227301

Yasmina (£££)

Overlooking the town's main beach, surrounded by greenery and with excellent view of the *kasbah*. Sun terrace, swimming pool and paddling pool; pizzeria with outdoor seating and a miniature golf course.

avenue Habib Bourguiba 72 280222 Fax 72 280593

El Haouaria

L'Épervier (££)

Situated off the main street and built round a pretty courtyard with jasmine and orange trees. A clean and comfortable hotel with almost the only restaurant in town.

avenue Habib Bourguiba 72 297017 Fax 72 297258

Kelibia

Palmarina (££)

Newish hotel with swimming pool, café/bar and restaurant. The sun terrace overlooks a small beach and the colourful fishing harbour. Friendly, helpful staff.

avenue des Martyrs 72 274062 Fax 72 274055

Nabeul

Hôtel Lido (£££)

A large complex with cottages in the grounds as well as the main hotel building. Every facility you would expect from a popular package destination.

3km east of Nabeul 72 285135 Fax 72 285487

Les Jasmins (££)

In a secluded tree-lined road five minutes' walk from a quiet beach. Popular with tour groups in summer, independent guests are still welcomed. Rooms are in two-storey blocks in gardens. Swimming pool and up-market seafood restaurant.

rue Abou el Kacem Chabbi (just outside Nabeul town centre) 72 285343 Fax 72 285073

Khéops (£££)

This hotel caters mainly for a mix of well-heeled business travellers and European tour groups.

avenue Mohamed V 72 286555 Fax 72 286024

Pension Les Oliviers (£–££)

A cut above average guesthouse with clean rooms and en-suite bathrooms in a large modern house surrounded by olive and citrus trees. Close to the beach and a minute's walk from the Hôtel Les Jasmins (► above).

11 rue de Havane 72 286865 Closed in winter

Don't be Star-Struck

Do not pay too much attention to hotel star ratings as they can be very unreliable. Introduced some years ago, the star system was only ever intended to grade the physical facilities of a hotel – ignoring the quality of service offered altogether. Now, even the assessing of facilities seems somewhat lax.

Central Tunisia

Food for Thought
Avoid beach resort hotels which insist that you book half- or full-board. Hotels find this a useful way to boost their income, but for guests it can mean an endless round of rather bland 'international-style' buffets. It is far more interesting and adventurous to eat out – and frequently cheaper as well.

Iles Kerkennah

Grand (££)
Recently refurbished secluded beachfront hotel with swimming pool and tennis courts. Cycling and horse-riding available nearby.
✉ Sidi Frej ☎ 74 281266 Fax 74 281485

Jazira (£)
Small family-run hotel in the Old Town district of Mahdia.
✉ Er Remla ☎ 74 281058

Kairouan

Splendid (££)
Probably Kairouan's classiest hotel – although it has seen better days. The big rooms are clean and comfortable and have private bathrooms. Bar and licensed restaurant.
✉ rue 9 April (off avenue de la République) ☎ 77 227522 Fax 77 230829

Mahdia

Corniche (£)
Good value, small modern hotel about 2km west of the town centre.
✉ avenue 7 Novembre (just before Zone Touristique) ☎ 73 694201 Fax 73 692196

Melia El Mouradi (£££)
Newish and fairly typical beachfront hotel aimed squarely at the package tourist market. Indoor and outdoor swimming pools, tennis courts and a nightclub.
✉ Zone Touristique ☎ 73 692111 Fax 73 692120

Monastir

Yasmine (£–££)
Family-run pension with single and double rooms and a licensed restaurant.
✉ route de la Falaise ☎ 73 462511

Port El Kantaoui

El Hana Hannibal Palace (£££)
One of Port El Kantaoui's longest-established hotels just a short stroll from the marina. Pleasant ambience with a popular lunchtime terrace restaurant.
☎ 73 348577 Fax 73 348321

Sfax

Abou Nawas (£££)
This well-located hotel, mainly aimed at business travellers, could do with sharpening up all round, from its dreary décor to its sluggish service.
✉ avenue Habib Bourguiba ☎ 74 225700 Fax 74 235960

Alexandre (£)
Very good value at this elegant old colonial-style building with enormous baths.
✉ 21 rue Alexandre Dumas ☎ 74 221911

De la Médina (£)
Cheap, cheerful but clean hotel in the *médina*. Shared bathrooms.
✉ 53 rue Mongi Slim ☎ 74 220354

La Paix (£)
Fairly basic hotel. Although rooms have showers, you have to be a bit of a contortionist to use them.
✉ 17 rue Alexandre Dumas ☎ 74 296437

Sousse

Abou Nawas Boujafaar (£££)
A mix of business travellers and holidaymakers at this plush beachfront hotel which is equally well placed for shopping and eating out. Facilities include a couple of

popular bars, a terrace restaurant and a thalassotherapy spa.
avenue Habib Bourguiba
73 226030 Fax 73 225521

Amira
Atmospheric *médina* hotel. All rooms have bath or shower and toilet. Staff are friendly and helpful. Breakfast is served on a rooftop terrace.
52 rue de France **73 226325**

Claridge (£)
Once the most superior place in town, now overshadowed by the string of beach hotels along the corniche. Plenty of character and a central location between the *médina* and the beach. The large comfortable rooms all have a bath or shower – but not all have en suite toilets.
10 avenue Habib Bourguiba
73 224759 Fax 73 227277

El Hana Beach (£££)
A popular family hotel in colourful gardens. Guests can use the facilities of two neighbouring hotels: the El Hana and the Chems El Hana.
boulevard de la Corniche
73 226900 Fax 73 226076

Ennasim (££)
Bed and breakfast only but well placed for restaurants and just 100m from the beach.
boulevard de la Corniche
73 227100 Fax 73 224488

Farès (££)
Busy city centre hotel next to the railway station. All rooms have bathrooms and balconies.
boulevard Hassouna Ayachi
73 227800 Fax 73 227380

Hadrumète (£–££)
A once-flourishing two-star hotel which has fallen behind the times. Close to the port, it still retains plenty of character. Ask for a room with a balcony and enjoy the hotel's faded glory.
place Assad ibn el Fourat
73 226291 Fax 73 226863

Jawhara (££)
Situated right on the beach and with good facilities.
boulevard 7 Novembre
73 225611 Fax 73 224123

Médina (£)
One of the best hotels in the *médina*. Rooms have en suite bathrooms and open on to a small courtyard.
15 rue Othman Osman
73 221722

Paris (£)
Beautifully maintained budget hotel just inside the walls of the *médina*. Friendly management, lots of atmosphere – but shared washing facilities!
15 rue Rempart Nord **73 220564 Fax 73 219038**

Sousse Azur (££)
Friendly, comfortable, close to the beach and good value for money.
5 rue Amilcar **73 226960 Fax 73 228145**

Tej Mahaba (£££)
A massive 700-bed hotel, 200m from the beach in large gardens with indoor and outdoor pools, tennis courts, Turkish bath and seafood restaurant.
avenue Taieb Mehiri
73 229800 Fax 73 229815

Women Travellers
Finding somewhere to stay presents extra problems for women travellers, whether holidaying alone or in pairs. Cultural differences mean that western women can face a certain amount of pestering although serious threats are rare. The best advice is generally to avoid small *médina* hotels and stay in family-run pensions or major tourist hotels instead.

Jerba & the South

Marhalas
The Touring Club de Tunisie runs a chain of cheap, traditional hotels known as *marhalas*. Priced slightly higher than youth hostels, they offer basic but clean rooms and a warm welcome. The most popular *marhalas* include the one in Houmt Souq and the underground hotel at Matmata.

Douz

Mouradi (££)
Indoor and outdoor pools, a gym and *hammam* at this newest of the *Zone Touristique* hotels.
✉ Zone Touristique ☎ 75 470303 Fax 75 470905

Sun Palm Hotel (££)
Atmospheric mid-market hotel attracting a mix of Tunisians and tourists. Rooms are comfortable if rather sparse and service is very casual.
☎ 75 475123 Fax 75 470525

Gabès

Atlantic (£)
Once-grand colonial-style hotel long past its best, but still with some character.
✉ 4 avenue Habib Bourguiba
☎ 75 220034 Fax 75 221358

Chems (££)
Enormous beachfront bungalow complex with single and double rooms.
✉ On the beach ☎ 75 270547 Fax 75 274485

Jerba

Dar Faïza (££)
A popular family-run hotel on the beachfront road near the harbour. Rooms are basic but spotless with crisp white sheets; huge baths with plenty of hot water. There is a small pool in the garden, a bar and good restaurant open to non-residents (► 98).
✉ rue de la République ☎ 75 650083 Fax 75 651763

Erriadh (£)
This delightful *fondouk* (► panel, 107) in the heart of Houmt Souq oozes charm and character. Built around a vine-covered courtyard, rooms are prettily tiled and have en suite facilities.
✉ 10 rue Mohamed Ferjani
☎ 75 650756 Fax 75 650487

Jerba Beach (£££)
Built in traditional Tunisian style with windsurfing and waterskiing facilities, a swimming pool, fitness centre and tennis courts.
✉ Zone Touristique (13km from Houmt Souq) ☎ 75 657200 Fax 75 657357

Lotos (£–££)
Very spacious rooms, many with large balconies overlooking the coast.
✉ 18 rue de la République
☎ 75 650026 Fax 75 650127

Marhala (£)
One of several character budget hotels run by the Touring Club de Tunisie (► panel). Small and basic rooms but loads of atmosphere and a busy bar.
✉ 13 rue Moncef Bey ☎ 75 650146 Fax 75 653317

Sables d'Or (£)
Converted house with a central patio in the centre of Houmt Souq. The 12 rooms are kept spotlessly clean and all have showers – but there are communal toilets.
✉ 30 rue Mohammed Ferjani
☎ 75 650423

Ulysse Palace (£££)
Beachfront hotel with several restaurants, a thalassotherapy spa and minibars and satellite television in all rooms.
✉ Zone Touristique ☎ 75 758777 Fax 75 757850

Matmata

Marhala (£)
This converted underground

house is run by the Touring Club de Tunisie (► panel). Popular, so book well ahead.
✉ off Toujane road ☎ 75 230015

Nefta

Marhala (£-££)

This former brick factory on the edge of Nefta's oasis is now a hotel run by the Touring Club de Tunisie. Comfortable and friendly, it has recently opened a new wing and swimming pool.
✉ route Touristique ☎ 76 430027 Fax 76 430511

Rose (£££)

Block-booked by mainly German tour groups in the peak summer season, this comfortable hotel is often almost empty in winter when room rates take a dramatic dive.
✉ route Touristique ☎ 76 430697 Fax 76 430385

Tamerza

Tamerza Palace Hotel (££–£££)

Stylish, well-run hotel overlooking the ruined village of Tamerza. A good base for exploring the desert region.
☎ 76 453722 Fax 76 799910

Tozeur

Abou Nawas (£££)

Palatial hotel on the edge of the palm grove with an elegant marble-floored lobby with gushing fountain. Bedrooms are in two-storey blocks in the gardens. French speciality restaurant or a gloomy cafeteria.
✉ route Touristique ☎ 76 453500 Fax 76 452686

Basma (£££)

Over-priced tourist hotel very popular with French tour groups. Attractive bar and lobby area. Dull bedrooms.
✉ route Touristique ☎ 76 452488 Fax 76 452294

Continental (££)

Long-established mid-market hotel on the edge of the palm grove with comfortable rooms and a swimming pool.
✉ avenue Aboul Kacem Chebbi ☎ 76 461411 Fax 76 452109

Grand Hotel de L'Oasis (££)

Popular hotel with tourists on desert safaris. The rooms are a bit like cells but the service is friendly and there is a decent bar and restaurant.
✉ avenue Aboul Kacem Chebbi ☎ 76 452699 Fax 76 452153

Palm Beach (£££)

The most expensive hotel in Tozeur. This was where the cast of *The English Patient* stayed when filming in the desert. Every comfort provided including a luxurious spa.
✉ route Touristique ☎ 76 453111 Fax 76 453911

Palmeraie (£££)

An upmarket hotel which offers a genuine touch of style and class. Plush bedrooms, a spacious lobby, decent restaurant, swimming pool and gardens backing on to the palm grove. Worth the price.
✉ route Touristique ☎ 76 454599 Fax 76 454833

Résidence Warda (£)

Very basic rooms with en suite showers and scorching hot water.
✉ avenue Abdel Kacem Chabbi ☎ 76 452597

Fondouks

Similar to *marhalas* in offering simple accommodation at cheap prices, *fondouk* hotels – of which there are several in Jerba – have all been built round old courtyards. Originally these would have been used for stabling horses and storing goods while merchants lived in rooms above. *Fondouk* hotels are some of the most atmospheric in Tunisia and well worth a night or two's stay.

Shopping in Tunisia

Hassle...
Do not expect to be allowed to shop in peace in Tunisia. There is little understanding – or desire to understand – the concept of browsing. Enter a tourist shop and an 'assistant' will immediately shadow your every move continuously pointing out the obvious, informing you very graciously that there is 'no charge for looking' and seizing upon even a slight flicker of interest in any item.

Markets

No trip to Tunisia would be complete without at least one visit to a local market. Outside the main towns they are the driving force and economic hub of rural communities. Lives are planned around the event: it is not only where all purchases are made for the week ahead but is a chance to see friends and catch up on local gossip. Tunisian markets are noisy, bustling and colourful and – even if you are not planning to buy anything – they have a wonderful atmosphere, are great for photographs and provide a fascinating insight into the Tunisian way of life.

Market Days

Monday: El Jem, Kairouan, Matmata, Houmt Souk
Tuesday: Kebili
Wednesday: Menzel Bourguiba, Gafsa
Thursday: Douz, Le Kef, Nefta, Hammamet
Friday: Nabeul, Tabarka, El Haouaria, Mahdia, Sfax, Midoun
Saturday: Monastir
Sunday: Sousse, Tozeur

Carpets

Carpet-making is one of Tunisia's most traditional crafts dating from as early as the 14th century. While not cheap, they make a handsome and long-lasting souvenir and are readily available all over Tunisia particularly in Tunis, El Jem, Sfax and, of course, Kairouan – the King of the Carpet Centres. Make sure any carpet you purchase has a label of authenticity attached.

The most expensive carpets are knotted, and are priced according to the number of knots per square metre. As a general rule, the firmer the pile and the sharper the definition of the pattern, the greater the value of the carpet and the longer it will last. You can also purchase the woven carpets known as kilims, which usually feature traditional Berber motifs – these are reasonably cheap to buy.

Pottery

Cheap, colourful and very collectible, Tunisian pottery makes the ideal souvenir. Nabeul and Guellala on the island of Jerba are the two big production centres although pottery is sold all over the country. Nabeul's industry dates back to Roman times with many of today's most popular designs and colours (blue and white, and yellow and green) the same as those used 2,000 years ago. Best buys include plates, bowls, vases and tiles which – if you buy several – can make a very attractive wall panel.

Jewellery

Almost every *souq* in the country has its jewellery section. Most Tunisian gold is only 12 or 14 carat while silverwork is often *metal argente* (silver plating). Houmt Souq in Jerba is one of the best places for silver and gold pieces. Common motifs include fishes and the Hand of Fatima, Islam's principal female cult figure who was the daughter of the Prophet Mohammed.
The Berber regions of the south specialise in chunky

silver jewellery often set with semi-precious stones. In Tabarka you will find a lot of coral jewellery – but since coral is endangered and protected, it has probably been gathered illegally.

Woodwork and Metalwork

The best wood carving is to be found in Sfax where olive wood is turned into bowls, spoons and chess boards. The tapping of hammers and chisels on brass is a familiar sound in any of the *souqs* where ashtrays, plates and trays are among the most popular items. Craftsman will often offer to engrave a name on pieces bought.

Clothes

Traditional clothes like the *burnous* (a heavy woollen coat) and *chechias* (the traditional red felt hat still worn by many men) can be tempting, but it is as well to question whether it will ever be worn back at home! All the *souqs* sell this kind of souvenir.

Leatherware

Pouffes and *babouche* slippers are good value but be wary of jackets, handbags and belts which can appear to be bargains but need checking carefully for the quality of stitching and overall workmanship. All the *souqs* sell leatherware.

Stuffed camels and bird cages

Lined up in rows outside dozens of souvenir shops – particularly in Port El Kantaoui and Hammamet – few holidaymakers can resist buying a stuffed camel which range from the pocket-sized to those scarily close to the size of the real thing. Equally cumbersome to carry on homeward-bound flights are decorative blue and white bird cages often seen in tourist hotel reception areas where they are used to collect letters and postcards.

Official Shops

ONAT/SOCOPA Shops

In the major tourist centres there is a chain of craft workshops and outlets run by the Organisation National de l'Artisanat Tunisien (ONAT or the National Organisation of Tunisian Craftsmen). The prices are fixed and may be higher than you could pay by haggling, but these shops are less hassle and the goods are generally fairly high quality. The stock tends to be very similar throughout the country, but local produce is always promoted. Opening hours are about 8:30–noon and 4–7PM, but may be shorter in smaller towns.

Bizerte
Quai Khémais Ternane, Old Port

Gabès
Avenue Farhat Hached

Houmt Souq
Avenue Bouguiba

El Jem
Avenue Farhat Hached

Monastir
Rue Abdessalem Trimeche

Nabeul
144 avenue Farhat Hached and 93 Habib Thameur

Sfax
10 rue Lt Hamadi Taj

Tunis
Le Palmarium, avenue Bourguiba

...and Haggle

Bargaining is a way of life throughout the Arab world and, with the notable exception of food and medicines, applies to most commercial transactions. As a general rule, do not express any interest in anything you do not really intend to buy, and always start at a figure that is roughly half of what you would actually be prepared to pay.

Most tourist towns have at least one official shop where prices are fixed (► left).

Children's Attractions

Children's Car Seats
Tunisia has no laws concerning the safety of children in cars which means that most rented vehicles and taxis will not have rear seatbelts. If you are concerned about this and planning to rent a car, you will need to inquire in advance. However the reality is that international firms are no more likely than local ones to be able to provide them and it is recommended that visitors take their own strap-in child seats.

Children in Tunisia

Children can be assured of a warm welcome in Tunisia. As with many Mediterranean countries children are treated with great affection – and in Tunisia they represent a sizeable proportion of the population. Latest figures show that more than 50 per cent of the people are under 18 while around one-third are under 14.

But visitors should be aware of the cultural differences which exist in attitudes towards young people. In Tunisia it is not unusual for children to work in shops and markets, to play unsupervised, ride on the back of motorbikes without any sort of protective headgear, and to hitch lifts from complete strangers. This can cause astonishment and concern to first-time European visitors.
They, in turn, can take offence when Tunisians begin fussing over their children, admiring them, occasionally touching them, complimenting the parents and asking what may seem like nosy questions. As always, the best advice is to be relaxed and diplomatic and to remember that half the reason for travelling is for it not to be like home.

Activities for children

Since Tunisia is still developing its package tourism industry there are very few attractions aimed specifically at children such as theme parks and adventure playgrounds. Most museums are not even adult-friendly let alone geared to the minds of children. So most families tend to stick to the beach resorts as children will prefer playing in the sand and sea than touring Roman ruins or walking round *souqs* and markets.
However, the list below gives information on some places designed specifically for children.

Hammamet

Fabiland
This small funfair with rides and slot machines is primarily aimed at the eight to 15 age group.
✉ 6km south of Hammamet (close to Hotel Safir) ☎ 72 226868 ⌚ 9:30–6:30, summer only

Hergla

Hergla Park
A new go-kart park, featuring a separate track specially for children.
✉ 30km north of Sousse ☎ 73 251485 ⌚ Daily 9–7 On-site pizzeria and café

Port El Kantaoui

Acqua Palace
This new waterpark is fairly modest in scale, but it offers a large swimming pool, wave machine, various waterslides and a paddling pool.
✉ 9km north of Sousse ☎ 73 348855 ⌚ Daily 9:30–6 On-site pizzeria, self-service restaurant and bar

Tunis

Zoo du Belvédère
This zoo houses a selection of wild cats, birds, snakes and camels.
✉ Park Belvédère ☎ 71 281846 ⌚ 9–7 (9–4 in winter)

Buses, camel rides and water taxis

In Hammamet, Sousse, Port

El Kantaoui and Monastir, so-called 'Noddy Trains' – open-sided tourist shuttle buses – are always popular with small children as are short camel rides which are available on many beaches. Watersports are always popular with children and many resort hotels offer tuition for pursuits such as windsurfing. Taking a picnic to another beach by water taxi or making an excursion in a glass-bottomed boat to look at the underwater life is always a popular option.

Pools and playgrounds

One of the reasons why Tunisia has become so popular as a beach destination is that it offers long, warm, sunny days, safe seas and clean beaches which makes it particularly well suited to families. Many of the bigger hotels have separate children's pools and playgrounds. Some also provide children's clubs with qualified helpers arranging day-long programmes of organised activities. In addition, some hotels offer child discounts or will put a child's bed in an adult's room free of charge.

Food and drink

Do not expect to find children's menus except in tourist hotels; normally they will be expected to eat a smaller portion of the adult meal. In resorts, there should be no problems finding hamburgers, hot dogs or pizzas. Pasta dishes also feature prominently on many menus, and the usual fizzy drinks, such as cola and lemonade, are widely available. Some children may find Tunisian dishes too spicy, particularly those containing the fiery *harissa* sauce made from chillies. You can always ask for dishes to be 'sans piquant', but this is not always possible. Salads are often a safe choice as they are invariably based around tuna or eggs. Most children will also enjoy the sticks of crispy white bread which accompany any meal or save up their appetite for a honey-soaked pastry like *baklava* or *makroud*. Finding provisions for a picnic can be a challenge with most supermarkets stocking a very limited range, but markets are where most Tunisians shop and there is always a vast choice of food.

Necessities for babies

Small-size disposable nappies are available at all chemists, although the larger sizes (over 15kg) can be difficult to find. You are not likely to experience problems in finding dried baby milk or bottled and tinned baby food.

Sun precautions

Always remember that the sun is extremely strong in Tunisia, particularly in the summer months. Apply plenty of sunblock and insist they wear wide-brimmed hats, particularly if going on a boat trip: the cooling influence of the wind can be misleading, and the reflective effect of the water makes the rays even more powerful. Make sure you have a dense parasol for the pram if you are taking a baby along.

Public Toilets

There are very few public toilets in Tunisia except at railway stations and airports and these may not be up to the standard usually found in Europe and North America. The best bet is to head to the nearest café or restaurant. Always carry toilet paper as it is rarely supplied. Hand-cleaning wipes can also come in useful.

Sport

Flying Falcons
El Haouaria in the Cap Bon region is Tunisia's main falconry centre. Local enthusiasts catch young peregrine falcons and sparrowhawks in March and April and train them up for an annual Falconry Festival in mid-June. The Club des Fauconniers provides very helpful information for those interested in falconry. Located just outside El Haouaria, it is open from 10-4 daily.

Diving
Tunisia is steadily gaining recognition as a leading scuba-diving destination. The strongest interest is centred on Tabarka which has three major diving sites: Cap Tabarka, Grouper Rock and Tunnels Reef, which is an extraordinary complex of tunnels, caverns, caves and gullies.

Tabarka
Aquamarin
☎ 78 673508

École de Plongée
☎ 78 644344

Mehari Diving Centre
☎ 78 673136

Yachting Club de Tabarka
☎ 78 671478

Diving is also available at the Port el Kantouai resort, accessible by bus from Sousse (► 70).

Fishing
There is no river fishing in Tunisia but plenty of sea fishing is available. No permit is required and most harbours have boats for hire with or without crew.

Football
Football is the country's national sport and obsession, and is a useful opening conversational gambit with any Tunisian male. All over the country there are organised matches on Sunday afternoons. Tunisia also has its own football league. In Tunis, two local teams – Espérance Sportif and Club Africain – share the El Menzah ground at Cité Olympique.

Golf
Tunisia's temperate year-round climate provides ideal golfing conditions. Many first-time visitors are often surprised by the golf courses in Tunisia which are generally lush and well maintained. A former golf-loving minister of tourism was partly responsible for persuading the government to invest heavily in the sport to provide an added attraction for holidaymakers. Most of the big resorts now have international standard courses. There are no membership requirements and while golfers with their own kit are welcome, those who prefer to travel light will find that everything from clubs to caddies are available for hire – all at very reasonable rates. Many hotels will organise pre-set tee-times and provide complimentary transport to and from courses.

Hammamet
Golf Citrus
Designed and landscaped with six lakes, olive trees and forest, Golf Citrus comprises two 18-hole 72-par championship courses. There is also a schooling course, driving range and putting greens.
✉ Bir Bou Rebka, 13km west of Hammamet ☎ 72 226500 Fax 72 226400

Golf Yasmine
Glof Yasmine is a more intimate course adjacent to Golf Citrus. It offers a single 18-hole course, constructed around twin lakes.
✉ Bir Bou Rebka, 13km west of Hammamet ☎ 72 227001 Fax 72 226722

Port El Kantaoui

El Kantaoui Golf Course

A 36-hole course particularly popular in November, February and March.

✉ Opposite the Hotel Green Park ☎ 73 231755 Fax 73 348755

Skanes

Palm Links Golf Course

Ideally suited to beginners, an 18-hole, 72-par course with a nine-hole schooling course and driving range.

✉ Dkhila ☎ 73 466910 Fax 73 466913

Tunis

Carthage Golf Course

Tunisia's oldest golf club, established in 1927, provides an 18-hole, 66-par course.

✉ Choutrana 2, La Soukra ☎ 71 765 919 Fax 71 765915

Horse riding

There are horses for hire on most tourist beaches and a few coastal hotels even have their own stables. Jerba is particularly well supplied with horses and ponies, and prices are very reasonable. In the Tunis area lessons and escorted rides are available.

Tunis

Club Hippique de la Soukra

✉ La Soukra, 15km north of Tunis ☎ 71 203054

Hunting

The shooting season (Dec–Feb) is centred on the Khroumir Mountains around Ain Draham and Tabarka. The main prey are jackals, foxes, mongooses and wild boar. Permits are necessary and can be arranged by hotels, but it's best to organise these through a tour operator before arrival.

Sailing

Tunisia has some of the best marinas in North Africa which attract wealthy Europeans in the summer and 'yachties' from all over the world in the winter. Facilities are generally high quality and security good. Marinas can be found at:

Bizerte
El Kantaoui
Monastir
Sidi Bou Saïd
Tabarka
Tunis (La Goulette)

Swimming

All major beach hotels have at least one swimming pool, and many now offer indoor pools to attract winter guests. Even if you are not staying in a hotel it is usually possible to use the pool for a small charge. Sea swimming is usually safe and pleasant but jellyfish can be a problem in some areas.

Tennis

Most tennis courts in Tunisia are attached to beach hotels and can usually be used by outside guests as well as residents. Some of the most extensive facilities are at the Club Mediterranée resorts in Jerba and Monastir – but these are closed to non-residents.

Tunis

Cap Carthage

A 30-court complex.

✉ 15km northeast of Tunis ☎ 71 740064

Walking

Ain Draham, Le Kef, Tamerza and Zaghouan are among the main hill-walking centres in Tunisia.

Watersports

One of Tunisia's biggest attractions as a beach destination is that all its major beach resorts are well-equipped with a wide variety of watersports facilities. From hiring a pedalo to more energetic pursuits such as windsurfing, waterskiing, sailing and paragliding, facilities and equipment are available at very reasonable rates. Hammamet alone has more than more than a dozen watersports centres.

Nightlife

Bars

Outside of the main tourist hotels, drinking in most Tunisian bars is confined to early evenings, from around 6 to 9PM. Grimy and smoky, the bars are a meeting place as much as anything else; men of all ages sit together playing cards, smoking *chichas* (through a water pipe) and drinking beer.

The range of night-time entertainment on offer in Tunisia is quite limited. Outside the capital, most evening activities are centred around the tourist hotels, many of which provide free entertainment several times a week. This generally involves local musicians playing easy-listening, internationally known songs – which, after all. is probably what most tourists want after a long day spent in the sun.

Most tour operators will also offer holidaymakers the opportunity to book an evening excursion to a local nightspot for a 'Tunisian Evening' where a specially-tailored version of a traditional Tunisian meal is provided – served with generous amounts of wine and beer. The entertainment on offer normally comprises young women in silk robes and head-dresses performing traditional dances to the accompaniment of folk music. Sometimes there will also be a juggler, snake charmer or belly-dancer – although it is rare to see a performance by a genuine belly-dancer.

Cabaret Dinners

Tunis

Chez Gaston
Traditional music is played to accompany pleasant food served in a convivial atmosphere.
✉ 73 rue de Yougoslavie ☎ 71 340417 🕐 Fri, Sat evenings

El Mawel
✉ rue Amine Abbassi ☎ 71 790321

El Mazar
Live music in a cosy atmosphere with a mix of local people and tourists.
✉ rue de Marseille (above La Mamma restaurant) ☎ 71 340423 🕐 Nightly from 6–8.30

Mbrabet
Dinner, Berber dancing, traditional folk music and a glimpse of a belly-dancer.
✉ Souk et Trouk ☎ 71 261729 🕐 Nightly

La Privé
✉ rue de l'Abrabie Saoudite ☎ 71 891633

Nightclubs

Bizerte

Hôtel Corniche Palace
✉ rue de la Corniche ☎ 72 431831

Hôtel Jalta
✉ route de la Corniche ☎ 72 431169

Hammamet

Ben's
✉ avenue Moncef Bey ☎ 72 227053

Calypso
✉ avenue Moncef Bey ☎ 72 226803

Manhattan
✉ Hammamet Sud ☎ 72 226226

Nirvana
✉ route Touristique, Hammamet Sud ☎ 72 278408

Ranch Club
✉ avenue Moncef Bey ☎ 72 226462

Tropicana
✉ route Touristique ☎ 72 227200

Mahdia

Club Cesar
✉ Hôtel Thapsus, Zone Touristique ☎ 73 694495

Samba
✉ Hôtel Mehdi, Zone Touristique ☎ 73 671287

Skanès

Hôtel Kuriat Palace
✉ Zone touristique
☎ 73 521200

Hôtel Sahara Beach
✉ Zone Touristique
☎ 73 461088

Sousse

King Nightclub
✉ Hôtel Samara, boulevard Abdelhami Kadhi ☎ 72 226699

Marcana
✉ Hôtel Tej Marhaba
☎ 73 229800

Tabarka

Hôtel Abou Nawas Montazah
✉ route Touristique
☎ 78 673532

Tunis

Club 2001
✉ Hôtel El Mechtel, avenue Ouled Haffouz ☎ 71 780450

Le Jocker Club
✉ Hôtel El Hana, 49 avenue Habib Bourguiba ☎ 71 331144

Club Sheherazade
✉ Hôtel Abou Nawas, avenue Mohammed V ☎ 71 350355

Casinos

Casinos have only recently been recognised as another way of attracting tourists and are at present few and far between, but new ones are being built all the time. To gain entry you will need to be over 21 and non-Muslim, so take your passport. Since it is forbidden to gamble with Tunisian dinars, you will need US dollars or some other form of hard currency. Travellers' cheques, Eurocheques and credit cards are also accepted. Opening hours are usually noon–4AM, and the dress code is smart casual.

Hammamet

Casino Emeraude
✉ boulevard Assad ibn el Fourat ☎ 72 278655

Grand Casino
✉ Sol Azur Beach Hotel, route Touristique, Hammamet north
☎ 72 240777

Jerba

Grand Casino
✉ Sidi Mehrez ☎ 75 757537

Sousse

Casino Club Caraïbe
✉ boulevard 7 Novembre
☎ 73 211777

Cinemas

Cinemas are found all over the country and are one of the most popular forms of entertainment in Tunisia. With only a tiny film-making industry of its own, the cinemas rely largely on a programme of violent American films, kung fu movies and Arabic films, mainly from Egypt.
In Tunis there are more than 20 cinemas, including one at the Hôtel l'Africa Méridien (► 101) which sometimes shows more highbrow French language films. Matinées usually start at 3PM with evening performances at 6PM and 9PM.

Hammams

One of the most leisurely ways of spending an evening or afternoon is by visiting a *hammam* – a traditional steam bath. Found all over Tunisia and popular since Roman times, most Tunisians will visit a *hammam* at least once a week, not only for relaxation and cleanliness but as a place to meet and chat. Visitors keen to learn more about the Tunisians will find a visit to a *hammam* very rewarding. Avoid hotel *hammams* which are a travesty of the real thing.

What's On When

Ramadan

Ramadan is by far the most important festival in any Muslim country and is adhered to by the vast majority of Tunisians. The Koran demands that during the month-long festival (the date of which varies from year to year) no water and no food must pass a Muslim's lips during daylight hours. Some tourists avoid travelling to Muslim countries during Ramadan but it can be quite an exciting time as each evening eating and drinking continue into the early hours. The end of Ramadan is marked with a massive celebration – the Aid es Seghir.

As a Muslim country, Tunisia celebrates a number of national festivals and feast days related to Islam, including the month-long fast of Ramadan (▶ panel). The dates of these religious events are calculated according to the Muslim calendar which is lunar. Dates are thus eleven days earlier each year. Aid el Adha is a celebration of Abraham's devotion to God who told him to sacrifice his son, but 'stayed his hand' when He saw that Abraham was prepared to follow out the order. A sheep is killed and all the family feast. *Mouled* is a celebration of the Prophet Muhammad's birthday, and Al-Hijra is the Muslim New Year.
The following are among the most popular local festivals:

March–April

Ksars Festival: Berber traditions and folklore,Tataouine.
Festival of Oranges: timed to coincide with the start of the orange-picking season and supported by a programme of cultural events, Nabeul and Menzel Bouzelta.

June

Falconry Festival: falcons trained by villagers take part in a series of competitions to catch partridge and quail before being released into the wild. El Haouaria.
Classical Music Festival: El Jem.
Music Festival: week-long festival of *maalouf* music which was exported to North Africa by Andalusian refugees between the 12th and the 15th centuries. Testour (75km southwest of Tunis).
Ulysses Festival: folklore festival including a re-enactment of the arrival in Jerba of Ulysses, Jerba.

July–August

Festival of Carthage: the biggest cultural festival in Tunisia. Staged within the restored Roman theatre at Carthage and including dance, film, theatre and musical events, Carthage.
Dougga Festival: theatrical performances in the spectacular setting of the Roman theatre within the archaeological site, Dougga.
Festival of Theatre: folk music, dancing and plays, Sousse.
Coral Festival: aimed purely at tourists and at promoting the town's coral shops, Tabarka.
Jerba Folklore Festival: held every other year (even years), Jerba.
International Festival: music, dance and theatre, Monastir.

September

Cavalry Festival: displays of horsemanship, Kairouan.

November

Date Harvest Festival: Kebili.
Festival of Tozeur: oasis folklore and traditions, Tozeur.
International Film Festival: held bi-annually (even years), Carthage.

December

International Festival of the Sahara: attracts up to 50,000 Bedouin, nomads and tourists for camel races and folklore displays. Held in the desert on the edge of town, Douz.

Practical Matters

Above: *Tunis has an efficient metro system*
Right: *a decorative postbox in Hammamet*

TIME DIFFERENCES

	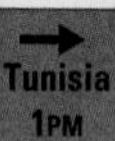				
GMT	Tunisia	Germany	USA (NY)	Netherlands	Spain
12 noon	1PM	1 PM	7AM	1PM	1PM

BEFORE YOU GO

WHAT YOU NEED

● Required
○ Suggested
▲ Not required

Some countries require a passport to remain valid for a minimum period (usually at least six months) beyond the date of entry – contact their consulate or embassy or your travel agent for details.

	UK	GERMANY	USA	Netherlands	Spain
Passport	●	●	●	●	●
Visa (Regulations can change – check before your journey)	▲	▲	▲	▲	▲
Onward or Return Ticket	▲	▲	▲	▲	▲
Health Inoculations	○	○	○	○	○
Health Documentation (➤ 123, Health)	▲	▲	▲	▲	▲
Travel Insurance	●	●	●	●	●
Driving Licence (national or international)	●	●	●	●	●
Car Insurance Certificate (if own car)	●	●	●	●	●
Car Registration Document (if own car)	●	●	●	●	●

WHEN TO GO

Tunis

High season

Low season

16°C	17°C	20°C	21°C	23°C	27°C	30°C	32°C	29°C	25°C	22°C	17°C
JAN	FEB	MAR	APR	MAY	JUN	JUL	AUG	SEP	OCT	NOV	DEC

 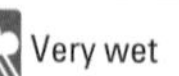 Very wet  Wet  Sun  Sunshine/ Showers

TOURIST OFFICES

In the UK
Tunisian National Tourist Office
77A Wigmore Street
London W1H 9LJ
☎ (0171) 224 5561
Fax: (0171) 224 4053

In the USA
C/o Ambassade de Tunisie
1515 Massachusetts Ave NW
Washington DC 20005
☎ (202) 862 1850
Fax: (202) 862 1858

In Germany
Fremdenverkehrsamt Tunesien
Goethe Platz 5, 60313 Frankfurt
☎ (49) 69 2970640
Fax: (49) 69 2970625

POLICE 197 (National emergency telephone number 197)

FIRE 198

AMBULANCE 481 313/284 808

WHEN YOU ARE THERE

ARRIVING

There are two major gateways. Tunis-Carthage International Airport handles scheduled flights from all over Europe. (There are no direct services from the US). Tunisia's domestic airline TunInter operates flights to Jerba, Tozeur and Sfax. Monastir-Skanès International Airport is used by charter flights.

Tunis-Carthage International Airport

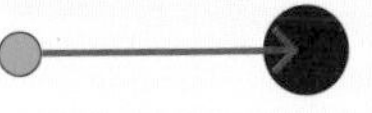

9 kilometres

Journey times

 20–25 minutes

12 minutes

Monastir-Skanès International Airport

5 kilometres

Journey times

 20 minutes

10 minutes

15 minutes

MONEY

The monetary unit of Tunisia is the dinar which is divided into 1,000 millimes.There is a one dinar coin and coins for 5, 10, 20, 50, 100 and 500 mills. Banknotes come in 5D, 10D and 20D denominations. The dinar is a 'soft' currency which means that exchange rates are fixed artificially by the government and cannot be traded on world currency markets. It is illegal to import or export dinars so you will be unable to obtain local currency in advance.

TIME

Tunisia is one hour ahead of GMT all year round which means that flying from Britain in summer there is no time difference while in winter watches have to be put forward one hour.

CUSTOMS

YES

Alcohol:	spirits 1L
Still table wine:	2L
Cigarettes:	200 or
Cigars:	40 or
Tobacco:	400gms
Perfume:	50ml
Toilet water:	1L
Cameras:	2
Video camera:	1

10 rolls of black & white film and 20 rolls of colour

Jewellery with a precious content: up to 500 grms.

Musical instrument: 1

A car, motorcycle, caravan or boat.

NO

Drugs, firearms, ammunition, offensive weapons, obscene material, unlicensed animals.

EMBASSIES AND CONSULATES

UK	USA	Germany	Netherlands	Spain
71 793322	71 782566	71 786455	71 799442	71 782217
Fax: 01 792644	Fax: 01 789719	Fax: 01 788242	Fax: 01 785557	Fax: 01 786267

WHEN YOU ARE THERE

TOURIST OFFICES

Bizerte
1 rue de Constantinople
72 432897
Fax: 72 438600

Jerba
route de Sidi Mahrez, Houmt Souk
75 650016
Fax: 75 650581

Monastir
Zone Touristique de Skanès
73 461205
Fax: 73 463219

Nabeul
avenue Taieb Mehri
72 286737
Fax: 72 223358

Sousse
1 avenue Habib Bourguiba
73 225157
Fax: 73 224262

Tabarka
boulevard 7 Novembre
78 671491
Fax: 78 673428

Tozeur
avenue Abdul Kacem Chabbi
76 454503
Fax: 76 452051

Tunis
31 rue Hasdrubal
71 845618
Fax: 71 842942

NATIONAL HOLIDAYS

J	F	M	A	M	J	J	A	S	O	N	D
2	1	2	1	2	1	1	1	2	1	1	3

1 January	New Year's Day
18 January	Anniversary of the Revolution
2 February	La Candelaria (Candlemas)
20 March	Independence Day
21 March	Youth Day
9 April	Martyrs' Day
1 May	International Labour Day
1 June	National Day
25 July	Republic Day
13 August	Women's Day
7 November	Anniversary of the Events of 1987

In addition to these secular holidays there are also various Muslim feast days which follow the Gregorian calendar and move backwards by roughly 11 days a year. The biggest holiday is the three-day feast called Aid es-Seghir, marking the end of Ramadan.

OPENING HOURS

Shops
Restaurants (lunch)
Banks
Museums
Post offices
Pharmacies

9 AM | 10 AM | 11 AM | 12 PM | 1 PM | 2 PM | 3 PM | 4 PM | 5 PM | 6 PM

9:30 | 10:30 | 11:30 | 12:30 | 1:30 | 2:30 | 3:30 | 4:30 | 5:30

Opening hours can be flexible according to region, time of year and even individual whims. In the peak season it is not unusual for shops to stay closed for much of the afternoon and then re-open again in the evening when it is cooler. During Ramadan working hours are also generally shortened all round. Many museums and archaeological sites are closed on Mondays. Pharmacies are found in every village and are generally clean and well-stocked with staff speaking fluent French. In large towns, there will be a pharmacy open 24 hours a day, but closed Sundays.

PUBLIC TRANSPORT

Internal Flights Tunisia's relatively small size means there is not much demand for domestic air travel. The two busiest routes are between Tunis and Tozeur and Tunis and Jerba which is used as a major gateway into Libya. All internal flights are operated by TunInter.

Trains Tunisia's small but efficient rail network is operated by the Societé Nationale des Chemins de Fer Tunisiens (SNCFT). The main line runs north to south from Tunis to Gabes. Three trains daily, whole route; eight services from Tunis to Sousse, six from Tunis to Sfax. Trains offer three classes – second, first and *confort*. Some have air-conditioned carriages.

Buses There is a wide network of bus routes operated by a variety of companies – some of which refuse to recognise each other's existence. Bigger towns usually have a central bus station. Local buses are usually filled to the brim, especially on market days when you may find yourself sharing the journey with chickens or sheep.

Ferries The busiest ferries in Tunisia are those operating between Jorf and Ajim on the island of Jerba. There are year-round services between Tunis and the Italian ports of Genoa and Trapani, with summer connections between Tunis and Naples. Compagnie Tunisienne de Navigation (01 346572) operates between Tunis and Marseille.

Urban Transport Tunis has a *metro leger* (tram) network and a very limited suburban rail service connecting the capital with Carthage and La Marsa. Services are punctual if not exactly frequent. There is also a metro service between Sousse and Monastir which is particularly useful for holidaymakers staying at hotels in Skanès.

CAR RENTAL

Car rental in Tunisia is expensive. Even vehicles from international rental companies can be poorly-maintained, and there are many potential hazards, from people driving at night without lights to pedestrians walking out into the road without looking.

TAXIS

Official taxis are yellow and equipped with a meter. Some drivers will try not to use it, in which case insist, fix a fare in advance or get out and use another taxi. There is a 50% surcharge between 9pm and 6am. In several resorts you can also hire *calèches*.

DRIVING

Speed limit on motorways: **110kph**

Speed limit on main roads: **90kph**

Speed limit in built-up areas: **50kph**

Seat belts are not compulsory and are absent from all but the most modern vehicles. Even then, hardly anyone uses them.

Random Breath Testing: No breath-testing but there are a lot of traffic police and local people are regularly asked to produce their papers. It is almost unheard of for a tourist to be booked unless they cause an accident.

Petrol: Fuel is cheap by European standards and costs the same everywhere.
It is sold as super, regular and *essence sans plomb* (lead-free petrol). Although petrol stations are reasonably plentiful, never make the mistake of running short on fuel especially when driving in more remote areas.

Breakdown: Do not expect to be able to call a motoring assistance organisation – although some of the major international car rental companies will provide replacement vehicles and help. Garage mechanics can normally fix most problems. Punctured tyres are common, so if planning a long journey take food and blankets.

0 1 2 3 4 5 6 7 8
CENTIMETRES
INCHES
0 1 2 3

PERSONAL SAFETY

Tunisia is a very safe country with a relatively low crime rate. Sadly, petty thieving is on the increase particularly in busy resorts. Beware of groups of small children distracting you with posies of flowers or cheap souvenirs. To reduce the risk of theft or assault:

- Beware of pickpockets, especially in crowded markets and *souqs*.
- Keep cameras and other valuables in closed bags.
- Do not carry more money and valuables than you need.
- Make use of hotel safes.
- Do not walk alone around *médinas* at night.
- Women should dress modestly, covering themselves when away from the beach or hotel.

Police assistance:
☎ **197** **from any call box**

TELEPHONES

Tunisia's telephone system is quite efficient. Many households do not have phones, so public facilities are always busy. In major towns and cities look out for Taxiphone offices – easily identified by their bright yellow signs – where there will be several booths under one roof with an attendant to give change. You can make a direct dial international call very easily using one dinar coins. Some shops have public phones, usually indicated by a blue sign.

International Dialling Codes from Tunisia to:

UK:	**00 44**
Germany:	**00 49**
USA and Canada:	**00 1**
Netherlands:	**00 31**

POST

Post offices are known as PTTs (Poste, Telephone, Telegraph) and are well-represented throughout the country. They sell stamps – although these can also be bought from hotels, newsagents and kiosks. Postboxes are generally small and yellow. Postcards and letters to Europe tend to take about a week to arrive.

ELECTRICITY

The voltage is 220/240v.

The power supply in Tunisia is 220 volts although a few more remote areas are still on 110 volts. Sockets accept two-round pin plugs so an international adaptor is needed for most non-continental European appliances. A transformer is needed for appliances operating on 100-120 volts.

TIPS/GRATUITIES

Yes ✓ No ✕

Restaurants (if service not included)	✓	10%
Cafes/bars (if service not included)	✓	A few coins
Tour guide	✓	
Hairdressers	✕	
Taxis	✓	Optional
Chambermaids	✕	
Hotel porters	✓	(500mills to TD1)
Theatre/cinema usherettes)	✕	
Cloakroom attendants	✓	(a small coin)
Toilets	✓	Optional

PHOTOGRAPHY

What to photograph: Busy market scenes, the dramatic desert landscape, Sidi Bou Said, camels, mosques, archaeological sites.
What not to photograph: Government buildings, people in uniform, anything military, airports, the Tunisian flag.
When to photograph: Very early morning and early evening.
Where to buy film: It is probably best to bring as much film as you think you will need although most major brands are available from camera shops and souvenir kiosks.

HEALTH

Insurance

Do not try to skimp on travel insurance, which is well worth the investment should problems occur. If you fall ill, all major tourist hotels or a pharmacist should be able to recommend a good doctor – although any treatment would have to be paid for and then reclaimed. If you end up in hospital, immediately contact your insurance company which is there to provide support and advice.

Dental Services

Most tourist hotels should be able to recommend a reputable dentist. Any treatment will need to be paid for and then reclaimed on insurance. It is advised to have a thorough dental check-up before leaving home.

Sun Advice

The sun in Tunisia can be very hot, particularly between June and September in the main beach resorts and in the deep south. Wear a hat, loose cotton clothing and a high factor sunscreen. Drink plenty of bottled water, avoid excess alcohol and caffeine as these aid dehydration – and restrict the amount of time spent in direct sunlight.

Drugs

Pharmacists are knowledgeable and well-respected in Tunisia. Their shops are generally well-supplied although it is always worth checking the date stamp on any medicines which can deteriorate quickly in the heat. Pharmacists can supply drugs for many minor complaints such as sore throat, upset stomach or diarrhoea. Never buy illegal drugs.

CONCESSIONS

Students/Youths: Students with valid identification may get reductions at historical sights and museums. There is a small network of youth hostels in Tunisia, five of them run by the country's Youth Hostel Association. Clean and cheap, there is strict segregation between men and women and a 11PM curfew is imposed. In theory you need to produce a relevant membership card – but it is not always asked for.
Senior Citizens: Tunisia is a very popular destination with older travellers – although they receive no special discounts. Senior citizens tend to be more respected by society than they are in many western countries. It is not unusual for several generations of a family to live together and there is generally much greater interaction between young and old.

CLOTHING SIZES

Tunisia	UK	Rest of Europe	USA	
46	36	46	36	Suits
48	38	48	38	Suits
50	40	50	40	Suits
52	42	52	42	Suits
54	44	54	44	Suits
56	46	56	46	Suits
41	7	41	8	Shoes
42	7.5	42	8.5	Shoes
43	8.5	43	9.5	Shoes
44	9.5	44	10.5	Shoes
45	10.5	45	11.5	Shoes
46	11	46	12	Shoes
37	14.5	37	14.5	Shirts
38	15	38	15	Shirts
39/40	15.5	39/40	15.5	Shirts
41	16	41	16	Shirts
42	16.5	42	16.5	Shirts
43	17	43	17	Shirts
34	8	34	6	Dresses
36	10	36	8	Dresses
38	12	38	10	Dresses
40	14	40	12	Dresses
42	16	42	14	Dresses
44	18	44	16	Dresses
38	4.5	38	6	Shoes
38	5	38	6.5	Shoes
39	5.5	39	7	Shoes
39	6	39	7.5	Shoes
40	6.5	40	8	Shoes
41	7	41	8.5	Shoes

- There are no airport taxes, but you should exchange your spare dinars at the airport as it is illegal to export Tunisian currency. Have your exchange slips with you as you are only allowed to reconvert up to 30 per cent of the total amount of money exchanged in Tunisia.
- Tunisia's airports can be very busy in the summer so allow plenty of time to check-in for your homeward flight.

LANGUAGE

Tunisia is almost bilingual. Although the official language is Arabic, nearly everyone speaks some French and increasingly common among wealthier classes and the business community is for people to speak 'Frarabic'– a rather odd mixture of the two. Not content with two languages under their belt, a lot of young Tunisians are also learning English or German. Tourists can do their bit by learning a few words of Arabic, which is well worth the effort as it usually brings instant friendship.

English	French	Arabic
hotel	*un hôtel*	otel/fondouk
I want a room	*Je voudrais une chambre*	B'gheet beet
Can I look at it?	*Est-ce qu'on peut la voir*	Yoomkin ashoofa?
How much?	*Combien?*	Kaddésh?
too expensive	*c'est trop*	yessir
shower	*la douche*	doosha
open	*ouvert*	mahoul
closed	*ferme*	msaker
bank	*une banque*	bank
post office	*une poste*	bousta/barid
1, 2, 3, 4, 5	*une, deux, trois, quatre, cinq*	wahed, jooj, tlata, arba, khamsa
6, 7, 8, 9, 10	*six, sept, huit, neuf, dix*	setta, seba, tmenia, tse'ud, a'chra
100, 1000	*cent, mille*	mia, alf
the bill	*l'addition*	el-hisaab
fish	*poisson*	samak/huut
meat	*viande*	lahm
vegetables	*légumes*	khodra
fruit	*fruit*	fawakih
water	*de l'eau*	maa
soup	*potage*	shorba
coffee	*café*	kahwa
tea	*thé*	shay
wine	*vin*	sharab
bread	*pain*	khoubz
airport	*l'aéroport*	al-matar
bus	*l'autobus*	autobees
car	*la voiture*	sayara
train station	*gare*	mahata el tran
garage	*le garage*	garage
petrol	*l'essence*	benzeen
puncture	*le crevaison*	tokob
yes	*oui*	naam
no	*non*	la'a
please	*s'il vous plaît*	birabee
thank you	*merci*	shukran
hello	*bonjour*	assalama
good morning	*bonjour*	sabah el khir
good evening	*bon soir*	missa el khir
goodbye	*au revoir*	bislémah
excuse me	*pardon*	samahanee
how are you?	*ça va?*	ashnooa ahwalik?

INDEX

Acknowledgements
The Automobile Association wishes to thank the following photographers and libraries for their assistance in the preparation of this book.

THE J ALLAN CASH PHOTOLIBRARY 39, 57c; BRUNO BARBY/MAGNUM PHOTOS 14b; MARY EVANS PICTURE LIBRARY 10b, 14c; INTERNATIONAL PHOTOBANK 8c, 91b; MRI BANKERS' GUIDE TO FOREIGN CURRENCY 119; ROBERT HARDING PICTURE LIBRARY 21; SPECTRUM COLOUR LIBRARY 51b, 52b, 73b, 79b; TUNISIA NATIONAL TOURIST OFFICE 9b, 87a; WORLD PICTURES LIBRARY LTD 61.

The remaining photographs are held in the Automobile Assocation's own library (AA PHOTO LIBRARY) and were taken by Steve Day.

Peter Lilley would like to thank Ann Noon of the Tunisian National Tourist Office, London; Jason Nicholls, GB Airways; Panorama Holidays; Abou Nawas Hotels.

Copy editor: Hilary Hughes Managing editors: Apostrophe S Limited

Dear Essential Traveller

Your comments, opinions and recommendations are very important to us. So please help us to improve our travel guides by taking a few minutes to complete this simple questionnaire.

You do not need a stamp (unless posted outside the UK). If you do not want to cut this page from your guide, then photocopy it or write your answers on a plain sheet of paper.

Send to: **The Editor, AA World Travel Guides, FREEPOST SCE 4598, Basingstoke RG21 4GY.**

Your recommendations...

We always encourage readers' recommendations for restaurants, nightlife or shopping – if your recommendation is used in the next edition of the guide, we will send you a ***FREE*** **AA *Essential* Guide** of your choice. Please state below the establishment name, location and your reasons for recommending it.

____

____

____

____

Please send me **AA *Essential*** _______________________

(*see list of titles inside the front cover*)

About this guide...

Which title did you buy?

AA *Essential* _______________________

Where did you buy it? _______________________

When? m m / y y

Why did you choose an AA *Essential* Guide? _______________________

____

____

____

____

Did this guide meet your expectations?

Exceeded ☐ Met all ☐ Met most ☐ Fell below ☐

Please give your reasons _______________________

____

____

____

continued on next page...

Were there any aspects of this guide that you particularly liked? ________

____

____

____

Is there anything we could have done better? ______________

____

____

____

____

About you...

Name (*Mr/Mrs/Ms*) ______________________________

Address ______________________________________

____

______________________ Postcode ______________

Daytime tel nos ________________________________

Which age group are you in?

Under 25 ☐ 25–34 ☐ 35–44 ☐ 45–54 ☐ 55–64 ☐ 65+ ☐

How many trips do you make a year?

Less than one ☐ One ☐ Two ☐ Three or more ☐

Are you an AA member? Yes ☐ No ☐

About your trip...

When did you book? m m / y y When did you travel? m m / y y

How long did you stay? ____________________________

Was it for business or leisure? ______________________

Did you buy any other travel guides for your trip?

If yes, which ones? ____________________________

____

Thank you for taking the time to complete this questionnaire. Please send it to us as soon as possible, and remember, you do not need a stamp (*unless posted outside the UK*).

Happy Holidays!

The AA and the Automobile Association Limited, their subsidiaries and any other companies or bodies in which either has an interest ('the AA Group') may use information about you to provide you with details of other products and services, by telephone or in writing. The AA Group as a matter of policy does not release its lists to third parties.
If you do not wish to receive further information please tick the box... ☐

The Atlas

Steve Day: desert scene

The Automobile Association
www.theAA.com
The Automobile Association's website offers comprehensive and up-to-the-minute information covering AA-approved hotels, guest houses and B&Bs, restaurants and pubs in the UK; airport parking, insurance, European breakdown cover, European motoring advice, a ferry planner, European route planner, overseas fuel prices, a bookshop and much more.

The Foreign and Commonwealth Office
Country advice, traveller's tips, before you go information, checklists and more.
www.fco.gov.uk

Tunisian National Tourist Board
www.tourismtunisia.com

GENERAL
UK Passport Service
www.ukpa.gov.uk

Health Advice for Travellers
www.doh.gov.uk/traveladvice

UK Travel Insurance Directory
www.uktravelinsurancedirectory.co.uk

BBC – Holiday
www.bbc.co.uk/holiday

The Full Universal Currency Converter
www.xe.com/ucc/full.shtml

Flying with Kids
www.flyingwithkids.com

www.discover-tunisia.co.uk
www.tourist-offices.org.uk/tunisia
www.tunisiaonline.com

TRAVEL
Flights and Information
www.cheapflights.co.uk
www.thisistravel.co.uk
www.ba.com
www.worldairportguide.com

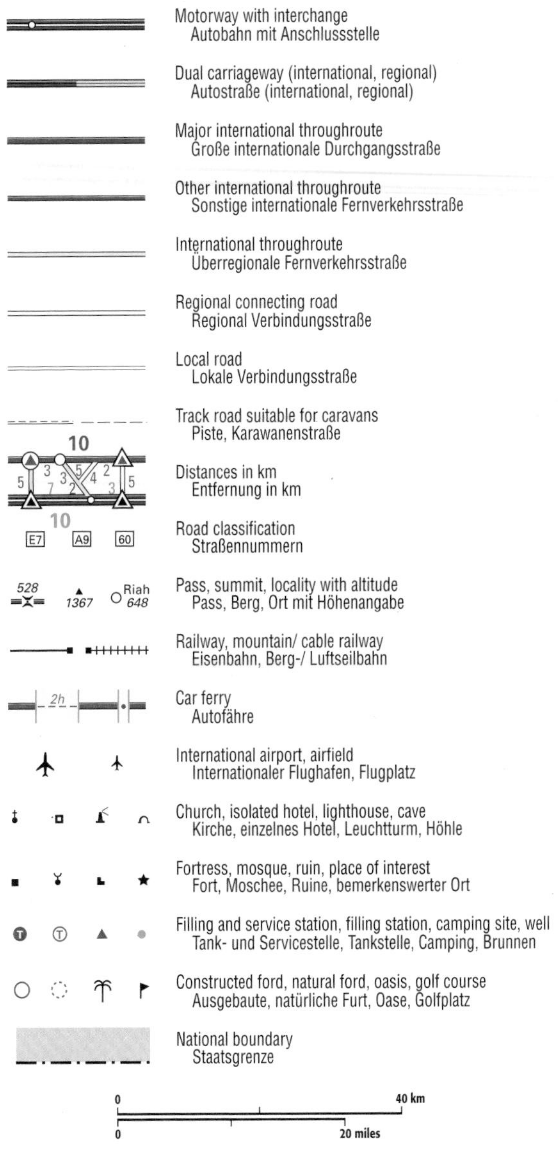
Motorway with interchange
Autobahn mit Anschlussstelle
Dual carriageway (international, regional)
Autostraße (international, regional)
Major international throughroute
Große internationale Durchgangsstraße
Other international throughroute
Sonstige internationale Fernverkehrsstraße
International throughroute
Überregionale Fernverkehrsstraße
Regional connecting road
Regional Verbindungsstraße
Local road
Lokale Verbindungsstraße
Track road suitable for caravans
Piste, Karawanenstraße
10
5 3 3 5 4 2 5
7 2 3
10
Distances in km
Entfernung in km
E7 A9 60
Road classification
Straßennummern
528 1367 Riah 648
Pass, summit, locality with altitude
Pass, Berg, Ort mit Höhenangabe
Railway, mountain/ cable railway
Eisenbahn, Berg-/ Luftseilbahn
2h
Car ferry
Autofähre
International airport, airfield
Internationaler Flughafen, Flugplatz
Church, isolated hotel, lighthouse, cave
Kirche, einzelnes Hotel, Leuchtturm, Höhle
Fortress, mosque, ruin, place of interest
Fort, Moschee, Ruine, bemerkenswerter Ort
Filling and service station, filling station, camping site, well
Tank- und Servicestelle, Tankstelle, Camping, Brunnen
Constructed ford, natural ford, oasis, golf course
Ausgebaute, natürliche Furt, Oase, Golfplatz
National boundary
Staatsgrenze
0 40 km
0 20 miles

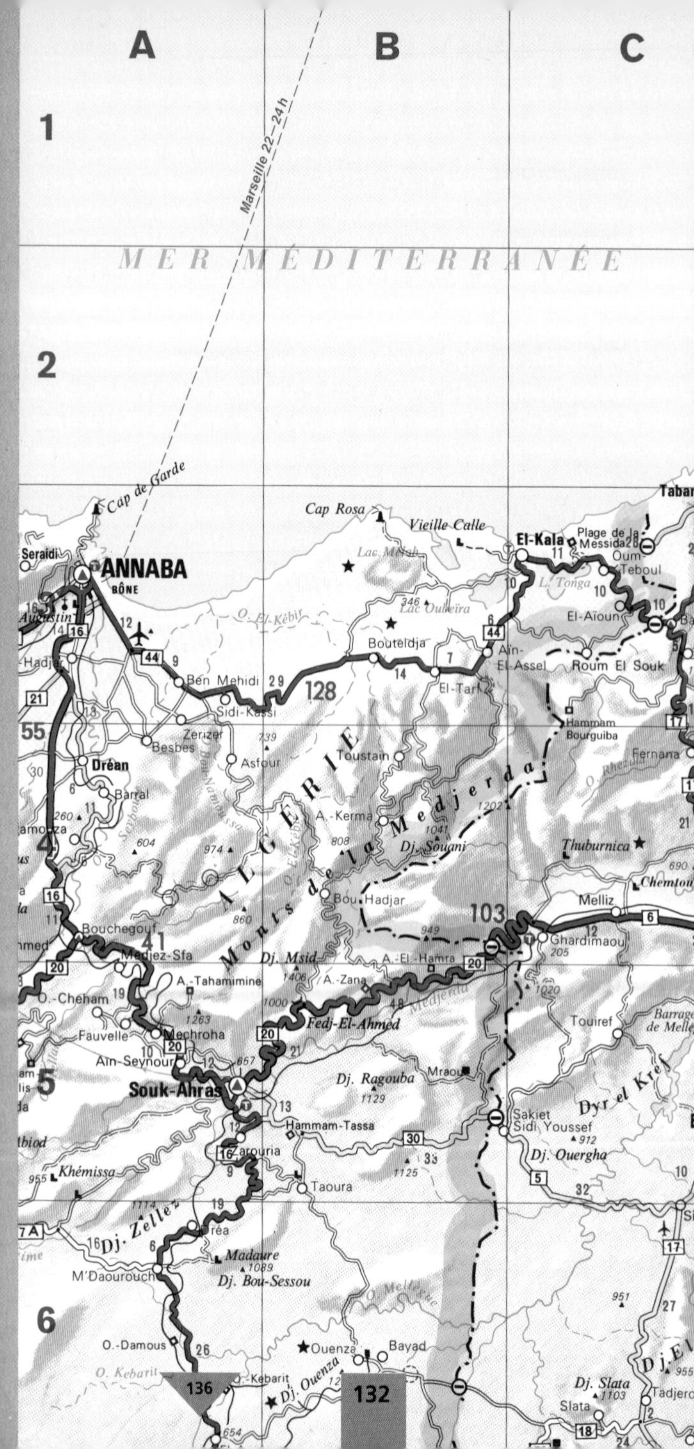

A
B
C
1
2
5
6
Marseille 22—24 h
MER MÉDITERRANÉE
Cap de Garde
Cap Rosa
Vieille Calle
Tabark
El-Kala
Plage de la Messida
Oum-Teboul
ANNABA
BÔNE
Seraidi
Lac Melah
Lac Oubeïra
L. Tonga
O. El-Kébir
El-Aïoun
Bouteldja
Aïn-El-Assel
Roum El Souk
Ben Mehidi
128
El-Tarf
Sidi-Kassi
Hammam Bourguiba
Zerizer
Besbes
Toustain
Fernana
Asfour
Dréan
Barral
ALGERIE
Monts de la Medjerda
A.-Kerma
Dj. Souani
Thuburnica
Chemtou
Bou Hadjar
Melliz
103
Ghardimaou
Bouchegouf
41
Medjez-Sfa
Dj. Msid
A.-El-Hamra
A.-Tahamimine
A.-Zana
O.-Cheham
Fauvelle
Mechroha
Fedj-El-Ahmed
Touiref
Barrage de Mellegue
Aïn-Seynour
Souk-Ahras
Dj. Ragouba
Mraou
Dyr el Kef
Hammam-Tassa
Sakiet Sidi Youssef
Zarouria
Dj. Ouergha
Khémissa
Taoura
Dj. Zelles
Tréa
Madaure
M'Daourouch
Dj. Bou-Sessou
O. Mellègue
O.-Damous
Ouenza
Bayad
O. Kebarit
O.-Kebarit
Dj. Ouenza
136
132
Dj. Slata
Slata
Tadjerou

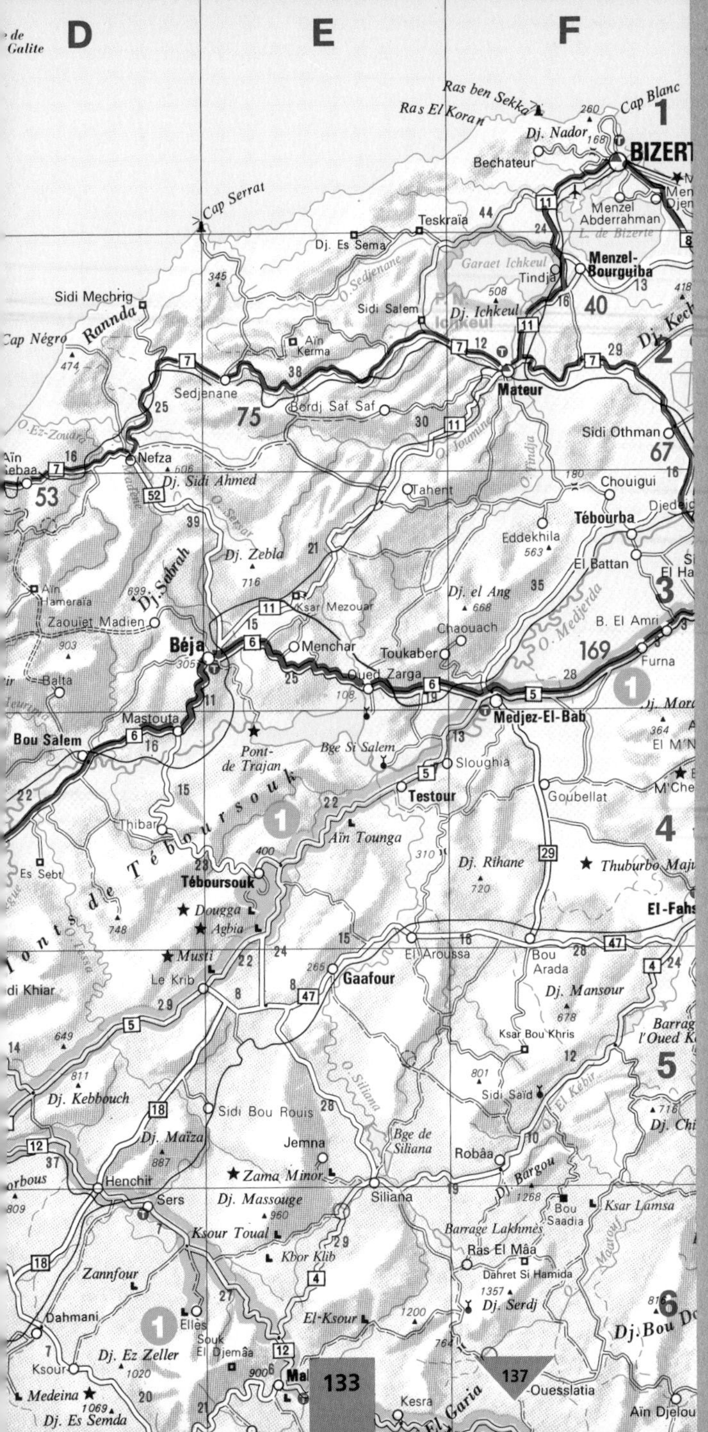

D
E
F
Ras ben Sekka
Ras El Koran
Cap Blanc
Dj. Nador
BIZERT
Bechateur
Menzel Abderrahman
L. de Bizerte
Cap Serrat
Teskraïa
Dj. Es Sema
Garaet Ichkeul
Menzel-Bourguiba
Tindja
Sidi Mechrig
Sidi Salem
Dj. Ichkeul
Rannda
Cap Négro
Aïn Kerma
Sedjenane
Mateur
Bordj Saf Saf
Sidi Othman
Nefza
Dj. Sidi Ahmed
Tahent
Chouigui
Tébourba
Eddekhila
Dj. Zebla
El Battan
Dj. Sabrah
Dj. el Ang
Aïn Hameraïa
Ksar Mezouar
Zaouiet Madien
Chaouach
B. El Amri
Béja
Menchar
Toukaber
Furna
Balta
Oued Zarga
O. Medjerda
Mastouta
Medjez-El-Bab
Bou Salem
Pont-de Trajan
Bge Si Salem
Sloughia
Testour
Goubellat
Thibar
Aïn Tounga
Monts de Téboursouk
Es Sebt
Dj. Rihane
Thuburbo Majus
Téboursouk
Dougga
Agbia
El-Fahs
Musti
El Aroussa
Bou Arada
Le Krib
Gaafour
Dj. Mansour
Ksar Bou Khris
Dj. Kebbouch
Sidi Bou Rouis
Sidi Saïd
O. Siliana
Dj. Maïza
Bge de Siliana
Jemna
Robâa
Henchir
Zama Minor
Siliana
Dj. Bargou
Sers
Dj. Massouge
Bou Saadia
Ksar Lamsa
Ksour Toual
Barrage Lakhmès
Kbor Klib
Ras El Mâa
Dahret Si Hamida
Zannfour
Dj. Serdj
Dahmani
Elles
El-Ksour
Souk El Djemâa
Dj. Ez Zeller
Dj. Bou Dabouss
Ksour
Medeina
Dj. Es Semda
Kesra
Oued El Garia
Oesslatia
Aïn Djeloula
133
137

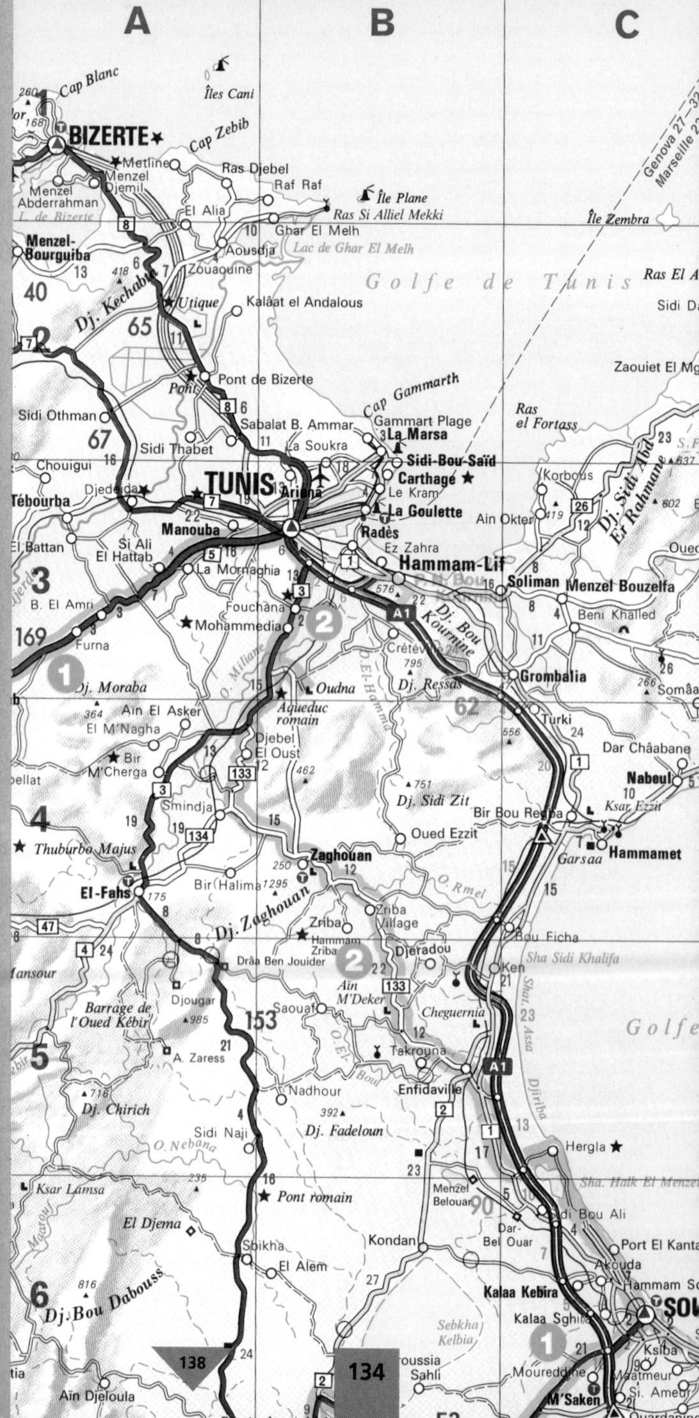
A
B
C
Cap Blanc
Îles Cani
BIZERTE
Cap Zebib
Metline
Menzel Djemil
Menzel Abderrahman
L. de Bizerte
Ras Djebel
Raf Raf
Île Plane
Ras Si Alliel Mekki
El Alia
Ghar El Melh
Lac de Ghar El Melh
Aousdja
Menzel-Bourguiba
Zouaouine
Dj. Kechabta
Utique
Kalâat el Andalous
Golfe de Tunis
Île Zembra
Genova
Marseille
Ras El A
Zaouiet El Mg
Pont de Bizerte
Cap Gammarth
Gammart Plage
La Marsa
Sidi Othman
Sabalat B. Ammar
Sidi Thabet
La Soukra
Ras el Fortass
Sidi-Bou-Saïd
Chouigui
TUNIS
Ariana
Carthage
Korbous
Djedeida
Tébourba
Le Kram
La Goulette
Dj. Sidi Abd Er Rahmane
Manouba
Radès
Ain Okter
El Battan
Si Ali El Hattab
Ez Zahra
Hammam-Lif
La Mornaghia
Soliman
Menzel Bouzelfa
B. El Amri
Fouchana
Dj. Bou Kournine
Beni Khalled
Mohammedia
Furna
Crétéville
Dj. Moraba
Oudna
Dj. Ressas
Grombalia
Somâa
Aqueduc romain
Turki
Ain El Asker
El M'Nagha
Djebel El Oust
Dar Châabane
Bir M'Cherga
Nabeul
Dj. Sidi Zit
Smindja
Bir Bou Regba
Ksar Ezzit
Thuburbo Majus
Oued Ezzit
Zaghouan
Hammamet
Garsaa
El-Fahs
Bir Halima
O. Rmel
Dj. Zaghouan
Zriba Village
Zriba
Hammam Zriba
Bou Ficha
Djeradou
Drâa Ben Jouider
Sha Sidi Khalifa
Mansour
Ain M'Deker
Ken
Djougar
Barrage de l'Oued Kébir
Cheguernia
Saouaf
Golfe
A. Zaress
Takrouna
Enfidaville
Nadhour
Dj. Chirich
Dj. Fadeloun
Sidi Naji
O. Nebana
Hergla
Ksar Lamsa
Pont romain
Menzel Belouar
Sha. Halk El Menzel
El Djema
Sidi Bou Ali
Dar-Bel Ouar
Kondan
Port El Kanta
Sbikha
El Alem
Akouda
Hammam So
Kalaa Kebira
Dj. Bou Dabouss
Kalaa Sghira
Sebkha Kelbia
Ksiba
Moureddine
Messaadine
Sahli
Aïn Djeloula
M'Saken
Si. Ameur
Ouardanine
138
134

D
E
F
1
2
3
4
5
6
Ras Addar (Cap Bon)
393
Dj. Sidi Abiod
El Haouaria
Garaet El-Aouaria
Chichou
Kerkouane
25
Zaouiet Azmour
27
Ras El Melah
Hamman Rézèze
Kelibia
12
Ras Mostefa
Menzel Temime
Menzel Heurr
MER MÉDITERRANÉE
mmamet
Îles Kuriate
Ksibet el Mediouni
Khniss
Lamta
Saïada
Hellal
135
139

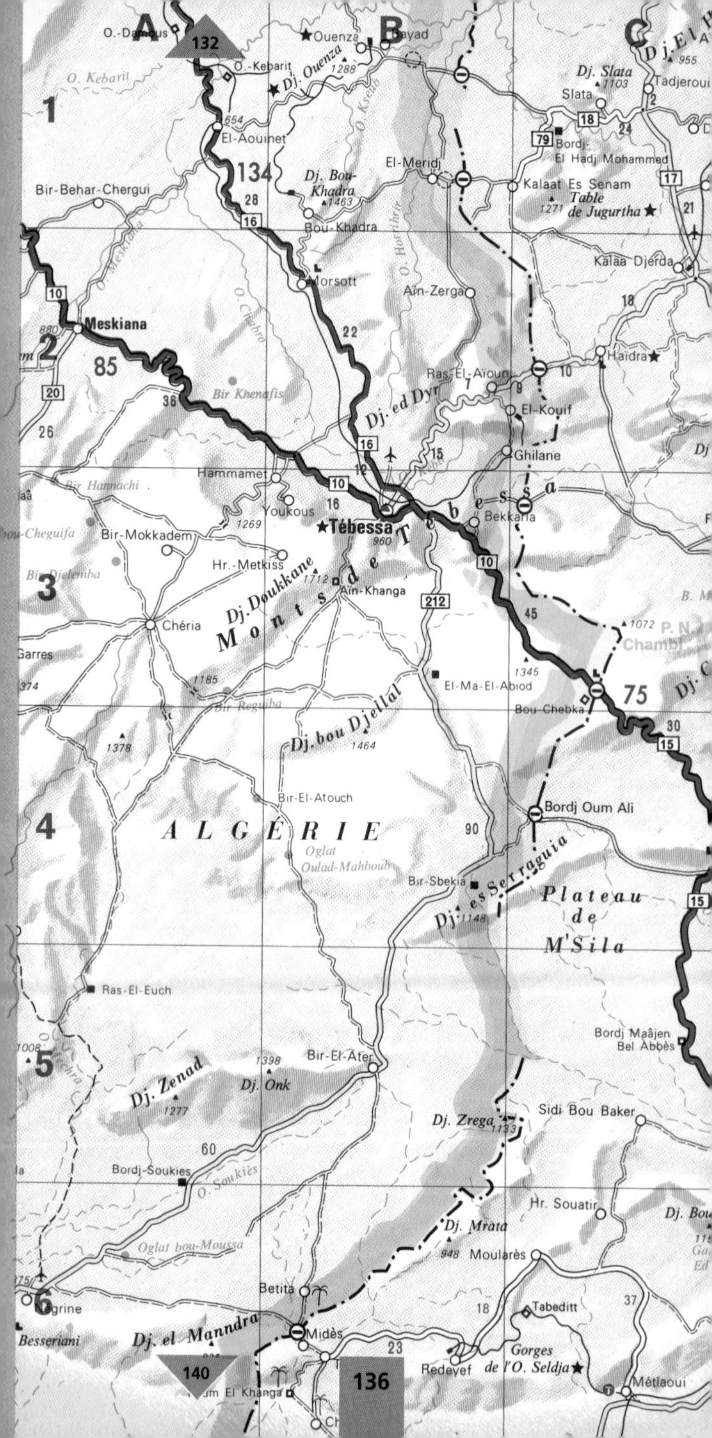

A
B
C
132
134
136
140
1
2
3
4
5
6
O.-Damous
Ouenza
Bayad
O.-Kebarit
O. Kebarit
Dj. Ouenza
1288
Dj. Slata
1103
Slata
Tadjerouine
El-Aouinet
El-Meridj
Dj. Bou-Khadra
1463
Bou-Khadra
Bir-Behar-Chergui
Bordj-El Hadj Mohammed
Kalaat Es Senam
Table de Jugurtha
1271
Kalaa Djerda
Morsott
Aïn-Zerga
O. Chabro
O. Meskiana
O. Horihrir
Meskiana
Bir Khenafis
Haïdra
Ras-El-Aïoun
El-Kouif
Dj. ed Dyr
Ghilane
Hammamet
Bir Hannachi
Youkous
Tébessa
960
Bekkaria
Bir-Mokkadem
Hr.-Metkiss
1269
Dj. Doukkane
1712
Aïn-Khanga
Monts de Tebessa
Chéria
Garres
1185
Bir Reguiba
El-Ma-El-Abiod
1345
1072
Bou-Chebka
Dj. bou Djellal
1464
1378
Bir-El-Atouch
Bordj Oum Ali
ALGÉRIE
Oglat Oulad-Mahboub
Bir-Sbekia
Dj. es Serraguia
1148
Plateau de M'Sila
Ras-El-Euch
Bordj Maâjen Bel Abbès
Dj. Zenad
1277
Dj. Onk
1398
Bir-El-Ater
Dj. Zrega
1133
Sidi Bou Baker
Bordj-Soukies
O. Soukies
Hr. Souatir
Dj. Mrata
948
Moularès
Oglat bou-Moussa
Betita
Negrine
Besseriani
Dj. el Manndra
Midès
Tabeditt
Gorges de l'O. Seldja
Redeyef
Métlaoui

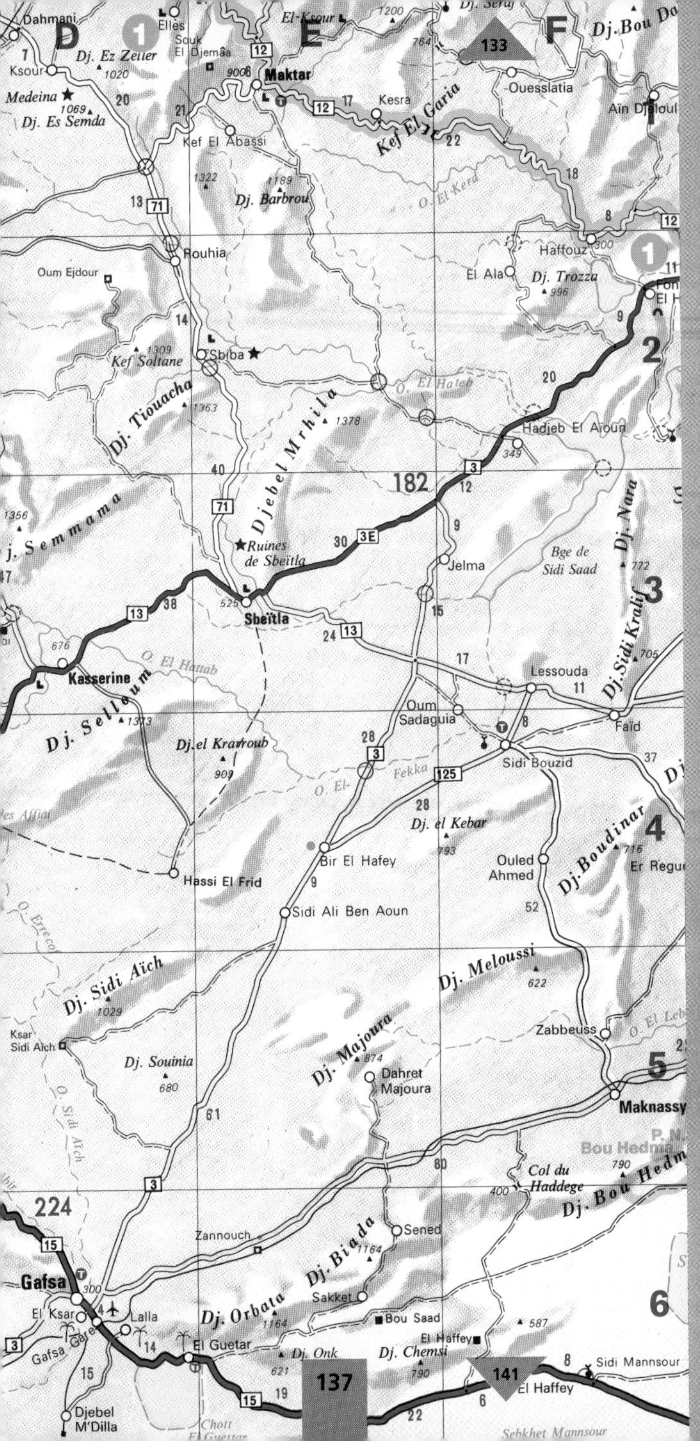

D
E
F
1
133
Dahmani
Elles
El-Ksour
Dj. Bou Da
Ksour
Dj. Ez Zeller
1020
Souk El Djemâa
Maktar
Medeina
Dj. Es Semda
Kesra
Ouesslatia
Aïn Djeloul
Kef El Abassi
Kef El Garia
Dj. Barbrou
O. El Kerd
Rouhia
Haffouz
Oum Ejdour
El Ala
Dj. Trozza
Kef Soltane
Sbiba
Dj. Tiouacha
O. El Hateb
Djebel Mrhila
Hadjeb El Aïoun
2
182
Dj. Semmama
Ruines de Sbeïtla
Jelma
Bge de Sidi Saad
Dj. Nara
Sbeïtla
3
Kasserine
O. El Hattab
Dj. Selloum
Dj. Sidi Kralif
Lessouda
Oum Sadaguia
Faïd
Dj.el Kranroub
Sidi Bouzid
O. El-Fekka
Dj. el Kebar
Bir El Hafey
Dj. Boudinar
4
Ouled Ahmed
Er Regue
Hassi El Frid
Sidi Ali Ben Aoun
Dj. Meloussi
Dj. Sidi Aïch
Ksar Sidi Aïch
Zabbeuss
O. El Leb
Dj. Souinia
Dj. Majoura
Dahret Majoura
5
Maknassy
O. Sidi Aïch
P. N. Bou Hedma
Col du Haddege
Dj. Bou Hedma
224
Zannouch
Sened
Dj. Biada
Gafsa
Dj. Orbata
Sakket
6
El Ksar
Lalla
Bou Saad
Gafsa Gare
El Guetar
El Haffey
Dj. Onk
Dj. Chemsi
Sidi Mannsour
137
141
Djebel M'Dilla
Chott El Guettar
Sebkhet Mannsour

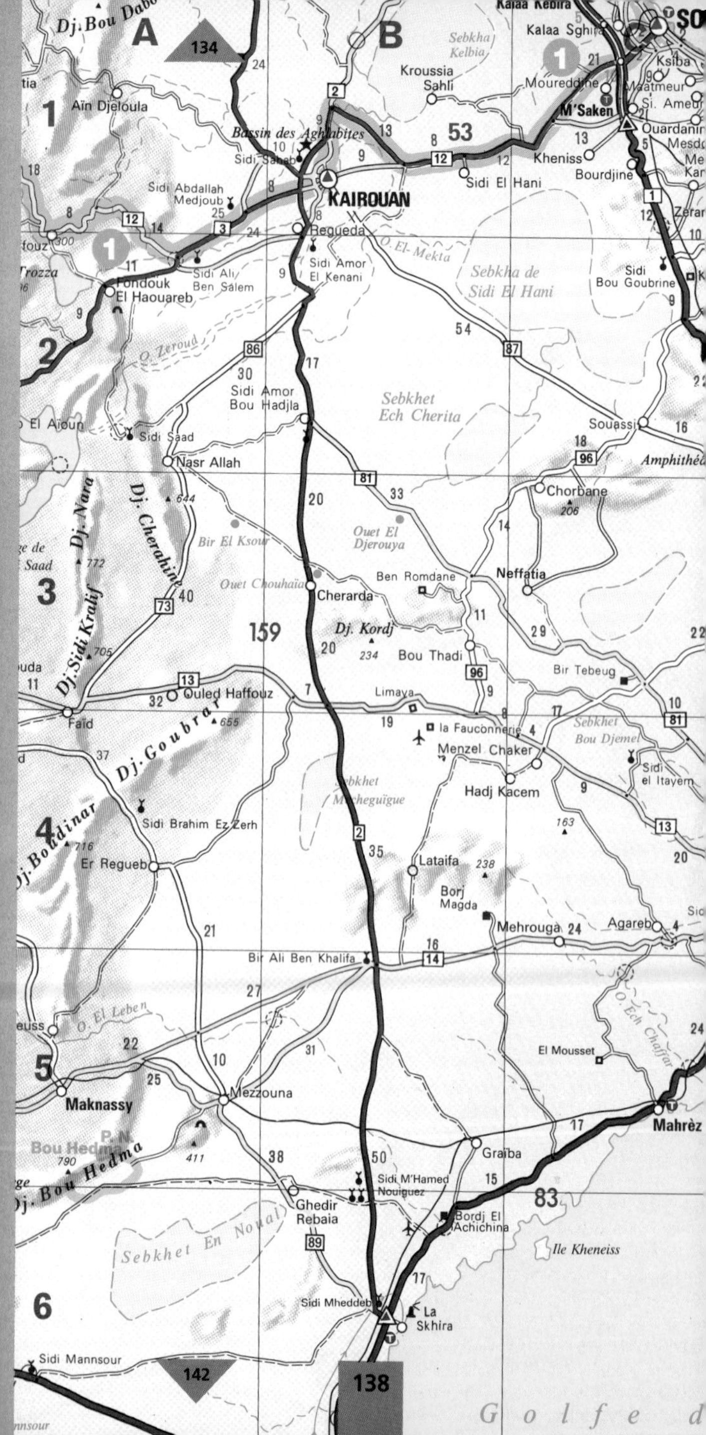

A
B
134
Kairouan
Bassin des Aghlabites
Sidi Sahab
Sidi Abdallah Medjoub
Regueda
Sidi Amor El Kenani
Aïn Djeloula
Fondouk El Haouareb
Sidi Ali Ben Salem
Kroussia Sahli
Sebkha Kelbia
Kalaa Kebira
Kalaa Sghira
Moureddine
M'Saken
Ksiba
Maatmeur
Si. Ameur
Ouardanin
Kheniss
Bourdjine
Sidi El Hani
Sebkha de Sidi El Hani
Sidi Bou Goubrine
O. El-Mekta
O. Zeroud
Sidi Amor Bou Hadjla
Sebkhet Ech Cherita
Souassi
Amphithéâ
Sidi Saad
Nasr Allah
Chorbane
Dj. Nara
Dj. Cherahine
Bir El Ksour
Ouet El Djerouya
Ouet Chouhaïa
Cherarda
Ben Romdane
Neffatia
Dj. Sidi Kralif
159
Dj. Kordj
Bou Thadi
Bir Tebeug
Ouled Haffouz
Faïd
Limaya
la Fauconnerie
Menzel Chaker
Sebkhet Bou Djemel
Sidi el Itayem
Hadj Kacem
Dj. Goubrar
Sebkhet Mcheguïgue
Sidi Brahim Ez Zerh
Dj. Boudinar
Er Regueb
Lataifa
Borj Magda
Mehrouga
Agareb
Bir Ali Ben Khalifa
O. El Leben
O. Ech Chaffar
El Mousset
Maknassy
Mezzouna
Mahrès
P.N. Bou Hedma
Dj. Bou Hedma
Graïba
Sidi M'Hamed Nouiguez
Ghedir Rebaia
83
Bordj El Achichina
Ile Kheneiss
Sebkhet En Noual
Sidi Mhedheb
La Skhira
Sidi Mannsour
142
138
Golfe d

D
E
F
135
Îles Kuriate
1
2
3
4
5
6
Ksibet el Mediouni
Lamta
Saïada
Ksar Hellal
Teboulba
Bekalta
Ras Dimasse
Thapsus
Moknine
Sidi Neya
Hiboun
Cap Afrique
Madhia
Sidi Bennour
El Zghana
Rejiche
Ksour Essaf
Rass Salakta
Salakta
Sidi Alouane
Tlelsa
El Bahira
La Chebba
Ras Kaboudia
Meiloulèche
Ras Djezira
Ras Bou Tria
La Louza
Djebeniana
Hazeg
El Amra
Île Roumedia
Île Sefnou
El Gheraïb
Chergui
Île Rhermedi
Sidi-Mansour
Sakiet Eddaier
Île Chergui
El Attaïa
Remla
Kellabine
SFAX
Sidi Fredj
Oulad Bou Ali
Île Gharbi
Oulad Kacem
Oulad Yaneg
Sidi Youssef
Mellita
Îles Kerkenna
Ras es Semoun
MER MÉDITERRANÉE
139
143
Gabès

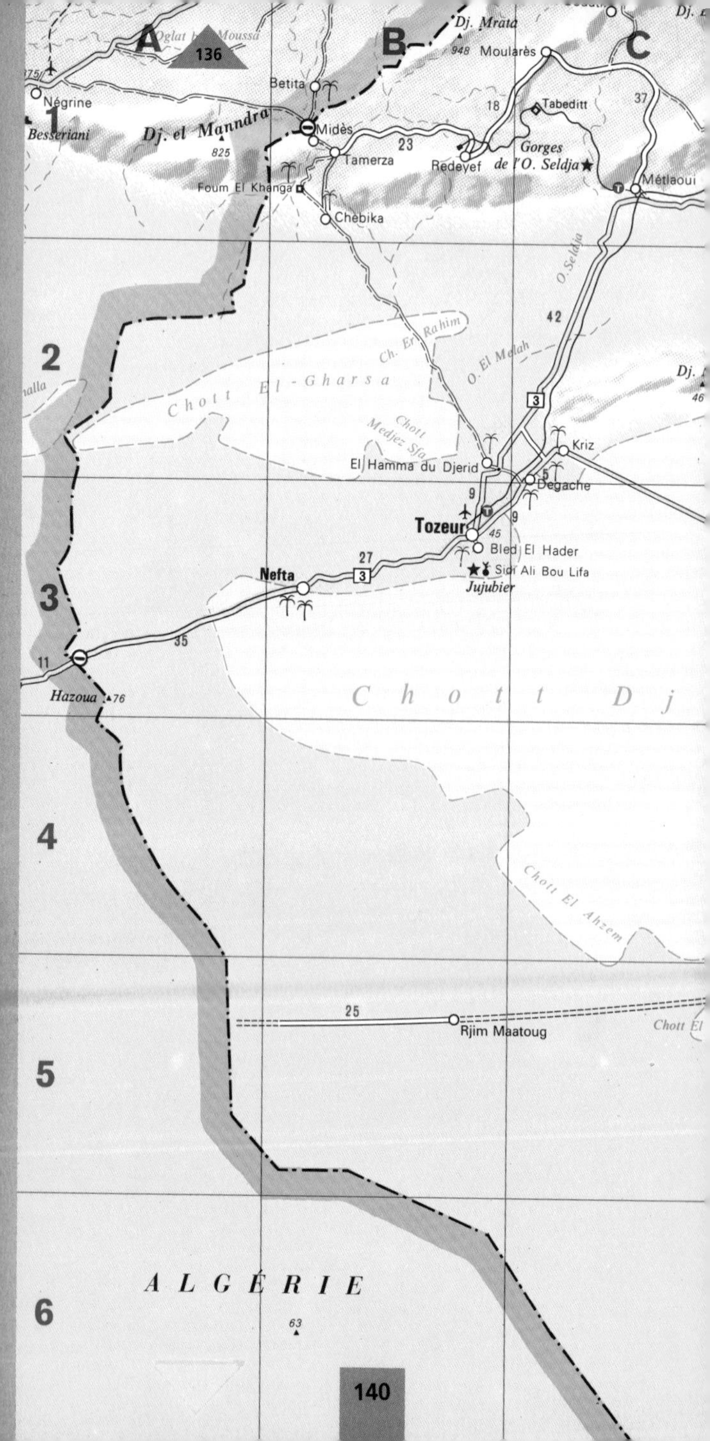

A
B
C
136
Oglat b... Moussa
Dj. Mrata
948
Moularès
Dj.
Betita
Négrine
1
Besseriani
Dj. el Manndra
825
Midès
18
Tabeditt
37
23
Tamerza
Redeyef
Gorges
de l'O. Seldja
Foum El Khanga
Métlaoui
Chebika
O. Seldja
42
Ch. Er Rahim
2
O. El Melah
Chott El-Gharsa
3
Dj.
46
Chott
Medjez Sfa
Kriz
El Hamma du Djerid
5
Degache
9
Tozeur
9
45
Bled El Hader
27
Nefta
3
Sidi Ali Bou Lifa
Jujubier
3
35
11
Hazoua
76
Chott Dj
4
Chott El Ahzem
25
Rjim Maatoug
Chott El
5
ALGÉRIE
6
63

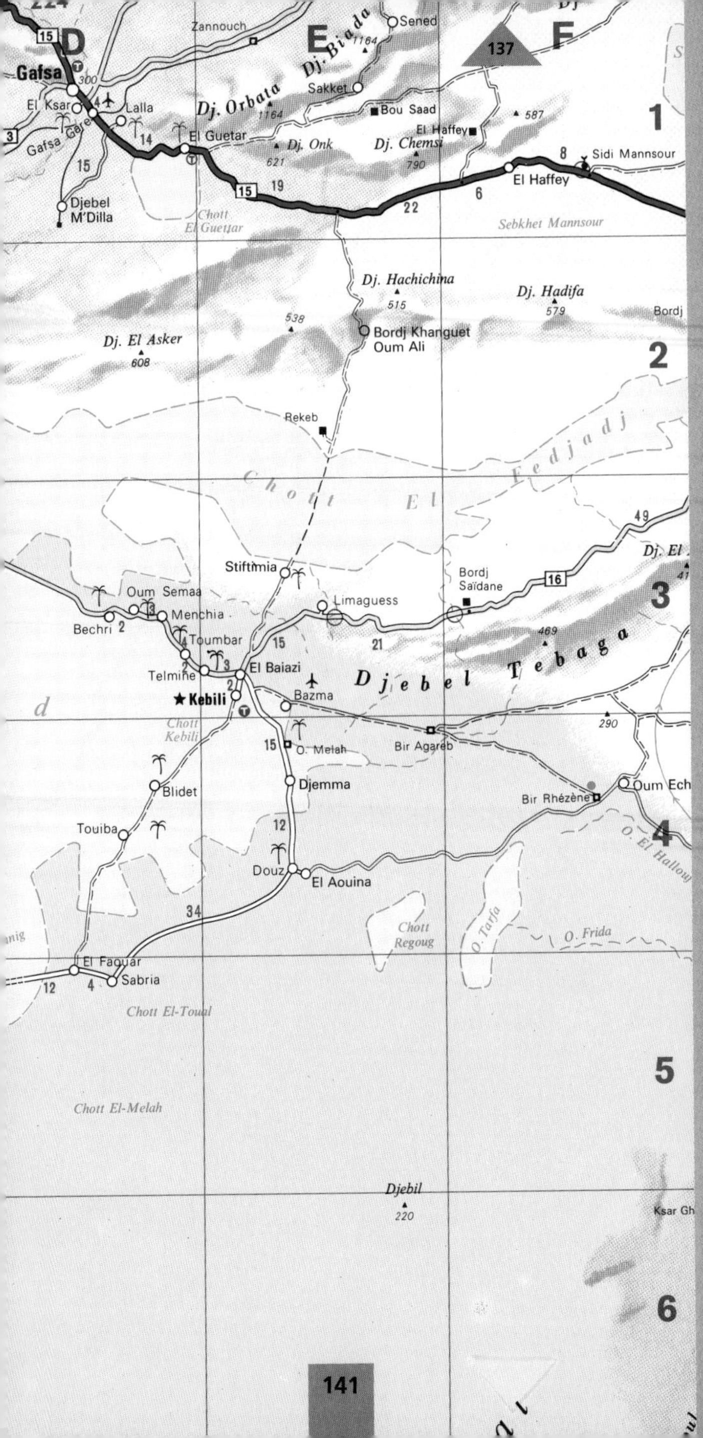

D
E
F
137
1
2
3
4
5
6
Gafsa
300
El Ksar
Lalla
Gafsa Gare
El Guetar
Djebel M'Dilla
Chott El Guettar
Zannouch
Sened
Dj. Biada
1164
Sakket
Dj. Orbata
1164
Bou Saad
Dj. Onk
621
Dj. Chemsi
790
El Haffey
587
Sidi Mannsour
El Haffey
Sebkhet Mannsour
Dj. Hachichina
515
Dj. Hadifa
579
Bordj
538
Bordj Khanguet Oum Ali
Dj. El Asker
608
Rekeb
Chott El Fedjadj
Stiftimia
Bordj Saïdane
Oum Semaa
Bechri
Menchia
Limaguess
Toumbar
Telmine
El Baiazi
Kebili
Chott Kebili
Bazma
Djebel Tebaga
469
290
Bir Agareb
O. Melah
Djemma
Blidet
Touiba
Bir Rhézène
Oum Ech
O. El Hallouf
Douz
El Aouina
Chott Regoug
O. Tarfa
O. Frida
El Faouar
Sabria
Chott El-Toual
Chott El-Melah
Djebil
220
Ksar Gh
141

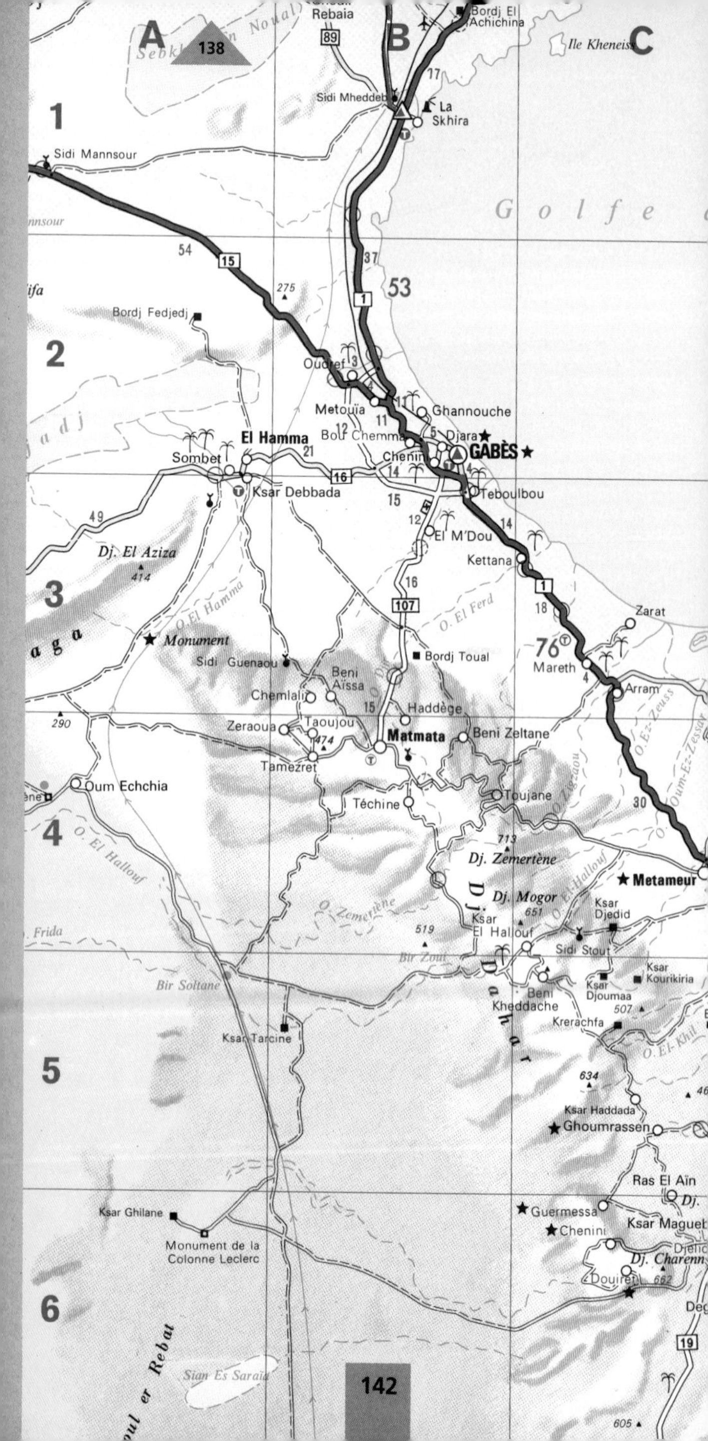
A
B
C
138
Rebaia
89
Bordj El Achichina
Ile Kheneiss
Sidi Mheddeb
La Skhira
17
1
2
3
4
5
6
Sidi Mannsour
Golfe
54
15
37
53
275
Bordj Fedjedj
Oudref
Metouïa
Ghannouche
El Hamma
Bou Chemma
Djara
GABÈS
Chenini
Sombet
Ksar Debbada
16
Teboulbou
49
El M'Dou
Kettana
Dj. El Aziza
414
107
O. El Hamma
O. El Ferd
Zarat
Monument
Sidi Guenaou
Bordj Toual
76
Mareth
Arram
Beni Aïssa
Chemlali
Haddège
Zeraoua
Taoujou
474
Matmata
Beni Zeltane
Tamezret
290
Oum Echchia
Téchine
Toujane
O. Ez-Zeuss
O. Oum-Ez-Zessar
30
O. El Hallouf
713
Dj. Zemertène
Metameur
Dj. Mogor
651
Ksar El Hallouf
Ksar Djedid
O. Zemertène
519
Sidi Stout
Bir Zoui
Bir Soltane
Beni Kheddache
Ksar Kourikiria
Ksar Djoumaa
507
Krerachfa
Ksar Tarcine
O. El-Khil
634
Ksar Haddada
Ghoumrassen
Ras El Aïn
Ksar Ghilane
Monument de la Colonne Leclerc
Guermessa
Chenini
Ksar Maguel
Dj. Charenn
Douiret
662
19
Sian Es Saraïa
605
142

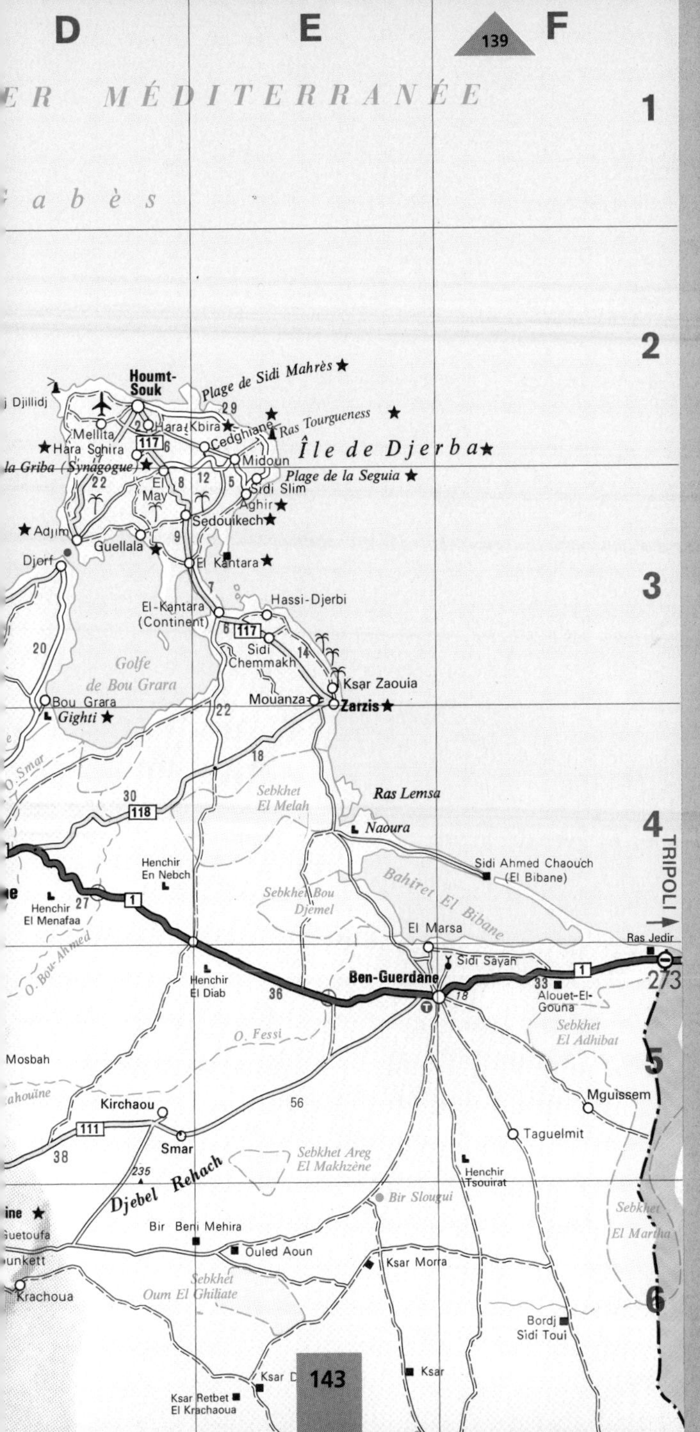

D
E
F
139
1
2
3
4
5
6
MER MÉDITERRANÉE
Golfe de Gabès
Houmt-Souk
Plage de Sidi Mahrès
Djillidj
Mellita
Hara Kbira
Hara Sghira
Cedghiane
Ras Tourgueness
Île de Djerba
la Griba (Synagogue)
Midoun
Plage de la Seguia
El May
Sidi Slim
Aghir
Sedouikech
Adjim
Guellala
Djorf
El Kantara
El-Kantara (Continent)
Hassi-Djerbi
117
Sidi Chemmakh
Golfe de Bou Grara
Ksar Zaouia
Bou Grara
Gighti
Mouanza
Zarzis
O. Smar
Sebkhet El Melah
Ras Lemsa
118
Naoura
Henchir En Nebch
Sidi Ahmed Chaouch (El Bibane)
TRIPOLI
Henchir El Menafaa
Sebkhet Bou Djemel
Bahiret El Bibane
El Marsa
Ras Jedir
O. Bou-Ahmed
Sidi Sayah
Henchir El Diab
Ben-Guerdane
Alouet-El-Gouna
273
O. Fessi
Sebkhet El Adhibat
Mosbah
Mguissem
Kirchaou
111
Smar
Taguelmit
Sebkhet Areg El Makhzène
Djebel Rehach
235
Henchir Tsouirat
Bir Slougui
Sebkhet El Martha
Bir Beni Mehira
Guetoufa
Ouled Aoun
Ksar Morra
Sebkhet Oum El Ghiliate
Krachoua
Bordj Sidi Toui
Ksar
Ksar Retbet El Krachaoua